The Miranda Complex

Volume 1:

Munchkinland

Barry Smolin

For the Zoo

CONTENTS

Prelude

I have a bad heart.

Countless failures have groomed the stars out of it.

My heart cries to be alive.

My heart is the sad fact of time moving irreversibly forward.

My heart is a demiurge, freely allegiant, an anchor in the void.

And right in there somewhere is the brokenness, Georgie Porgie, right there where you left it . . .

. . . I went to a party last night at Madeline Baker's house up in the Hollywood Hills and ran into Miranda Savitch after not having seen her since graduation like over a year ago.

Miranda Savitch.

The first that e'er I sigh'd for

I was seated at the host's vintage Hammond Chord Organ, playing the opening drone-tones of "Blue Jay Way," avoiding involvement with the mingling minions, when a pair of hands covered my eyes from behind.

A false female baritone rumbled, "Lance Atlas."

There's a fog upon L.A. . . . and my friends have lost their way . . .

She sang the first two lines and stopped.

"What ho?" I played Shakespearean.

"Jane Gallagher," the voice warbled in a different timbre, more familiar.

Even more familiar was her smell like fruit still on the tree.

"In sooth, reveal thyself," I said.

"Hence, bashful cunning!" she removed her hands and stepped back.

It sounded and smelled like Miranda Savitch, but when I turned around to see her face, she looked different enough that it took me a few moments to connect the voice with my memories of the girl I used to know.

"Hi, Lance! My God . . ."

"Admir'd Miranda," I croaked, barely audible because I hadn't said a word all night to anyone.

She was wearing a white tank top with a *Disco Sucks* button pinned to her bosom, white jeans, barefoot.

"You have a beard! Bitchin' . . . you look like Jesus."

"All us nice Jewish boys look the same."

"Yeah, huh. Right on."

"What about you?" I wondered, "Something's different."

Miranda turned sideways and pointed to her profile.

"Nose job," she said.

"You look great," I ached, "I liked the old nose also, though."

"Eh, too jewy."

"So, where are you now?"

"UCLA," Miranda said, "And you're at . . .?"

" . . . Cal State Northridge," I admitted.

"Righteous. English major?"

"No duh," I affirmed.

"Right on," she said for want of anything else.

We shared a subtle panic at the first dangle in the conversation. I brought

8

up the obvious.

"How's Freddy?"

"Um, I actually have no idea . . . we broke up last summer, like right after graduation."

"Oh, sorry to hear that," I said in mock sympathy.

"Nyeah, it's good. It'd kinda run its course, you know."

"Fizzledy fizzle."

"Yeahzackly."

"The smile on your mouth was the deadest thing alive enough to have the strength to die . . . right?"

"There you go, totally," she said, "I remember that poem from Megiddo's class! But, um, yeah, that about sums it up."

"Mr. Megiddo's AP English class, the source of all wisdom."

"For sure," she Cali-drawled, "I remember you broke up with Diana Hitchcock. Like right before prom, wasn't it?"

"Yikes, yeah. That was gnarly times 9," I said. "It was a similar fizzle to yours probably," I said.

"Probly, right?"

"Yeah," we spoke in unison.

A joint was making its way around the living room.

Someone we went to Fairfax with (I've gone blank on her name) passed it to Miranda who inhaled deeply then wheezed, "Coolness," on exhale, handing the joint to me.

I took a hit, but the smoke made me cough.

"Dang, dude, that shit's harsh," I waved at the smoke.

"Nah, you're just all spoiled by that sweet Thai Stick Whitman Rust always used to get."

"I suppose," I handed the joint to this dude Harold Monarch I was on the

9

track team with in 10th Grade. "Spread the news, brother," I told him, "Spread the good news."

"Blessings," Harold said as he prepared to partake of the sacrament.

I was fighting off memories. Memories are enemies.

Miranda was glancing around the room. Looking for a way out, perhaps. Where was her savior?

"So, what're you up to besides school?" she continued, turning back to me.

"Uhhhm, I'm writing a lot of music and playing in this band called Tin Man Alley."

"Brill."

"Yeah, cool name, right? Manny Shepherd's in the band also. We played at The Troubadour last month."

"The Troubadour . . . bitchin'," Miranda said, "Hey I heard Buzzy Lagniappe went all the way cuckoo or something."

"Yeah . . . he still lives next door . . . I don't know . . . he seems pretty far out there."

"What happened?"

"I'm not really sure. He'd been getting weird for a while though."

"I remember . . . like when they first showed *Sybil* on TV and Sally Field reminded me of Buzzy Lagniappe. That was 11th Grade, right? . . . man, Buzzy Lagniappe . . . wow."

"Yeah, all those voices he used to do, he was really hearing them."

"I loved his voices."

"Most of them sounded like Bugs Bunny though."

"Oh yeah, huh. I never thought of that but may be."

"Or like Hobo Kelly meets Augustus Gloop."

"Too funny."

"Or like Scarecrow meets Dorothy."

Miranda smiled sweetly at the shared memory.

"I see him in the front yard. He sits on the porch and writes in a spiral notebook. Sometimes he waves, other times he's just too far out there."

I shrugged.

I didn't know what else to say.

"Sucks," Miranda said, "I wonder what kind of stuff he's writing."

"Maybe he lets all his voices talk to each other."

"Maybe. That'd be trippy," Miranda offered a polite smirk.

"What about you, what're you doing?"

"Oh, not much really. Just kicking back mostly. Working in my dad's office part time for the summer. I'm reading *Swann's Way* right now."

"Right on, Marcel Proust," I said, "English translation?"

"Oh, yeah, forget the French, no way am I ready for that."

"Someday, though."

"For sure. I'm working on it. I've grown beyond *The Little Prince* at least."

"That book reminds me of Madame Couchée's class," I fudged a bit.

"Proust is a whole nother thing," she said, smiling 'cause she knew what I meant.

"Remember Megiddo's lecture on 'stream-of-consciousness'? 'It's like dropping a pebble in a still pond,' he used to say, right?, 'which sets in motion ripples in random directions outward from the source,' right?, 'and each of those ripples is a memory.'"

"I, uh, yeah, I think I kind of remember. Or, wait, I might've been absent that day, maybe?"

"I don't know, Megiddo cracked a lot of things open for me," I said.

"You gonna be the next Megiddo?"

"I'd rather be the next Bob Dylan actually."

"Ah," she humored me, "well, right on."

Harold Monarch tapped me on the shoulder and offered me what was left of the extinguished joint.

I couldn't figure out how to light it though without singing my lips and nose, so I declined.

"Nah'm cool," I said, handing the roach back to him.

Miranda seemed increasingly anxious to move on.

"When does UCLA start back up again?" I asked, trying to hang onto her for a just a few more moments.

"Third week of September."

"Oh, no fair, I have to go back end of August."

"Bummer."

"Yeah, what a drag, right?" I said, "it's fuckin' hot in the Valley in August."

"I bet," she responded robotically, "Cal State Northridge."

Aaaaaaah-ha, loser . . .

"So . . . yeah . . ." I filled the elongating void.

"You look great, Lance," Miranda said.

I smiled an ancient painful smile, gazing upon the hearth.

"No, same old amorphous blob in the scheme of things," I parried away the compliment, a lifelong talent.

Miranda shook her head and looked at the carpet. Then she met my eyes and shrugged. Again. For the billionth time. She shrugged the shrug of eternal exasperation.

"Well anyway your vision has declined in old age."

"We *are* getting old, aren't we?"

"18. Yes. Positively primeval. 1979 is already more than half over, can you believe it? Scary . . . 1972 feels like yesterday," I said.

"Ha, 7th Grade."

"Ms. LaBouche! Wicked Witch of the West!"

"Dang, to me it seems like forever ago. I can hardly remember what I was like then."

"I remember," I said, though I'm pretty sure she'd stopped listening.

The room's party-babble filled the empty solemnity between us.

I remembered I had a quaalude waiting in my pocket.

Miranda waved and smiled as if at someone across the room.

"Listen, Lance, I've gotta split. It was wonderful to see you again," she held out her hands to me.

"Likewise." I maintained a cool demeanor, keeping need invisible and want subterranean as ever, and took her hands in mine.

Miranda leaned swiftly toward my face and kissed me softly on the cheek as I inhaled her scent.

"Bye, Lance," she said.

I nodded profusely and watched her walk away.

She didn't glance back.

Her ass looked awesome in those white jeans.

Miranda's kiss and the smell of her body carried me back to the birthplace of feeling, love awakening in its discordant manger.

I turned to face the organ and performed a memorial tune, a little Elton John to eulogize the passing decade.

I began with the synthy organ bits from "Funeral For A Friend," as best I could remember them (but mostly making shit up), with a rumble in my gut and an ache in my brain and a fracture in my humanity.

Time to drop that 'lude, dude.

The music was a form of dissolution.

I followed a revised map to "Love Lies Bleeding" and eventually found my way to "Goodbye Yellow Brick Road."

Forever a dance with Miranda.

But I only got through the first two lines.

When are you gonna come down?

When are you going to land?

I had to stop. It was time.

Distracted in sadness back to Miranda, back to this thing that never happened.

I went into the kitchen to fetch a glass of water . . .

The Girl From Zody's

By the age of 11 I had already harbored a fascination with girls and their bodies and had also already experienced erections, but up to that time the two sensations bore no connection to each other.

Catching glimpses of Gina Dichlich's underwear when she hung upside down on the monkey bars in the 4th Grade, though enjoyable and sought out whenever possible at recess, was not associated with wanting to fuck her nor were my various boners on bumpy bus rides or sliding around in the tub associated with any penetrations.

No, the first time I ever saw a pretty girl and got an erection because of it happened when I went to the psychedelic department store Zody's with my grandparents.

Zody's was a brightly-lit low-end retail outlet where the trippy colors and acid-drenched wall designs made it at least more entertaining than venues like the steely cold White Front or else this drab store called The Akron which sold merchandise guaranteed to break within hours of bringing it home.

Zody's had concession stands near the entrance that sold snack foods like popcorn and ice-cream and frozen bananas (plain or chocolate covered) on a stick.

In fact, my first girl-related hard-on occurred near those concession stands, where I saw this gentle, brilliant creature with curly black hair and enormous purple eyes working a frozen banana in her mouth.

She held the frozen banana in her left hand and moved her lips back and forth across its girth.

I couldn't stop watching her do that, and the longer I watched the harder my pubescent tumescence grew accompanied by thoughts of my body touching her body.

And I do believe that I was ashamed of those thoughts.

Ashamed of wanting.

The recurring theme.

And the shame doesn't stop the wanting.

Oh, to be android.

I rode the exacting blade's edge of staring at her and not getting caught staring at her.

While strolling the aisles with my grandparents, who were shopping for some gadget or other which would undoubtedly be useless by the next day, I passed the black-haired beauty several times, each instance averting my eyes from her but longing terribly to look.

I sneaked enough peripheral vision to know she still had the frozen banana.

But it was really her eyes I wanted to gaze at again, not her mouth.

I couldn't bring myself to risk interest. As if by instinct. I didn't even know why yet.

It's called the fear of being human. Of dabbling in the actual. It's called trying to be a good warrior and avoid confrontation.

I didn't talk to her.

Ashamed of wanting.

It was 1972, the summer "Alone Again, Naturally" was in heavy rotation on 93 KHJ, the perfect soundtrack for wallowing in one's own social paralysis. I loved that song when I was 11, very much God's own lurch-left sediment dweller.

I remember feeling her gone forever while riding back to my grandparents' house from Zody's.

I resurrected the image of the girl from Zody's nightly for quite a while; she was a leading player in the fantasy pantheon. Sometimes she'd have the aspect of an Egyptian bird-god; sometimes she'd have a more human plumage.

But the reality of the girl from Zody's, the bird made flesh, I felt, would never be encountered again.

As it turned out, though, my premonition of finality was (almost for certain) incorrect.

Because, weirdly, I'm pretty sure I go to college with the girl from Zody's, what, these 7 years later (when I first saw her in lit class I thought she was Dorothy from *The Wizard of Oz*, but then I saw her face and realized in a mind-gasp that, no, it was the girl from Zody's), and a fellow English major at that.

From the moment I noticed the lavender flash in her eyes I exerted tremendous energy downplaying my awareness of her, diligently avoiding contact through two different literature courses in Freshman year, but trying to drink her in clandestinely at oddly focused moments, or openly when I had permission to look at her, like when she'd answer a question or comment in class.

In the stretch between Zody's 1972 and Cal State Northridge 1979, I had mythologized her in a perverse sequined imaginary shrine to lust and shame, but I was not entirely positive the English major I ogled from the side in *Major British Authors II (Romanticism to the Present)* was in fact the sapphire-eyed beauty I had peeped *in flagrante delicto* with her frozen banana at Zody's a different lifetime ago.

I had no indication she had any sense of my existence at all until this one stilted conversation she initiated in Oviatt Library.

I was reading Volume II of *The Norton Anthology of British Literature*, tripping out on Blake's imagery, and she sat down next to me and just started talking.

"Hey," she said, "from Dr. Acorn's class, right?" and I was forced to look at her eyes, which were of course still beautiful, born but to smile and fall, "Are you ready for the test tomorrow?"

"Hey, how's it going."

"Pretty good."

"Yeah, I'm pretty much ready. I'm also taking Romantic Lit with Professor Hickok this semester, so there's a lot of overlap," I stumbled in fixation with her face, nearly lost in self-conscious awareness that I was talking to the girl from Zody's.

"Ah, well, you have a distinct advantage then," she said, herself perpetuating the eye-lock for a number of rubbery moments until she averted her stare downward at my book. "Blake," she pointed, "I'm not sure about him."

"What aren't you sure about?"

"No, I mean, I don't think I'm getting him completely. It doesn't seem like poetry to me."

"What does it seem like?"

"I don't know. Something else. Ecstatic scripture maybe."

"It's that too, definitely. But why can't it also be poetry? What's it missing? Look at this passage," and I read to her, in a library whisper from "The Book of Thel."

Ah! Thel is like a wat'ry bow, and like a parting cloud;

Like a reflection in a glass; like shadows in the water;

Like dreams of infants, like a smile upon an infant's face;

Like the dove's voice; like transient day; like music in the air.

Ah! gentle may I lay me down, and gentle rest my head,

And gentle sleep the sleep of death, and gentle hear the voice

Of him that walketh in the garden in the evening time.

"I mean, come on, all the music you need is right there. It's got dance, it's got rhythm, it's got the perfect virgin in paradise unwilling to give it up for the pleasures of the world."

"That was me once," she said.

"I bet there are plenty of people out there who wish they'd made the same decision as Thel," I said, "I think the poem is a word concerto."

"I love that. A word concerto. I'm Lily, by the way."

I didn't automatically tell her my name according to accepted custom so she took up my dropped end of things: "And you're Georgie, right?"

"No, I'm Lance. I sometimes refer to myself privately as Georgie Porgie, but how would you know that?"

"Well, maybe I'm psychic."

"I don't groove on psychic phenomena."

"I don't know, for me it's more of a character study than anything else," she replied with the bohemian air of someone who isn't quite sure what she means.

"All right, if you're psychic then what am I thinking of right . . . now?" I challenged her, immediately thinking with great focus of her body in total submission to me.

This was my very feeble way of flirting with her. Just in case she really *was* psychic.

"Um," she closed her eyes as she concentrated (I wanted her to leave them open). "You're thinking of the fat kid from *Willy Wonka and the Chocolate Factory*. Buzzy something."

"Augustus—"

" . . . Lagniappe."

"—Gloop. Augustus Gloop."

"I thought his name was Buzzy Lagniappe."

"Augustus Gloop is the fat kid from *Willy Wonka & The Chocolate Factory*."

"Then who the fuck is Buzzy Lagniappe?"

"Well, actually, I grew up next door to a guy named Buzzy Lagniappe, if that's who you're talking about."

"Is he fat?"

"He was at one time, yeah. And his real name is Augustus. You know him?"

"No, I don't."

"Then how did you know he was fat?"

"I didn't. That's why I asked *you*, dum-dum."

I hadn't heard the term *dum-dum* since before my Zody's days.

"Well, Buzzy looks nothing like Augustus Gloop. Buzzy's more of a Danny Partridge-looking motherfucker."

She looked at me like she knew something.

Was she on the verge of realizing she's the girl from Zody's?

Instead, "So, you're one of those people people talk about," was her ambiguous innuendo.

"Sorry?"

"*Mr. Big Stuff,*" she started singing , "*who do you think you are?*"

"Could you, um . . . ?" I tried to get her to stop.

Heads turned and stared as she did her impromptu number.

"*You made 'em cry, many poor girls cry.*"

"I still don't get what you're—"

"—I do that song with my band, The Girly-Q's. We're playing Wednesday night at the Bla-Bla Cafe. You should come check us out," she handed me a flier for the show. While I looked at the flier without really reading it, she added, "You remind me of somebody . . ."

(Looking up into her eyes again, I was ready for the great Zody's revelation. Alas.)

". . . This guy I've been stalking for a while. I wrote a poem about him. You want to see it?" she asked as if I had the option.

Lily pulled a worn hard-bound journal out of her backpack and opened to the page where she had written the poem in elegant cursive.

"Here," she said, "tell me what you think."

She handed the book to me, and even though I think she wanted me to read it out loud like I had done with Blake I decided to ingest it silently.

The title told immediately that this infatuation would grow ugly if it went on long enough. It would all depend on her attention span.

The Iceman Liveth

When you first meet him
he looks like Willy Wonka
addicted to heroin

Then his magic face starts to throb
with layers of potent attraction
You are drawn to his wild brown eyes

But there is only so far you're let in

A sudden freeze-out numbs you into desperation
You want to follow him
Find out where he's hiding
Win back the balmy conversations
the fascinating plank

The Iceman Liveth
Right here
He will overwhelm you with his kiss
until your swoon embarrasses yourself and others
You are becoming one of those females and you hate it

You fixate

You unleash a barrage of pathetic beggings

Be careful in his midst

For he is a vile magnet

"Sounds like most guys I know," I said, "English major?"

"No duh," she said with a scurvy snarl. "One night he kissed me on the beach with such caveman passion I thought he was totally into me. Then when I asked him, 'What's going on between us?,' he said, like, all formal, 'Uh, I have enjoyed your company tonight,' and I was confused. 'But that kiss felt real,' I told him, and he just said, 'Oh, it was. I loved it.' And then I said, I said, 'Wait a sec,' I said, 'But you only loved the *kiss*, you don't love *me*,' and he goes, 'Hey I don't even know your name, girl' as if that's some kind of excuse. Oh, but he's such a fox. I must have him."

"So, what, you started following him around?"

"Well, basically . . ."

"Do I know this guy?"

"He knows you. Tony Crumb?"

"Oh, yeah, sure. Really into 18th Century stuff. He's a Pope/Dryden dude. And a total Pepys-head. The biggest one I know."

"You know more than one?"

"Pepys-heads? They're everywhere."

"So you know Tony then."

"He's cool, yeah."

"Well, he thinks you're an arrogant prick."

"He's half right," I said, disguising the cold rush of shit to my heart.

"I think it's 'cause he heard you making fun of Dr. McMichaels' vocal tic or something over on the roof of Sierra South."

I smiled, "Oh, the 'hmm?' thing McMichaels does at the end of each sentence?"

"Yes!" she laughed too loudly for the library, "the beep sound!"

"My theory is it's because McMichaels is Canadian and tried to swallow saying, 'eh?' at the end of his sentences, and it got stuck in his throat: 'hmm?'"

"Fuckin' McMichaels," she scoffed, "what a hard-ass. If you answer one of his questions wrong in class he never calls on you again. I had Medieval Lit I with him last semester, and the class got so hypnotized by the 'hmm?' at the end of each sentence that we all unconsciously started beeping 'hmm?' in unison with him 'cause we were so caught up in the rhythm. It was really funny when some of us would become aware of the group 'hmm?' and look at each other and start giggling. The best though was when he'd look up after a classwide unison 'hmm?', thinking that somebody was asking a question, and'd go, 'Hmm?' Oh, it was so hard not to bust up right then."

"And McMichaels never figured out what you were doing?"

"Hell no! But I always thought about what it must sound like to somebody walking by in the hall or sitting out there waiting for the next class. You could probably not hear McMichaels, just a classroom full of students beeping 'hmm?' together every few seconds. I got a 'D' in that class. But Tony thinks McMichaels is God, so when you were lampooning the deity it bugged him."

"And that's what you mean by I'm one of those people people talk about, hmm?"

"Oh, no. I was referring to something else."

"Like what, hmm?"

She laughed as she stood up to leave.

"I'm going to go get a frozen banana from Zody's, wanna come?," I thought I heard her say.

"Hmm?"

"I'm hoping to suck your cock like a pony's, wanna come?," was the next version there's no way I actually heard her say because I was too busy thinking about the first time I'd laid eyes on (I think it was) her with a frozen banana in her mouth.

"Sorry," I motioned, pointing, "rock and roll ears. One more time?"

"I'm going to go stalk Tony, wanna come?"

"No, I need to work on Blake. I've got a paper due on Thel next week."

"Well, if you wanna study together later for the test, here, give me a call," and she proceeded to write her phone number in the palm of my hand while continuing, "And can I ask you a question? Why do guys have to be such assholes? Before I started dating them, I thought they were awesome. Reality changed my understanding of . . . um . . . reality. It's been my saddest heart-fall."

"That's a cool image. You should use it in a poem."

"Maybe I will. I'm working on a poem about following Tony around campus. It's perfect for the last stanza. *Reality changed my understanding of reality*," she wrote in her journal.

I was actually referring to the image *my saddest heart-fall*. That's when I realized she was not a poet but a journalist.

"I still want to know what you meant by I'm one of those people people talk about," I made one last plea.

"Oh, I don't mean anything by it. People talk about you. You are a topic of conversation. Code Name: Georgie Porgie."

"But what are they saying, other than calling me an arrogant prick?"

"Hey, gimme a buzz tonight and I'll be more specific, 'k?"

"All right. And let me read that poem when it's done," I whispered as she left.

"I will," she promised without meaning it. I tried to turn my attention away from Lily and back toward Blake and Thel:

Why cannot the Ear be closed to its own destruction?

the glist'ning Eye to the poison of a smile?

Why are Eyelids stor'd with arrows ready drawn,

Where a thousand fighting men in ambush lie?

Or an Eye of gifts and graces show'ring fruits and coined gold?

Why a Tongue impress'd with honey from every wind?

Why an Ear, a whirlpool fierce to draw creations in?

Why a Nostril wide inhaling terror, trembling, and affright?

Why a tender curb upon the youthful burning boy?

Why a little curtain of flesh on the bed of our desire?

I was pretty sure I had just talked to the girl from Zody's.

And I was a little more heart-fallen because of it.

I never did call Lily.

By the time I worked up the courage my sweaty palm had blurred the ink beyond deciphering.

That probably wasn't her real phone number anyway.

Frenching

I am, either by nature or by nurture (not sure which), drawn to the ironic art of the straight-faced put-on, or, in the jargon of post-graduate academia, the *legitimated hoax* (public performances that purport to be authentic but wherein the perceiver knows the content is fake and chooses to believe in it anyway): professional wrestling, magic shows, Santa Claus, The Monkees, *The Oidar Wavelength*, Andy Kaufman, Sherlock Holmes & Dr. Watson, the State of the Union Address, Peter Pan, the Harlem Globtrotters, softcore pornography, *Fernwood Tonight*, the *War Of The Worlds* radio broadcast, fortune cookies.

And of course no such roster would be complete without roller derby, the most erotic and volatile legitmated hoax of all.

Our local roller derby team was the Los Angeles Thunderbirds.

We dug the guys too, of course— Ralphie Valladares, "Psycho" Ronnie Rains, Danny Reilly, Big John Johnson and his gangly windmill jamming, Dave Pound for a time—but it was really the ladies we loved, the real reason we watched—Shirley Hardman, Skinny Minny Miller, Honey Sanchez, Earlean Brown, Sally Vega, Colleen Murrell, Cathy Traylor, Sherry Jackson, Terri Lynch, our goddesses.

All that hot girl-on-girl catfighting.

All those first stirrings.

Our bodies and minds were just beginning to get it on.

And then into our skate-girl loving lives came Raquel Welch, the big vavoom at that time, starring in *Kansas City Bomber*, a roller derby movie, with Raquel in curve-tight uniform, acres of woman, a living symbol.

I had a beloved poster of Raquel Welch bikini-clad up on the wall of my bedroom.

She'd replaced an earlier poster of Marlo Thomas in *That Girl*.

My tastes and passions were in transitional shift. And Raquel ruled the sanctified land of pre-horny nerdboys.

We all went to see *Kansas City Bomber* at the Paramount Theater on Hollywood Blvd., riding our bikes betwixt and between the tourists, junkies, and teenage runaways who peopled the Walk-of-Fame.

The guys I did stuff like that with—Whitman Rust, Manny Shepherd, and Gus Lagniappe—enjoyed obscenity and racial slurs and inappropriately loud mockery of passers-by whom they'd often compare to the likes of Sonny Bono or Mr. French or Spiro Agnew.

I would get embarrassed at such goofball dumbjerk public rudeness. But I wasn't sure if I was embarrassed because my friends were assholes or embarrassed because I thought they were funny.

I was a goody-goody with a wicked imagination.

I'd always let other people express my demons for me.

"My name is Pancho, I work on a rancho, I make pfipty pesos a day," said Whit in reference to nothing in particular as we sat in the theatre waiting for the movie to start with our Milk Duds and tubes of FLICKS chocolates, which, if you held the tube with your thumb over the bottom of the "L" and the "I" looked like it said FUCKS (later they changed the label to read *Flicks*, the lower case letters essentially ruining the naughty fun of children . . . we always wondered if that was the reason they changed it, that somehow they'd gotten wind of our little delight in the obscene . . .).

"I go to see Lucy, I play with her pussy, she take all my pesos away," Whit continued with exaggerated Mexican accent.

As 11-year-old boys we (or at least I) didn't fully understand such humor nor how much that humor grew out of real-life sexual experiences; we just thought it was funny to have a joke with the word *pussy* in it.

I had not spilled any man-seed as yet, so when Gus told a joke about a 'blowjob' I didn't quite understand the concept.

"You know, she sucks on your dick, dude, and stuff comes out," said Gus to my inquiry regarding what a 'blowjob' was.

"What stuff?" I wondered, thinking of some weird secretion of unknown penile insides.

27

"Think about it, dorkwad," Gus taunted.

"Ah, yeah, heh," I pretended to 'get it.'

With the onset of the cocksucking imagery, we all, naturally, began thinking of our classmate Gina Dichlich, whose perfectly realized name conjured the most confusing rumble of suggestions.

We'd gone to school with Gina Dichlich since kindergarten.

Every year, on the first day of school, her new teachers would get to Gina's name on the attendance roster and try any possible pronunciation except the correct one, hoping it wasn't what they thought it was.

"Deetchleetch" they'd say or "Deeshleesh" or "Ditchlitch" or "Dykelike" if they had to.

Gina always took great pleasure in raising her hand and saying, "It's DICK-LICK," with a knowing and amused smile.

We worshipped her spunk and her mini-skirts.

"Dichlich's a spitfire," Whit used to love saying, "Gonna get some o' dat Dichlich lipstick on my dipstick, yuh-huh," an event that would never occur in real life.

Gus rode the residual laughter by starting in, "So this guy is eating this girl's pussy out," (the first time I'd ever heard of such behavior), "and he starts getting like particles of food and stuff in his mouth, like fruit and other type of chunks, and he says to the girl, 'Hey, are you sick or something?,' and the girl goes like, 'No, but the guy before you was,'" and Manny and Whit just went into hysterics, joined by Gus then laughing at his own joke, and I laughed along without fully grasping the concept, though I did think about that punchline for quite a while afterward.

The film was disappointing, riding a lot on the fascinating wonder of Raquel's ample breastage.

The roller derby sequences seemed 'fake,' which we all noted with ironic glee afterward, and the story was predictable. The usual triumph of the human spirit crapola. I hate pretty much any movie that ends with a slow-motion victory lap. And the inevitable freeze frame. Dang, dude.

The part I remember best is when Raquel Welch kissed her boyfriend, and they had their mouths open, and they were sticking their tongues in each other's mouths.

I'd never seen that before.

Movie kisses, like all the real world kisses I'd seen until then, were with lips together, smooches, pecks. Even when I'd pass by young couples making out at the Tar Pits I never imagined their mouths were open and their tongues were touching.

I leaned over to Gus during the first kissing scene and asked what they were doing.

"They're frenching!" he whispered loudly.

There were a couple more frenchings in the film and at each occurrence I'd hear, in my head, Gus whispering, "They're frenching!" over and over; the sound of the word gained a liquid animation in my thought-responses.

Frenching, a mouth-melting splendor castle, a drawbridge to girlness, a hot and salty visitation, a tingly uproar of the body and all its blood.

Frenching.

"They're frenching!"

"Dang, dude, Raquel is foxy as all get-out," said Gus after the movie, using a comparative phrase I've never quite understood, "all get-out."

One of his Kansas sayings.

The Lagniappes had moved to Los Angeles from somewhere in Kansas when Gus was in 3rd Grade.

"Lance doesn't know what frenching is!" taunted Manny.

"Yes I do!" I said in defense.

"Yeah, now, after Gus told you!" Manny retorted.

"Lance is a gay golita," giggled Whit.

That term "gay golita" was Whit's description of any dude who wasn't into girls.

We were in that tweeny corridor during which puberty grabs hold of each boy at different times, some, like Whit and Gus, already sprouting pubes

29

and fantasizing about oral sex and variant copulations with the girls we knew, others not yet having made the full transition.

Those were the "gay golitas" Whit would take pleasure in accusing.

I was often identified as one by Whitman Rust.

Except I was already more into girls than the three of my chums realized, ignorant of specific sex practices beyond the most basic, but definitely feeling the feeling inside.

There was this one girl . . . Miranda . . . I kept my infatuation a secret, silenced by the shame of wanting, suspended in solipsis. Still, I would eventually be the first among us to do any frenching . . .

. . . It would have been a year after the *Kansas City Bomber* outing, so Fall semester of 8th Grade, that I got a phone call from Miranda Savitch, the object of my burgeoning lust, a constant presence in my attention since 7th Grade English, the predominant face in fantasy, Miranda Savitch, font of sweet sarcasm, a goddess and a scholar.

Why had she called me?

"Hey, so, Candy Stoner and I, Candy's here by the way, say hi, Candy . . ."

"Hi, Lance!" I heard Candy's voice giggle from across the room.

"Hi, Candy," I twinkled back fake-adorably.

"He says, 'Hi Candy,'" Miranda relayed to Candy in pitch perfect mimicry of me, ". . . So, Candy and I are going to the movies this Saturday, and we were wondering if you and Oliver want to come too?"

"Ummm, yeah, I guess. What're you seeing?" I asked.

"It's a double-bill at The Fairfax: *Soylent Green* and *Westworld*. Yul Brenner is in it. Et cet-er-a, et cet-er-a, et cet-er-a."

"Ah, coolness, yeah, I'll go," I sputtered, already picturing sitting next to Miranda in the movie theatre and realizing I wouldn't really know what to do.

I was 12 years old by then.

The first time I ever spoke to Miranda Savitch beyond awkward greetings was the year before when we were assigned to work together on literature questions—we had been reading "The False Gems" by Guy De Maupassant—in Ms. LaBouche's class.

Tackling the question on M. Lantin's emotional reaction to his wife's death—the answer was 'despair'—we started discussing *The Omega Man*, a movie from a couple of years before, which I had seen at the Gilmore Drive-In when it came out but which Miranda had just watched the previous weekend on television.

"Movies like that make you realize there's always hope," she said in response to my complaining that the film was depressing. "Despair was one of our vocab words last week, remember?, and so when I watched *Omega Man* while I was babysitting Saturday night, I noticed Charlton Heston never gave in to despair."

I'll admit that in 7th Grade I didn't really understand the Maupassant story, few of us did, but in that moment, listening to her speak of matters that . . . well . . . mattered, I entered a recurring state of fascination with Miranda Savitch, one that would glimmer and fizzle and glimmer and fizzle regularly for years thereafter, adrift beyond the current, always failing to catch the wave.

The more she spoke the more I wanted to french her.

"You might find it depressing," she continued, "but I find it uplifting. There's always hope. Remember that, monsieur."

And then she wrote on my exercise answer sheet:

you remind me of the little prince! luv, Miranda

I spent countless amounts of time staring at that message, partly flattered, partly not really sure what she meant. Was she making fun of me?

We didn't talk much at length after that for the rest of 7th Grade.

I did find it highly amusing that she wrote in my yearbook, *Good luck with Raquel.*

She'd been listening.

I said, "So yeah I'll go, but I don't know about Oliver. I'll have to ask him," but Miranda informed me:

"Oh, that's done. Oliver already said he'd go with me, and now you're gonna go with Candy, how bitchin'," followed by a whisper, "Candy likes you!"

"You are so fucking dead," I heard Candy scold in the background and then the sound of tussling over the phone.

"She does!" Miranda squealed, then, recovering from the scuffle, added, "See you at school tomorrow and we'll figure out a time and everything, 'k?"

"Um, yeah," I offered, from a sinking position.

"OK, bye, Lance," then quickly, "and your new girlfriend says bye too!"

"You bit—," most of Candy's epithet got through before the dial tone.

Dang. Miranda liked Oliver.

It was worse than getting stuck on the Small World ride at Disneyland.

Worse than pantomime in the park.

Worse than buttered popcorn flavored jellybeans.

Worse than mothballs.

Worse than Saturday afternoon television.

Worse than The Valley.

Worse than meatloaf.

Worse than stomach flu.

Worse than pre-algebra homework.

Worse than having to read *Island Of The Blue Dolphins*.

Worse than the oral polio vaccine.

Worse than carnival music, the soundtrack of organized fun.

Worse than holiday meals in an old-age home.

Worse than cotillion.

Worse than visiting friends of your parents who have "kids your age" with whom you are expected to bond immediately and have a bossa nova time for untold hours.

Worse than the fact that said friends of parents never have beautiful daughters, always only sons of two stripes: delinquent slackers who like to play with fire and shoot birds with BB guns or else drippy pillboxes who collect Star Trek memorabilia and are members of the Junior Count Dracula Society, usually making a stop-motion animation Super-8 film in their backyard using their Major Matt Mason dolls and all ready to tell you more than you ever wanted to know about the complete works of Ray Harryhausen.

Worse than that gnarly bitch Yocheved who sits next to you in Hebrew school.

Worse than having to go see The Carpenters at the Hollywood Bowl with your parents.

Worse than the *I Love Lucy* episodes that take place on the farm in Connecticut.

Worse than an orthodox cousin's bar mitzvah.

Worse than the arts & crafts table at day camp.

Worse than tetherball.

There's always hope. Remember that, monsieur.

We all met up at the Fairfax Theatre, a dingy cavern whose floors were slippery with butter topping, and the whole place smelled like wet dogs had peed all over the moldy carpeting in the aisles.

But you could see a double-bill for $1.50, and for those of us on allowance that made socializing happily affordable.

Oliver bought a tube of FLICKS, which he called 'Ghetto Kisses', and which he kept holding up with his thumb covering the bottom part of the "L" and "I," snickering, "Dang, check it out, FUCKS."

Candy giggled uncomfortably while eating a hot dog.

Miranda rolled her eyes and ate popcorn.

I had a Wonka Scrumdiddlyumptious bar.

Wonka chocolate was a phenomenon in a kind of subset of the *legitimated hoax* tradition.

A fake candy company that was also real.

Based entirely on the popularity of the Gene Wilder movie *Willy Wonka and the Chocolate Factory*, Wonka chocolate nevertheless was 'real' candy, sold in stores and movie theatres, and yet it was a fabrication at the same time.

And the whole time you were eating Wonka chocolate you'd be thinking, whoa, this is really the chocolate that Willy Wonka made, knowing full well that Willy Wonka is a fictional character (and the Gene Wilder character in the film a double fiction).

Thus, I consumed Wonka chocolate with dogged fascination.

Oliver taunted, "Dang, dude, I thought only Buzzy Lagniappe ate that shit."

"You mean Gus?"

"No, dude, Buzzy Lagniappe, the fat kid from *Willy Wonka and The Chocolate Factory*."

"That's Augustus Gloop," said Miranda, who looked at me and Candy and mouthed the word "retard," which made Candy almost choke on her hot dog.

"I thought it was Buzzy Lagniappe," said Oliver.

"Augustus Gloop is the fat kid from the book *Charlie and the Chocolate Factory* by Roald Dahl, which was later made into a movie starring Gene Wilder called *Willy Wonka and the Chocolate Factory*," Miranda told Oliver.

"Sometimes we call Gus Lagniappe Augustus Gloop," I tried to explain.

"Gus looks nothing like Augustus Gloop," said Miranda, "that's stupid."

"I think it's more the Augustus thing since that's Gus's real name."

"Boys," muttered Miranda.

"I like boys even though they're stupid," Candy said.

And Oliver shook his head, "Dang, dude, where did I get Buzzy from? I'm such a retard."

Miranda shot me a look that almost made me gloop the scrumdiddlyumptious chocolate in my mouth. Then she flicked a piece of popcorn at me which glanced off the lens of my glasses into Candy's coke.

"Hey, that's not nice," said Candy to Miranda, then turning to me asked, "Are you ok, baby?" and kissed my lens, smudging it with lip gloss (*Cerise Sauvage* the flavor was called, I still remember) and a dab of mayonnaise that had lingered on her lips.

The movies themselves were irrelevant.

I had to go back and see both *Soylent Green* and *Westworld* again another time because I was unable to pay attention to either.

My head was preoccupied with the agony of not knowing what to do, and that included what I was expected to do, what I'd end up wishing I'd done, what I wanted to do.

Did I even want to do anything with Candy Stoner?

She was beautiful and sweet but.

I looked over at Miranda and Oliver.

Oliver seemed to be going through a similar paralytic crisis.

Miranda, who caught my glance, stuck her tongue out at me and then flicked another a piece of popcorn which lodged itself in my voluminous jewfro.

"What is your problem, Mandy? Leave my boyfriend alone," Candy said, rushing to my defense (and disentangling the popcorn from my frizz).

Hearing her use the word boyfriend, knowing Candy Stoner liked me "like that," was flattering enough to be persuasive, and I found myself rolling with the vibe of having something going on with her, even though nothing official, verbal or otherwise, had happened between us.

But then what?

I bargained with myself, "The next time Charlton Heston speaks I'm going to put my arm around her."

At Heston's subsequent move-busting line I shifted the stakes, "The next time Charlton Heston speaks to Edward G. Robinson then I'll . . ." and postponed my advance several more times until eventually I did in fact put my arm around Candy Stoner . . . and just sort of left it there . . . for a long time . . . waiting for inspiration . . . until my arm fell asleep . . . and Candy's shirt was getting damp . . . but if I took my arm away she'd think I didn't like her or something . . . so I left it there . . . numb and sweaty . . . until the end of *Soylent Green*.

When the lights came up in the theatre, I couldn't move my right arm, so I had to hoist it with my left hand off Candy's shoulders.

Candy and Miranda went to wait in line for the bathroom, and Oliver and I talked about our respective conquests.

"Dang, dude, I felt some titty during *Soylent Green*, right through Miranda's shirt, and, dang, she got some tig ol' bitties, dude. I just put my arm around her and kept on reaching down till I got my left hand on some of that, you know," Oliver said while slunked all the way down in his chair, his feet hoisted up on the back of the seat in front of him.

I had glanced regularly over at Oliver and Miranda throughout the film and saw no hand anywhere near Miranda's tig ol'. But I let Ollie have his brag, sort of, giving him only a wee bit of a hard time.

"Through the shirt doesn't count, man," I proclaimed with authority.

"Where's it say that?"

"My baby sister told me."

"Um, Atlas, your baby sister has Down Syndrome."

"Yeah, but still, Joy knows the rules. And she told me once that feeling titty through the shirt doesn't count."

"You a damn lie," Oliver scoffed, "She never said that shit to you."

"No, for real, she did, she said you can do that by accident on a crowded bus anytime. Through the bra will get you points because that takes some skill and finesse. But through the shirt ain't shit."

"Dang, dude, that's cold. Like you're Mr. Joe Pussy over there, Mr. Make-out Artist. What'd you get off Candy anyways?," Oliver called me out with playful hostility.

"I wasn't trying to get anything.."

36

"Yeah, well, dang, dude, Candy's got those itty bitties; you'd need like a geiger counter and a magnifying glass and tweezers and shit to find 'em. Dang, that'd been dog in the movie if Soylent Green was made from titties, dude. Charlton Heston'd be yellin' 'Soylent Green is titties!' dude, 'Soylent green is titties!,'" he cracked himself up. "But, so, wait, you didn't do shit with Candy, did you?"

"I put my arm around her . . ."

"Aaaaah-ha, loser," he teased.

The girls returned having had, no doubt, a similar if more truthful conversation, waiting in line for the bathroom.

When *Westworld* started, Candy reached over and took my hand, eliciting an electric gooseflesh as our skin slid together and our fingers enmeshed.

I didn't make eye contact with her in that moment, but I smiled at this new dark pleasure.

After a minute or so, she squeezed my hand.

I squeezed back.

Several seconds later she squeezed my hand twice.

I squeezed back twice.

Several seconds after that she squeezed my hand three times.

And, yeah, I matched her again but I started wondering if I had to squeeze back every time. Like if it just kept increasing indefinitely and how much concentration that would eventually require.

Later in the film she put her head on my shoulder, and I kind of leaned my head against hers.

She squeezed my hand when I did that.

A few seconds later she squeezed my hand twice.

And a few seconds after that . . .

Dang, dude.

Our hands grew sweatier the more I twisted my soul into resolution, until she whispered, "It's ok to let go once in a while," while disentangling from my shvitzy grip.

That was the extent of our lovemaking.

I am the lamest excuse for a human male.

While walking back down Fairfax Avenue toward Miranda's and Candy's houses after the movies, we stopped at Jack-In-The-Box on the corner of Drexel and Fairfax for some french fries.

Oliver asked for 20 packets of ketchup and proceeded to flood his fries by making use of every single packet.

During the deluge, he said, "Remember that *I Love Lucy* episode when they're in France and Lucy gets arrested for putting ketchup on escargot? That was fuckin' funny, dude."

"She didn't get arrested for putting ketchup on escargot, she got arrested because her money was counterfeit. She had fake francs," Miranda scolded.

"Whatever, it was fucking funny, dude."

"That's the best Europe episode," I opined.

"Oh, no, my favorite is when she's stomping grapes in Italy," squealed Candy, "I just wanted to like get in that big-ass barrel and get all squishy."

"It's a vat, not a barrel," Miranda corrected.

"I got that doll for my 7th birthday, too," said Candy, "the Lucy-Stomping-Grapes Barbie, and I got in trouble for using it to smash a whole mess of grapes my mother had brought home for a barbeque we were having, oh, man . . . 'but we're playing *I Love Lucy*' I kept saying to my mom. She put me on punishment anyways."

"Dang, that's dog, dude," consoled Oliver.

"Anything is better than the farm episodes in Connecticut," Miranda chimed in.

"Totally," I agreed, "those are the worst. It's like not even really *I Love Lucy* anymore." Miranda looked at me briefly with great tacit vehemence and then looked away.

Standing on the corner of Fairfax and Drexel, none of us wanting to let go of the moment, Miranda suggested we walk over to the Tar Pits and hang out there for a while.

The 6th Street side of the Tar Pits was quieter than the Wilshire side and so we usually hung out there, away from the main Tar Pit where the tourists congregated.

There was a little stream that didn't really move (a 'crick' Gus Lagniappe used to call it), mostly tar and barely liquid, over on the north side of the park.

One could watch the river not flow with great deliberate stillness, feeling the bog of time get all sludged up and bubbling.

It was a sweet and mild November afternoon in 1973, with air like silk and as motionless as the water in the stream, the evergreen foliage showing no sign of autumn.

An exquisite Los Angeles day.

We would always be 12 years old . . . If we just stayed right there by that stream . . . A future preserved in tar.

I sat on the grass along the north bank of the stream with Candy.

Miranda and Oliver crossed the Japanese footbridge to the other side of the stream and sat down together over on the south bank, facing us. Miranda waved.

"So, did you like the movies?" Candy asked me, diverting my gaze from Miranda across the way.

"Uhm, I wasn't really able to pay attention."

"No? Why?"

"I was distracted."

"By?"

I shrugged and blushed.

"Hey," she said, tapping my hand with her index finger, timidly inviting me to pounce.

Our fingers interlocked.

Even at 12 I had seen enough films to know this was a kissing moment, though I had never made that move before.

In this strange instance, though, I wasn't struggling with the shame of wanting, the weakness of needing.

I didn't really want Candy.

It wasn't the usual neurotic barricade.

No, another stitch arose in its place, one which involved the unexpected reality of accepting that Candy desired me.

That was a worse obstruction.

The shame of wanting, it turned out, was trumped by the deeper shame of being wanted.

But somehow . . .

After several minutes of silence and discomfort and Candy squeezing my hand once, twice, three times, again, dang, dude . . . I finally silently commanded myself, "Do it now," leaned forward, and kissed Candy Stoner on the mouth, lips together, puckered, smack, over in a millisecond.

Then, as I pulled my head away from that first feeble kiss, Candy placed her left hand on the back of my neck and drew me back toward her face, saying, barely above a whisper, "Come on. For real," and proceeded to insert herself, lips parted, into my mouth, finding my elusive, tentative tongue and coiling round it, slithering along my teeth, braces and all, and then around my tongue again, her bubblegum breath a perfume of the most ecstatic splendor.

I was doing it . . . my eyes were closed . . . savoring every sensation . . . beyond the barricade . . . I was . . .

"Frenching!" shouted Miranda, disrupting the breakthrough with immediate buzzkill accuracy, "They're frenching!"

Our lips and tongues unlocked, and we both looked over at Miranda and Oliver.

Oliver was holding two thumbs up in the air.

"Dang, dude! Go for that Soylent Green, baby!" he shouted.

Miranda transmitted a passionless glare at both of us, as Candy lay back and pulled me into face-dock with her and again we were at it.

Nothing else happened but lips teeth and tongues.

It was clear what Candy wanted. But what did Miranda want? And was she ashamed of it?

I realized as I was frenching Candy Stoner that there was no way Miranda Savitch had any real interest in Oliver Gelding.

What would they talk about?

His baseball card collection? His *MAD* Magazine obsession? *Twilight Zone* trivia?

Her ashen aspect betrayed the wrongness of it all.

By the time Candy and I were done frenching, Oliver was alone, leaning over the Japanese footbridge letting loogies dribble from his lips into the stream.

Miranda had left a while before, he told us, deciding to walk home alone.

The next day after school, I rode my bike over to Candy's house, following an invitation from her that ended with the tantalizing, "My mother won't be home."

And, indeed, her mother wasn't home, but her older sister Desirée was, blasting the new Who album *Quadrophenia* on the stereo, bopping around the house in Levi's cut-offs and an excellently skimpy pink halter top.

I was greeted at the front door by her singing along with the blaring music.

"You say she's a virgin? Well I'm gonna be the first in," she spun, stopping to shimmy in my general direction, then continuing around to face me straight on in delivery of the lines, *"What is it? I'll take it. Who is she? I'll rape it,"* turning away but looking over her shoulder at me, *"Gotta bet there? I'll meet it,"* and heading up the stairs, *"Getting high? You can't beat it,"* doing a full on joint-smoking pantomime and head gestures to indicate I should come up.

Nah, I motioned her away, I'd come to see Candy.

"Your boyfriend came," Desirée yelled at a closed bedroom door before disappearing into her own sordid chamber of venery.

Candy came down the stairs and led me into the living room, where we sat on the couch and just simply started frenching without even exchanging meaningful greetings, two bodies suffused with newness.

A few minutes into our session, however, the doorbell rang, and, looking out the window, Candy could see, "Oh, jeez-louise, it's Miranda, why is she—"

When Candy went and opened the door, Miranda said, "Hi, I just came by to see what you were doing and—"

"—You know exactly what—"

"—Oh, hey, Lance is here, I'm sorry, I didn't—Hi, Lance!" Miranda greeted me from the entry hall.

"Hey," I said.

Candy and Miranda whispered intently for a couple of minutes at the front door, and then Miranda left, shouting, "Bye, Lance!" from outside.

I waved back through the window at her furrowed brow and impossibly mismatched glinting smile.

Candy returned to the couch and nestled expertly into the contours of my flank.

"Hi, Lance," she said, imitating Miranda, as she beckoned me to another excellent lesson in frenching.

I relaxed and basked in the sweet sadness.

I had a girlfriend.

It wasn't Miranda.

There's always hope. Remember that, monsieur

I succumbed to the bliss of not wanting.

I Want To Tell You

1

"The correct answer is always 'I don't know,'" Miranda Savitch said to the weird and mysterious Lorelei Lux who was in the midst of some vague perplexity (one never got details from Lorelei Lux, only cryptic glimpses and innuendos, so it didn't much matter).

I would know her quite well one day, Lorelei Lux.

Anyway, on that day her words were mostly gobbledygook through the impenetrable filter of male-resistant gibberish, that schoolyard giddy-guy-giddy-goo girl language.

It was December 1973. My bar mitzvah was coming up the following April. Life was starting to get interesting.

I had come to the arcade in the Town & Country shopping center at 3rd & Fairfax, across the street from Farmers Market, with Gus Lagniappe, Claude Moss (known to his tormentors—which sometimes included us, depending—as "The Fungus"), Whitman Rust, Oliver Gelding, and Chester Flinch, an unpredictably fun but sometimes out-of-control member of our unofficial cool nerd crew.

The arcade was a sanctified parent-free zone, a place where cigarettes were in full fume, forbidden couples shared their star-crossed love, uber-dorks competed for the top pinball scores, and girls were almost easy to talk to.

That day we were particularly interested in checking out the new arcade game, Pong, neither pinball machine nor shooting gallery, all of the action taking place on a TV screen. Pinball purists shunned the new invader, but we were hot to experience this latest incarnation of fun.

The reality did not live up to our fantasies, however.

Everything is kind of like that, though.

Pong was a rudimentary joke compared to the flashing lights and bumper bells and random pathways of pinball.

Nevertheless, I played a game of Pong with Gus for the sake of trying it out, and while making sure my little white video paddle hit the oncoming dot-ball I contemplated going over to Fisher's for a mediocre hamburger or maybe some fishsticks with tartar sauce because that shit tasted good.

Amid the din of useless thoughts I heard Miranda's voice coaching Lorelei through her vexation, and so I diverted my attention from the comfort food at Fisher's and the bland amusements of Pong to the much more compelling prospect of scavenging useful wisdom from the secret life of girls.

"The correct answer is always 'I don't know.' Lance will agree. Right, Lance?" Miranda said from behind me.

"Oh, definitely. 'I don't know' will get you out of just about anything," I offered as support despite my ignorance of the context, "You know, look at Nixon."

"No thanks, I'd rather not," snapped Miranda.

"Do you prefer crunchy or puffy Cheetos?" Lorelei Lux asked me with the gravitas of Nostradamus.

"Um, crunchy," I said, "The puffy ones feel like you're biting into week-old cat shit."

"I see," Lorelei said as she pondered my answer, "week-old cat shit . . . that changes a few things . . . interesting . . ." Lorelei Lux often said, "interesting . . ." with great menacing inscrutability.

"Tell me, sir," she pursued further.

"Depending," I warned.

"Do you hyphenate week-old, or is it two words?"

"Hyphenate," I confirmed.

"Interesting . . ." Lorelei did her thing, " . . . And what about cat shit? Hyphenated or two words?"

"Two words."

"Interesting . . ."

"It should be one word though: catshit. That's what I think, like bullshit."

"I'll have to take that into consideration for later," Lorelei waxed prophetic, "and there will be a later . . . for you and for me, Lance Atlas."

"And for everyone," I peered into the cold and unforgiving gaze of Ms. Lux.

Miranda turned her face to me, her brown eyes dampening the onslaught of flashing and flourescence, and asked, "How's your Christmas vacation been?"

"Pretty mellow," I said, "I've just been very laid-back, listening to the radio, records, you know, reading *The Exorcist*." I moved away from the Pong game and let Chester take my place.

"I know what you're doing, dude," said Chester as he took over for me, "Yeah-uh, Miran-duh, Yeah-uh, Miranduh . . ." he chanted while playing Pong with his right hand and grabbing and squeezing one of my pectorals in rhythm to the incantation with his left.

One day he'd be either a drummer or a piano player. I never did find out which.

Miranda looked briefly and efficiently at Lorelei who immediately wandered off to share her indecipherable crisis with somebody else.

"Are you going to see the movie?"

"Definitely. Day after Christmas. Right when it opens. That's why I'm reading the book."

"I'm going that day too. In Westwood? The crowds are going to be crayzee."

"For damn sure," I agreed, "Me and Gus and Chester and Claude are going anyway, though. Maybe Whit too. The book is pretty scary. At least so far. So we'll see about the movie."

"They're saying the movie's going to be more popular than *American Graffiti*."

45

American Graffiti had infiltrated and then pervaded Southern California youth culture quickly. We all went to see it when it had come out that past August and were immediately sucked into '50s cool.

American Graffiti took place in 1962, but to us anything before The Beatles was the '50s.

The nostalgia wave was swelling, with the *American Grafitti* soundtrack album a staple at adolescent parties, the TV show *Happy Days* soon to be bursting into prominence, KRTH-101 and KRLA pumping out the oldies to teen bedrooms and backyards and cars across the Southland; Wolfman Jack became a visible icon instead of just a voice hovering up from Mexico; school dances overnight turned into "sock hops," and I think we were all drawn to the simple rules of teen life—at least as we perceived it—in the '50s as opposed to the tangled up angles facing those of us coming of age circa 1973/1974, when there were still rules, but nobody seemed to know which ones applied anymore and which ones didn't.

Plus, some of us had youngish parents who had been teenagers in the '50s so we grew up with that mythology, hearing the stories and records, seeing the photographs and the yearbooks, visual and sonic patterns deeply engrained in our inherited psyches.

American Graffiti was also a welcome departure in a summer spent watching the heinous disgraces of Watergate get unveiled daily on television.

Ooh, we fuckin' hated Nixon, dude.

"Well maybe I'll see you there!" Miranda continued, "Which showing are you going to?"

"I don't know yet. Probably the earliest. We like to be the first ones to have the best lines memorized. Yup. Geeks, basically," I said.

"Defenly," Miranda concurred, smiling and looking at her shoes.

"Defenly," I teased in mimicry.

"Don't make fun of me."

"Well you're smiling to yourself because you agree I'm a geek, right?"

"Defenly," she nodded.

"Defenly," I imitated her again with deadpan earnestness.

"Stop."

"OK."

"Really," she made me swear.

"Really."

We paused in thought. Separate but equal. I looked down.

"You have fluffy balls hanging from your socks."

"Those are my tennis socks. They bring me good luck," she said.

"Neat," I said, for want.

I perused the room searching for a topic to keep the conversation going.

Miranda got there first. That was her job.

"So, Lancelot Link Secret Chimp, what happened with you and Candy?
You're not together anymore?"

I thought Miranda and Candy were still best friends, but it's easy to fall
behind in the swiftly shifting sagas and allegiances of girl-world, so I had to
fill her in on the details of the Lance-Candy derailment.

"I guess the answer is I don't know, I'm not sure really. We pretty much
just stopped frenching. One day I didn't go over her house after school and
that was it. We didn't officially break up or anything."

"Kind of the way it started, right?" Miranda observed spot-on.

"Yeah, huh," I admitted, "Alls I know is she's pretty much ignoring me.
I've tried to say hi but."

"Well, she's being a real bitch to me too right now for whatever reason. Do
your friends know?"

"Nyeah, I don't know, it barely lasted long enough for them to notice it was
even happening, but, yeah," I sort of sighed, "They mostly went, 'Dang,
dude, you didn't even make it to the next menstrual cycle.' Sorry about the
rudeness."

"No, that's funny if you're a boy I guess," Miranda said.

"No no, my friends are rude. I'm sorry," I apologized again.

"If it was that rude you wun't have told me it, right? I mean, you din't have to. You wanted to tell me."

I did.

"That's right, I wun't," I imitated her again.

"How's Pong?" she changed the subject.

"Pong stinks," I said, "like why would you give a fuck about getting good at something like that? Maybe it's 'cause they left the ping out. That's what's missing. Right now, it's all pong."

"No ping, just pong," she hung with my dorkological driveling.

"Zackly," I said as if I were chewing bubblegum.

"Not like the real thing then," she said.

"Hell no. *Ain't nothing like the real thing, baby,*" I half-sang, feebly, "The real thing rules the universe," I spoke with attempted cute exuberance.

These were my early nerdacious attempts at flirting.

"You mean 'universes,'" Miranda giggled, referring to Chester Flinch's now infamous showdown right before Thanksgiving with our 8th Grade science teacher Mrs. Roebuck, whom Chester grappled with over the nature of reality.

Chester had claimed that there were multiple universes.

"My father is a physicist, and he says that there are many universes and that each universe is connected to all the other universes by a kind of hinge. That's what black holes are," Chester said to her during a heated classroom discussion.

I remember Oliver Gelding leaned over to me during the brouhaha and said, "Black holes make me horny."

Dang, dude.

Mrs. Roebuck was a conservative Christian lady and staunch Republican with a picture of President Nixon, Watergate be darned, hanging on one of her storage cabinets, but she was also *shiksa*-sexy and wore achingly short dresses which we all craned our necks to see up every time she bent over to get something out of her filing cabinet.

"Please make it the bottom drawer, *please*," every heterosexual male in the room would hope.

Roebuck answered Chester's new physics with a blistering diatribe about the "Book of Genesis" which Chester described as "a fairy tale," whereupon Mrs. Roebuck sent Chester Flinch to the Dean, Mr. Gilligan, to be punished for what she cited as his "defiance."

She didn't write "blasphemy" on the referral slip.

You know she wanted to, though.

"Yes, universes, of course, sorry," I said, "Defenly," breaking my promise but hoping for forgiveness.

Her face was at its most beautiful when being teased.

"Stop. I told you," she said and meant it.

"I'm sorry."

"You're so not sorry."

Ever since Nixon's trip to China and his meeting with Chairman Mao, ping pong fever had found its way into Saturday afternoon television sports programming and into the patios and rec rooms of freedom-loving Americans everywhere.

A crossroads of politics and culture.

By December of 1973, Nixon's treasons overshadowed his successes in the public eye, but ping pong still held recreational sway all over the American leisure time funscape.

"I rule the table at home," Miranda boasted of her ping pong prowess.

"Oh, I fuckin' dominate the game. Wherever I play," I came back triumphantly.

"You should come over to my house and take me on sometime. Receive a few lessons from a true champion."

"Hey, anytime you want to submit yourself to a lickin' from me, I'm ready."

"Your humiliation will occur on the day of your choosing. You name it," she got formal, like a roller derby queen challenging me to a match race at the Olympic Auditorium.

"How about New Year's Eve Day because it sounds so funny when you say it out loud?" was my suggestion.

"Let's do it on New Year's Eve Day then, and giggle when we say it out loud."

"Chuckle."

"Fine, chuckle when we say it out loud."

"Or you can giggle if you want," I backtracked.

"And do one or the other then when we say it out loud."

"Or both," I had to.

"And do what the fuck ever when we say it out loud," she finished with determination.

"Agreed. A duel with destiny. Loser gives all," I sealed the deal by extending my hand, which she took, and we had a firm shake on it, like the shaking of my interior fault lines.

"Oh wait, I can't. Dang. We're going to be in Palm Springs," she pouted.

"You're *deserting* me," I said, mockingly pained but also sincerely so.

"Pun-o-rama City," she pointed and followed up quickly, "How about after Christmas vacation? After school one day?"

"I can do that," I said with business-like confidence despite the seismic activity across my body.

"You can just come home with me on the bus after school."

"I look forward to overwhelming you with my power moves."

"You'll have to get past my serve."

"Maybe the Wednesday we get back?"

"Um, Thursday is probly better."

"Probly," I broke my promise again.

"Stop," she said, I think surprised that I went back on my word a second time.

"Probly," I continued out of nervous inertia.

"You shun't do that."

"Shun't?" I pressed her good will, "Wun't?"

"Stop!"

"Cun't?"

"Fuck you," she said as she swatted my chest and then patted it.

We both looked away into a fake distance.

"Well, I think Lorelei and I are going to go get something to eat," Miranda broke the silence again.

"Fisher's?" I inquired.

"Yeah, I guess. Fisher's is depressing. But the fishsticks are pretty good. They kinda taste like chicken."

"The tartar sauce does it. But dang, the burgers are a joke. They're like the fast food version of Pong," I said, "definitely go for the fishsticks."

"So true!" she sniffled with mild amusement, "that's probly why they call it *Fisher*'s and not *Burg*ers, duh?"

"Yeah, huh," I said, one-upped by lusciousness.

"Maybe see you at *The Exorcist*?" She was looking around the arcade for Lorelei.

"'May be," I echoed into her field of distraction.

"And defenly ping pong when we get back."

"I'll be there," I said, resisting the temptation to mimic her 'defenly.'

"And maybe accidentally between," she dandled herself before me.

"It could happen," I smiled at her.

"Bye, Lance . . . Lori, let's go now, or else we're gonna be—," she said heading off for Fisher's mid-sentence, making her usual quick get-away.

Miranda Savitch didn't like to hear other people say goodbye.

2

The day after Christmas, my buddies and I went to, yes, the first showing of *The Exorcist*.

It was rated 'R,' but there was always an adult in line who'd agree to take you in.

We found our "uncle" immediately—a cool dude named Walter Simmons who, crazily enough, ended up being one of our teachers in high school like 3 years later.

We remembered him from the *Exorcist* line as soon as we walked into his Cinema class in the 11th Grade.

Simmons claimed to recognize us, too, but we couldn't tell if he was just saying that.

He was the kind of guy you imagined had taken lots of young boys into movie theatres.

After Mr. Simmons accompanied us into the theatre, he invited us to sit with him, but we declined and he told us to be good boys before finding his own corner of the dark to nestle into.

We all bought ourselves the requisite FLICKS and Milk Duds and started doing the usual goofball pre-screening screw-arounds which was a lot of times the best part of going to the movies.

"So, they bring in the Mexican guy, and he's all like blindfolded and shit," said Gus Lagniappe, finishing up the joke known as The Taste Test, "and sit him down in front of the girl's pussy and tell him to go ahead and start eating, and then he nibbles a bit and says all confused, 'Ay, caramba, eet smell like feesh but eet tace like cheeken!'" and the boys all rumbled with love for the punchline.

"Check out Mr. Howell," said Whitman Rust, pointing to a straw-hatted gentleman walking down the aisle in our direction.

"Hey, Thurston, where's Lovey, dude?" shouted Chester Flinch at the old guy who looked up at first bewildered and then just irked at us crazy kids.

I continued to feel bad about those public obnoxions. I knew even then that one day I'd be an old guy and rowdy kids would be yelling shit like that at *me*.

"Do you think Gilligan and the Skipper were gay golitas?" Claude asked.

"Totally," said Whit, "Gilligan would slip into Skipper's hammock every night, dude."

"Not the Professor, though," said Claude.

"Nah, dude, he and Mary Ann had a thing going on, for sure," said Whit.

"*The Professor and Mary Ann,*" sang Gus.

"See, they're even together in the theme song," observed Whit.

"You think Thurston Howell III and Lovey ever did it?" asked Claude.

"Hell no," said Whit.

"Dude slept with his teddy bear, dude," said Gus, "Mr. and Mrs. Howell had separate beds."

"Gay golita," said Whit.

"Nah, dude, be honest: would *you* wanna fuck Mrs. Howell?" challenged Claude.

"Lucy and Ricky slept in separate beds," said Chester.

"Yeah, but they had little Ricky, dude, so they fucked at least once," Claude came back.

"Fred and Ethel Mertz never fucked," said Gus.

"Nyeah, dude, that is flagrant," said Chester, "thanks for the gnarly picture I get to carry around in my head for the rest of the day. Dang, dude. Fred and Ethel. No."

"Ethel Mertz can be sexy sometimes," I said but nobody reacted.

"Mike and Carol Brady sleep in the same bed," said Claude.

"But Mike Brady's a fag so it doesn't count," said Gus.

"Gay golita, totally," said Whit.

"Alice is a lesbo, don't you think?" Claude asked the group. Nobody was interested in his question.

"Oop, oop, Augustus Gloop," chanted Chester Flinch, in thickly bad German accent, to rile up Gus.

In retaliation, Gus Lagniappe, with kung-fu quickness, performed a magnificent two-fisted titty-twister on Chester Flinch's pendulous breasts.

"Ow, dang, dude, that hurt worse than fucking your mother's jagged pussy," complained Chester, cupping himself and turning away.

"Speaking of your mother, there she is," said Gus, pointing out a yellow haired middle-aged woman making her way down the aisle sucking on a brobdignagian candy cane.

"Damn, that's like some shit Little Bo Peep would carry," said Whit.

"Check it out: Mary Ann and Ginger!" Claude spat forth to direct our attention to a pair of women walking past.

"Hey, Atlas, who would you rather fuck: Mary Ann or Ginger?" asked Gus.

My head was not in the game-space, though.

Without appearing to be looking for Miranda, I had been looking for Miranda everywhere. In line, in the lobby, in the aisles, in the rows in back of me. She did not appear. It was just me and my geeky freak brothers.

"Um, I don't know," I said, out of the rhythm of the banter.

"Gay golita," said Whit, on cue.

"Really, Lance, oh mighty titan Atlas, only one among us who's actually frenched, who would you rather fuck: Mary Ann or Ginger?" Gus asked me again.

"Did you ever notice that Ginger looks like a mermaid?" I asked the group, diverting the question with a question.

"Yeah, well, when I go fishing, I know what I want to catch!" said Claude.

"*Chick*en of the Sea tuna, dudes," said Chester.

"Eet smell like fish but eet tace like *chick*en!" said Gus.

"My dad says that's where mermaids come from," said Chester.

"A tin can?" I asked.

"Nah, man, fishy chick smell. That's where the idea for mermaids comes from. They're like beautiful chicks from the stomach up and like fish from there on down," he explained.

"Whoa, that's deep," said Whit.

"Dang, I never thought about it like that," said Claude Moss, "I'd rather fuck Mary Ann then."

The movie was a phantasmagoria of weird visual effects, unforgettably great lines ("*Your mother sucks cocks in Hell!*" seeming to be everyone's clear favorite immediately), enough genuinely scary demonic shit to keep you on edge, green vomit, tinkle on the carpet, a girl saying lots of dirty words and raping herself with a crucifix, and Linda Blair's angelic-whore face to embrace and repel throughout. We loved it.

Upon exiting the theatre, we bumped into Miranda, waiting in line for the next showing with Lorelei Lux, Claire Farnaway, and Dolly Ferris, a trio of girls in Miranda's immediate orbit who would have varying degrees of significance in my life over the next several years).

I stopped to bid hello, and so, naturally, my friends chose to be on their worst behavior.

"How'd you like it?" Miranda asked.

"*Your mother sucks cocks in Hell!*" said Gus Lagniappe over my left shoulder.

"I Um—"

"*Let Jesus fuck you, let Jesus fuck you! Let him fuck you!*" said Chester Flinch over my right shoulder.

"Dang, dude, it's the day after Christmas," I said to Chester, peeved. "Forgive them. They were born this way," I then begged the pardon of Miranda and everyone near her in line.

"*Stick your cock up her ass, you motherfucking worthless cocksucker,*" Claude Moss then said right into my ear in possessed-Linda-Blair-voice that sounded more like the devil-conscience in a cartoon.

"*Captain Howdy, that isn't very nice,*" I shrugged him off me, fighting geekery with geekery.

Miranda looked annoyed.

"Enjoy the movie, girls," I said and wished Miranda a "hot" time in Palm Springs, as the boys dragged me down Westwood Boulevard chanting, "*Fuck me, Jesus!*" and rousing repetitions of "*Your mother sucks cocks in Hell!*"

"Bye, Lance," I heard Miranda say, "Ping pong! Don't forget!"

I turned briefly to hoist two thumbs up before being forced to move on. I also shouted bye to her, but I think I was too far away for her to hear me.

I spotted Candy Stoner further back in the line as we walked to the Wilshire bus.

She appeared to be with some guy who must've been like 16 years old or something and who most definitely looked like he wanted (and would be able) to kick my ass, so I chose not to attempt any sort of greeting. Not even a nod.

3

Winter is an illusion. A joke that Los Angeles plays on the rest of the world.

And yet, the Thursday we got back from Christmas vacation was as wintry as L.A. gets, daytime temperatures in the lower 60s, thunderstorms, lots of slow traffic and car accidents.

Angelenos have no idea what to do when it rains. The rain is a nuisance and a nemesis.

And it was that kind of day in L.A., a day of flooded storm drains and short-circuited traffic lights, exasperated motorists, wading pedestrians who don't own umbrellas because why should they, general mayhem all around.

That was the day I would go home with Miranda Savitch.

Miranda and I avoided speaking for much of that school day, and I was suffering from a nervous anxiety that chose to locate itself, as usual, in my stomach.

I was in the greatest panic during the last class of the day, 6th period PE, which meant dodge-ball in the gym because of the weather.

I sat along the side wall with Chester, Gus, Oliver, and Claude.

I was afraid to reveal my fear. It would be a dishonor and a violation of the code. Admitting that girls are scary. Never.

"So, you and Miranda today, dude, right?" said Chester Flinch.

"She'll finally find out what a fag you are," Gus chimed in.

"What base are you trying for?" Oliver asked.

"I'm not going to play baseball, I'm going to play ping pong," I said.

"Yuh-huh, meaning you're gonna paddle her ass, what," Oliver pantomimed.

"No, straddle her ass," said Chester, making pelvic thrusts.

"And you know there will be titties involved," Claude Moss felt compelled to add.

"Dang, dude, Miranda got some tig ol' bitties, though, dude, I felt 'em," Oliver made sure everyone knew.

"And then you're gonna play Leggo My Eggo, right, Sir Lancelot?" said Gus, making some kind of sexual gesture I was not able to make sense of.

"Leggo my pussy," Oliver corrected, to more general guy laughter.

"I can't even tell if she likes me, though," I said, "I don't know."

"Dude, she likes you," Chester said, "Lori and Claire told me. And they wouldn't've told me unless Miranda wanted them to tell me and wanted me to tell you. Get it? That's how girls operate, dude. Every leaked 'secret' is intentional. You've gotta learn this girl-strategy shit, golita. Miranda is hot and ready for your wussy love."

Chester Flinch was pretty reliable about that sort of gossip.

He never had a girlfriend, but he was friends with pretty much every cute girl in the school.

They often used him to relay female interest to a chosen male entity or to gauge male interest in the aforementioned female entity, and Chester dug that line of reconnaissance work.

Chester Flinch disappeared from our lives after 8th Grade.

The "official" story was that he had moved and was going to Samohi. But we all believed he joined the CIA.

"Well, I don't know, dudes, I don't know how to tell if she does or not," I said.

Gus walked behind me as we got ready for dismissal, giving me a boxing trainer's between-round shoulder rub.

"Remember, she's just a girl, it doesn't matter, she's just a girl, it doesn't matter. Keep saying that to yourself, dorkwad. She's just a girl, it doesn't matter . . . Don't ever forget it. A year ago you didn't even care about girls, right?"

When the bell rang at the end of class, my cue to go meet Miranda at her locker (adjacent to mine), my chums all wished me luck.

"Dang, dude," Oliver Gelding said as I left for my rendezvous, "don't forget Soylent Green, baby, Soylent Green," he encouraged, grabbing the air with both hands.

"Let's go," Miranda said matter-of-factly, and we walked to the bus stop at Wilshire and Highland.

Lorelei, Claire, and Dolly all took the same bus, so they bore witness to the first journey of Miranda Savitch and Lance Atlas.

The social circle that had coalesced among the group of cool nerds at John Burroughs Jr. High circa '72-'75 already considered us a couple, and the

Lorelei-Claire-Dolly triumvirate that surrounded Miranda stared and whispered like the Fates themselves, ready to publish every detail of this pre-ordained relationship to the members at large.

Miranda huddled briefly with the sisterhood before we exited the bus at Fairfax, right outside May Company.

She wore a pink cardigan sweater, no raincoat, over a white blouse and tan linen skirt that came down over her knees, Jack Purcells and the tennis socks with the little fluffy dangly-balls in back.

I'd been thinking about those socks since the arcade.

She was wearing tights which reminded me of this time in Mr. Swanson's class I told her I liked her tights and she got embarrassed.

Miranda had skinny legs. Wasn't she cold? I was. I was shivering. And I was wearing a jacket.

We walked in relative silence, occasionally pointing out which of our friends lived in which of the houses we happened to be passing.

My nervousness abated some as I breathed the damp chilly air.

There was a strange elation, felt from my heart to my perineum, elevating my mood.

I was walking in the rain with Miranda Savitch.

We each had our own umbrella.

It was like a movie.

The murky birth-story of my sexual awareness.

I didn't come out of the gate all cock-hard and rocking,

I didn't wake up one morning wanting to fuck everything.

Rather, the onset was gradual, nuanced.

Stirrings at first were vague and ephemeral. Very much a snake that uncoiled slowly.

The early whirlpools were oddly girl-related but not attached to this or that one.

A slinky underneath feeling of wanting that hot otherness.

I first began masturbating when I was about 11, in the bathtub, sort of sliding forward and back on my stomach as I'd let the water drain, a wondrous discovery.

The porcelain was smooth girl skin.

It wasn't anybody in particular.

It was just the sensation of skin on skin, me on girlbody.

There were climaxes, yes indeed, dry climaxes, no spunk or other utterances, just sweet-'n'-dreamy soft porcelain paradise, just a really neat thing for the body to do. An intensely peaceful reward.

And even when it had to do with specific females, like the girl from Zody's, it was still just skin on skin, body on body, face against face, even later with Candy Stoner, right up until I came upon a new impending verge . . . the canyons of Miranda.

It was sitting in Miranda Savitch's bedroom, alone with her, wanting to talk to her about everything, wanting to enfold her body, wanting to enchant her heart, wanting to occupy the center of her being, that I entertained, right there, with consciousness-shaking revolt, my first cock-in-pussy thoughts.

Specifically, my cock in her pussy, on the bed, with her skirt still on.

And her tennis shoes. And her tennis socks with the little dangly-balls. And the pink sweater.

This was a new paradigm. A sudden drastic alteration in my approach to the world.

I wanted to fuck Miranda Savitch.

That's what my cock had been pointing to all that time. That's where the rocket was supposed to land, Tyrone. That's what all the bathtub calisthenics were about.

I knew about cock-in-pussy and how that business got done for the sake of propagation. But I'd never applied it to my own cock in someone else's actual pussy. That was brand flashing new, and I was thunderstruck.

I sat inches away from Miranda's porcelain body and thought about fucking her.

Lust, 'til then, had been just a miasma of attraction, undirected, ambiguous.

Although I deeply enjoyed the hours I spent frenching Candy Stoner, I never thought about my cock being in her pussy.

At the edge of Miranda's bed, her legs extending from under that skirt, her eyes alternately on me and looking away, I swelled with mammal passion, having entered a new cuntcentric universe, shivering to contain a fountain of starry-heart jazz.

But amid the hugeness I found myself afraid of so much feeling. More feeling than I was ready to be feeling.

It was too real. And too torrential. And too soon.

I was in love with Miranda Savitch. And it vanished every other thought.

The smell of her girlness pervaded the air, the house was full of it.

I was a jungle monkey horny to climb her contours.

But for all my slutty rumblings I felt embarrassed and unsure.

Need is a weakness. To want is to lack. Don't display your human frailty. Be cool. Be that cat who never needs a thing.

I wanted to tell her. I wanted to tell her I wanted to.

In a way I forebade myself from touching her. It would only stir up her revulsion or her disappointment. Those were the only two possible outcomes.

I hovered nonplussed, sitting next to Miranda Savitch, at the edge of her bed. It would have been so easy to.

Dang, dude.

"What music are you listening to these days?" Miranda asked, apparently unaware of my entire psychic turmoil.

"Um, I'm really into the *American Graffiti* soundtrack right now. And *Aladdin Sane*. You like David Bowie? *Quadrophenia* is cool too, the Who. John Lennon solo; have you heard the *Plastic Ono Band* album? And The Beatles are always in my ears, of course," I said.

"The Beatles, yes! *Revolver* is my favorite album of all time," Miranda enthused, "I listen to it every single night." She strode over to her record player and put the needle on "I Want To Tell You." George Harrison's memorable lick faded up and cascaded forth as the great insane piano track entered steadily into the loony swirl of the psychedelic vocal:

I want to tell you

My head is filled with things to say

When you're here

All those words, they seem to slip away

"I love this song," Miranda said, singing along.

Was she singing to me?

Or was I singing to her?

I lost track.

Every word was resonant.

At least it was from my side of the tango.

Or was I just singing to myself?

When I get near you,

The games begin to drag me down

It's all right

I'll make you maybe next time around

Miranda had her eyes closed.

She could have picked any song from side B. Why that one?

Though I couldn't determine any definite intentionality, the lyrics were just too suspiciously relevant to be accidental. Or was I simply connecting random dots in pursuit of some imposed pattern that might grant my wish?

But if I seem to act unkind

It's only me, it's not my mind

That is confusing things

Her younger brother wandered into the room and sat down in a rocking chair.

"Are you Lance?" he asked.

I nodded confirmation.

"Are you my sister's boyfriend?"

I shook my head with prideful denial.

"Why are you here?"

I want to tell you

I feel hung up but I don't know why,

I don't mind

I could wait forever, I've got time

Miranda opened her eyes and looked at me. And then at her brother.

Sometimes I wish I knew you well,

Then I could speak my mind and tell you

"Jeremy, get out of here, please," Miranda yelped at her brother. He was just young enough not to realize he shouldn't be in her room under such circumstances. He picked up enough via sibling subtext, however, to get the exit message and find his entertainment elsewhere.

I want to tell you

I feel hung up but I don't know why,

I don't mind

I could wait forever, I've got time, I've got time, I've got time

"*I've got time*," Miranda continued past the fade, "God, I love it. Isn't it the best?"

I looked at her for a moment while I contemplated my answer.

I wanted to say, "You're all I think about" and then fuck her all over that California-thin quilt, but instead I said, "Yeah, George did a lot of great songs that people never talk about," and continued sitting next to her, behind the self-imposed barricade.

Put your hand on her bare leg, Lance, just put your arm around her and get to frenching, you know how to do that at least, I told myself amid the barrage of cock-in-pussy, cock-in-pussy, cock-in-pussy thoughts.

I had an erection the size of a frozen banana from Zody's.

Could she tell?

"But that song just says it all," Miranda gushed, "Every night before I go to bed I listen to that song. And then again when I wake up in the morning. I love how hopeful it is. *I could wait forever, I've got time* . . . I should make that my motto."

I wasn't sure if the intensity with which she held my gaze was real or if I was just duping myself out of unilateral desire.

Nobody had ever looked at me the way Miranda Savitch looked at me.

She's just a girl, it doesn't matter . . .

Nausea and an irrepressible case of the shakes overcame me at that inopportune moment, and in an attempt to break the vortex of fear, I suggested, "Are you ready to get your ass kicked in ping pong?"

"I'm ready to swat you into submission, yeah," she came right back, always on call for sassy repartee, "But I have to pee first."

While Miranda was in the bathroom I calmed my boner with thoughts of Richard Nixon.

The Savitch family ping pong table stood in an enclosed patio which was chilly and dank in the rain.

"You haven't got a hope in Hell, you know," Miranda said, referring, I think, to my chances in the ping pong match, but I don't know.

"*Captain Howdy, that isn't very nice,*" I spoke in falsetto fake-girl voice, grasping at the essence of Linda Blair, "and, plus, I thought hope was your thing."

"I'll take pink," said Miranda, choosing which color paddle she'd use.

"Why, 'cause you're the girl?" I asked.

"No, because it matches my sweater," she stuck her tongue out at me, "And you take blue because—"

"—it matches my jeans," I finished for her.

"No, because you are a blueberry."

"Just like Violet Beauregarde," I said.

"Yeah, you remind me of her," Miranda made playful. "Ready?" she asked as she sent her first serve my way.

We volleyed back and forth gently . . . There was no competition here . . . No championship to be won . . . The only lesson was in finding the rhythm and jiving with it . . . Plugging into the eternal . . . A sweet reprieve from the mental tempest.

"I thought I reminded you of the Little Prince."

She had to think for a moment.

I had obviously spent longer looking at the note she wrote me in 7th Grade English than she had spent writing it. My myth, not hers.

Finally she raised an embarrassed oh-yeah smile recalling the year-old scribble on my literature worksheet:

you remind me of the little prince! luv, miranda

I still have that note somewhere.

"I could never figure out what you meant by that," I said.

"Oh, God, I don't know. I think I just meant, I don't know, whatever, it's not important," she said with some consternation.

"Violet Beauregarde, huh?"

"That's right," she said. "Hey, I could've said you remind me of Augustus Gloop, you know, so."

"You mean Buzzy Lagniappe?" I took the bait.

"Oh, man," she giggled, getting the allusion, "Where did Oliver come up with Buzzy Lagniappe instead of Augustus Gloop? That was cray-zee," she laughed.

"I swear, I'm just going to start calling Gus 'Buzzy' from now on. It fits him. Buzzy Lagniappe. The fat kid from *Willy Wonka and the Chocolate Factory.*"

"*Charlie and the Chocolate Factory,*" Miranda said.

"That too," I said, "And, you know what? You remind me of Mary Ann from *Gilligan's Island.*"

"I think of myself more as Ginger," Miranda replied, "Mary Ann's too much like Dorothy from *The Wizard of Oz.* I'm not a farm girl, I'm a movie star."

"Did you ever notice Ginger dresses like a mermaid?"

"Like I said . . ." Miranda flipped her hair back in response.

I wanted to tell her she reminded me of everybody 'cause she was all I thought about. I don't know. I didn't. I just got ready for her next expertly ginger serve.

Just as Miranda and I started a new round of volleys, her little brother came onto the patio.

"Can I watch?" he asked.

"Jeremy, please," Miranda whined, "MOM!"

Mrs. Savitch responded quickly to the SOS, appearing in the doorway.

"Jeremy, come with me right now," she said, and to me, "I'm Tamar."

"Lance."

"We've heard a lot about you, Lance."

"Good, I hope!"

"Eh," she see-sawed.

Wise-ass sarcasm is genetic, I learned.

"No," she assured me, "Miranda talks about you all the time and says you're just the—"

"—Mom," Miranda warned, cutting her mother off.

"Are you staying for dinner?" Tamar asked.

"No, my dad's coming to get me at six," I said.

"Well, do come join us some night," she said, "I have to go finish making dinner, and, Mandy, don't forget to set the table after Lance goes home."

"What're we having?" Miranda asked her mother.

"Pork chopsh and appleshaush. Ain't that shwell?," Jeremy bogied à la Peter Brady.

"Fishsticks," Tamar interjected, "can't you smell?"

Miranda nodded and looked at the ping pong table.

"Parents are embarrassing," she said after her mother was out of hearing.

She put her paddle down.

"What's wrong?" I asked.

"I don't know," she shrugged.

"Done with ping pong?" I guessed.

"Yeah. My mother always ruins everything," she said, looking down.

"You don't want fishsticks?" I tried to be cheery.

I walked around the table to get closer to her.

"I'm sure they're not as good as Fisher's, but," I touched the back of her head, "Hey what happened?" I asked, overcoming the Lagniappe/Flinch-inspired desire to say "*Your mother sucks cocks in Hell!*" in creepy-devil voice.

"I don't know," she answered.

"What do you want to do?"

"I don't know what I want to do, Lance," she said, "What do *you* want to do?"

I avoided the honest-to-goodness cock-in-pussy answer to that question.

"It's not raining right now. Let's go outside and hang out," I suggested.

"'K," she muttered, looking up at me, then looking away.

It was already dark outside with a mist soft like talcum, the air menthol brisk.

This kid we sort of knew from school rode past on his bike delivering copies of the *Herald-Examiner*.

"We only get the *Times*," Miranda said.

"Oh, man, my dad loves the *Herald*. He sits on the front porch and reads it every afternoon. Cigarettes, coffee, and the *Herald-Examiner* are my dad's only necessary possessions. He loves Melvin Durslag.."

"Melvin Durslag. That's a funny name, Melvin Durslag," Miranda giggled, "Is that real?"

68

"Yeah, sports writer at the *Herald*. Here, I'll show you," and I walked over to her next door neighbor's house to pick up their copy of the paper, pulled it out of the protective rainy day plastic, pulled off the red rubber band, uncurled the bundle, and removed the Sports section, showing Miranda the Melvin Durslag by-line. There was a drawn picture of him, too.

"Cray-zee," she grinned.

"Made you smile," I teased.

"No, Melvin Durslag made me smile," she said, back in decent humor.

"No, his name made you smile," I re-rolled the *Herald* and wrapped it back in its rubber band and slid it into the protective rainy day plastic.

"Hey, you're good at that," Miranda admired.

"I used to deliver the *Herald*, so I've had lots of practice," I crowed about my first and only job.

"Do you still like Candy?" Miranda asked, out of a sudden nowhere, "You seem sad about breaking up with her."

"I'm not sure I ever did like her really," I said, pausing to put the idea together, "I liked frenching with her, definitely, but I don't know."

"Defenly," Miranda said in half-smirk.

"Defenly," I taunted.

"Stop it, you're evil!" she swatted at me, almost knocking my glasses off.

"You wun't," I parleyed harder, in response to a raised fist of hers apparently poised to slug me on the shoulder. I grabbed her hoisted fist which opened to meet my hand, but, dang, dude, our fingers did . . . not . . . enmesh, it didn't happen. I do not know why.

As we separated, Miranda looked at the ground.

"Do you like anybody right now?" she asked.

I wanted to tell her.

"*Stick your cock up her ass, you motherfucking worthless cocksucker,*" the voice of demon-voiced Claude Moss crept into my consciousness.

"I don't know," I said, from the cringing bowels of my wimpitude.

"That's always the correct answer," she said and backed away a few steps, turning to go inside, "Let's go back to my room," she said, "It's getting cold," and I followed.

Miranda removed *Revolver* from her record player and pulled *Introducing The Beatles* out of her stack of LPs.

The first song on side B was "P.S. I Love You."

She stood and looked at the LP spin while it played.

"*You you you*," she sang along, "*You you you* . . . god I love that part of the melody, *you you you*. What does P.S. stand for?"

"Postscript," I said.

"Latin, right?" she answered.

"Yeah, post means after and script is writing."

"Right, the writing that comes after the other writing, that makes sense. How do you know stuff like that?" she wondered.

"I read the dictionary for fun," I said, not joking.

"P.S. is in the dictionary? I din't know that."

"You din't?" I couldn't help saying.

Her "don't start" glare tamed me into remorse. "Nah, sorry. It's in the dictionary, yeah," I said.

She pulled a dictionary off one of her shelves and sat on the bed looking it up.

"Hyphenated, or two words?" she asked.

"I don't know, I think it's one word, not sure," I said.

"Yeah, one word, here it is, 'postscript, noun, an additional remark below the signature of a letter. Example,'" she paused, "no way," she motioned me over next to her on the bed.

I sat and leaned into her right shoulder as she read while pointing on the page, "*Example: P.S. I love you.*' They should say it's a Beatles song," and she looked at me, our faces but centimeters apart, ready for frenching. "Here, sign the page," she pushed the dictionary onto my lap.

"Why?" I asked, a bit dazzled by her proximity.

"I want your autograph," she got up to get a pen, a Bic 4-color. Medium point. My favorite pen ever. I carry one with me always.

I signed in a blankish space near the word 'postscript,' I started writing *You remind me of* but then I ran out of room so just finished with my still evolving signature, *Lance Atlas*.

I heard the unmistakable sound of our lumbering Chevy station wagon pulling up in front of Miranda's house.

My dad's shave-and-a-haircut signature horn tap pattern confirmed my imminent departure.

I put on my beloved UCLA letterman's jacket, grabbed my backpack, and Miranda walked me out.

Stopping at the front door, we faced each other. Miranda held onto the sleeve of my jacket.

"Lancelot Link, Secret Chimp," she said.

"Mata Hairi," I spoke back, in the spirit of the allusion.

"Violet Beauregarde."

"Ginger the mermaid," I said in turn.

"I want to tell you," she said as she moved her face closer to mine, "that," and she paused, looking groundward.

"That?" I waited.

"That," she closed her eyes, "Mmm . . . yeah . . . hmm," she stalled, then she looked at me with wet directness, "well, if we had played ping pong for real . . . I would have been nice and let you win."

"Loser gives all," I restated the stakes.

"Something like that," she rasped, "Defenly."

"Miranda is hot and ready for your wussy love," I heard Chester declaim in my head.

But what if he was wrong?

I don't know. Dude. Here's the thing:

I didn't kiss her. I don't know.

Dang, dude.

She's just a girl, it doesn't matter

"I gotta go," I said and trotted to the waiting Kingswood Estate.

"Bye, Lance," I heard Miranda meander off.

Before I got into the car I turned around to say bye back, but she had already closed the front door.

Who Knows What

1

Rabbi Hamlisch was talking to me about unholy fire and who knows what else, but I was preoccupied with thoughts of the soggy note from Miranda Savitch—a love-struck summons perhaps, a beacon from the burning bush—waiting folded and unread in my backpack.

Was it about our weekend schoolyard trespass last Saturday? Her shivery whispers? Her darkly sparkling eyes? My blushing bumblings? The genius of hamburgers? The shame of wanting? Our feet in sand? The corner of Curson and Curson? The sharing of solitaire? Or nothing to do with any of that?

The previous Saturday afternoon, during a game of spin-the-bottle in the bushes at the Tar Pits, Miranda and I split off from the group and strolled through the maze of Park La Brea to Hancock Park Elementary School, Miranda's alma mater.

Having almost but not quite kissed in the aforementioned spin-the-bottle game, the conversation was, at first, awkward.

She had suggested we break away mid-game, but she didn't explain why.

We mainly talked about friends of ours who lived in Park La Brea—a carefully planned apartment community in the heart of the Fairfax area, one of those complexes wherein all the buildings are identical and the streets maddeningly labyrinthine.

"I hate going over Misty's house 'cause I can never find her building," Miranda said, "it's like where the fuck are you?"

"Oh, man, yeah, last time my dad had to pick me up at Chester's place he was totally pissed at how hard it was to find where Chester lived. 'You can take the bus home from now on,' he was saying all crazy, 'because I am never under any circumstances doing this shit again.'"

"Your dad said shit to you?"

"Yeah. Ever since I said shit in front of him he's cool with saying shit in front of me now."

"When'd you say shit in front of your dad?"

"Back a while ago. We were walking the dogs at night, and these three unattended doberman pinschers turned the corner and started walking right towards us—"

"Nazi dogs."

"—Totally, and I said 'shit' right at that moment. My dad just said, 'Turn around slowly and start walking back toward the house.' I apologized for 'using the s-word,' and my dad patted my head and went, 'No worries, son. That's what the word's for.'"

"For when you're scared shitless."

"No shit, yeah. But also for when shit sucks. Like my grandmother, behind her back we call her cooking shitalicious. Even my mom says it. That's pretty flagrant."

"Shitalicious. Sounds yum. You got away from the dobermans though?"

"Yeahyeah, they didn't really follow us at all," I explained as we stopped at a curious corner. "Oh, here, check out this intersection," I said, pointing to the sign that showed two perpendicular streets both called Curson, "this is where Curson crosses itself."

"Meet me at the corner of Curson and Curson," Miranda said, "what a great place for a date. 'Meet me at the corner of Curson and Curson.' I want to say that to somebody someday."

"You just did."

"No, I mean I want to say it and mean it."

"Nice, thanks," I feigned insult.

"No, no, I mean we're already on the corner of Curson and Curson, so I don't have to tell you to meet me here," she was squirming her way out of it with undeniably foxy charm.

I shook my finger mightily. "A curse on Curson!" I said just to be saying something (though I do admit I was hoping she would find it adorable. I couldn't tell if she did or not. Dang, dude.).

We stood at the corner of Curson and Curson, looking at each other in silent acknowledgement of who knows what.

Miranda's eyes were a fireplace. They filled me with the shame of wanting.

"You do realize neither of us would have any idea how to find our way back here," I said.

"Lance . . ."

"Ya," I offered my ear to her foggy silence.

"Nothing, just . . ." Miranda scanned the landscape, "This reminds me of the crossroads scene in *The Wizard of Oz* when Dorothy meets the Scarecrow."

"Yeah kinda," I said.

"*Now which way do we go?*" she intoned quoting Judy Garland in the movie.

"*That way is a very nice way*," I said, doing Scarecrow, continuing the movie vibe. A flirting technique.

"*Who said that?*" Dorothy looked about bemusedly.

"*It's pleasant down that way, too.*" Scarecrow said, pointing in the other direction.

Miranda didn't know her Dorothy line there. Neither did I.

"*Of course, people do go both ways!*" I went back into Scarecrow character, all Ray Bolger rubbery.

It was too late.

"So, which way *do* we go? Curson or Curson?" Miranda asked as herself.

"I think if we stay left it'll take us to Colgate, but who the fuck knows," I slipped back into Lancehood, "Maybe we'll end up at Misty's building."

Miranda laughed.

"You do a good Scarecrow," she said.

"Well, it's easy: I haven't got a brain—only straw. I can't make up my mind about anything . . . I *am* the fuckin' Scarecrow."

"No you're not. You're just doing a good imitation of the Scarecrow. You're really someone else."

"Ah, the Little Prince, right?"

"Wrong."

"The fat kid from *Willy Wonka & The Chocolate Factory?*"

"Not Buzzy Lagniappe, no," Miranda grinned.

"Um, Captain Howdy?"

"Nyeah, wrong again."

"Well, *who?*"

"You're *Lancelot Link, Secret CHIMP*," she sang to the melody of the show's theme song.

She moved toward me, brushing my shoulder with hers, making like she was trying to run me off the road or something.

I didn't put my arm around her.

I was probably supposed to right then. And I really wanted to. But I couldn't do it.

I was scared of starting.

The spin-the-bottle game had been one of those dreaded suggestions that erupted spontaneously while all of us were just messing around at the Tar Pits.

Lorelei Lux found an empty bottle of Schlitz beer, and I believe it was Dolly Ferris who uttered, "Hey we should play spin the bottle," with which every girl agreed immediately.

In addition to Dolly and Lorelei, Justine Balthazar was also there, Misty Winters, Sharon Rose, Claire Farnaway, Candy Stoner, and Miranda: the newly coined *Chick Clique*.

The boy contingent, less inclined to want to suffer the psychic discomforts of spin-the-bottle, included me and Gus Lagniappe, Chester Flinch, Claude Moss, Whitman Rust, Oliver Gelding, and also Dolly's newly official "boyfriend" (they had frenched) Freddy Snow, one of those bronze-faced, godly-looking Jewish guys with feathered brown hair parted in the middle, the kind of guy who'd grow up to be a doctor or a lawyer or a media executive if his ambition didn't get derailed in adolescence by cocaine and quaalude cocktails. He stood in stark contrast to me with my dorky teardrop glasses, braces, zits, and jewfro. I'm fairly convinced he didn't like me very much.

And, dang, dude, Freddy Snow was hanging pretty close to Miranda for somebody who was officially going with Dolly Ferris.

When he spun the bottle it stopped at Miranda, and Freddy didn't just lean across the circle and kiss her; Freddy pushed Miranda onto her back and gave her a long tongue-involved kiss, at the conclusion of which he turned and looked intently at me.

"Dude, that's cool, right?" Freddy asked as he sat back down.

Dolly glared at Miranda.

Miranda looked at the ground.

Dang, dude.

Candy Stoner's first bottle spin stopped at me.

She crawled across the circle we had formed in the bushes near 6th Street, and kissed me on the mouth, attempting to french and yeah I let it happen 'cause it felt good and maybe I wanted to get back at Miranda or something.

It had been like 4 months since Candy and I'd stopped being a couple, but the rhythm of the tongues was intact.

A general "oooh" permeated the circle.

"Aaaah-ha sexes with the exes," Oliver taunted.

My spin, as fate dictated, landed on Miranda, who was sitting next to me.

Following the briefest eye contact I leaned toward her, but as my mouth approached hers she turned her face and then sidled up to my ear and whispered, "Can we get away from here?" I pulled back and nodded yeah.

We separated without kissing.

"Dang, dude, rejection in spin-the-bottle? That's dog," said Oliver.

"Why'd you do that, Mandy?" scolded a cross Candy Stoner.

"That's cold-blooded," Claire Farnaway joined in.

"Actually, Lance and I are going to go somewhere more private," said Miranda as suggestively as her 13 years could muster, and thus began our romp through Park La Brea.

Another "ooooh" swept across the group.

"All right, Soylent Green, golita, Soylent Green," we heard Oliver say as we journeyed forth.

"Mandy, later, 'k?" Dolly shouted and gestured "Call me."

I looked back and saw the girls huddle before turning my attention to Miranda and our sudden oneness.

We had followed the left Curson which led us to Colgate and the Hancock Park Elementary School playground.

On that soothing blue April afternoon we had the entire schoolyard to ourselves.

Oh, holy emptiness.

Hopping the chain-link fence, we entered what seemed to me a standard issue LA Unified playground: a covered eating area with tables and benches, 3 beige handball courts, a couple of tetherball poles, monkey bars, rings, and other climbing equipment installed over black rubber padding, painted four-square and two-square games, two kickball/sockball diamonds, a couple of basketball courts with 8-foot hoops hung with chain-link netting, and also a bunch of hopscotch boxes, oh, and three tetherball poles.

In 3rd Grade I threw up while watching Sally Campos play hopscotch one morning before school.

The puke looked and smelled like rotten eggs.

My mother had to come and take me home.

What I remember best about that day is that I got to lie on the couch and watch TV.

The Los Angeles Kings were playing the Montreal Canadiens in the late afternoon.

Ross Lonsberry, "Cowboy" Bill Flett, Eddie "The Jet" Joyal. Frenchie Lemieux. Jiggs McDonald calling the play-by-play. I loved that team.

They were sacred.

They sucked, but I loved them anyway.

The very essence of love.

I was not a Hancock Park alum.

I had spent my grammar school years at Melrose Avenue Elementary School, right behind hotdog heaven Pink's.

So, the Hancock Park yard was not buzzing with wonder for me, but for Miranda it harbored a fleet of beloved memories.

I enjoyed learning about her past and her nostalgic thrall for that distant life of two years before. What was she like then?

"This is where Freddy Snow fell backwards and cracked his head open in 6th Grade. He was trying to imitate some Kung Fu movie guy—"

"—Bruce Lee—"

"—YES! and he tripped over this bench and cracked his head on the ground. He was awake but bleeding really bad."

I will admit a certain joy at hearing of Freddy's injury.

"Is Freddy a good kisser?" I tortured myself by asking.

"Well, you know, he's experienced," Miranda blushed and then countered, "How was it kissing Candy again?"

"She seemed like she was into it, but the thing is I saw her with some older guy at *The Exorcist*, and he looked like he wanted to kick my ass. So I thought she had a new boyfriend. I couldn't figure out why she was kissing me for real in the game."

"Doofus, that was her cousin Nick at *The Exorcist*. He goes to Uni. You are Mr. Gullible's Travels, totally," Miranda said.

I still don't know what she meant by that, but I pretended like I did at the time.

"Defenly," I said.

"Stop."

"Why did you want to get away from everybody back there?"

"I don't know. I din't want to be there. With them. Right then."

"You din't?"

"Don't."

"Did it have to do with Freddy?"

Miranda looked down.

"No, not really, I guess," she mumbled.

"Candy?"

Miranda nodded a sort of yes.

"What about Candy?"

"She's just . . . going out of her way to be against me. I guess that's how I'd describe it. But we have all the same friends so I have to be around her all the time. And who knows what I did wrong?"

We strolled over to the Kindergarten yard, a fenced off area next to the main playground.

"I remember being in Kindergarten," Miranda said, "I'd come to school in the morning and then go home and watch TV."

"I was in afternoon Kindergarten," I said, "I watched TV all morning, then my mother would make me a Swanson's chicken pie, and I'd eat it while watching *Sheriff John*. After that I'd go to school."

We climbed the little fence into the enclosed Kindergarten area.

A copy of *My Darling, My Hamburger* lay carelessly tossed open near the sandbox.

Miranda took off her Jack Purcells and the tennis socks with little fluffy balls dangling in back, picked up the book, and stood barefoot in the sandbox.

"How's the sand?" I asked.

"Mmm, warm-cold. Come try."

"Warm-cold?" I didn't understand.

"Yeah, the sand is warm from the sun but cold underneath once you dig your feet in. Warm-cold. It's yum," Miranda beckoned, "like a hot fudge sundae."

I removed my Adidas and sweat-socks and joined her.

"I can't believe elementary school kids are reading this," she said of the Zindel book.

"Yeah, and we're in the *Kindergarte*n yard. Is it dirty?" I tried to grab it away from her.

"There's a lot of stuff in it they wun't understand. It's about high school. There's a lot of stuff in it I din't understand, I guess, and I'm 13. Maybe it belongs to one of the teachers."

"Let me see it," I made another grab.

"No, it will give you ideas," she dangled it at arm's length.

I reached for the book and she pulled back playfully, sometimes almost letting me snatch it.

Miranda interrupted the struggle and looked over at the handball courts.

"I wish we had a handball," she said.

"So I could whoop your ass at it?"

"No, so I could show off my cuts and slices."

"Ah."

"And then whoop *your* ass."

"At Melrose Avenue we called them slicees," I said.

"Slicees?"

"Yeah. Cuts and slicees. And I'd always get stuck sitting in line on the bench next to Wayne Paul Nader."

"Hey, what is that guy's trip? He says really creepy stuff to Lila Saddleback all the time, and she's always telling him to fuck off."

"Let me 'splain something, Lucy," I said in my best Ricky Ricardo voice because Miranda was an *I Love Lucy* freak. It seemed like another good flirting technique.

"'Splain," she mocked, Lucy-style.

"You know how Wayne is now?"

"Of course. Creepazoid of the year. You went to elementary with him?"

"Yeah. All through. And he was always way out, even when we were in like 5th Grade. So, during handball we'd be sitting on the bench waiting for our turns, and if you were sitting next to him, he'd say to you, in this, like, fucked-up munchkin voice, 'Tickle my legs,' like all Lollipop Guild and shit, 'Tickle my legs,' and then he'd, like, tickle your legs a little, but in this majorly feeble way. It felt like a spider was crawling on you. I don't know, dude. Dang, and he wore purple pants all the time too. Dang, dude."

"Do the munchkin voice again," Miranda demanded.

"Follow the yellow brick road," I said.

Miranda reminded me of Dorothy from *The Wizard Of Oz* sometimes. So the munchkin thing was more flirting. She laughed and asked me to do it again.

Miranda Savitch and I were in 8th Grade when we stood face to face barefoot in the sandbox and nothing happened save the warm-cold pleasance of our feet in sand, separate and together. Miranda had just turned 13. I was still 12, but on the verge, my bar mitzvah less than a month away.

"Why didn't you have a bat mitzvah?" I asked her.

"I dunno. My parents thought it'd be too jewy, I guess. 'We're just people,' they always say, 'we aren't anything.' We get presents for Chanukah and we go to my aunt's house every year for Passover but that's it. There are several trees growing in Israel in my name I think. People gave them to me on my 13th birthday even though I din't have a bat mitzvah." She put the book back down on the ground where she found it. "I want to go on the monkey bars," she shifted the focus.

"Oh cool. I love watching girls go on the monkey bars. Except you're not wearing a skirt. No fun."

"Letch."

"No, it's not like that. It's natural. It can't be helped. It's a thing."

"Do I want to know this?" she asked.

I shrugged. I waited.

"Well now you have to tell me."

"All right, it's simple. The basic idea is this: Dresses and skirts were made to be looked up."

"That's perverted," she scoffed.

"But it's not. Perverted is when things are all sick and twisted. Like the stuff Wayne Paul Nader probably says to Lila, that's for sure some perverted-ass shit. But looking up a girl's dress isn't sick and twisted; it's just what you do," I attempted to defend my gender. "I mean, it's not even a sex thing really. You know Gina Dichlich, right?"

"Yes. Of course. How could I not?"

"Nyeah, well, she went to my elementary school, too. In like 4th Grade a bunch of us would always watch her go upside-down on the monkey bars so we could see her underwear."

"That's pathetic."

"True, it's pathetic, but it's not perverted. Pathetic I agree with. But it's what we do. To everyone."

"Ew gross. Really?"

"Pretty much, yeah. Any opportunity. That's the thing I was telling you."

83

"Everyone?"

"Well, basically . . ."

"That means you've tried to look up my skirt," she gasped.

"Tried?" I groucho'd my eyebrows.

"Oh I'm so—What's the big deal about underwear?"

"It's not the underwear; it's the promise."

"Huh?"

"You want the promise before you even know what the promise is."

"You mean like hope?" Miranda asked.

"Nyeah, sort of but not really."

"Or more like wish," she tried again.

"No defenly not wish."

"Stop."

"Sorry. I din't remember."

"You are bad, you swore not to," Miranda slapped my arm.

"Wishes make me sad," I confessed.

"Everybody wishes," said Miranda.

"That's what's so sad about it. And also that wishes are a disappointment either way. If they don't come true you're disappointed. And if they do come true you're disappointed in a different way."

Miranda was watching me talk. Who knows what she was thinking.

I continued, "I also don't like getting presents. Whenever my parents ask me what I want for my birthday or for Chanukah or something I always tell them nothing. I don't want to want anything."

"Sometimes you're like a girl, Lance."

"I think it'd be weird to be a girl."

"Being a girl feels like the normal way to be," she said, "I dunno. Boys are the mutation. I mean, please, the male thingy, you know, it looks like a mistake."

"Seen many, have you?" I taunted. Miranda blushed and looked away. "You know that joke about the boy and the girl playing doctor?"

"Which one?"

"This little boy and this little girl get naked, and the little girl points to the boy's thing and says, 'Oooh, can I touch that?' and the little boy says, 'No way, look what you did to yours.'"

"Ha ha," Miranda endured the humor.

She sat down in the sandbox and started mounding up the foundation of a castle.

She had abandoned her plan to go on the monkey bars.

"Hourglasses make me sad," she said. "What else makes you sad, besides presents and wishes?"

"Carnivals. I don't feel like I'm part of the human race when I'm at a carnival. I come from a planet that doesn't need carnivals," I confessed. "What about hourglasses makes you sad?"

"They make me think of everything I can't keep."

"Isn't there a big hourglass in your room?"

"Yeah, you remember? Neat. That was my grandmother's. I got it when she died. Another reason hourglasses make me sad."

"Kinda the same reason."

"Yeah, huh," she looked at me for a moment. "I want to live in a castle," Miranda said as she turned her attention to the sand and the erection of her fantasy palace.

"*And so castles made of sand*," I scraped the Hendrix tune with my nasal drone, "*fall into the sea eventually . . .*"

Miranda didn't know Hendrix.

"You know, the deserts get bigger every year?" Miranda said, "One day the entire earth will be a desert. But things can grow even in sand. That's what you have to remember. I love sand."

"Except in hourglasses . . ."

"Yes," Miranda Savitch offered up all intensity.

She was wearing brown corduroy pants.

I could see her brassiere through her white blouse.

And so arose the inevitable knotty eruption of cock-in-pussy thoughts.

"I think it's unlikely the entire earth will be a desert," I said with controlled breath.

"Unlikely," Miranda said, "I like when things are unlikely. If I'm thinking of the word unlikely when I'm falling asleep at night I always have the best dreams."

"I didn't know you were so weird, Miranda."

She smiled, "Wowie kazowie."

"What?"

"You called me Miranda."

"Yeah so? It's your name."

"You never use my name."

"I use your name."

"Never."

"Really?"

"Yeah."

"Really? Never?"

"Yes. And in fact if I didn't start conversations with you we'd probably never talk even."

Our exchange was starting to remind me eerily of *American Graffiti*. I don't know why exactly, but it was. She was right, though. I never called her by her name.

"Dang, dude, I suck," I waited, "I'm sorry . . . Miranda."

"I like the way that sounds," she said.

Who knows what she meant by that.

Miranda was beautiful.

"I thought it was funny in Ms. Roebuck's class when she said, 'Miranda is a moon of Uranus,'" I recalled, "I wrote it in my science notes."

Every time I looked at that phrase in my science notes I thought of Miranda's ass.

"Ha, yeah, huh? Almost as good as that time Roebuck said 'Uranus is mostly gas.' Yes, a moon of Uranus. That's me. Hey, did I tell you about Palm Springs?"

"I know you went."

"Yeah yeah, when I was in Palm Springs over Christmas vacation we stayed in this really ultra-modern hotel, and it was weird because I was lying by a concrete pool—"

"The sea-meant pond," I said in my durndest Jethro Bodine voice.

"—Yeahzackly, on a plastic lounge chair at an air-conditioned hotel, but still when I looked up at the stars I felt like I was in the wilderness; I cun't believe how many of them there were, and I thought, dang, those are there every night and I don't get to see them, that sucks," she thought for a moment.

"You got to see what you're missing."

"All the way real . . . " Miranda's mind meandered. "What was it like to be the first humans and look up there and see the Milky Way? Do you ever think about that?"

"Every night," I wanted to say but didn't. I just wanted her to keep on talking so I could keep on looking at her. And listening. I loved the way her voice scratched at the air.

"What did they think it was? Freaky," Miranda continued, "It's the best movie I've ever seen, the Milky Way."

"Better than *Willy Wonka & The Chocolate Factory*?"

"You would've liked it," Miranda said, and added, after a pause, "I thought about you a couple of times when I was out there looking at the sky."

"Only a couple?"

"OK, like 3 times. Yeah, no, like I wondered if you were also looking at the sky."

"I do that."

"Yeah, no, I know, no, but I wondered which stars you were able to see. Like maybe we were looking at the same one at the same time or something? I could see the whole thing but you were looking at the same sky and could only see a couple of those stars, right?"

"Like maybe four or five. Like Orion. Or The Big Dipper. Gemini. The Pleiades if I squint."

"Yeahyeah," she was putting the finishing touches on her sand castle, "and so, Lancelot Link Secret Chimp . . . here's the big question . . . do you think we were looking at the same star at the same time?"

I had no idea.

"I look at the sky every night," was my honest but evasive reply.

"I love the sand and you love the stars," Miranda said, "you ever notice that?"

"Is that why I remind you of the Little Prince?"

"I dunno," Miranda shrugged, "but I will tell you my favorite line in *The Little Prince* though: 'What makes the desert beautiful is that somewhere it hides a well.' That's my life motto."

"I don't get it."

"You will. But anyway you're somewhere between the Little Prince and a blueberry."

"With a bit of chimp thrown in?"

"Yessireebob."

"My dad always says that!" I said.

"Mine too!"

"Dads all know the same jokes."

"They learn them at the Dad Convention," Miranda said with authority.

"Yeah, like 'shave and a haircut, two bits,' right? And 'Pull my finger,' dang."

"Right, or how about this one?" Miranda said as she stood up. "Here, get up." I rose. "Shake . . . come on, hand out . . . Shake," she said, shaking my hand, "Spear," she said poking me in the ribs with her elbow, and then turning me around and kneeing me in my jean-tight buttocks, "kick in the rear."

It was not the last time I would let a girl kick my ass.

I turned to face her, and she held onto my arm.

We stood for a few seconds without saying anything.

"What?" she interrupted the silence.

"What what?" I returned and looked aside.

Miranda said, "What's that?" and pointed at a spot on my shirt. When I looked down she zipped her finger up my chest and onward across the length of my face, a fitting joke for the kindergarten sandbox, and, of course, I fell for it for the billionth time in my almost 13 years on the planet.

"Chimp!" Miranda ran and hopped the Kindergarten fence, dashing back out onto the big yard. "Let's play handball!" she shouted, though there were no balls on the premises save my own, however deflated.

I followed her over to the handball court, and we sat on the bench as if waiting our turn to play.

"Tickle my leg," she said in Wayne Paul Nader munchkin voice.

I allowed the tips of my fingers to touch her corduroy pant leg and began these wormboy sissy ticklings which she swatted away several times playfully.

"*Lance Link, whatcha gonna do?*" she half-sang. I wanted to run my hand up her leg and feel her crotch through the plush nexus of seams.

"What should I do?" I sort of lust-croaked.

"Follow the yellow brick road," Miranda said breaking into a nervous laugh.

Did she know I wanted her on her back, legs spread, taking my cock in the sandbox, yessireebob?

I placed the palm of my hand on her inner thigh, nearer the knee.

Miranda put her hand on my forearm, neither pushing nor pulling.

But I wouldn't let my hand move any higher.

Miranda looked at me with too much mystery to read.

I was supposed to kiss her at that moment, I knew.

But I didn't, again.

I remembered a similar constellation of feelings in the moments before I kissed Candy Stoner for the first time, that earliest frenching.

I didn't want Candy Stoner and kissed her anyway.

But here I wanted to entwine tongues with Miranda Savitch.

Her mouth was devourable, the voice that emanated from it a river I'd swim in, the mind it spoke for a magic lantern.

But the shame of wanting, the fear of being seen as human left me sunk in paralysis.

She'd think I was like everybody else.

"You wanna get a hamburger or something?" she said, gently pushing my hand away.

"Yeah, ok," I said, pulling back and getting up.

We retrieved our shoes and socks and made our way across Fairfax to Jack-In-The-Box.

An overriding silence accompanied us, though once we settled down at a table, the heavy tension subsided.

"Genius," Miranda said, pointing to her Jumbo Jack, "this hamburger is a work of genius."

"Mine's pretty good," I said, "It's the 'secret sauce,' that's what does it."

"No, this hamburger is a work of genius," she spoke as she chewed, "You don't understand. I've been wanting this all day and it's like the hamburger knew and was just waiting for me to find it. I've been thinking about this hamburger since I woke up this morning and I didn't even realize it. Genius."

She shook her head at the revelation.

"So, speaking of hamburgers," I said, "you liked that book *My Darling, My Hamburger?*"

"Yeah, it was good."

"But not a work of genius."

"Not like this hamburger, no."

"A Jumbo Jack from Jack-In-The-Box," I said in my best Rodney Allen Rippy 5-year-old voice (which bore a marked resemblance to my munchkin voice), "It's too big 'a eat." Miranda didn't laugh. "What's the book about?" I asked.

"I don't know, relationships I guess. Mainly 2 couples with problems. They're in high school. I din't get some of it."

"But you liked it."

"Yeah, it was good. But this hamburger is a work of genius."

Miranda took a sip of my milkshake. Using my straw. It was almost like frenching.

"You want to come over for a while?" she asked.

"Yeah, cool," I said, pondering the cock-in-pussy possibilities of the venture.

I hadn't been to Miranda's house since our ping pong date. Perhaps I would redeem myself.

We walked the few blocks to her house in the waning April afternoon.

The house was empty, which stoked my horny commotion of course, and we settled on her bed, some distance apart.

Miranda pulled two decks of cards from her nightstand drawer, one of which was a *Lancelot Link, Secret Chimp* deck.

"Here, you can use this deck because you are a chimp," she said and began taking the other deck out of its box, indicating I should do the same with mine.

"Um, what are we doing?" I asked.

"I wanna play solitaire with you."

"I've never heard of playing solitaire with someone."

"It's fun. Oh, wait, music," Miranda strode across the room and pulled a Jim Croce album from her small stack of records right next to the big hourglass.

Croce had died the previous autumn in a plane crash and had been splashing across the airwaves nonstop posthumously for months.

It was one of those things where you kind of had to say you liked Jim Croce's music even if you didn't 'cause he'd just died and he was a nice guy and stuff.

I actually did like Jim Croce's music, but I knew people who didn't and were waiting for the day they could fess up.

Miranda put on "Time In A Bottle" and re-joined me on the bed. As she was dealing her own hand of solitaire, she sang along.

If I could save time in a bottle

The first thing that I'd like to do

Is to save every day

Till eternity passes away

Just to spend them with you

"This is my first time," I said.

Miranda looked at me quizzically, then looked back down at her solitaire hand and continued singing.

If I could make days last forever

If words could make wishes come true

I'd save every day like a treasure and then,

Again, I would spend them with you

"It's my first time playing solitaire with someone," I clarified.

Miranda nodded, still looking down, and continued:

I've looked around enough to know

That you're the one I want to go

Through time with

"It's cool to be alone and together at the same time," Miranda said without lifting her gaze from the cards.

If I had a box just for wishes

And dreams that had never come true

The box would be empty

Except for the memory

Of how they were answered by you

Alone and together at the same time. That was us. That would always be us.

"You can learn a lot about people when you play solitaire with them," she said over an instrumental interlude, then joining the bridge's return:

I've looked around enough to know

That you're the one I want to go

Through time with

She looked up from her cards.

By the time the song was done, though, I had already reached an impasse in the solitaire game. Dead end. All my cards were spent.

Dang, dude.

"That was quick," Miranda said.

"Dang, that's embarrassing."

"Aaaah-ha . . . 3 minutes . . . loser."

"Man, sorry. I'm no fun," I said.

"Oh, stop, who cares, I'm just teasing," Miranda said as she crossed the room again to pick up another LP. She held the cover up to show it was *The Man Who Sold The World*, David Bowie.

"I got this 'cause of you," Miranda said as she laid the needle on the title track. The opening trippy riff got kicking.

"One of the greatest albums of all time," I said. "The other day on KMET I heard a new version of that song that Lulu just did. That's on my list," I said.

"You have a list?"

"Oh yes, I have a list for everything."

"Pick a list and tell me what's on it."

"OK, um, Lulu's version of 'The Man Who Sold The World.' "

"List of records to get. Give me something harder."

"Burning bush, unholy fire, false idols."

Miranda pondered, then said in fake Italian, "Beats-a me-a."

"List of shit I have to talk about in my bar mitzvah speech."

"Your bar mitzvah's coming up soon."

"Yeah, three weeks. Are you coming?"

"Of course. I already know what I'm wearing. You wanna see?"

Chicks, dude. They figure out what they're gonna wear way ahead of time and then they change their minds at the last minute and end up wearing something else.

She went to her closet and pulled out a yellow dress.

She held it up to herself.

It was short. The better to flash you with, my dear.

I thought of the big bad wolf . . . the yellow brick road . . . the burning bush . . . unholy fire . . .

2

"Lance, are you with me?" Rabbi Hamlisch's voice reclaimed my attention. "While Moses is communing with the burning bush up high on Mt. Sinai, down below in the desert sand there is unholy fire, right?"

I stared at the xeroxed words of my Torah portion without answering.

"Come on, Lance, concentrate. What is going on in this portion?" Rabbi Hamlisch asked me.

"Nadab and Abi'hu are killed when they try to bring unholy fire to the altar," I answered.

"Anything else about Nadab and Abi'hu?"

"They don't care about the difference between holy and unholy."

"Very good. What you have here is a clear demarcation between the sacred and the profane. One of the gifts of the Torah is its recognition of this duality, and in some ways our main duty as Jews is to observe and respect the separation. Read the passage to me."

"And Nadab and Abi'hu, the sons of Aaron, took either of them his censer, and put fire therein, and put incense thereon, and offered unholy fire before HaShem, which he commanded them not. And there went out fire from HaShem, and devoured them, and they died before HaShem."

"They go to the altar and don't perform the offering according to the prescribed priestly practice. Why would they do this?"

"Maybe they hadn't been taught the correct method?"

"They're the sons of Aaron, the head priest. Wouldn't they have been taught this by their father?"

"I suppose."

"What else? Skip down to verse 9."

"Do not drink wine nor strong drink, thou, nor thy sons with thee, when ye go into the tabernacle of the congregation, lest ye die: it shall be a statute for ever throughout your generations: and that ye may put difference between holy and unholy, and between unclean and clean."

"What does this tell you?"

"Nadab and Abi'hu were drunk?"

"It sure seems so. This blurred their understanding of God's requirement that we put a difference between holy and unholy. You see, Lance, there's nothing wrong with unholy fire, but it's important to know the difference between the burning bush up high (he pointed to his head) and unholy fire (he pointed crotchward) down below," Rabbi Hamlisch proffered, "it's important to know the difference."

Miranda Savitch in her short yellow dress was both.

The Torah didn't help with that circumstance.

I continued, "*'there went out a fire from HaShem . . .'*, I dunno, that sounds like the fire came from God."

"Well, sort of, yes, in the sense that everything comes from God, but look further down, you see, their clothes are not singed, the skin is not burned. They are consumed from within by the very same unholy fire they sought to offer before HaShem. And so what does this mean?"

"It means," I tried to focus, "we all have unholy fire inside us."

"This is true, of course, but not the correct answer. And there's an extra lesson for you," Rabbi Hamlisch went on, "it is possible for something to be true and still not be the correct answer. But back to the Torah question: what does it mean?"

"It means I have no idea."

"It means you have to pay much more attention to this than you have been. What do you want to say about this portion in your speech?" Rabbi Hamlisch asked.

"I want to talk about worshipping false idols, like money or celebrities or Nixon. He's really the falsest idol of all. And Watergate is the unholy fire."

"Heh, that's good. But you do realize Rabbi Saks is friends with President Nixon?" Rabbi Hamlisch warned.

"He is?"

"Yes. Your criticisms will not be well received."

"Dang, that sucks," I said, forgetting the difference between the sacred and the profane.

"But I'm going to let you take that approach anyway, as long as you remove President Nixon's name and replace it with 'politicians' instead. And say they are the falsest idols of all, plural."

"I will do that. Definitely. Thank you, Rabbi Hamlisch."

"All right. Go home and get that speech written. I want a draft to read by next Monday."

"I'll have one for you."

"You're very distracted, aren't you, Lance? You look like you're thinking about who knows what."

"Yeah, I suppose."

"Let me guess. You're thinking about the fat kid from *Willy Wonka & The Chocolate Factory* . . . what's his name? Buzzy—"

"Augustus—"

"—Lagniappe?"

"—Gloop. Augustus Gloop is the fat kid from *Willy Wonka & The Chocolate Factory*."

"Are you sure?"

"Mm-Hmm"

"Then why did I think it was Buzzy Lagniappe? Funny."

"I actually do know somebody named Gus Lagniappe and we sometimes call him Augustus Gloop."

"Is he fat?"

"Well, he used to be, yeah, but we call him that because his real name is Augustus."

"I know," Rabbi Hamlisch returned to guessing who knows what I was thinking about, "How about the girl from Zody's?"

"The hell you say?"

"I've got it, last guess: Pussy?"

"Come again?" I said, baffled.

"Baseball?"

"Yeah," (phew) "baseball. I thought you said something else."

"Think Aaron's going to do it tonight?" Rabbi Hamlisch asked.

"Yes. I bet it's tonight. I think the game's already started, actually. It's in Atlanta."

"Against the Dodgers, right?"

"Yeah, it'll be weird to have Babe Ruth no longer the homerun record holder. That's been the record since like my dad was born."

"Well, tablets were made to be broken," Rabbi Hamlisch said.

"Heh," I tried to muster a giggle.

"Exciting stuff," Rabbi Hamlisch said with the half-cocked enthusiasm of someone who doesn't really care about baseball, "Go enjoy. Let's hope Aaron hits that home run so you can get your mind back on figuring out what to say about his two sons in your speech."

"Thank you, Rabbi Hamlisch."

"And don't worry, you'll be rolling in pussy soon enough."

I'm 99.9% certain he didn't actually say that. But I carried the image with me well into my last waking moments that night.

When I got in the car after the tutoring session, the Dodger game had started. "You already missed Aaron's first at-bat," my father said, "He walked."

"Cool," I said, hand in backpack holding the note from Miranda Savitch, "I'm glad I didn't miss the big one."

When we arrived home I saw, for the first and penultimate time, our television had been moved into the dining room. "It's so we can watch during dinner," my father said, "This is history. We don't want to miss it."

"I'll come sit in a minute," I said as I headed toward my room, "Call me when Aaron comes up."

Once in my bedroom I removed the note from the backpack and lay supine on my bed to bask in Miranda's handwriting.

I carefully unfolded the soggy note (I had dropped it in the gutter waiting for my mom after school) to find the ink had smeared beyond legibility. The only readable text was:

Dear Lance, I hope

The rest was an abstract monochrome watercolor, like the secret of Miranda Savitch's rorshach heart.

4/8/74

Dear Lance, I hope

I looked at it 12 more times.

"Lance!" yelled my father, "Aaron's up!"

"Coming!"

"And dinner's ready!"

"'K!"

What did the rest of the note say?

I sat distracted at the dinner table, though I was watching when Hank Aaron swung on that 1-0 pitch from Al Downing in the bottom of the 4th and sent it over the left field wall.

As was our custom, we'd turned down the volume on the national TV broadcast so we could hear Vin Scully call the game on the radio, and Vinny was over-the-top as he narrated the moment.

It's a long drive to deep left, Buckner to the fence . . . It is GONE . . . What a marvelous moment for baseball. What a marvelous moment for Atlanta and the state of Georgia. What a marvelous moment for the country and the world. A black man is getting a standing ovation in the Deep South for breaking a record of an all-time baseball idol. And it is a great moment for all of us, and particularly Henry Aaron.

But for all of Vinny's hyperbolic eloquence, for all the social and cultural importance of Aaron's achievement, it wasn't the big climax I expected.

My father, on the same wavelength at that moment, said, "It's kind of silly the big deal we make about a game."

History is disappointing. A cauldron of false idols. Ghosts of old wishes.

I blew off my homework and instead put out my lights and listened to my only Jim Croce album.

His voice reminded me of last Saturday with Miranda.

I pictured myself on the bed with her, playing solitaire, Miranda singing along with Jim Croce.

I should have pushed her onto her back and kissed her, the way Freddy did.

I should have climbed on top of her and felt her body underneath me.

I could imagine myself going through with it.

I took hold of my cock and began fantasizing about Miranda on her back on her bed, my mouth on her mouth, tongue to tongue, fierce and gentle, fierce and gentle, my hands on her breasts, my fingers inside her, and finally the blazoned image of my cock entering her, St. Peter at the furry gates, 'I'm fucking Miranda Savitch,' I thought, repeated to the verge of climax and torqued down several times before absolutely letting go mindfully inside her tabernacle, until I was utterly empty. 'I love you,' I whispered to the eyelid image of her. My fingers and belly were wet with first jizz, immaculate ejaculate. I came in unto myself and knew myself.

Yeah, I know it's kind of strange

But every time I'm near you

I just run out of things to say

I know you'd understand

'Cause every time I tried to tell you

The words just came out wrong

So I'll have to say I love you in a song

I wondered if Miranda could feel it, the jazz cantata I'd just imagined all over her, the unholy fire I had just lurched into her burning bush? (represented here by my dirty sock which was the only available receptacle for the unexpected mess).

Was she seeing the same stars?

Would she be able to tell tomorrow?

Would she catch the shame of wanting in my eyes?

Would she know what I'd done to her?

Alone in the dark, I fell asleep to Jim Croce . . . and sweet images of the unlikely.

'Cause every time the time was right

All the words just came out wrong

So I'll have to say I love you in a song

3

I was afraid to make eye contact with her the next morning because of my profane debauchery of the night before, my first consummated fantasy.

What if she felt it somehow?

Girls, dude, you never know.

They're born with weird-ass radars and other built-in surveillance systems we don't have.

They can pick up shit like that.

Miranda sat next to me in Mr. Swanson's 5th Period history class.

We called him Sgt. Carter sometimes because he had a similar face and haircut to the TV character from *Gomer Pyle,* and he had that same superball-tight closet-homo intensity too.

I mean, everybody knew Gomer was gay, but we definitely also had our suspicions about Sgt. Carter.

Mr. Swanson stood daily, between classes and after Nutrition and Lunch, at the top of the main stairway at JB, busting kids for going "up" the "down" staircase. "Go down, little boy," Mr. Swanson could be heard to charge, "Go down!"

Mr. Swanson was a superfreak who had a doll named "Baby" hanging from the ceiling of his classroom by a noose.

He was very attached to Baby, so it was psychic mayhem walking into his class that day, when Mr. Swanson informed us that Baby had been kidnapped and that the perpetrators had left a ransom note.

Swanson swore brutal vengeance on anyone who did harm to Baby. "It will be swift and definitive," he vowed.

"After I've handed back your essays I will begin a thorough inquiry into this crime." Mr. Swanson strolled the room looking for guilty faces.

Everybody knew that Gus and Whit were responsible for the kidnapping.

They had duped one of the custodians—this pear-shaped dude who seemed kind of retarded—into unlocking Mr. Swanson's classroom door after school on the pretext that Gus had left his backpack inside (which, in fact he had done in preparation for the prank).

While Whit, remaining in the hall, asked the custodian questions about his personal life, Gus stood on a desk and pulled Baby out of the noose. They were planning to fuck with Swanson and ask for $1,000 ransom, maybe mutilate Baby, like singe the hair or something, but eventually return the doll to the noose one day after school again.

Quite suddenly, I, rather than Baby, became the main attraction.

"Mr. Atlas, I read your essay. The one entitled 'And The Eye Came With It.'"

Yes, that was mine.

The title was a reference to a story Mr. Swanson had told about Magellan getting killed on the beach, how he got shot in the eye with an arrow and pulled the arrow out, "and the eye . . . came . . . with it," Mr. Swanson had said in a really exaggerated Vincent Price kind of voice.

"The entire essay is devoted to the one story I told in class about Magellan and his death on the beach. That is not what the topic asked you to do, Mr. Atlas, you were to examine several factors which contributed to the death, so it is a failure in that regard, but there were two bigger problems with your essay. Would you like to know what those were, Mr. Atlas?"

"Sure," I shrugged.

"First, for some reason that is far beyond my ability to comprehend, although you are clearly writing about the death of Magellan, you refer to him throughout the essay as Galileo."

The whole class began giggling.

"Dang, I must've been tripping."

Miranda rolled her eyes.

"Well you certainly have fallen, Mr. Atlas. And now I'm about to kick you the rest of the way down the stairs. If you had paid more careful attention to the assigned topic you would also have noticed that you were supposed to be writing about Balboa, not Magellan, the death of Balboa, Mr. Atlas."

"Dang. I always get them confused. The two Pacific Ocean dudes, right?"

I looked around for sympathizers. Everyone was stifling laughter. Miranda had her head in her hands.

"How did Balboa die, Mr. Atlas?"

"Didn't he die under house arrest for heresy?"

"No, that, Mr. Atlas, was Galileo. And so you've come full circle."

"Hey, I knew the names at least and the circumstances. I just couldn't remember which dude did what."

"Yes, well, Mr. Atlas, history rides quite a bit on knowing 'which dude did what.' But enough. Class, tomorrow as you know we have a test. And remember: If you study, it will be crystal clear. If you don't, it will be as clear . . . as . . . mud," Mr. Swanson said, "I'd like you to spend the rest of the hour studying for tomorrow's exam, and I will begin my investigation into the disappearance of Baby. Oh, yes, and anybody with information leading to Baby's safe return will be handsomely rewarded."

Once Swanson had handed back the essays (I left mine face down), he ensconced himself at his desk.

Miranda tossed a folded piece of paper onto my desk. It read, "Did you get my note yesterday?"

I wrote back, "Yeah, but I dropped it in the gutter by accident and it got all smeared. I couldn't read it."

"CHIMP!" she scrawled.

"What'd the note say?" I added beneath her response.

"Too late. You blew it. CHUMP!" she scribbled.

"Aw, that's cold," I returned.

She read my comment and slit her eyes at me.

The following Saturday, Gus, Claude, Whit, Chester, and I walked over to the Piece O'Pizza on Beverly Blvd. near Fairfax, right next to Taco Tah.

As always we made lewd references to the Piece O'Pizza ad slogan, "Had a piece lately?" which was displayed across a large marquee in front of the restaurant.

Claude Moss boasted, "I'm gonna get me a piece at the sock hop next month, nyeah."

Student Council at John Burroughs had decided to have a 1950s-style "sock hop" instead of a regular dance in the Spring semester.

Gus responded to Claude's claims of bagging pussy at the sock hop, "Dude,

105

unless you're choosing to go outside the species, give up on getting any kind of piece 'cause, dang, dude, what human female would even come close to considering doing it with a green-toothed gay golita like you? I mean, you have like algae and paramecium and like trilobites and shit growing in your mouth. Who'd want her tongue climbing around that jungle of slime?"

"Justine Balthazar," Claude proudly announced.

"Absolutely no fucking way," said Gus. "You asked Justine to the sock hop?"

"Yuh-huh."

"And she said yes?"

"Yerse."

"You a goddamn lie," Gus said.

"Sit on it," Claude raised his middle finger at Gus.

"Ooh, and now the Fungus can quote *Happy Days*. The heighth of cool," Gus popped his finger in his cheek.

"Hey, I've got a date. That's more than Lance can say," said Claude.

"I don't want to go to the sock hop," I said.

"Dang, dude, you can't abandon us," said Whit, "you're closer to getting a piece than anybody. You have to blaze the trail."

Gus said, "You ever notice how chicks got their asshole and their pussyhole so close together? My brother says that's so you can carry 'em around like a six-pack of Schlitz."

"Or a bowling ball," Whitman Rust added.

"No, you need three holes for that shit," Gus said.

"Nyeah, good one, dude," Whit held out his hand to meet Gus's slap.

"Hey, I've got one," Claude Moss said, "Why shouldn't girls drink beer at the beach?"

I offered the obligatory "Why?"

"'Cause they might get sand in their Schlitz."

"Hey, Claude was actually funny," snickered Gus. "Schlitz," he said as he made a two-fingered holding-a-six-pack sign.

An instant code word was born.

Thenceforth one of our stock ways to crack one another up was we'd point to some girl and mouth the word "Schlitz" while making the holding a six-pack sign in reference to the lass in question.

"Look at me, I've got one in each hand," said Gus Lagniappe, hobbling along with both arms in pantomime burden.

"You look like Lancelot Link Secret Chimp when you do that," Chester Flinch said.

We entered Piece O'Pizza, and Chester Flinch couldn't resist messing with the oriental lady at the counter.

Chester fake-scanned the menu and asked, "You got any pizza with beaver meat? I'm really craving some beaver."

"Sorry, no beaver. Pepperyoni. Sausage. Tha's ah. Pepperyoni and Sausage go good."

'Nah, you know what, that's not cool. When I come here for a piece I expect there to be some beaver available. False promises, dude."

We were squealing with glee. The counter lady was not getting it.

"Sorry, no beaver," she said again, not realizing that her phrase would enter our horny-boy lexicon for years to come.

At the table, each of us chowing down our slice of choice, we settled in for a session of raucous talking.

"Why *do* they call pussy beaver?" Claude said, "I've never understood that one."

"'Cause it eats wood, dude," said Whit, making a chompy beaver face.

We giggled and snickered in the unventilated hotness of Piece O'Pizza.

Gus asked, "What kind of piece'd you get, Atlas?"

"Pepperyoni and sausage," I said.

"Sorry, no beaver!" Whit replied on cue.

"How about a Miranda samich?" said Chester.

"Yeah, so, how far'd you get with Miranda last Saturday anyway?"

"1st base at least with Monsieur Frenchingboy over here," Whit said.

"We didn't do anything. We just hung out and talked and stuff," I said.

"That's it?" Gus scoffed.

"We played solitaire together," I added.

"Dang, that's dog, dude," said Claude.

"Lance, you are such a fag," said Gus.

Chester Flinch said, "Miranda Savitch wants all of your hot monkey love, and you know it."

"I don't know shit. I can't tell. She sure seemed to enjoy frenching with Freddy during spin-the-bottle."

"Yeah but it's you she wants to go to the sock hop with," Chester said.

"No way," I said.

"Hell yes, dude, I have this on very good authority, as in the *Chick Clique*," Chester said, shifting suddenly into an Aunt Bee voice, "Mandy is randy for you," rubbing on my tit like I'm a chick or something.

"Come on, Lance, you know you've fantasized about fucking her," said Gus with startling clairvoyance, "so what's the big deal about getting to 1st base with her? Just grab her and kiss her."

"She's waiting," added Chester. "It's like duh."

"And then 2nd base!" said Whit, making the titty-grabbing sign with both hands.

Gus said, "Miranda's got some big ones, too."

"The Himalayas, dude," answered Chester.

"Which one's Everest?" joked Gus.

"Consult Atlas!" said Chester with unconscious brilliance.

"I bet when she's lying down they look like tostadas," said Claude.

"Dos titties," Whit added.

"What about 3rd base?" said Claude sticking his tongue through V-fingers.

"Nah, dang, dude, 3rd base is with your hand," said Whit, raising his middle finger and wiggling it up and down.

"Nuh-uh, you're both wrong. 3rd base is . . . Chester said pantomiming a blowjob."

Gus said, "All right, so whatever, let's just say that 1st base is tongue, 2nd base is titty, 3rd base can be either finger-in-pussy, tongue-in-pussy, or cock-in-mouth, and we all agree that the homerun is—"

All chimed in together, "Cock-In-Pussy!"

Gus raised his glass of lemonade, "Here's to Cock-In-Pussy!"

"Cock-In-Pussy," we all toasted, lemonades hoisted.

We didn't know what the fuck we were talking about.

"So are you gonna ask Miranda to the sock hop or what? We all know who we're going with. Even Claude has a date for fuck's sake," said Gus.

"I don't know," I said. "I don't really want to go to the sock hop."

"Yeah, but, dude, chicks dig that shit. You gotta do it. If you wanna pop the cherry," said Gus, "Don't be a gay golita."

"And you also have to pretend you're having a good time," Claude said.

"And then she'll be all over your body," Chester promised, "Cock-in-pussy solidarity, dude."

"How are you guys dressing for this thing? It's gotta be '50s, right?" I asked.

"We should all go in like tight white t-shirts with cigarettes rolled up in the sleeve and straight-legged Levis. Hair slicked back," Gus suggested.

"Yeah, like the Fonzie-dude in *American Grafitti*," said Claude.

"What Fonzie dude?" asked Gus.

"The one who's got the 12-year-old girl in his car," responded Claude.

"She's 14 I think, the one in Paul Le Mat's yellow car?" I observed, knowing who Claude meant.

"Yeah, Paul Le Mat, dude. He's cooler than Fonzie," Claude said.

"If we dressed like Paul Le Mat everyday at school we'd be rolling in pussy, dude," said Chester.

"You sound like my rabbi," I muttered. Nobody heard me.

Pizza chowed, lemonade swilled, Gus Lagniappe steered our course.

"All right, let's split the scene if you know what I mean," he said, and we all rose to go.

As we were leaving, Claude picked up a matchbook from the counter. He snorted, "Check it out," holding up the matchbook, which said on the cover: *Enjoy Life: Eat Out More Often!*

Everybody stuck tongues through v-fingers.

And Chester shouted to the cashier as we exited, "Sorry no beaver!"

4

My bar mitzvah was actually on my 13th birthday, April 20, 1974, an unusual day not just because it actually was my birthday instead of the usual "closest Saturday available" at a Bar Mitzvah mill like my temple but also because I share a birthday with Adolph Hitler, which always freaks people out anyway, but on that 4/20 I was being about as jewy as a Reform Jew could be.

I would often joke that I was the reincarnation of Adolph Hitler. That his punishment was coming back as me, an American Jew.

I stopped saying that once I figured out that nobody thought it was funny.

I remember my grandfather said of my little joke, "Only God would find that humorous."

I have no idea what the fuck he meant by that.

Only God would find that humorous

It's brilliantly meaningless.

The ceremony went smoothly.

I got through the *V'yahavta* and *Avot V'Imahot* and the lot without a glitch.

I read from the Torah with only a couple of stumbles, and my speech was received well by most save the more conservative wing of my family and Rabbi Saks himself who later castigated Rabbi Hamlisch for allowing me to do it.

Everybody could tell my speech was about Nixon, dude.

The funny thing is Rabbi Saks' sermon that morning was about how stupid the kosher laws are.

"I eat bacon cheeseburgers when I feel like it," he told the congregation.

I'd just spent months studying the importance of separating holy from unholy and the rabbi was saying that *kashrut* was bullshit.

I could see Miranda's yellow dress from the bima the whole time.

I didn't want one of the hotel ballroom type bar mitzvah receptions that so many of my friends had had.

Instead, mine was an intimate affair in my grandparents' backyard.

I brought over my stereo and my favorite records.

I wanted to be DJ at my own party.

I loved being the DJ. It kept you separate. Observing the party but not part of the party. You didn't have to interact and yet you were a presence in your own way, guiding things even.

There were no decorations, no themed anything, no hora dancing, no hoisted chairs, no corny-ass rhyming-couplet-narrated candle-lighting ceremony, no retrospective slide show, no speeches.

Just relatives and friends commingling in the yard and shmoozing.

Miranda made her entrance up the driveway and into the yard just as I had started spinning Redbone's "Come And Get Your Love."

The rest of the *Chick Clique* ran to greet her and after air kisses and a hushed huddle Miranda made her way over to me and handed me a gift.

"*Mazel Tov,*" she said, half-smirking.

"Aren't we jewy, today," I remarked. "I love the dress," I said as I laid her package on the gift table.

"Thank you. Even though you've seen it before."

"Not on you, though."

She smirked and looked downward.

"Are you relieved?"

"Hell yes. I just want to play lots of music today and not think anymore about the Torah. Oh, here this'll be fun," I said, as Redbone came to an end, and I put on Steve Miller Band's "The Joker."

The kids gathered on the concrete slab that would serve as a dance floor.

Some people call me Maurice

'Cause I sing of the Pompatus of Love

It was the most cryptic of all pop song lines in 1974. We loved that song. Especially the *Woo-Woo* guitar fill after "Maurice." You always sang that guitar part too when you sang the song. "Some people call me Maurice, *Woo-Woo . . .*"

Nobody had any idea what the Pompatus of Love was.

I wove together the group's favorite songs all in a bunch.

"Bennie & The Jets" by Elton John, "Smokin' In The Boys Room" by Brownsville Station, "Takin' Care Of Business" by Bachman-Turner Overdrive, "Billy Don't Be A Hero" by Bo Donaldson and the Heywoods, "Midnight At The Oasis" by Maria Muldaur, "Seasons In The Sun" by Terry Jacks.

I also couldn't resist playing Ray Stevens' novelty hit "The Streak."

The fad of running naked through public gatherings had found its way into mainstream media when a dude had streaked across the stage at the Academy Awards 3 weeks before.

We would later all pitch in a bunch of money to pay an intrepid classmate of ours to streak past the orthodox synagogues on Beverly Blvd. on a Saturday just as morning services were letting out.

Oliver Gelding brought Marvin Gaye's great *Let's Get It On* album to the party, and I spun a whole side of that record. It was during the Gaye album that the kids actually started doing a little dancing.

"Here, Mr. DJ, I brought you a coke," Miranda said, handing me a cup. "I'm your biggest groupie."

"Garsh, thanks. You like this song?" I asked.

"Tin Man" by America was coming through the speakers at that moment.

But Oz never did give nothing to the Tin Man

That he didn't, didn't already have

And cause never was the reason for the evening

Or the tropic of Sir Galahad

"I prefer Sir Lancelot to Sir Galahad myself," she said.

"*The perfect prize that waits upon the shelf,* eh?"

"Heh, defenly . . . This song really sucks, you know?"

113

"Yeah, I don't know why I'm playing it."

I put on the next record, a perfect thematic segue from "Tin Man" into "Goodbye Yellow Brick Road."

After I got the tune spinning, Miranda tugged on my arm and pulled me into the dance area.

I didn't really know where to put my hands or anything, but looking around settled on what appeared to be the conventional boy's hands on girl's hips.

Miranda put her hands on my shoulders.

Some of the other girls had their arms all the way around the boys' necks, but Miranda didn't do that.

When are you gonna come down?

When are you going to land?

As I held my hands on her hips I could feel the outline of her underwear and I began to get a hard-on.

I wanted to run my hands all along her body, feel her ass, her sides, her breasts.

I looked past her.

Trying to keep my crotch from brushing against hers lest she get a grind of the aching bone.

How soft would she be if I squeezed her?

At moments the tips of her breasts would brush against my chest, intensifying the swelling below.

She leaned into me a bit in order to speak in my ear.

"I know why Candy's been being a bitch to me," she said.

"Why?" I asked.

"She thinks I'm trying to steal her boyfriend."

"I thought you said that was her cousin."

"I'm talking about *you*, doofus," Miranda clarified.

"Um, I'm not Candy's boyfriend."

"You *were* her boyfriend."

"For like 3 weeks, yeah."

"That means you will *always* be her boyfriend."

"But she doesn't like me anymore."

"That doesn't matter."

"No?"

"No, you're hers."

"To all eternity."

"Correct."

You know you can't hold me forever

I didn't sign up with you

"That's how it goes then," I sighed.

"Yep," she said, "You will remain in her peripheral vision always."

My father was trying to get a picture of me dancing with Miranda.

"Cheat to the camera!" he kept saying as he followed us around the floor, never quite getting the shot.

"*Are* you trying to steal her boyfriend?" I asked.

Miranda smiled lopsided without looking at me.

"Right now I'm dancing with Sir Lancelot," she said.

So goodbye yellow brick road

Where the dogs of society howl

I leaned into Miranda's girlbody, boner be damned, and danced for real all the way inside the music.

Dancing with Miranda made the whole world slow down.

The boys were on remarkably good behavior.

Gus said "Schiltz" and did the holding-a-six-pack sign in reference to my 75-year-old great aunt much to the busting up of all who got the gag, and Chester Flinch blurted out "Sorry, no beaver" at an inappropriate moment when I was cutting the cake.

But otherwise the guys gave me the model citizenship I had pleaded of them the day before.

My golitas came through for me.

There *were* a number of attempts to sneak wine while distracting the bartender, but he was used to the 13-year-old crowd.

"I know your tricks!" he'd say as one of us would ask for a coke while another would reach behind the bar for a wine bottle. "I know your tricks!" he'd always catch us, laughing.

When Miranda informed me her mom was coming to pick her up any minute, I walked with her to the back gate. We stood half-facing each other.

"Thanks for coming," I said.

"Oh, no, thanks for inviting me," she answered automatically.

And rather than agonize any longer I convinced myself to blurt out, with a decided lack of romance and seductiveness, "You wanna go to the sock hop with me?"

Miranda did her downward smile again and answered with little pause, "I'd love to, yes," finally playing out a script she had written weeks before.

"Cool."

"Relieved?" she jabbed.

"Heh, I—yeah."

"You should call me or something," she said.

"I will."

"Probly or defenly?" she asked.

"Defenly," I promised.

"Cool." She turned around and saw her mom's car. Tamar waved. "Hi, Lance!" she shouted, "*Mazel Tov* on your bar mitzvah!"

"Hey your mom's all jewy too," I said and then fell into muteness, finally bumbling, "Well . . . "

"You did great today," Miranda rasped, tilting swiftly toward my face and kissing me softly on the cheek, then just as swiftly turning away and scurrying toward her mom's car, yelling, "Bye, Lance!" without looking back.

The sweetness of that moment would linger for adolescent centuries.

Miranda had kissed me.

I sort of stood and watched her get into the car, and when I turned back around to face the party, I could see the scenario had witnesses.

My pals didn't care; they were still busy trying to sneak wine behind the bartender's back.

But the *Chick Clique* was watching intently, all smiley and goopy-eyed.

They'd also read the script.

This would be the subject of many phone calls across the girl network later in the evening.

Miranda Savitch kissed Lance Atlas at his bar mitzvah.

They are going to the sock hop together.

Mission Accomplished.

At home that night, opening presents, I saved Miranda's for last.

After the stack of envelopes with generous checks, certificates for trees planted in Israel in my name, savings bonds, numerous books about The Jewish People, a couple of Cross pens with my initials engraved, and a subscription to *National Geographic* (available porn!), I finally tore the tissue paper off Miranda's gift: a book entitled *The Inner Game of Solitaire* and the new Lulu 45, her version of David Bowie's "The Man Who Sold The World." Also enclosed was a piece of Little Prince-themed stationery personalized with the name Miranda Raquel Savitch, upon which she'd written a note.

Dear Lance,

Cross this one off your list.

Love, Miranda

That night, alone in the dark of my own brain, I fucked Miranda Savitch in her yellow dress upstairs at my grandparents' house while the party was still going on.

My imagination reveled in lusty conduct with the fantasy Savitch who wanted me to fuck her and uttered the demand audibly until a massive ejaculation and shame overtook my sleepy accomplishment.

Lulu sang, "*Oh no, not me, I've never lost control . . .*" as I slid into unlikely dreams.

I woke up with crusty kleenex still in my hand. This time I'd been prepared.

5

The month that passed between my bar mitzvah and the sock hop had its jagged edges.

I didn't really know what our relationship was.

The words "boyfriend" and "girlfriend" had never been uttered.

We were each other's dates for the sock hop. Otherwise, not much else.

And, of course, I didn't call her.

I was always afraid I'd be interrupting something or I wouldn't know what to say if her mother or, worse, her father answered.

And if you called somebody up "just to talk," what did you talk about?

How did you start?

So my response to the confusion was not to call.

I dialed the first 6 numbers quite a few times, pulling the hallway phone with the long cord all the way into my bedroom and locking the door.

A couple of times I even dialed the 7th number and hung up when it started to ring.

And though we hung out during Nutrition and Lunch at school it was always with the group.

Some days Miranda was nice to me, other days I felt her unspoken scorn.

When, on very short notice I was informed of a practice dance session for the sock hop at Misty's apartment in Park La Brea the next night, I opted out immediately.

"I don't want to practice," I said.

"Well, guess what, we're going to a '50s dance and we don't how to dance to that music, so you need to come practice with us," Miranda spoke in a tone that admitted no decline option. I was going. I just was. Choice was not on the menu. There *was* no fucking menu.

How do girls do that?

Once I was finally able to find Misty's building (near the corner of Curson and Curson, actually), I was late to the practice, which aggravated Miranda's peeve at me, and Freddy Snow was there with Dolly, which aggravated my discomfort.

119

Misty was going to the sock hop with Gus, but she was unable to force his presence at the practice.

He'd said no fucking way.

Gus was my hero.

When I failed in my attempt to lift Miranda so she could straddle me as part of a dance step (it kind of looked like fucking when it was done right, but we never got to the spread-leg straddle move), Freddy Snow came over and demonstrated how it's done, lifting Miranda masterfully, lowering her, legs a-spread, onto his hips; for an unbearable second it looked like Freddy Snow was fucking Miranda Savitch.

My humiliation was complete when I made another attempt at that particular dance move and Miranda waved me off with a "don't bother" glare.

Our bodies simply didn't jive.

Who knows what was the reason.

The rest of my energy that evening was spent swallowing mucus-thick back-of-the-throat tears invisible to the outside world.

The night of the sock hop, my mother drove me to pick up Miranda, and when Miranda opened the door I could immediately sense her disappointment with my appearance.

I couldn't tame my jewfro into '50s jewboy ducktail and so my curls spouted freely. And my mom wouldn't let me dress tough-guy so I wore a nerdy v-neck sweater over a button-down shirt.

I looked less like Paul Le Mat in *American Grafitti* and more like "Clair"-era Gilbert O'Sullivan.

"Hi," Miranda said flatly.

"Hey. You ready?" I tried to be chipper.

"Yeah," she returned as if burning me in effigy. "You don't look '50s, " she eyed my pants, "Bell Bottoms? Jeezis, Lance."

My mother drove us in silence to JB.

The sock hop itself took place in the boys gym.

The gym wasn't decorated '50s, but the music was era-correct, mostly from the *American Graffiti* soundtrack album.

It had actually been a crazy day in L.A.

Earlier in the afternoon the LAPD had cornered suspected members of the Symbionese Liberation Army—the dudes who'd kidnapped Patty Hearst—in some house in Watts, and the SLA people inside the house were shooting back at the cops.

The boring-ass Watergate impeachment hearings were interrupted by on-the-spot live coverage of the SLA shootout.

It was the 2nd and final time that my father pulled the television into the dining room during dinner so as not to miss history.

The SLA shootout dominated all the talk in the gym.

Lots of "Did you see that shit? It was like wap! wap! wap!" imitations of gunfire.

Members of student council were telling people where to leave their shoes and to have a 'ginchy' time, but everybody else was going off on the SLA shootout.

"Keep Your Socks On!" read the sign over the entrance.

"Oh look, there's Dolly and Freddy, let's go say hi," Miranda said, almost nice to me, tugging me by the arm to the other side of the gym.

Claude Moss had indeed come with Justine Balthazar and they were already dancing.

Gus Lagniappe was sitting in the top row of the bleachers with Whitman Rust while their dates Misty Winters and Claire Farnaway walked arm-in-arm around the perimeter of the gym picking up on the latest gossip and spreading it forthwith.

Sharon Rose's mother wouldn't let her go, so she was home moping and waiting for her friends to call with all the dirt afterwards.

Oliver Gelding, who was planning to attend with Candy Stoner, got sick the day before and wasn't there.

Candy didn't want to go alone so she had tagged along with Chester Flinch and Lorelei Lux.

Chester pointed to Lorelei's ass, made the holding-a-six-pack sign and said "Schlitz" under his breath as they all three walked by.

"Hi, Mandy," Dolly warbled, "Hey, Lance."

"My Darling," Freddy said to Miranda.

"Hi, guys," Miranda chimed, "Isn't this great?"

"So far it's OK," said Freddy, "But I need to get dancing. Shall we?" he held out his hand, with dumbfounding surprise, to Miranda. Without a glance at me Miranda joined Freddy Snow on the dance floor.

They were gone.

For the rest of the night.

I spent the first few songs expecting the liaison to end, but by the 4th tune I realized I was not part of Miranda's picture for the evening.

Dolly, numbed, went and sat down in the front row of the bleachers. It was dark enough so that I couldn't tell if she was crying.

I sat down next to her eventually.

"Hello, Dolly," I said to her, perhaps the 40 billionth time she'd been greeted thus.

Dolly snorted and rolled her eyes.

"This is like totally fucked up," she said.

Freddy and Miranda were having a grand time, all bopping limbs and giddy smiles.

"Likewise. I don't get it." I said, "I'm so confused. She wanted me to ask her to this dance. And now look. What's her trip?"

"Mandy is Mandy. She freaks out about stuff. Freddy, on the other hand, I don't know why he's doing this," Dolly said, getting teary and watching the dancers, "Anyway, you know Miranda likes you, right?"

"Obviously not."

"You have no idea, Lance. Believe me. She's all switched-on-bitch tonight, though."

"Dang, dude, I don't know, I'm in pain," I shared with Dolly. I wanted to go home.

"Don't forget it's my fucking boyfriend she's dancing with. We're in this together it looks like," Dolly said.

"I guess so," I said.

"If you ever want to talk about stuff . . . "

"Yeah, right. From my mouth to Miranda's ears."

"No, Lance, really. Anytime. I can keep secrets," she swore. "I'm not exactly a Mandy fan at the moment."

Suddenly, following a string of authentic '50s tunes the PA started blaring "Crocodile Rock" by Elton John, a '70s nostalgia pastiche of the '50s.

It made perfect sense. There, in a 1974 gymnasium, amid a media swell of '50s imagery and homage, from *American Graffiti* to *Happy Days* to KRTH-101, we were listening to a 1970s recreation of that bygone era.

The music of "Crocodile Rock" was blaring from the shitty speakers, but I was hearing a different song. Elton John reminded me of my one and only dance with Miranda. That's the music that floated in my thoughts.

Maybe you'll get a replacement

There's plenty like me to be found

As I watched Freddy and Miranda dance, Lorelei Lux approached.

"Hi, Lori," said Dolly.

"Dahlia Ferris," Lorelei nodded, "I have come to dance with Lance Atlas."

"I don't want to dance," I said.

"You will dance with me, Lance Atlas." Lorelei ordered.

"I'm planning to dance with Miranda when she's done dancing with Freddy," I explained.

"Interesting . . ." Lorelei pondered, "Your girlfriend is dancing with someone else's boyfriend . . . interesting . . ."

"Lori, stop being a crazy-ass bitch," Dolly insisted.

"I am speaking with Lance Atlas, not you, Dahlia Ferris, whose boyfriend has been dancing with someone else's girlfriend all night," Lorelei scolded.

"Miranda's not my girlfriend," I countered.

"You need to see a doctor, Lori, really, get help, please," Dolly said.

"Come dance with me, Lance Atlas. They're playing Elton John . . ."

"Don't do it, Lance," Dolly half-warned.

I joined hands with Lorelei Lux, meandering onto the dance floor, and we began not dancing but spinning, facing each other, holding hands; the more intense the music got the faster we spun.

It felt like 2nd Grade.

What kept me from getting dizzy and nauseated was my focus on Lorelei's face, a face that would invade and overtake my future a few years hence.

I saw it.

I should have known the collision course ahead right then.

A titanic failure in the making.

If I looked away from Lorelei to try and see Miranda, I'd surely lose all balance in the blur and make a foolish stumble.

I kept my eyes riveted to Lorelei's.

By keeping me in a spin she knew I wouldn't be able to look at anybody but her.

At the conclusion of "Crocodile Rock," Lorelei, flashing a rare smile, threw her arms around me and hugged me tight.

Our embrace was interrupted by Chester Flinch, who said, "Sorry, no beaver," as he extracted Lorelei from my orbit.

Just two songs later the curfew brought an end to the sock hop, and everyone was ushered out onto McCadden to await parental pick-up. Another ride home in silence concluded with our station wagon pulling up in front of Miranda's house.

"See ya," Miranda said as she opened the car door.

My mother turned around and said, "Lance, you be a gentleman and walk the young lady to the door."

I would tell my mother the story later and get her apologetic sympathy, but at that moment I did as she said. Miranda kept her back to me as we walked, and she quickly removed her key and unlocked the front door. She would have simply walked in and closed the door on me had I not stopped her—

"Hey," I said. She paused and turned.

I shrugged. She shrugged.

"I don't know, Lance. I'm sorry if I hurt your feelings."

"What'd I do?" I said with a hidden whimper.

"Nothing. That about sums it up," Miranda said, "Nothing. . . " She backed into the doorway.

"Bye, Lance," she said as she closed the door.

On the way home my mother didn't ask me why I was crying.

Miranda and I didn't speak the last 4 weeks of school.

Freddy and Dolly were still a couple, so the Freddy/Miranda thing didn't materialize as expected and obviously Dolly got over Freddy's dalliance at the sock hop.

I asked Chester Flinch to go on a reconnaissance mission for me, and he came back with the following report:

"OK, so I talked to Miranda . . ." Chester said.

"And?" I inquired.

"You're the hamburger," he said.

"Huh? What's that mean, I'm the hamburger?"

125

"I was talking to Miranda and I asked her what her trip was, why she wanted to go to the sock hop with you and why she danced with Freddy all night and she said to me, and I quote, 'Lance is the hamburger,' all serious and mysterious and shit, and I'm wondering 'What the fuck kind of Lorelei Lux type bullshit is that? please 'splain it Lucy?' and she, check this out, she goes, this is me being her, she goes 'It's like when you go to a restaurant and you see this big juicy hamburger on the menu and you think right away, like, Ok, this is what I want, and then you like fantasize about how great the hamburger's going to be when they bring it, but then when they put it on the table in front of you you look at it and you realize it's not really what you want.' And so I ask her again 'What the fuck does that mean?' and all she says is, 'Lance is the hamburger.'"

Genius, I thought.

"So I don't know what the hell else to tell you, man. You're the hamburger."

"I'm the hamburger. Wow," I said, without much air.

During the last week of the semester my yearbook filled up with signatures the majority of which ended with some form of the phrase, "Good Luck with Miranda," but when I reluctantly approached Miranda to sign my yearbook, I don't know why, just 'cause I couldn't imagine my 8th Grade yearbook without the most important person's signature in it, Miranda declined to sign it.

She took the book from me, even turned to a page as if she were going to sign. But then she closed up the yearbook and handed it back without writing in it.

"You know what?" she said, "There's nothing to say."

"OK," I said, in all my accumulated wimpery, and walked across the quad in search of silence and solitude for my mucus-thick tears aback the throat.

On the very last day of school, I was purposely slow taking down my science project from Ms. Roebuck's wall, partly feeling sorry for myself, partly avoiding seeing Miranda at locker clean-out after school, partly trying to get one last glimpse up Ms. Roebuck's dress when she bent over to pick stuff up, and so by the time I got to my locker to clean it out for the summer, everybody was already gone.

The hall floors were strewn with the detritus and desolation of term's end. Meaningless tests and worksheets and assignment logs and Pee Chee folders and pencil stubs and Cliffs Notes and tattered book covers fashioned from brown grocery bags and comic books and collages made from magazines.

There's nothing emptier than a school hallway after the last student has gone home for the summer. A haven for ghosts and ghouls and other souls in denial.

And there I was.

In the midst of the void.

This was of course intensified by my own inner emptiness and utter bafflement as to who knows what I did to make Miranda Savitch not like me anymore.

Nothing . . . that about sums it up . . . nothing . . .

As I opened up my locker to pull out the last remaining papers and deliver them unto the muck heap, I found a folded note wedged into one of the slats. It was from Miranda.

Dear Lance,

I'm sorry for not signing your yearbook. That was mean. It's not that there's nothing to say, it's that there's so much I could say. I realized and found out a lot recently. You 'probably' don't know what I'm talking about so forget it. I 'didn't,' 'shouldn't' and 'couldn't' explain. Maybe someday when I throw out my tennis socks and forget all my inside jokes with myself you'll figure it out.

Love always,

Miranda

I experienced a rush of happy-sadness, similar to the warm-cold feel of sand.

I'd spend the summer sniffing for tidbits.

The living disappointment of a wish come true.

Don't Make A Move

1

Halloween was hotter than hell.

Nothing unusual there.

Summer in Los Angeles can last until Thanksgiving some years.

Most folks tend to forget from fall to fall.

That old temptation to believe in paradise.

Even before the bristling Santa Ana winds drag desert heat in their wake across the Southland, and hackles rise in step with the temperature, even when it's still just a plain old lingering summer no different from last year, rather than register the sense memory and relax into "Oh, yeah, this again," Angelenos rather wail and gnash their teeth as if the sweltering autumn is something new that just came tumbling down out of the sky from some celestial brouhaha.

"What did we do to deserve this furnace?" they gripe at rope's end, "It's fall! Oh hell! The garden will be ruined!"

In the days leading up to Halloween 1974, the asphalt quad at John Burroughs Jr. High had been rippling with liquidity, a scatter of phantom puddles really, mirages aquiver with wavy vapors redolent of sulphur and burning tar.

You didn't know whether the sponginess of the blacktop was due to the ground itself softening in the heat or the rubber soles of your Adidas beginning to melt.

We were constantly hot and horny anyway, so the external inferno was merely a corollary to the boiling blood within, the triple blister of wanting what you're afraid to have and being ashamed of both the wanting and the fear.

Such is the seemingly eternal torment of the 14-year-old libido.

And it didn't help that the hot sticky pavement smelled like girls.

Our oasis from the baking was the so-called 9th Grade Court, a fenced off area available to JB Class of '75 only, where, during Nutrition and Lunch, sheltered by shade, we would argue about sports, repeat lines from Monty Python sketches and Marx Brothers routines and our favorite movies (*"Your mother sucks cocks in hell!"* from *The Exorcist* being a perpetually popular exclamation still, nearly a year after the film had come out), eating pieces of sinfulicious JB coffee cake, bitching about homework, and trying to get girls to notice us.

I was still hanging around with Whitman Rust and Gus Lagniappe in those days, unacknowledged leaders of the cool nerd set, awkward dorks who played at being bad-ass while getting good grades and high test scores.

I was spending more time alone with Claude Moss too, who, when with the group, was always vying for Gus and Whit's approval, making lame attempts at gross-out humor, setting himself up for ridicule with every misfired quip, but who, in private, had superb taste in music, a willingness to check out new books and films that weren't mainstream treacle, and a romantic attachment to baseball.

The 1974 Dodgers were a great team, with that Garvey-Lopes-Russell-Cey infield, and the rest also soared: Bill Buckner, Jimmy Wynn, Willie Crawford, Steve Yeager, Joe Ferguson, pitchers Don Sutton, Andy Messersmith, Tommy John, and, of course, the 104 relief appearances of Iron Mike Marshall. Their 4-1 loss in the World Series to the Oakland A's brought a depressing end to a gleeful season.

On the other hand, that Oakland A's team was also tremendously fun and colorful, with the likes of Blue Moon Odom, Sal Bando, Rollie Fingers, Catfish Hunter, Bert Campaneris, Joe Rudi, Vida Blue, et al. A rogues gallery of subversive talent, all mustaches and renegade bravado. So the World Series was entertaining despite the humiliation of our beloved Big Blue Wrecking Crew.

"At least it wasn't the damn Yankees," I said in consolation the day after the Series ended, just two weeks before Halloween.

"Damn Yankees. They are fucking evil, dude," said Claude.

"Satan in pinstripes," said Eddie Gurges, the newest of our crowd, "Fuck the damn Yankees. The A's are cool, though, I have to admit. I hate them and I wish they'd lost, but still, they are cool."

Eddie Gurges was about 5'1" with curly hair unsuccessfully tortured flat and a chipped front tooth.

He too loved The Beatles, Monty Python, the Dodgers, *MAD* Magazine, and the Marx Brothers.

Together we would pore over the books *Why A Duck?* and *Hooray For Captain Spaulding*, reading the lines out loud at lunch like the dorks we were and snorting and chortling at Groucho's language and Harpo's lack of it.

Funny, brilliant, nervous, and utterly consumed with the visual world, Eddie Gurges drew cartoons obsessively and with phenomenal skill for his age.

His early style was heavily influenced by Don Martin from *MAD* Magazine, floppy tongues and gangly limbs afluster, but he also had a subtle Sergio Aragones way of telling a story in pictures.

Eddie was defined by his drawing, and he was incessantly at it.

Everywhere he went he had his sketchbook with him, in class, standing around the 9th Grade Court, on the beach, at the movies, in the car, talking on the phone, browsing the $1 bins at Aron's Records, watching Dodger games, even using the bathroom (Eddie once showed me a drawing of Richard Nixon he did "while taking a shit," to use his apt description).

"You know, the Dodgers would have won the Series if they had used Jim Brewer more instead of Mike Marshall," Eddie contended.

"Bonehead Brewer?" mocked Whit, "He needs an arm transplant."

"Well, you'll see," Eddie countered, "Marshall will be crap next season and Brewer will still be there in the bullpen coming through when the Dodgers need him."

"So what do you think about the Dodgers fucking up this year?" I joked, holding an invisible microphone up to Sandy Clay's mouth.

Sandy had recently become a folk hero among our crowd when, during the World Series, he called in to Dodger Talk—the pre-game show on KABC TalkRadio 790—on a bet that he'd be able to say fuck on the air without getting bleeped and, in fact, he pulled it off.

An hour before Game 1 started, near the end of Dodger Talk, Sandy's call was taken on the air, and he asked that day's guest, Dodger General Manager Al Campanis, regarding the 1973 team, "What do you think about the Dodgers fucking up last year?"

And it wasn't bleeped. He said it. We heard it: *"What do you think about the Dodgers fucking up last year?"*

"Sorry, I didn't catch that, the Dodgers what?" Campanis asked back.

"Uh, the Dodgers, henh, messing up last year," Sandy revised, having won the bet.

"Sandy said fuck on the radio!" we all cheered for months thereafter.

I had known Sandy Clay since 7th Grade.

 He wore his hair in a wonky jewfro much like my own, twin sons of Harpo Marx (the jewfro godfather).

What drew us closer together eventually was our mutual desire to be DJs and a shared love of radio that led to an ongoing exchange of tapes we'd make in our bedrooms of fake 'radio stations' we'd create, manufactured 'airchecks' of the stable of 'DJs' who were on our 'stations,' featuring us doing all the voices.

We'd listen to each other's tapes and offer critique. In our earlier childhoods we had both been galvanized by Boss Radio 93 KHJ and the manic patter of uber 'boss jock' The Real Don Steele, and we both sought to emulate his incendiary assault.

Sandy called his station KSIN, "the place where the devil's music gets its due."

Mine was KMRS, in honor of my heart's insatiable devotion, Miranda Raquel Savitch.

Miranda Savitch and the rest of the *Chick Clique* were still hanging together:

Dolly Ferris continued to rule the group which also included bopping curlytop Claire Farnaway, gossip-hub Sharon Rose, herbal hippie-chick Justine Balthazar, Misty Winters the innocent coquette sometimes called Little Miss Muffet by a growing harem of geeky fanboy admirers, Candy Stoner (the first and only girl I'd thus far frenched) with hair sometimes processed and sometimes in a tight natural, cryptic enigma Lorelei Lux, and a new addition to the hive: a striking *shiksa* goddess named Arabella Mayflower, whose social catch phrase —"I don't know which fucking boat my ancestors came over on"—might have left an impression of snarl, but she was in fact mostly a gentle swan in our little scene. And Arabella, unlike her clique-sisters, understood the supreme importance of the Los Angeles Dodgers and would often engage in ball talk with us.

Gina Dichlich and her friend Samantha Coventry were also a sexy presence in the 9th Grade Court, but they weren't part of the *Chick Clique*. Gina and Samantha mostly hung around in a dark corner, at their own table, away from everybody.

"Planning their next ritual sacrifice probly," Miranda Savitch once said, a sardonic reference to their both being self-proclaimed witches.

Gina Dichlich wasn't *really* a witch.

She did move through the world fully aware of the power she wielded because of her name, though, that's for sure.

Samantha Coventry, on the other hand, as I later learned traumatically, was actively pursuing witchcraft. A haunting beauty who wasn't all the way connected somehow, Samantha gave the same answer to seemingly every question: the simple, predictable imperative, "Suck my cock." No matter what you asked her about—the weather, music, yesterday's math quiz, *Twilight Zone* reruns, salvation and damnation, it didn't matter—she'd answer, "Suck my cock."

Gus loved baiting Samantha with contrived set-ups for her inevitable answer.

"Hey, Samantha," he'd taunt, "what does your daddy do for fun after work?"

"Suck my cock," she'd say to our delight, as we'd exchange gimme fives and gimme tens.

"What's my homework tonight?"

"Suck my cock."

"What is Ms. Cummings going to do after school?" Whit might ask.

"Suck my cock," Samantha would most certainly answer.

When school had started in the Fall, we were majorly bummed to find that our English teacher was not the one we had expected.

Since 7th Grade we had all been looking forward to having the best teacher at JB, Victor Fleming, when we were 9th Graders, but it turned out Mr. Fleming was taking a year-long sabbatical to finish his PhD, so we had this new teacher named Ms. Cummings.

For some of us, though, the upset ended when Ms. Virginia Cummings walked into the room and began, "When I was your age I would normally introduce myself by saying, 'I'm Virginia. That's Virgin for short, but not for long!'" and a pause ensued during which we ogled her voluptuous womanhood, and then she punctuated, "I can't use that one anymore."

She had a voice like maple syrup.

We were hers.

"Oh, great," Dolly Ferris said as she and the other girls watched all male attention sucked into the Cummings vortex immediately.

We also had a strikingly sexy history teacher, Ms. Barrows, who, we learned, would be team-teaching the year with Ms. Cummings.

"Double whammy, terrific," Dolly complained, "This is going to be fun."

Ms. Cummings, also on that first day of school—as so many teachers before her over the years had done—tried every way but the right way to say Gina's famous last name when calling roll. "Gina Ditchlitch? Deeshleesh? Dykelike?" she squirmed.

And Gina—as she had likewise done so many times before over the years—raised her hand and said, salaciously, "It's DICK-LICK."

I usually blushed when talking to Gina Dichlich.

Partly because of her name, of course—she could be talking about anything but you'd just be thinking 'Dick-Lick, Dick-Lick, Dick-Lick'—and partly because of all the pre-lecherous moments Manny Shepherd and I spent looking at her underwear when she'd hang upside down on the monkey bars in 4th Grade—and partly because I liked Gina Dichlich but couldn't ever seem to click with her.

On one of those flaming hot afternoons around Halloween, Gina Dichlich and Samantha Coventry came up to me laughing during lunch.

"Hey, Lance," Gina said, "Wanna try something funny?"

Samantha looked at me like Lucretia McEvil from the Blood, Sweat & Tears song.

"Um, yokay," I bumbled with embarrassment.

"Cool. Close your eyes. All right, now, picture me standing in front of you, and point to where my head would be . . ."

That was easy. I pointed.

"Good, now point to where my boobs would be . . . don't touch, just point . . ."

I wanted to make the two-handed titty-grabbing sign, but instead I merely pointed one finger toward each imagined breast.

"OK, now point to where my belly button would be . . ."

I sensed what was coming next.

"All right, now point to where my, um, pussy would be."

I pointed with a downward thrust in the general vicinity of her, um, pussy, at which moment I felt my finger inserting itself into a moist groove which made me jerk my eyes open in surprise. Looking down, I saw Gina, knees to the brimstone, my finger in her mouth, head atilt to make her lips vertical, looking up at me with one eye, and all I could think seeing her there looking up at me was, "Dick-Lick, Dick-Lick, Dick-Lick . . ."

Gina stood up laughing with Samantha.

"Aaaah-ha loser . . . you thought it was real," said Gus ". . . you thought that was really her pussy," and upped his voice to broadcast volume, "Aaaah-ha, Lance thought he was just touching Gina's pussy!" shouting to everybody in the vicinity.

"I wouldn't let *you* touch my pussy with a six inch pole," Gina sniped at Gus.

"More like a 2 inch pole," joked Whit.

"The hell you say, dude, 10 inches right here," countered Gus, grabbing his crotch, "soft."

"Yeah? Get a ruler, let's verify," challenged Whit.

"You'll need a yardstick, dude," Gus blustered, "'Cause I've got a frozen banana in my pants right now way too vast for a ruler."

"Like from Zody's," Claude chimed in, snickering.

"What the fuck are you talking about, asswipe?" Gus shot at Claude.

"A frozen banana like they have at Zody's," Claude explained.

"Dude, I hope we don't meet in the afterlife because otherwise I'm going to be forced to kick your ass in the pit of hell for all eternity," Gus said.

Gina Dichlich was the only girl who still wore skirts to school, most Angelenas that year opting for Dittos jeans or cords from Fred Segal or extra-wide flares over platform shoes. You never saw skirts unless you were at a bar or bat mitzvah or something. Chemin-de-Fer was everywhere.

Our talk was caught up mostly in anticipation of the Rumble in the Jungle, the upcoming big fight in Zaire between Mohammed Ali and George Foreman for the heavyweight title, and then Halloween right after. Unfortunately they were both weeknights.

"Dang, dude, why does Halloween have to be on a Thursday?" Gus Lagniappe complained.

"Yeah, that's retarded," said Claude. "Who planned that shit?"

"You're the tard, tard. Halloween is on October 31 no matter what day of the week it is," Whitman Rust said.

"I know, dang dude," Claude tried to cover up his tardness.

"You don't know shit about shit, you fungusoidal incubus," Whit replied.

"Claude is the syphillitic afterbirth of a mongoloid gangfuck," Gus felt compelled to add.

"Ooh, face!" said Sandy Clay, piling on, "you are moted."

"I think Ali is going to kick Foreman's ass," claimed Oliver Gelding.

"I don't know, Foreman's fists are like sledgehammers," I countered.

"My dad and I are going to see the fight on closed circuit TV at The

Forum," bragged Whit. He always got to go to things like that.

In response, Gus did the finger-in-cheek Big Whoop twirly sign.

The late season heat wave added discomfort to an already discomfited ritual 'cause Halloween had gotten all awkward recently anyway.

When we were little kids it was all about the candy, and trick-or-treating was a means to that end.

But for the last couple of years it'd been all about the adventure of being out on the streets at night without your parents and again trick-or-treating was a means to that end though we didn't really give a shit about the candy anymore.

As 9th Graders ruling the school with our own private lunch court and senior privilege passes, we found ourselves in the days leading up to Halloween torn between having another night of raucous mayhem on the streets of the Fairfax area with our boy's club of doofus nerdball hooligans or going to the costume party at Dolly Ferris' house where there would be girls in abundance.

The consensus was to go where there would be girls in abundance. And though I was leaning that way myself, instead I ended up deciding to skip the party.

"I think I might go see *Phantom of the Paradise* with Manny on Halloween," I said.

"Wussy boy's still traumatized by the sock hop," Gus Lagniappe taunted, "He's avoiding Miranda Savitch."

"Nah," I insisted, "Miranda and I are cool again. No biggie. She sits next to me in English class."

"You're the hamburger, dude!" teased Whit.

"Dang, dude, I wouldn't put up with that junk," Gus blustered, "Bitch tried that shit with me I'd go, 'Bitch, you don't dance with another dude all night when you're my date,' and then I'd smack her upside the head with the back of my hand so she'd know what's what."

"Hell, yeah, like Harry Reems, dude. All caveman and shit," Whitman Rust said, "Dude, tell them."

Gus snickered, "Whit and I snuck into the Pussycat Theatre and saw *The*

Devil in Miss Jones last weekend."

"No way. How?" I asked.

"We were walking down Santa Monica Blvd. and noticed there was no one at the door of the Pussycat Theatre so we just strolled in. Nobody stopped us," Gus said.

"Nobody gives a shit anyway," said Whit.

"Totally," Gus added, "it's just a bunch of flashers there to beat the meatles."

"So, Harry Reems plays this, like, devil-type dude who teaches Georgina Spelvin all about sin," said Whit.

"Meaning fucking and sucking," Gus explained.

"She sold her soul for some rock and roll," Whit proclaimed.

"Rock and roll hoochie cooze," Oliver Gelding sang in what might be the only instance in the known universe of a black guy imitating Rick Derringer.

"Dang, dude, but when Harry Reems pulled her by the hair and fucked her on the pool table that was flagrant," said Whit.

"Sho nuff, Pufnstuf," gloated Gus, "that's the way I do it too."

The big news of the summer (besides Nixon resigning) was that Gus Lagniappe claimed to have lost his virginity while spending a month at his Aunt's house in Kansas.

"Dudes, I got laid when I was there," he told us when he first got back from his visit.

"Your pillow doesn't count," chided Whit.

"Or sheep, farmboy," Sandy prodded.

"No, for real. I gave up my purity to a lady named Helen . . ." Gus maintained.

We couldn't tell whether or not to believe him. It became one of those things you resign yourself to never knowing for sure.

". . . This fat old bitch, I think she was like 28 or 29 or something, and she was totally hot for my foxy bod—can you blame her?—and she just started hitting on me in the backyard at my Aunt's house like a few days after we met and was like feeling on my chest and arms and and saying shit like, 'I think you should come pay me a visit,' and I was like, dang, dude, this is getting pretty flagrant. So she invites me over to her house, and I go there the next day, and we sit down in the living room and the first thing she says to me is, 'So let me ask: Have you fantasized about fucking me?'"

"No way," I said.

"No, dude, it's true. 'Have you fantasized about fucking me?' I swear to fucking God that's what she said. And I had actually jacked off with her in mind the night before because, well, you know, she was around and she had a pussy and I'm not related to her, so . . . Anyway I told her yeah. And then she goes, and I'm not lying, 'Do you want to fuck me for real?' And I went, 'I guess, yeah.'"

"You guess?" we all said at once like in a bad musical.

"And, dudes, she was like on me, frenching, pulling my shirt off, biting my nipples and shit, and, oh yeah, dang, dude, there were like upside-down crosses and red candles and crystals everywhere, and she burned these gnarly incense that smelled like those big-ass trash bins in the alley behind Bob's Big Boy, then she undid my pants and grabbed ahold of my dick, I almost blew my spunk right then, that was a close call."

"You're making this shit up. It sounds like one of those 'Letters to the Sexpert' in *Beaver Slam* magazine," I challenged.

"Solly, no beava," said Oliver in an exaggerated unidentifiable oriental accent.

"Or like some *Hollywood Press* article," I added another suspicion.

"*Penthouse* Forum, dude," said Sandy.

In a very short span of time we had accumulated myriad avenues for the acquisition and consumption of pornography.

From the underwear ads in the Sears catalogue and the droopy boobies of sundry tribeswomen in *National Geographic*, we had graduated to 50 cent news rack copies of the *Hollywood Press*, filled with raunchy erotica written by older versions of dorks like us who somehow managed to get laid (so their horny ramblings were inspiring because it meant there was hope for us someday), and then, during the summer, in the garage behind Gus's house, we happened upon the porn stash of his Uncle Eddie, who sort of lived back there sometimes, an extensive collection of the revelatory *Beaver Slam* magazine.

All cock-in-pussy all the time, dude.

Gus held firm against our skepticism, "Nuh-uh—dudes, don't even, I am totally telling the truth."

"Any fellatio?" asked Whit.

"Not that first time no. But later on. . ." Gus smiled widely. He had very small teeth.

We all digested this latest fact. Gus Lagniappe had gotten a blowjob. Or several. Or so he claimed.

"And, dudes . . ." Gus drawled, "Dudes . . . when I got on top and started fucking her I thought to myself, 'Dang, dude, my cock is in a real pussy,' and I came right when I thought that. 30 seconds."

"Dang, dude," I said.

"3 pump chump," Whit scoffed.

"Minute Man Service, Minute Man Service," Sandy chuckled out the Union 76 gas station ad.

"Put some lipstick on this dipstick, ma'am?" said Oliver in Union 76 service attendant voice.

"I got better with practice, dudes. Lots of practice. Like three times a day practice."

"The hell you say," Claude quipped.

"Yeah, that's more than you whack off daily, weenis boy."

"Nah, dude, " Claude contested, "In summertime I'm especially busy."

"And dig this: one time she turned over and got on all fours, and she was like 'Fuck me doggy-style the way I like it,' and, dang, dude, that was cool 'cause her ass was really fat so it was all like a Halloween carnival moonbounce and shit, and then she said, 'Finger my clit while you're fucking me from behind,' and let me tell you, dude, that shit worked, she was all 'Enh enh enh oh god you little devil' and I was just pounding that moonbounce like Buzz Aldrin and shit. Zero gravity. Dang, dude. Tranquility Base here . . ."

". . . The Eagle has landed," Oliver continued, thrusting his hips in solidarity.

"And she would do some surprising-ass shit," Gus continued straight through our razzing, "like this one time we were fucking and when she was about to come she took my finger and stuck it in her asshole, saying, like, 'Close the circuit, baby' and she started coming like your mother getting it from the milkman, like exploding and shit, and all I could think, dudes, was, 'Schiltz.' Dang, dude."

"HA! Oh, man, that's flagrant," Claude said, "Schlitz," and we all made the holding-a-six-pack sign and were just totally busting up.

"What did you guys talk about when you weren't having sex?" I asked.

"Aw, dang, dude, I don't know. She just watched soap operas and shit most of the time. All she really talked about was shopping for pantsuits and gossip about TV stars, and she always had Helen Reddy on the stereo, especially fuckin' 'Delta Dawn' over and over. 'I like her music because we have the same first name,' she used to say.' Dang, dude."

"HICK!" Whit yelped.

"We were listening to 'Angie Baby' one night, and she said, 'This song is about me,' which kind of freaked me out considering the main character is a total psycho lady," Gus said, "And the song during my first blowjob was 'Ruby Red Dress.'"

"Dang, dude, does Helen Reddy only do songs about crazy ladies who talk to themselves?" wondered Claude Moss.

"Doesn't sound like much going on upstairs there," I gave my estimation of Gus Lagniappe's imaginary lover.

"I spent most of my time downstairs, dude, so I didn't care how country she was," Gus said, "But I know, I know, Lance Atlas is into that 'brainy-lady' thing."

"Miranda Savitch," Whit coughed the name recognizably enough.

"Miranda's got Lance in her pants," Eddie Gurges said.

"Not even," I discouraged them.

"Fuck her doggy style the way she likes it," Oliver teased, "Apollo 11, baby. Pound that moonbounce."

Gimme fives were slapped all around at my expense, though instead of "gimme five" Claude said to Gus, "Slip me some skin" like a jazz hepcat from the olden days.

"Dang, dude," said Oliver Gelding, "Slip me some skin? Negroes stopped saying that shit in like the Depression."

"Well, that's what my dad says when he's trying to be cool," said Claude.

"Well, dude, that's like some shit Oscar Brown, Jr. would say," and Oliver launched into a snappy tune:

Permit me to introduce myself

The name is Mr. Kicks

I dwell in a dark dominion

Way down by the River Styx

"My dad has that album," I said.

"*Between Heaven And Hell,*" Oliver acknowledged.

"So, dude, when she gave you head did you come in her mouth or on her face or her tits or what?" Whitman Rust wanted to know. We all did, actually. What does one do in that situation?

"Well, like, the first time, when she could tell I was about to come she said, 'You can come in my mouth if you want,' and I said, 'I want to come in your pussy,' and she said, 'You can do that too.'"

"You are so making this up, dude," I accused, "You are like getting this shit from *The Devil in Miss Jones* or something. People don't really talk like that. Especially not in Kansas."

"Hell no, Lance, it's real," Gus defended himself.

"I'm from another planet, I guess," I said.

"Yeah, the planet Gay Golita in the Wuss galaxy," said Whit.

"Wouldn't you rather dive into a sea of tits and do the breast stroke instead of going to that faggy glam-rock movie?" Gus's question about my Halloween plans yanked me back into October.

"I don't know, I haven't made up my mind yet," I said, even though I had.

2

In Gus's absence during the summer I'd started hanging out more with Manny Shepherd, and I found his company stimulating.

Manny Shepherd and I had met in kindergarten at Melrose Avenue Elementary School and were what I guess you'd call 'best friends' throughout our years there.

Together we had endured Indian Guides, played Little League together, watched Gina Dichlich hang upside down on the monkey bars, a bounty of bonding.

Upon culmination in 6th Grade, we went to different Jr. Highs, he to Bancroft and I to John Burroughs.

We stayed in touch and hung out during 7th Grade despite our different schools and that summer even made a super-8 film together called *Judo Jew*, a take off on *Kung Fu*, but after that we pretty much fell out of touch for all of 8th Grade.

And yet, independently of each other, we had followed similar paths.

We had both been playing piano a lot with aspirations to write songs.

We both had switched to KMET as our radio station of choice.

We were both also majorly into reading.

In that summer before 9th Grade Manny was engrossed in *Stranger In A Strange Land* by Robert Heinlein, and I was reading Bram Stoker's *Dracula*.

We spent hours sitting on my front porch drinking cokes and talking about our respective reading books, our favorite shared music discovered over the past couple of months—David Werner's *Whizz Kid* album was our obsession all summer—and, of course, girls.

I told him about my frenching sessions with Candy Stoner and my several misfires with Miranda Savitch, confessing an ongoing flame for her despite the recent estrangement.

And he spoke of his 8th Grade passion, Denise Galileo, whom he described as voluptuous and unattainable.

One hot August morning, I brought Manny along with me to a cool nerd conclave at Farmers Market on 3rd and Fairfax, a tourist destination but also frequented by locals, an outdoor collection of food stalls and souvenir shops with an indoor annex adjacent.

The whole place smelled like peanut butter and candy.

Dolly Ferris had invited everybody over to watch Nixon leave the White House following his resignation speech the night before. The plan was to gather at Bob's Donuts in the Market to eat, goof around, then all go over to Dolly's place to watch Nixon get gone from our lives for good and cheer and jeer.

The morning crowd at the Farmers Market was a mixture of old Jews speaking Yiddish and comparing bodily discomforts, TV execs from the CBS Television City complex up the street, out-of-work entertainers "between gigs at the moment," masses of tourists buying schlocky souvenirs to commemorate their whirlwind adventure in Hollywood or killing time before going to watch a taping of *The Price Is Right*, and, during the summer months, Farmers Market had to deal with gaggles of obnoxious teenagers looking for a place to play and flirt and make fun of the tourists and otherwise be juvenile together.

I did not have the luxury of being rowdy at Farmers Market because everybody there knew me.

It was my surrogate backyard.

My father had his podiatry practice there.

Although the sign, *Theodore Atlas, Doctor of Podiatric Medicine*, sounded fancy and official, his "office" was really just a little cubicle in the back of the Farmers Market Beauty Shop.

The telephone number listed in the Yellow Pages was a pay phone in the hallway outside his cubicle.

There, in his little curtained stall, Doctor Theo Atlas, or "Doc," as he was mostly known, would shave down the corns and bunions of old Jewish ladies, put arch supports in their department store pumps, and give each a soul-smoothing foot massage (which, he said, was really the key to everything).

Because my dad, "Doc," was a superstar in the Farmers Market community, that made me easily identifiable as "Doc's Son," as my dad had been carrying me around the Market since my infancy, anytime my mom would take me over to visit, showing me off, introducing me, letting me goof around and chase the pigeons or wander in and out of Kip's Toyland throughout my childhood.

"Hey, there goes Doc's Son," they'd all say when I was a youngster running amok, and then, when I got to be a teen, "Hey, Doc's Son, how the hell are ya?"

Because of the recognizability factor, I was held to a higher standard than my more obstreperous and rambunctious peers.

When the commotion got surly, I'd keep my distance, go try on a pair of moccassins perhaps or visit the mynah bird in the pet store (whom the owner had taught to wolf whistle at women walking by) to make sure the vendors at the Market saw that I was not one of those unruly youths causing trouble.

I introduced Manny to the kids he didn't know, making no big deal when I said, "And this is Miranda Savitch," and Manny was equally cool about it.

I hadn't seen or talked to Miranda since she refused to sign my yearbook at the end of 8th Grade last June.

I had been dreading the meeting since the night before.

Manny had gone to Melrose with Gus and Whit and so was immediately comfortable, though admittedly disappointed that Gina Dichlich wasn't around.

"She doesn't hang with our crowd," I consoled.

"Well, ordinarily I'd be majorly bummed," Manny joked, "but, you know, just saying her name is almost the same as actually seeing her."

"She wears skirts that almost show her panties," Whit enthused, "and sometimes she bends over just right . . ."

"That's called 'A Dichlich Moment,'" I explained the new term to Manny, "and dang, dude," I continued to all, "I sat across from her in English," I said, "and when she'd lean over to talk to Samantha Coventry you could, like, see the whole megillah right there. It was like the monkey bars in 4th Grade." Manny put out his hand for a slap.

"I can't wait to see his gnarly ass waving goodbye for the last time," Claire Farnaway said of Nixon, breaking us out of our boy talk.

Nothing like Richard Nixon to deflate the adolescent swell brought on by thoughts of Gina Dichlich's panties and the promise thereunder.

"Hell, yeah, get that sweaty-lipped Droopy Dog-looking motherfucker out of my sight forever, dude," said Whitman Rust.

I had already had my usual apple fritter and hot chocolate from Bob's Donuts and so began wandering Farmers Market until we headed over to Dolly's house. Claude, Gus, Whit, Manny and I strolled over to the news stand to flip through a few comic books, see if the new *MAD* was out yet, maybe catch a glimpse of some girly bits over in the porn section without attracting the attention of the cashier who'd for sure shoo us away and then go tell my father.

The *MAD* they had on the shelf was still the July/August '74 "*MAD* Leads the Fight To Conserve Energy" issue.

But there was indeed a new issue of *Beaver Slam*, featuring a buxom brunette.

"Hey, dude, does your uncle have that issue yet?" Claude asked Gus of the copy of *Beaver Slam* shelved subtly in the bottom right-hand corner of the rack.

"Hell yeah, I've already fucked her twice," Gus gloated.

"She looks like Miranda Savitch!" Whit added at the worst possible moment, as I realized that Miranda was standing at the other end of the newsstand looking at the paperback books.

She had obviously seen me, even if only out of the corner of her eye, looking at porn.

I left Manny to cavort with Gus and Whit while I walked over to Miranda.

She was flipping through a *MAD* book, of all things, specifically a volume called *Mad About Mad*, a collection of totally visual humor by Sergio Aragones.

I knew the book well.

"His characters always seem like they're in hell," I remarked, without greeting or invitation.

"I don't know, I like how he doesn't need to use words," said Miranda, who looked me in the eye for the first time since June.

Despite our several ill-fated attempts at romantic couplehood, Miranda Savitch and I remained in this ongoing state of amorphous attraction that somehow would neither consummate nor dissipate.

Following the unexpected rejection at the school-sponsored sock hop and her refusal to sign my yearbook, a long summertime silence had ensued.

"I have an autographed copy of that book," I boasted, "I'll have to show it to you sometime. My aunt knows Aragones."

"Cool," she answered uncomfortably.

"Having a good summer?"

"I miss talking to you," Miranda shrugged.

"Well, maybe we don't need to use words," I tried to bullshit my way out of facing the situation.

"You never called or anything after my note. That was me apologizing for not signing your yearbook."

"Well this is me accepting your apology and apologizing for not calling you," I said, "And I miss talking to you, too."

She smiled.

We just kind of fell back into it.

I began meandering, Miranda joining me, into the western annex of Farmers Market, a ratty makeshift barn of a building that ran parallel to Fairfax.

It was mostly a useless ghetto of candlesticks and picture frames and overpriced junky jewelry, but it was worth it 'cause The Fun Shop was in that corridor, a place that sold magic tricks and whose owner, Dale Goody, was himself an avid magician ever eager to show customers the latest trick, gadget, gizmo, novelty, so I always braved the awfulness of the west wing in order to check out what Dale had up his sleeve.

His main clientele consisted mostly of the 9-12 year old set just getting into magic.

"Tricks Are For Kids!" boasted a colorful sign in the window.

"Hey, it's Doc's Son! How the hell are ya, guy?" Dale Goody greeted me.

"Staying clean," I answered using one of my dad's stock phrases.

"He called you dachshund!" Miranda giggled.

"That's dog, dude," I joked.

"Well, you're a wiener so it fits," she couldn't resist.

"You gonna introduce me to your girlfriend?" Dale asked.

I blushed and considered my response.

At first I wanted to say, "She's not my girlfriend," but I thought that might make her feel bad even though she really and truly wasn't my girlfriend.

As usual, Miranda got there first.

"I'm Miranda," she held out her hand.

"You like magic, Miranda?" Dale took control of the moment.

"Sometimes, if it's good," Miranda said.

"Well, I've got a wicked trick you might want to check out."

Dale reached under the counter and pulled out a round red plastic box.

"Now this one," he said, "is called 'The Devil's Coin Bank.' You got a quarter?" he asked me.

I reached into my pocket and pulled out the only quarter I had left and handed it to him.

Dale placed the quarter in the round box, shook it, and when he opened the box, the quarter had disappeared.

He shook the box again, re-opened it, pretended not to be able to get my quarter back, let me squirm momentarily, then shook it a third time and pulled from the Devil's Coin Bank nine quarters, which he handed to me and said, "Now go buy this lady an ice cream soda," like it was 1957 or something.

"What about that one?" Miranda pointed to another trick on the counter.

"Oh," said Dale, menacingly, "I don't think you're ready for that one yet. You'll have to come back another time with Datsun here," he said, winking at me as if he were helping the cause of my nonexistent dating life with Miranda Savitch, "This one's called 'The Devil's Handkerchief.' It's for kids with a little more experience in black magic," he explained, "like your boyfriend." He winked again.

That time Miranda blushed.

Then he turned back to me and said, "I'm glad your dad is taking care of himself. We sure missed having Doc around when he got sick a while back. He's looking a lot better now."

"He's trying," I said, "Still too much coffee, too many cigarettes, peanut butter and butter sandwiches, schmaltz herring, always the same demons."

"I can't imagine Doc otherwise," Dale smiled.

My dad had suffered a heart attack a couple of years before, September of 1972.

We had to disconnect the TV in his room at Cedars-Sinai hospital when the Israeli athletes were murdered in Munich during the Olympic Games so that he wouldn't get all upset and set off another coronary.

I had spent that afternoon with my grandparents at Zody's, the day I saw the girl eating a frozen banana there, but my bliss blew away when I walked in the house after getting home from Zody's and my mother told me, ashen and drained, about my dad's heart attack, a "myocardial infarction," she called it.

I went into my room and listened to "Alone Again, Naturally" over and over and cried until my mom took me and my sisters to the hospital to see him.

He didn't go back to work for several months, but my mother would bring us to Farmers Market once a week to report on how Doc was doing to the Market community.

Dale at The Fun Shop was always one of our stops.

"You gonna buy your girlfriend something?" Dale asked.

Once again I wanted to say, "She's not my girlfriend."

And, once again, Miranda got there first: "We actually have to get a move on," she said, "We're having a Good Riddance Nixon party; we're gonna go watch him leaving the White House."

"Well, say good riddance from me, too," said Dale, "and tell him he can go to hell. And hey, Lance, I'll tell your dad I saw you."

Miranda and I waved as we left The Fun Shop to go looking for the rest of us.

We all took the RTD down Fairfax to Olympic and then walked over to Dolly's house on Commodore Sloat.

Dolly's place was always in a state of polite disarray.

It was one of those warm houses where people actually live their lives and allow themselves to feel comfortable.

My favorite room in that house was the living room, a kind of heaven for me, floor to ceiling bookcases filled with brilliance and allure, a Steinway baby grand piano, a vintage globe from before the Soviet Union.

I would always make sure to sit down at that piano and play something.

When we arrived, Dolly's father was listening to an opera in the living room, and I stopped in to say hello.

Miranda continued into the den with the other kids.

"Lance, come listen," Leonard Ferris gestured that I should join him on the couch, "Listen to this passage . . . " The music swelled to crescendo, and Leonard closed his eyes to savor the climax. "Ah, perfection," he said, "Don't you think?"

"It sounded cool," I said.

"Stravinsky. *The Rake's Progress*. Do you know it?"

"No, I don't really listen to opera," I apologized.

"Ah, rock and roll, right. Shame. Nick Shadow, great character."

"Cool name, Nick Shadow," was the only thing I could think of to say.

I looked around the room.

A Thomas Mann novel was sitting on the coffee table.

"Is he worth reading?" I asked of Mann.

"Mann is for grown-ups," Leonard said. "He wrote this book while he was living in Los Angeles. Did you know that? You'll read it one day I'm sure."

"Lance, are you gonna come watch? Nixon's about to give his farewell speech to his staff," Miranda poked her head into the living room.

"Oh, yeah, for sure," I told her, and then to Leonard, "I've gotta go watch Nixon leave."

"He left long ago," Leonard said as he put another record on the turntable.

Everybody was sitting around in Dolly's den watching the replay of Nixon's farewell.

Miranda was on a bean bag chair in the corner, and I started to head in that direction when Dolly, freshly broken up with Freddy Snow, grabbed my hand and cooed, "Here, come sit next to me," pulling me onto the couch then putting her left arm around my shoulders and resting her left leg on my right.

I looked over at Miranda whose eyes were glued unnaturally to the TV screen watching Madge the manicurist soak some lady's hand in Palmolive dishwashing liquid.

"DISHWASHING LIQUID?" we all yelled in unison with the shocked customer, and echoing Madge all together, *"Relax, it's Palmolive."*

Then there was a Prell Concentrate commercial and a Biz commercial. We knew those by heart too.

"Put it in the Biz Bag!" we intoned like a brainwashed choir.

Finally, when Nixon's face appeared on screen everybody booed.

"Dang, dude, he looks like Herman Munster today," Gus said.

"Yeah but like post-nuclear Herman Munster," Claire added.

"He could star in vampire movies, I swear, that's his new career," Candy Stoner chimed in.

"He's already got the hairline," Dolly added, "He just needs a cape and Dracula teeth."

"I still have the vampire teeth my dentist gave me when I was like 10. Nixon can have those if he wants," Claude offered.

"Yeah, I'm sure he'd want to put *that* in his mouth," Misty Winters snarked at Claude.

"We should invite Nixon to our Halloween party," Claire suggested.

"Can you imagine opening the door on Halloween and Richard Nixon was there dressed like Dracula and carrying a pillow case and saying trick or treat and shit?" Gus said.

"Flagrant," said Claude.

"I can't wait to see his first vampire movie," said Candy.

"Totally. *Dracula Vs. Deep Throat*," I said.

"The whole thing could take place at the Watergate," said Miranda.

"Harry Reems reprising his role as Satan," added Whit.

"*It is only a beginning always*," Nixon was saying to his staff, many of whom were crying.

Nixon's voice was shaking.

After the speech he and Pat boarded a helicopter.

Nixon turned and flashed his trademark victory sign with both hands and was essentially extricated from the mess he'd created.

Time for the country to pull the covers over itself and hibernate for a few years.

Dang, dude.

Richard Nixon.

You kind of felt bad for the guy, even though you didn't want to.

I stood up and went back into the living room.

Dolly's dad had left by then, but Lorelei Lux was in there looking at the globe.

"You think Nixon sold his soul to the devil?" Lorelei asked me as I joined her.

"Nyeah, he *is* the devil."

"Interesting . . ." Lorelei Lux proffered, "I think Nixon started out with good intentions and then got lost in everyone else's inentions and mistook them for his own. "

"I don 't know. He started out hunting communists. So."

"Your opinions don't matter to me, Lance Atlas."

I fell into my usual uneasiness with Lorelei even though I did also at the moment very much want to make out with her on the couch.

"Hey, Lance, I'm going," Miranda called out from the entry hall, "You coming, Lori?"

"Yes, thanks for rescuing me," Lorelei said to Miranda and brushed past me toward the front door.

Dang, dude.

"Hey, we should hang out before summer ends," Miranda said to me, lightly pounding my chest with her fist, "Gimme a call?"

"OK, I will."

"No, you won't."

"Nyeah, I know."

"Well, I'll call *you* then," she said, turning away and heading out the door, saying, "Bye, Lance," without looking back.

And in fact on an unusually humid afternoon a few days later, the phone rang, and it was Miranda.

I was watching a re-run of my favorite *Rifleman* episode.

"This is me calling you," she said.

"This is me answering," I replied.

"What're you up to?" Miranda asked.

"Watching my favorite episode of *The Rifleman*."

"Oh, cool, what channel's it on?"

"5. It started about 10 minutes ago"

"Found it. Who's the guy in the sleeping bag?" Miranda wondered.

"It's a bedroll. That's Lucas McCain. He's the Rifleman."

"What's wrong with him? His face looks crazy. Is he sick?" Miranda wondered.

"No, there's a rattlesnake in his bedroll. But only Lucas knows. But he can't tell the others 'cause if he moves the snake will bite him."

"Whoa, shit. That's cool."

"Yeah, this episode is far out. I've seen it a whole bunch of times. The kid kneeling next to him is Lucas's son Mark, and the old guy is the sheriff, Micah Torrance. That other mangy looking dude is a murderer named Scully Potter that Micah is bringing to jail. They're just about to figure out about the rattlesnake."

I let Miranda watch *The Rifleman* for a while, then I told her, "I was just thinking of you the other night."

"About what an evil witch I am?"

"Well, yeah, of course, but I was also listening to *Revolver* and wondered if you still put it on every night before you go to bed."

"Every night, yes . . . Dang, look at the Rifleman sweating," Miranda said.

"Yeah, that's the next complication. It's hotter than hell. And getting even hotter."

"Micah has to decide whether or not to make a deal with the devil here," I said to Miranda right as Scully was asking Micah to take off his handcuffs so he could help kill the rattlesnake and then promise to put in a good word on Scully's behalf with the judge.

"It's like the serpent in the Adam and Eve story," Miranda observed, "I give you knowledge, you give me your eternal soul."

"Ooh, you smart. My rabbi says what Adam and Eve get from the fruit is the ability to separate the holy from the unholy. But it also makes them separate from nature," I shared.

"Cool," she said, "You smart, too."

"Nah, I just remember shit."

"You still stargazing I hope?" she asked.

"*Never go to bed without looking at the sky.* That's what my father always tells me."

"Mmm, I like that. I have a great view of Orion from my bedroom window right now," she said.

"But it's daytime," I said.

"No, I mean at night, dorkus," she play-scolded, "I look for it ever since you showed it to me."

"Oh, wait, here's the climactic scene . . ."

In one very quick motion, Scully grabs the bedroll with the snake in it, pulls it off Lucas who rolls away swiftly, then Scully throws the blanket at Micah to distract him and grabs Lucas's rifle from Mark.

"Oh, no!" yelped Miranda.

"Pa!" Mark yells, as Micah deflects the blanket and shoots Scully dead then kills the snake.

"Whoa, that was cray-zee," Miranda said, relieved.

"Usually, Lucas is the one that does the fancy shooting. I love that it was Micah this time," I said.

154

After the final commercial break, the show came back on for the tag scene at the end, usually either humorous or poignant, in the case of this episode, a little of both.

"This is where they ride off into the sunset. Dig the music," I said to Miranda.

"Mmm, yeah, that was great, yum," Miranda said.

"You like that?"

"So awesome . . ."

"Fun watching TV with you over the telephone," I said.

"Totally. Kind of like playing solitaire together," Miranda said.

"Yeah, huh. Let's do it again sometime."

"I'd love that," she agreed.

"Coolness. Call sometime whenever you're in the mood."

"How about *you* call *me* sometime?" Miranda said.

"I could do that," I said.

I didn't call, not even when, a little less than a month later, just a couple of days before school started, President Ford pardoned Richard Nixon, exonerating him of all high crimes and misdemeanors. There would be no trial.

"That's not right," my sister Mimi said, "Nixon should go to jail."

"You're goddamn right," my father agreed, "this is outrageous."

"Republicans," my mother added.

"He sucked the blood of the country," my father said.

3

Halloween night that year, sitting inside the air-conditioned Chinese Theatre on Hollywood Blvd., I felt good about my decision to join Manny at opening night of *Phantom of the Paradise* rather than go to Dolly's party.

Although I regretted giving up an opportunity to see Miranda, I beheld her presence anyway throughout the evening.

Upon walking into the lobby, Manny and I saw a poster for the upcoming film version of *The Little Prince*, an immediate Savitch association and definitely something to tell her about.

Maybe she would suggest we see it together.

And then *Phantom of the Paradise* itself, a rock and roll re-telling of the Faust legend about a guy who's writing a rock and roll re-telling of the Faust legend, conjured and reconjured images of the girl.

When Winslow Leach sang of his soul's longing for the true beloved, the life-transcending connection, I thought of Miranda and Miranda and Miranda.

Winslow was the lonely artist, my cool nerd progenitor.

The actress who played Phoenix was damn cute herself, but when she sang Winslow's song about love, I saw not the freckle-faced doe-eyed waif Jessica Harper but instead only my sloe-eyed jewess Miranda.

Our paths have crossed and parted

This love affair was started long long ago

This love survives the ages

In its story lives are pages

Fill them up

May ours turn slow

Phoenix sang of rising from the ashes of past lives, of a love that is eternal and unbound by earthly spans of time.

And of course there was the brilliance of Beef, Gerrit Graham's glam-rock grotesquerie played to perfection, whose line "I know drug real from real real" became the immediate favorite line spoken daily at school once all the geeks had seen the film.

Manny did a great imitation of Beef.

"Can't you feel the vibes in your own house, man? Bad, sport, real bad. The karma in here is so thick, you need an aqualung to breathe," Manny would say with faux-fag sibilance.

We loved the movie, an instant touchstone for us.

"Dang, the music was good," I said.

The score was like *Whizz Kid* but with a slightly more Top 40 polish.

"I only know the songs Paul Williams wrote for The Carpenters," I said.

"Yeah, same with me."

"Life at last, salutations from the other side," I sang with a snarl as we walked down the street.

"BEEF!" enthused Manny.

"And I totally relate to Winslow Leach. He's like my bad conscience," I said.

"And let me guess, Phoenix reminded you of Miranda," Manny spoke.

"Nyeah, I guess, you know."

"I do know. You're in love, dude. I have my own fucked-up version of that going on," Manny sighed.

"Every lyric you hear relates, right?"

"Absotively posilutely," Manny agreed and sighed, "Denise."

"Dang, dude, how do chicks do that?"

"Voodoo, I think," Manny joked.

"You remind me of the guy," I sang the familiar tune.

"What guy?" he responded on script.

"The guy with the voodoo."

"Who do?"

"You do?"

"I do what?"

"You remind me of the guy . . ." I threatened to keep going.

"Dr. Demento, dude," we slapped hands.

Manny and I listened religiously to the Dr. Demento show on KMET on Sunday nights. 4 hours of oddball freak and novelty music that delighted our ears and minds.

"Let's play some music together sometime. We can write a song about chick voodoo," Manny suggested.

"That'd be great, for sure," I agreed.

When I got home, my sister, who, as it turned out went to Dolly's party (Mimi was only 11 months younger than I and a grade lower, so we ran in overlapping social circles), was also just getting home.

She had gone to the party costumed as kid show host Hobo Kelly.

"I saw your girlfriend at the party tonight," she said.

"She's not my girlfriend," I maintained.

"Yuh-huh . . . then how'd you know who I meant? Anyway she said for me to tell you she's going to call when she gets home."

"How was the party?" I asked.

"Oh, good enough I guess, nothing special."

"How were the costumes?"

"I dunno, lots of Satans and witches. And of course hobos. Tons of hobos."

"But only one Hobo Kelly, I hope."

"Of course," she said and entered her room closing the door behind her.

When Miranda called, I let the phone ring 3 times.

"Hi, it's me," she said.

"Who's this?" I asked.

"More than one girl calls you?"

"No but—"

"—You're such a phony baloney; you knew it was me."

"Busted and disgusted."

"This is me calling with a party report."

"This is me wanting all the dirt immediately. Fun?"

"Nyeah, it was OK. Wayne Paul Nader came dressed as John Lennon, and Lila Saddleback was totally hitting on him like he was some cute guy she didn't know, and then she figured it out and kept on talking to him anyways. She's so weird. Normally he totally creeps her out. "

"Who'd Lila go as?"

"Pussy Galore, from the James Bond movies."

I wanted her to say Pussy Galore again but I couldn't ask.

"Oh, and Gus came as Augustus Gloop, of course. Perfect."

"Yeah, I knew he was gonna do that. It must've been hilarious."

"Totally, he had pillows in his shirt and pants and had chocolate smeared on his face. He was trying to get girls to lick it off."

"Anybody do it?"

"Hell no, ew. Dolly dressed as a vampire's victim. She said you'd know who."

"Lucy probably, from *Dracula*. We both read it over the summer. You ever read *Dracula*?"

"No, I saw the movie though. 'I vant to suck your bluhhhd,' right? Anyway, she looked great. She made her face all pale and her lips purple and she had fake vampire bite on her neck. Oh, and I forgot, Whit came as a vampire with a cape and everything, except he was wearing a Nixon mask."

"That dude's a crack-up."

"And Lori came as Witchiepoo from *H.R. Pufnstuf*. She looked more like the Wicked Witch of the West, though."

"You know I live across the street from H.R. Pufnstuf?"

"No way. You mean like the guy in the costume?"

"No, the dude who does the voice. He lives in this big-ass house on the corner."

"That show is trippy."

"Oh, yeah. There's a reason he's called 'puffin' stuff,'" I said, making the sound of deep inhale.

"Ha ha. I've never thought of that actually. Cool! What's he like?"

"My neighbor? Well, he's pretty large."

"Like fat?"

"Yeah. And he's really funny. He used to stand in his front yard and watch me and my sisters play when we were younger, and sometimes he'd come across the street and talk to us and do all these different voices. Gus still goes across the street and hangs out with him quite a bit in the front yard."

"Oh, yeah, huh, I forgot you guys live next door to each other."

"Like since forever, yeah."

"Hey, speaking of your sisters, I saw Mimi at the party."

"Yeah, I know. She told me."

"And she told you I was going to call."

"Uh, yeah."

"And still you pretended you didn't know it was me when I called."

"Uh huh."

"You are such a chump. But that's why we love you."

"We?"

"Shut up . . . so, Mimi is like only a year younger than you?"

"11 months. My mother used to take us for walks in this double stroller up Fairfax to Farmers Market to visit my dad, and old ladies would come to the stroller, and look at me, this 1 year old kid sitting up, talking, and then look at my sister, a 1 month old infant lying flat and asleep, and they'd actually ask my mother, 'Oh, are they twins?'"

"No way."

"And dig it, my mom'd answer, 'Yes, they are, but something's horribly wrong with the little one.'"

"Ha, that's evil."

"Or at least that's how my mother tells the story anyway. I have no memory of those walks obviously."

"Where did you live when you were little?"

"On Colgate right near Fairfax. If we hadn't moved I'd've gone to Hancock Park Elementary with you guys."

"In a way I'm glad you didn't," Miranda said.

"Why?"

"Um, hmm, I guess I think I met you at the right time and any earlier wun't have been right."

"It wun't?"

"Hey hey, don't, I'm serious."

"Sorry."

"And your youngest sister is handicapped, right?"

"Yeah, Joy has Down Syndrome and also a heart defect."

"Oh, That's sad."

"I don't know, we have fun. Her heart condition makes her skin and lips all purple, so Mimi and I call her a purple-lipped mongoloid when we're trying to get her riled up."

"Oh my god, that's terrible!"

"No no, she's into it. Joy will strike this really sassy pose and come back with, 'I'm not purple I'm fine.' Sometimes she says, 'I'm not mongoloid, I'm Jewish.'"

"Ha!"

"Mimi said there were lots of Satans at the party."

"Yeah, like 9 Satans, but they all kept their masks on, so I didn't recognize any of them."

"I know Eddie Gurges was one of them."

"Oh, of course, the short Satan!"

"Yeah, probably. Who'd you go as?"

"I was going to go as Lucy Ricardo in Connecticut, but I couldn't get the red hair thing to work out, so I used the same gingham dress, and went as Dorothy from *The Wizard of Oz.*"

"How'd it go over?"

"Well, everybody thought I was Mary Ann from *Gilligan's Island.*"

"But you're really Ginger underneath it all, of course."

"Yes, of course."

"Oh hey," I changed the subject, "are you watching TV right now?"

"No, sir."

"Turn on Channel 9. They're playing this really cheesy vampire movie."

"'K, hold on. What's it called?"

"*The Satanic Rites of Dracula*" I said.

"Yeah I'm there now. Wanna watch together?"

"Defenly."

"You're evil. Who's that guy playing Dracula?"

"Christopher Lee. Doesn't he look like Nixon?" I joked.

"Ha Ha. Did you ever watch *Fright Night* when Seymour was doing it?"

"Oh, of course," I said like the *Fright Night* announcer, "*The Master of the Macabre, the Epitome of Evil, The Most Sinister Man to Crawl the face of the earth,*" and then shifting into Seymour voice, "*Good evening, my Fringies.*"

"Yeah. I miss Seymour on that show. He was warped."

"Like you," I flirted.

"Not even. You're the twisted letch in this relationship."

"After this they're showing *To Hell And Back*, the Audie Murphy World War II movie, if you want to keep talking."

"I'm not into war movies," Miranda said, "Hey, how was *your* movie tonight?"

"Oh, man, *Phantom of the Paradise* is great. You should totally go see it. It's about a songwriter who sells his soul to this devil guy named Swan in return for his true love getting to play the lead in his rock opera."

"That sounds kinda weird," Miranda said.

"It is weird; it reminded me of you."

"This is me sticking my tongue out at you."

"And this is me doing the same thing back, nyeah."

"Oh, I know what I have to ask you," Miranda remembered, "Bella, Lori, and I are writing our film for the multimedia project, and we want you to play my husband. We'll be Mr. & Mrs. Link. Ha ha."

"What's it about?" I asked.

"This lady who owns a priceless hourglass. The sand is actually tiny diamonds. She doesn't know what the hourglass is worth though. To her it's just some cool thing she picked up at the Rose Bowl Flea Market. And she also doesn't know that people are plotting to kill her in order to get the hourglass. It's about not knowing the value of what you have. S'anyway, the film takes place when she sends her husband to have the hourglass fixed—the diamonds keep getting stuck—and he gets ambushed by a hit man."

"That sounds cool. I'll do it. I like the thing about the sand really being diamonds."

"Yeah, we're going to call it *Diamonds In The Sky*. We still haven't decided if you die or not."

"I'm cool dying or not dying, either way. Do we get to do a love scene?"

"Uh, no," she said.

"Like on the kitchen table?"

"You are twisted!"

"Bending over a hot stove?"

"Hey! You're supposed be my knight in shining armor, not my perv in flashing trenchcoat."

"I know I probly shun't say those things."

"You are EVIL! I told you, stop!"

"A thousand pardons," I said with a vague foreign accent.

"What are you doing your multimedia project on?"

"I don't know, Claude and Dolly and I are probably gonna do like a chase film thing at the beach and on the pier. Pretty stupid compared to yours. Originally we were gonna do a movie version of *Quadrophenia* but realized it would be too long and hard to pull off."

"Too long and hard to pull off, huh?"

"I'm an accidental pervert," I admitted.

"There are no accidents, letch."

"Really."

"Lurch."

"No, I mean it."

"Uncle Fester."

"Low blow," I conceded, "but, hey, that dude can light up bulbs with his mouth, and that's a pretty cool thing to be able to do at a party."

"Hey, did I tell you I went to the Huntington with my parents last weekend?" Miranda shifted gears, "And they had this Zen garden there which was just sand with patterns in it and rocks here and there. Mostly just sand though. They had these little rakes, and you could make designs in the sand. I made Orion and Ursa Major and pretended I was looking at the sky."

"Coolness! Oh, and, dig, I almost forgot: I saw a poster for a movie version of *The Little Prince* in the lobby of the Chinese."

"We have to go!" said Miranda.

"It probably stinks worse than *Bedknobs and Broomsticks*."

"So what, it's *The Little Prince*. I can't see that movie with anyone else but you."

"Willy Wonka's in it."

"Then we *really* have to go. When does it open?"

"Thanksgiving weekend, I think."

"Oh, dang, I'm busy all that weekend with family stuff."

"Well, hey, we didn't get to do New Year's Eve Day last year. Let's go then."

"Can't. I'm gonna be in Palm Springs again."

"Dang, dude."

"I know, I know. Christmas Day, though. We can have a Jewish Christmas."

"Movie and chinese food."

"Totally. Let's do it."

"OK."

"Bitchin' . . . but, um, my mom's gonna get mad if she catches me still on the phone. See you at school tomorrow?"

"Fershures. I have to go see Ms. Cummings after school to ask her a couple of questions about *Great Expectations*. The book report is due next week, and I don't understand some of it."

"You know, everyone thinks Ms. Cummings has a crush on you!"

"That's crazy."

"*Oh, well, Lance Atlas will know the answer,*" Miranda said, imitating Ms. Cummings's dixie-drawl, "*won't you, Lance? Oh, yes, that's right, Lance my darling! Okay, class, in this balcony scene, I'll play Juliet and Lance Atlas will be my Romeo. Class, isn't Lance clever? Isn't Lance charming? Isn't Lance insightful? Isn't Lance sexy?*"

"She's never called me sexy."

"She doesn't have to use the word," Miranda said, "But she has called you 'cute-face' on more than once occasion."

"Nyeah, she's just an old lady joking around."

"Dude, she's like 24. This is her first year teaching. But whatever. I'd better hang up before I get in trouble. Bye, Lance!" Miranda said and was disconnected.

I stayed after school the next day to talk to Ms. Cummings about Pip and Estella's relationship. Throughout my reading of *Great Expectations* I was confused by Estella. I couldn't tell whether she liked Pip or not.

"Maybe Dickens couldn't tell either," she said, "or maybe he preferred to keep it ambiguous."

"What does ambiguous mean?"

"Having more than one possible meaning," she explained.

"Why would Dickens do that?"

"It allows us to see Estella with the same confusion Pip has. The ambiguity is there because that is Pip's experience of his relationship with her."

I loved the way the word ambiguous sounded, especially in her foxy southern accent.

I did in fact have a crushy kind of love for Ms. Cummings.

She dug books and understood the places they can take you.

She had a sex-oozing smile.

I was trying to figure out ways to get her to say *ambiguous* again.

I'd've even settled for *onomatopoeia*.

"You like to read, don't you, Lance?"

"Yes. That's what I do mostly. I read. And play the piano. And listen to music."

"What's your favorite book?"

"*Alice In Wonderland* I think."

"When did you start loving reading?"

"Oh, uh, back in my Dr. Seuss days. I read those books over and over. I especially loved *Dr. Seuss' Sleep Book*. But for real books it was definitely *Treasure Island*. Then *The Phantom Tollbooth*. And after that *Charlie and the Chocolate Factory*."

"Ah, *Charlie and the Chocolate Factory*. I was around 13 when that book came out. What was the fat kid's name again? Buzzy?"

"Augustus—"

"—Lagniappe!"

"—Gloop."

" . . . Lagniappe! That's what it was: Buzzy Lagniappe."

"Um, actually, Augustus Gloop is the fat kid from *Charlie and the Chocolate Factory*."

"Really?"

"Yeah."

"I thought it was Buzzy Lagniappe. Was he called Buzzy Lagniappe in the movie?"

"No, he was Augustus Gloop in the movie also."

"Wow, that's weird. Where did I get Buzzy Lagniappe from?"

"Well, see, sometimes we call Gus Lagniappe Augustus Gloop because his real name is Augustus."

"Ah, well maybe that's it. His name is Augustus Lagniappe on the roster. When I saw the roster on the first day of school and saw Augustus Lagniappe's name, I was going to ask him if he was related to the fat kid from *Charlie and the Chocolate Factory*. But then I remembered Buzzy Lagniappe is fictional."

"You mean Augustus Gloop."

"Yes, right . . . So, you're reading *Great Expectations* now. What're you going to read for your next book report?"

"I was thinking of *Journey To The Center Of The Earth*."

"Try this instead," she handed me a copy of *The Picture of Dorian Gray* by Oscar Wilde, "I think you'll really get into it."

"It looks difficult," I said as I glanced at some of the language.

"Oh, not for a bright boy like you, Lance," Ms. Cummings said and smiled at me fiercely.

I tucked Dorian Gray away in my backpack for Christmas vacation reading and sort of sidestepped out of her room.

"Thank you," I mouthed as I left.

She blew a kiss with her forefinger. It was a great visual for bedtime later.

4

When the two week Christmas vacation finally arrived I attempted as always to balance the ease of freedom with the burden of responsibility (i.e., school projects due upon our return after New Year's).

On the one hand, days were unencumbered, and one did not pay a dear price for staying up late. On the other hand, every afternoon one spent lazing and playing meant that much more manic panic during the last weekend of break to get everything done.

Especially nice during vacation times were Sunday nights which, freed from "school night" stigma, became sumptuous occasions to hang out with pals, listen to Dr. Demento, crank up the music, and luxuriate in thoughts of sleeping late on Monday morning.

And 1974 carried a few extra days of vacation because New Year's Eve was a Tuesday night, so we wouldn't have to go back to school until January 6, giving us almost three weeks.

And we needed it.

The biggest assignment was the film for our mutltimedia project, due the week after we got back which meant the filming all had to be done during break.

Groups of us, manning super-8 movie cameras and four cartridges of film, set about telling a story that could be communicated without words in 12 minutes or less.

That first Sunday, I got together with Dolly and Claude to map out our film which we had already decided would be a chase film taking place at the beach.

Listening to KMET, waiting for Dr. Demento to start, we threw around ideas.

Dolly liked the idea of a boyfriend and girlfriend at the beach (played by me and her) who get harassed by a bully and the girlfriend encourages the boyfriend to confront the bully, leading to a chase onto the pier and on all the carnival rides and would end with the bully (Claude) getting pushed off the end of the pier.

Claude and I agreed it was a cool idea, though Claude wanted to play the boyfriend, an idea vetoed by Dolly.

"Nuh-uh, Lance is my boyfriend," she insisted.

KMET caught our attention in the background.

That was 'The Devil Came From Kansas,' Procul Harum, and before that we heard Captain Beefheart and his Magic Band doing 'Yellow Brick Road' on the Mighty Met, little bit of heaven 94.7. I'm B. Mitchell Reed. Up next is the Dr. Demento show. Stay tuned for that, and I'll leave you with this, some Rolling Stones to help keep the moss off.

Our conversation fell to silence as we began listening to the Stones, grooving to the sounds of the whiteboy jungle.

Pleased to meet you

Hope you've guessed my name

But what's puzzling you

Is the nature of my game

A couple of years before, I had started an informal Dr. Demento fan club called the Tar Pit Kids, a group which included Claude and Gus and Whit. Sandy Clay had recently joined on, as had Sharon Rose and Justine Balthazar.

Each week we would pick a Dr. Demento tune and circulate petitions as well as call in to the show to get our chosen song into that week's Top Ten.

In 8th Grade we had a stretch of about 6 consecutive weeks during which we got our chosen song—"Walter Wart, The Freaky Frog" by the Thorndike Pickledish Pacifist Choir—to number one on the Top Ten.

We did this by inundating the poor Doctor, as well as his assistants Captain Chaos and Jungle Judy, with our petitions and incessant phone calls.

Dolly and Miranda found the enterprise "geeky" and "embarrassing" and didn't participate in the group.

While listening to Dr. Demento that night (we had taken the night off from Tar Pit Kids activities to work on our project), Dolly, who was mostly irritated by the off-kilter loopiness of the music and the good Doctor's scholarly approach to it ("Are we gonna watch *Star Trek* re-runs next?" she asked sarcastically at some point, not realizing what a distinct possibility that in fact was later), flipped through the booklet that came with The Who's *Quadrophenia* album, when she suddenly blurted out—I think it was during either "Shaving Cream" or "Pico & Sepulveda"—" Unholy Shit,

LOOK!" as she pointed to a picture in the booklet of the rock opera's main character Jimmy lying in his bedroom surrounded by naked centerfold pictures, a masturbation panorama, and she kept jabbing at this one centerfold hanging on Jimmy's wall, "LOOK! It's Ms. Barrows!!!"

And, yes, the centerfold in question, on full bare tit and crotch display, bore an undeniable resemblance to our 9th Grade history teacher.

"Dang, dude, we have to show this to Gus and Whit. They will totally do something with it," Claude said.

Indeed, when we showed the picture to Gus and Whit a couple of days later, Whit took the booklet to his dad's real estate office and xeroxed it about 50 times, and they ended up posting the picture all over John Burroughs in January, much to Ms. Barrows's rage at the insinuation that that was her.

In fact we never did find out if that was really her.

We all went on believing it was, though, and the fantasies fueled thereby for the next several weeks were universal and incomparable.

The first week of Christmas vacation was a week of rampant filming among all the groups, and everybody ended up helping everybody else out with their films in some way.

Dolly, Gus, and I took the RTD to Santa Monica Beach on Tuesday, an 85 degree December day in L.A., to do our filming.

First Claude filmed me and Dolly acting like a couple on the beach, complete with me rubbing suntan lotion on Dolly's back, she in floral bikini, I in dorky purple Laguna swim trunks.

The feel of Dolly's skin, though, as I massaged her with Coppertone, the girlness of her body, imprinted itself on my prolific fantasy life and accentuated an already vibrant admixture of lust and affection between me and the feline Ms. Ferris, an ever fluctuating attraction content to sit precipitously on the eternal verge.

Our film was shallow, flashy, stupid, and we didn't really care.

Claude kicked sand on us. I chased him along the beach and onto the pier, onto the bumper cars, the roller coaster, the merry-go-round, eventually catching him at the end of the pier and pushing him into the ocean, at which point Dolly ran up and kissed me, tongueless, on the mouth, much to the eventual hoots of our classmates when we showed the film a couple of weeks later. We got our "A" from Ms. Barrows on the project and were fine with the half-assedness of it all.

The film that Lorelei, Arabella, and Miranda were making, however, was a much more serious project. My scenes were filmed on Thursday of the first week of break, first at Lorelei's house and then at the Tar Pits.

Miranda was in full-on housewife regalia, pink bathrobe, curlers, furry slippers, a '70s smartass playing a '60s mom in shellframe glasses, making a mess of Lorelei's kitchen, slopping pancakes on my plate, blowing bazooka gum-bubbles, treating me like shit and enjoying it.

I was thinking, like, dang, dude, this is my future, I suppose, this totally deep and sardonic assimilated jewchick.

Even though it was just a dumbass Jr. High School movie, *Diamonds In The Sky* was like a portrait of our future together in some predefined star-crossed sandtrap, an unconscious fate embedded forever in the Lance/Miranda collective mindscape. Perhaps never a fulfilled destiny but most inescapably the underlying pattern against which all other outcomes get measured, projected, assumed.

The hourglass whose sand was really tiny diamonds was represented in the film by the hourglass Miranda had inherited from her grandmother.

The climactic scene—in which I, Mr. Link, the husband, innocently taking his wife's hourglass to be repaired, is ambushed by an assassin while walking through the Tar Pits—was marred by Gus Lagniappe, the "assassin," showing up dressed as a cowboy, with hat and vest and boots and bandanna kerchief over his face, wielding a Lucas McCain style carbine rifle.

"Don't make a move," Gus said as he held the barrel of the rifle up to my head as a joke.

"Dude, this isn't a western," I said on behalf of the filmmakers.

"Oh, what's the dang difference?" Gus asked.

"But I told you on the phone this is about an average guy in modern day Los Angeles. You are playing a professional hit man," said Miranda, "not an outlaw from the wild west."

"Dang, dude," I ribbed, "You should be wearing a suit or something.

You're supposed to be like *Day of the Jackal* and you show up dressed like a bad guy from *The Rifleman*."

"He looks like Mike Teevee from *Willy Wonka and the Chocolate Factory*," Arabella Mayflower said.

"And hit men don't sneak up on people from behind and say corny stuff like 'Don't make a move,'" Miranda spoke with a director's scorn.

"It's a silent movie, so they won't hear that part," I pointed out.

"Maybe he could be a psycho hit man who likes to dress up as a cowboy," offered Lorelei Lux.

"What other choices do you have?" asked Gus, belligerent.

"I suppose," conceded Miranda, "We've got to get it done today 'cause I'm too busy for the rest of break."

Of course, Cowboy Gus ended up being a big campy hit when the girls showed their film in class in January.

The next six days were spent alternately rapt in *The Picture of Dorian Gray* and being intermittently distracted by my Jewish Christmas date with Miranda Savitch.

"Should we meet at the corner of Curson and Curson?" she had asked when we were done filming that day.

"It might take me forever to find the damn spot," I joked.

"*If it takes forever I will wait for you . . .*" Miranda sang in an exaggerated crooner's voice.

"That sounds like something you'd hear an old dude sing on *The Mike Douglas Show*."

"Totally," she giggled, "Or *Merv Griffin*."

"I always get those two confused," I confessed, "like Mike Wallace and Morley Safer."

"Or Balboa and Magellan?" she said.

"Ooh, that's cold," I winced.

173

"The Pacific Ocean dudes," Miranda giggled, "But just come over to my house and we'll walk. It's at the Fairfax isn't it?"

The ensuing days were hobbled by trepidation and misgivings. I was the usual brand of no-food nervous.

Sitting on the front lawn with Gus, still unsure if his loss of virginity and subsequent sexual schooling in Kansas was real or not, I listened to his coaching.

"Take control of the situation, dude. Show her that you are the boss of her life. And remember the lesson I've been teaching you since 8th Grade: She's just a girl, it doesn't matter. Picture her sitting on the toilet picking her nose," Gus advised.

"Thanks for that image."

" . . . taking a shit . . ."

"Enough, dude."

"That'll put an end to your Cowardly Lion bullshit," Gus promised.

Christmas afternoon I rode my bike to Miranda's house.

The streets of L.A. were quiet, almost empty, even the Orthodox corridor near Beverly & Fairfax was fairly deserted, though Canter's Deli had a crowd of hungry Jews in attendance.

Nothing was open in Farmers Market.

Miranda's mom let me in and told me Miranda was in her bedroom waiting for me, and, indeed, there she was when I entered, lying across her bed reading *Lord of the Flies*.

With my mind's cock I had fucked her on that bed countless times.

In the real world, I had sat on the bed wanting to fuck her exactly three times.

Her bedroom door was open, and I did that stupid thing where you knock on somebody's open door and say 'knock knock' at the same time.

"Hi, Lance!" Miranda said, sitting up.

"Hey," I said, "y'ready?"

The room looked pretty much the same. There was a new poster on the wall, a Fred Astaire poster, from the movie *The Band Wagon*.

"When did you get into Fred Astaire?" I asked.

"Oh, I've always liked him. But I saw *The Band Wagon* on TV over the summer and was majorly into it, and then I saw this poster at The Frigate—you know that place? 3rd & Crescent Heights?"

"I love The Frigate, yeah. I've found some really weird books and records there."

"Anyway I saw the poster and I was all hot on the movie so I bought it."

"Well, it looks like it belongs there," I said.

"That's 'cause it does!" she said, "Let's go," and she grabbed me by the sleeve, pulling me out the front door.

The Little Prince had been out for a month and had gotten terrible reviews, but the Fairfax was pretty full with Jews out having a traditional Christmas.

"How are you liking *Lord of the Flies*?" I asked, waiting for the movie to start.

"Oh, it's neat," she answered.

"Which would you be, Ralph or Jack?"

"That's what I keep thinking about, actually," Miranda said, "I'm pretty sure I'm a Ralph."

"'Cause Ralph has hope," I said.

"Correct, sir," Miranda said, pressing her forefinger to my nose, "Sir Lancelot . . ."

I pinched the tip of her finger between my thumb and forefinger and then squeezed her whole finger in my hand.

"Lemme go," she struggled feebly, laughing, trying to unpry my grip.

I let her go, and we looked at each other for several moments.

"So, you feel more like Ralph because—"

"—he was able to keep on believing they were going to be rescued," she finished my thought.

"He wasn't just maintaining rules out of habit?"

"No no, I think it's really clear from the stuff he says that they have to keep their Englishness because they're gonna be saved and go back into that society, but Jack thinks it's all hopeless and so he gives up his Englishness because he's never going back into that system as far as he's concerned. You know?"

"The rules are useless."

"Zackly."

"But what if Jack is right? What if the rules are just phony anyway and not the real way people are supposed to live?"

"Then why is Jack's tribe so icky? See, I don't think Jack is right."

"Well, yeah, of course, in the end when the boys—"

"—Don't tell me! I'm not done yet!"

"I'm a Ralph too."

"Defenly," she said, "But Ralph's hope is real, I think. I bet they get rescued—the movie's starting," Miranda said in the dimming lights.

"Or else you're going blind," I teased.

"Shush."

The critics were right.

The film version of *The Little Prince* was indeed terrible, and, worse, a musical.

We talked through much of it, pausing to watch the scene with Gene Wilder as the Fox.

I sat next to Miranda, contemplating putting my arm around her, holding her hand, frenching, none of which I actually did nor even attempted.

I thought of the note from 7th Grade.

176

Occasionally she moved her hand closer to me.

At one point she tapped my thigh to get my attention.

She missed my erection by a millimeter.

I'm glad it was dark.

"Isn't this horrible?" she asked.

"Painful."

"My favorite book, jeez-o-man," she lamented. "What are you reading for the next book report?" Miranda whispered in my ear.

It felt like she was about to nibble my earlobe but she didn't.

"Ms. Cummings gave me this book to read called *The Picture of Dorian Gray*," I said.

"Oh, your girlfriend, you mean?"

"Now now . . ."

"*Lance knows the answer, I'm sure, don't you Lance?*," Miranda did another breathy version of Ms. Cummings, "*Oh, Lance is the smartest boy, he knows everything!*" she continued, batting her eyelashes awkwardly, "*Lance is my loverboy.*"

"Dang, dude," I complained.

She snickered and stuck her tongue out at me. I should have met hers with my own and set on to frenching.

"Hey," Miranda said, poking my shoulder, "Are you and Mimi *really* only 11 months apart?"

"Yeah. I wasn't making that up. Busy parents. After Mimi was born they wouldn't let my dad in to visit my mother, you know."

Miranda went on, "It's just so weird to me. Nick and Lil are like 5 years

177

older than I am. And Jeremy is like 5 years younger. I can't imagine going to the same parties and stuff with my siblings."

"Do all the Savitch siblings have such big earlobes?" I asked.

"Hey, that's not nice, you with your little baby ears," she came back, touching my tiny earlobe with her thumb and forefinger.

"Well, you know some people are just born that way, Mrs. Dumbo," I said as I yanked on her earring and moved my mouth toward her.

"Mrs. Jumbo," she said, closing her eyes. She held my forearm.

"Well, for heaven's sake, it's the Almighty Atlas!" we heard the voice of Sandy Clay emerge from the darkness, diverting my attention from the region of Miranda's neck I was about to lay my lips on.

Three figures were moving up the aisle toward the exit.

It was indeed Sandy along with Eddie Gurges and Claude Moss.

"This movie stinks worse than yo mama's week-old drawers," Sandy offered.

"Time to split the scene if you know what I mean," Claude added.

"What're you guys doing here?" I asked.

"Hey, we're the lonely Jews of Christmas," Eddie said, "What else are we gonna do?"

"That'd be a good name for a band," I said.

"Hell yeah, The Lonely Jews of Christmas," Sandy agreed.

"Totally," said Miranda.

"Except none of you plays an instrument," I pointed out.

"This is true," said Claude in a Maharishi Mahesh Yogi voice.

"We also came here to spy on you making out with your girlfriend," Sandy said.

"All right, anyways, golita, we're gonna book, see ya," Claude said, and the three of them ambled up the aisle and out of the theatre.

Miranda and I wouldn't be far behind.

"This movie is really unbearable," I whispered, brushing her ear with my lips.

"I hate seeing them ruin the book," Miranda said.

"Should we leave?" I asked with the intention of doing so.

"Yeah, let's split," she agreed.

We walked up Fairfax to this restaurant called Meng Po, a dingy cave that had great chow mein. It was a strange time of day for eating, about 3:30pm, so we didn't have to battle crowds of hungry Jews.

Miranda and I sat across from each other in Meng Po, sharing a pot of their special Tea of Forgetfulness, chicken chow mein, and fried rice.

"You ever been to Kelbo's next door?" I asked.

"No, I've always wondered what it's like in there."

"It's pretty corny cool looking. There are witch doctor totem poles and tons of voodoo shit everywhere."

"I do voodoo," Miranda said.

"Oh . . . really . . ." I remarked, remembering my date to write songs with Manny about chick voodoo.

"Totally into it, in a major way. When we go back to my house I'll show you my Lance doll."

"Um . . . yeah," I said with trepidation.

"Psych," she said with a wide grin, "I don't know shit about voodoo."

"I'm sitting here picturing you poking holes in my head with pins."

"That's not where I'd be poking the holes," she smirked, looking down at her plate.

The waitress brought us the bill along with 2 fortune cookies and 2 almond cookies.

"I love fortune cookies," Miranda said, "Don't you?"

"I'm fascinated by them," I said, "They were printed in some factory in Monterey Park or Alhambra and have nothing to do with the person who ends up reading them in some Chinese restaurant in Los Angeles. But people who totally know all that still look at the fortune, and somehow believe the illusion that the fortune was written specially for them. I love stuff like that."

"Oh, for me they always apply. They point things out about your life which maybe you weren't noticing before, that's all. I think that's what's going on with fortune cookies."

"Except the cookie itself is terrible."

"Yeah but nobody eats the cookie part. It's like parsley. And I mean, who eats parsley, you know?"

"Um, yeeeah," I said and thought of a dirty joke which led to picturing my mouth on her vagina, "But at least the almond cookies are good," I said, biting into one.

Miranda opened her fortune cookie. "*Your destiny is what's always happening,*" she read out loud.

"Does it work?"

"I give it a hmmm."

"A hmmm?"

"A hmmm means I have to think about it some more. What's yours?"

I cracked open the stale cookie and read my fortune on the little slip of paper.

"*Don't make a move,*" I read.

"What?"

"It says '*Don't make a move.*'"

"No way, let me see," Miranda snatched my fortune.

"See? Me no lie."

"That's the weirdest-ass fortune I've ever seen. Does it apply?"

"Hmmm," I said half-laughingly.

"Well?"

"I'm not going to try to figure out my life based on dessert. Dessert makes me sad," I said.

"Wishes, carnivals, dessert . . ."

"I bet you anything hell is some kind of carnival," I said.

"Where damned souls spend all eternity wishing for dessert."

"Ha," I appreciated her brain, "And watching an hourglass."

We left Meng Po and started walking up Fairfax back to Miranda's house, when a car pulled up honking.

"That's my family," Miranda said with some measure of horror and disbelief.

Her mother rolled down the window and said, "Mandy, you said you'd be home by 5:00. We have to go to Aunt Clara's house. Get in the car! Hi, Lance!"

"Oh, dang, I forgot," Miranda said to me, "I gotta go."

"I had fun today."

"Me too. And if you feel any tingling sensations later tonight, that's me with my voodoo doll."

"MIRANDA!" her mother yelled.

"Bye, Lance!" Miranda said as she turned and hopped in the car.

5

After Christmas, I set a bit of time aside each day to practice a showy maneuver on my Schwinn 10-Speed whereby I'd build up enough momentum to cruise while hoisting myself to a standing position on the bicycle seat.

I thought it was sure to impress Miranda.

My plan was to glide by her in all my glory one morning when she'd be walking down McCadden from the Wilshire Bus toward school.

On a fateful day in February, when I felt well practiced, I caught sight of Miranda getting off the bus and began picking up enough speed to achieve a safe seat-stand.

At the crucial instant, m'lady's ass in view, I maneuvered myself to a seat-top standing position, cruising beautifully, on full display before Miranda and much of the JB student body standing around outside before first period.

"Miranda!" I shouted, looking her way as I passed, trying to be both heroic and cute at the same time while failing to notice the row of parked cars I was veering toward.

My handlebars clipped the sideview mirror of a cherry red Datsun B-210, sending me into free-flight over the roof of the car and onto the sidewalk, a face-first landing which rendered my right profile a relief map of shredded skin and bloody contusion.

I don't remember the impact nor its aftermath.

I'm told I got to my feet, set my bicycle aright, said I was fine, and then collapsed.

Apparently Ms. Cummings saw the accident from her classroom window and ran out to help. Though I was conscious enough to get up and walk propped up by Ms. Cummings, I didn't regain full awareness until I was in the nurse's office, lying on a rock-hard cot.

Ms. Cummings was placing swabs wet with my blood in some kind of spooky looking container.

"How's my boy?" Ms. Cummings asked, smiling, "Are you here now?"

"What happened?"

"You had a little accident. Looks like you weren't keeping your eyes on where you were going," she accused knowingly.

"I don't remember," I said.

"She isn't worth it," Ms. Cummings admonished.

My mother came to pick me up from the nurse's office.

We loaded my bike into the back of the station wagon and went to the doctor who pronounced my wounds mere surface abrasions, treated them with some kind of disinfectant goop and sent me home to recover.

My father took a couple of dozen snapshots of my fucked up face on his Instamatic thinking it was very funny.

"Pretend you're in agonizing torment," he said.

"Pretend?"

"You look like something Seymour would've shown on *Fright Night*," said Mimi.

I was out of school for a week, more due to cosmetic embarrassment than any medical need.

I passed the time venturing through numerous complete listenings to the new Dylan album, *Blood On The Tracks*, and of course every song reminded me of Miranda, if not in detail then the general underlying emotional tone.

I wondered if I'd hear from her.

Everyday after school Gus stopped by to give me a hard time about it.

"Why you wanna go fuck up your face for some dumb girl?" he'd ask. "You don't let her be a bossy bitch, dude, you boss the bitch, that's how it works. Dig?"

Eddie Gurges gave me a framed cartoon he'd drawn of me flying through the air with my bicycle and shouting "Miranda!"

Sandy Clay made me a tape of all his KSIN 'DJs' dedicating songs to me and making fun of me at the same time: "And now here's the song 'Transfusion' by Nervous Norvus, all about a guy who can't keep his eyes on the road, and we want to send this one out to Lance Atlas who knows the feeling."

Dolly Ferris came over with Sharon Rose after school on the last day of my convalescence.

Dolly pulled a note out of her purse. It was folded, but I recognized the Little Prince stationery.

"Guess who," Dolly said.

"Your girlfriend," said Sharon.

"She's not my girlfriend," I said but didn't read the note until Sharon and Dolly left:

My dearest Lancelot Link Secret Chimp,

How sad you must be,

Sitting around watching TV,

Reading that magazine called Oui.

Sorry you messed up your face because of me.

Love,

Miranda

I had meant to call Miranda several times and felt bad that I hadn't, but I always just kept figuring, hell, I'll see her at school tomorrow.

But then, of course, because I hadn't been calling she wasn't especially friendly at school.

Our joint Samsara was tightly wound and bound.

A month after the accident, Ms. Cummings and Ms. Barrows took us on a field trip to a special screening of the film *Camelot* after our unit on medieval England.

On the school bus afterward, Miranda, who was sitting in front of me and who hadn't really been speaking to me much, suddenly turned around and asked, "So what'd you think of the film, Sir Lancelot?"

"I, um, liked some of it, but, I don't know, there's something wrong with the music. Like it's not as good as it should be or something." Miranda looked at me blankly. "I liked Richard Harris as King Arthur."

"He can't sing, though!" cracked Miranda.

"Oh, totally. Have you ever heard him doing "MacArthur Park?""

"I don't know that song."

"You have to hear it. It's hilarious," I said and then began singing, a la Harris, "*MacArthur's Park is melting in the dark, all the sweet green icing flowing dowwwwwwwwwwwwn . . . Someone left the cake out in the rain . . . I don't think that I can take 'cause it took so long to bake it and I'll never have that recipe agaiiiin, oh nooooooo,*" and I broke into laughter.

"That sounds funny."

"You must experience it one day," I said.

The collective babble on the bus overcame the cheesy AM radio music coming over the bus PA system.

Miranda said, "I bet I can beat you in a staring contest."

"How much?" I held out my hand. We were already staring.

"Voodoo lunch at Kelbo's," she said.

"Loser gives all?" I made sure.

"Damn straight, them's always the stakes between you and me, Lucas boy."

She'd been watching *The Rifleman*. Cool.

The hits scratched their way through the shitty bus speakers and over the laughter and patter.

My eyes adored you

Though I never laid a hand on you,

My eyes adored you

The established rules of staring contests dictated that one could blink but couldn't look away.

And so we engaged in this extended eye-lock, a competition, a communication.

It was splendid having permission to stare at Miranda.

She sat on her knees facing the back of the bus, I in the seat behind facing forward, our eyes intertwined, utterly stuck, lost in the allness, tapping into the marrow, formidable visions.

I loved Miranda, I wanted Miranda, I watched Miranda watch me watching her.

Her eyes were the kind of chocolate you get at Disneyland.

There would be no looking away.

The bus came to a wheel-screeching halt followed by a brief roll followed fast upon by another jerky halt, "a double Jew-stop" as Whitman Rust called it, bringing to a premature finish our staring contest, no winner decided.

Walking to our lockers from the bus, Miranda hooked her arm around mine.

Gooseflesh ensued.

"The old film version of *The Picture of Dorian Gray* is showing at the Vagabond next Saturday," I brought up, "Do you want to go? It's right near MacArthur Park."

"The one from the song?"

"Yeah. You ever been?"

"No. Saturday?"

"Yeah. Afternoon. We could take the Wilshire bus. There's a lake with ducks there."

"I'm . . . yeah," she accepted.

"Cool. Saturday."

"Come over like 11 or something?"

"Yeah yeah."

"I haven't read the book, though."

"I doubt it'll matter."

"Right on then," Miranda said and smiled, "Saturday."

On the way to Miranda's house Saturday morning, I stopped at The Frigate on 3rd & Crescent Heights to see if I might be able to find the "MacArthur Park" single.

Miranda's birthday was a few days later, and I thought it'd be a fitting gift.

The Frigate was a small, cluttered hodgepodge emporium.

Books, records, posters, movie stills, hand-made clothes, stationery, fondue sets, music magazines, knickknacks like you might see in the breakfront on *The Courtship of Eddie's Father.*

Above the door was a quote from Emily Dickinson:

There is no frigate like a book

To take us lands away

I asked Sid, one of the owners, if they had a copy of "MacArthur Park", and he said, "By Richard Harris? We do, except I don't know where it is. Hold on. Marty!" he called out to his partner, "where's that copy of 'MacArthur Park,' the one with the campy sleeve?"

"You mean with the photograph of Richard Harris feeding the ducks from his paddleboat?" called Marty from the stock room.

"Yes!" Sid yelled back.

"I've got it in here somewhere! I'll bring it out in a minute!"

"59, 58, 57 . . ." Sid started in chanting loudly, then stopped, snickering. "He hates when I do that."

The Rolling Stones were rocking on the store sound system.

She comes in colors everywhere . . .

"I bet she does," said Sid with a lascivious grin.

"A camp classic," Marty said, emerging through the curtain from the back holding up the single ensleeved in a color photograph of Richard Harris riding a paddleboat on the lake in MacArthur Park tossing bread crumbs to the ducks.

"Can you wrap it? It's a birthday present."

"Boy or girl?"

"Girl," I blushed.

"What's your girlfriend's name?"

"Miranda," I said, "She's not my girlfriend."

"Like Carmen Miranda . . ." Sid said.

"*Mamae eu quero,*" Marty started singing and wriggling.

"Oh, stop that. You're worse than Lucy Ricardo."

"I remember that episode," I said.

"Except that was *supposed* to be bad. Unlike the episodes that took place in Connecticut," Sid said, "good lord."

"Miranda is an *I Love Lucy* fanatic," I said, "and even she hates the Connecticut episodes."

"*Mamae eu quero,*" Marty continued singing and sashaying.

"Marty, please. You look like the fat kid from *Willy Wonka and the Chocolate Factory* when you do that," Sid said.

"Buzzy Lagniappe, baby," Marty said as he kept dancing.

"Shit for brains, Augustus Gloop is the fat kid from *Willy Wonka and the Chocolate Factory* . . ." Sid corrected while handing me the wrapped single.

I shuffled quietly out the door and headed over to Miranda's house.

"Oh my God, thank you, Lance," Miranda enthused when she opened her birthday present, "This is so cool. Is the picture serious or a joke?" she asked.

"Kind of ambiguous, I think."

"Huh?"

"A little of both," I explained.

"Do we have time to listen now? Oh, wait, no, look, it's 7 minutes long! Like 'Stairway To Heaven,'" she said.

"Or 'Nights In White Satin,' except no bad poetry at the end," I promised.

"Phew."

"The bad poetry's all in the lyrics."

"Ha!"

"No joke."

"Worse than 'Breathe deep the gathering gloom?'"

"Well, no."

When we got off the bus at MacArthur Park, Miranda gazed all about her. She had this way of drinking it all in.

We walked the block and a half back to the Vagabond across the street.

The Vagabond Theatre was sacred ground.

A small auditorium with famous old-time movie star silhouettes painted on the walls, the Vagabond specialized in great old black and white films.

I sat there in the dark with Miranda Savitch, squirming with paralytic lust.

Every time I'd get it in my mind to hold her hand, put my arm around her, nibble her earlobe, kiss her on the mouth and use my tongue, I'd flash on that fortune cookie at Meng Po.

Miranda found the movie "Kinda fake."

"Yeah, the worst thing for me was actually seeing the portrait," I said as we walked back across the street to MacArthur Park, "When I was reading the book, I imagined the most disgusting demon face, but in the movie the picture was just sort of, I don't know, corny or something."

"It kinda looked like Nixon during his resignation speech," Miranda joked.

Miranda and I found a bench near the lake.

I should've rented a paddle boat or bought bread crumbs to feed the ducks or gotten her a balloon or a churro or something from one of the Mexican vendors or pounced on her mouth and frenched the hell out of her, but I just plain old didn't know how to be a boyfriend.

Instead, we merely sat and watched the water.

Occasionally we would look at each other but then disengage immediately from the gaze.

I couldn't hold onto her. I didn't want to be held. Both of us drawn to the impossible.

"What's the most embarrassing thing about you?" Miranda asked me after a prolonged silence.

"You really wanna know that?" I asked.

"Make me blush," she said.

Saying to her, "I fantasize about fucking you every night of my life," would certainly have made her blush, but the consequences would have been far too dire to deal with. And so instead I confessed, "I do a radio show in my bedroom every Saturday morning from 6-10am."

"Wow, I didn't know that! On what station?"

"No no, I just do it in my bedroom. It's not on any station. I pretend people are listening," I said.

"Is it, like, a music show or?"

"Yeah yeah, music. I have two record players set up so I can crossfade, I rigged up the microphone from my tape recorder to look like a radio microphone. I make up a whole bunch of commercials for fake products, and I pre-record those and play them on my tape recorder between music sets. At the top of the hour I read the news from the *Articles in Brief* section of the *L.A. Times*."

"What kind of music do you play?"

"Everything I like, pretty much, mostly from my own collection, but I also play stuff from my parents' records. So I can go from, like, David Bowie to The Who to Ella Fitzgerald to The Beatles to The Weavers to Oscar Peterson. My favorite album since last summer has been *Whizz Kid* by David Werner, so I play cuts from that one a lot. And I close every show with 'Nights In White Satin.'"

"Haha."

"Psych . . ."

"What do you do while the music's playing?"

I let another opportunity to say, "I fantasize about fucking you," pass and said instead, "I drink hot chocolate."

"Does it ever get boring?"

"Sometimes."

"But you keep doing it," she puzzled.

"I want to be a DJ," I said.

"So it's kind of like practicing the piano then."

"Uh, yeah, I guess so," I said, having never thought of it that way.

"So then what's so embarrassing about that?"

"Well, because it's bogus. Nobody hears it."

"You do."

"I guess."

"Do you ever miss a show?"

"I didn't do the show today."

"Why not?"

"Cause of this, our, um . . ."

" . . . date?" she said.

"Nyeah I guess . . ." I blushed as I looked at the ducks, "Is that what this is?"

"Your little earlobes are turning red, Sir Lancelot."

"So are yours, Mrs. Dumbo."

"Jumbo."

"Mrs. Jumbolobes," I smiled and looked at her as I tugged on her earring and she swatted my hand away.

"Do you like me, Lance?" Miranda asked suddenly serious, looking at the lake, then, after a pause, "Just wondering."

"Nyeah, I-uh . ."

"You-uh?" she pressed.

"I-uh . . ."

"Hmm?"

"Well, I . . . love you," I said out loud in the real world for the first time to somebody I wasn't related to, "Yes."

Miranda didn't reply. She looked at the ground and grinned. A few minutes passed.

"Did you love Candy Stoner?" she asked.

"No. I liked Candy. But I love you," I said.

Another eon elapsed.

"I mean it," I said, holding her jaw and making her look at me, "I love you."

Miranda pulled away from my grip.

"What?"

"You make me cuckoo," she said, withholding all meaning.

Realizing she wasn't going to return with an "I love you, too," I nudged the conversation elsewhere. "What's the most embarrassing thing about *you* then?" I asked. "Your turn to try and make *me* blush," I ribbed.

"Oh, mine won't make you blush."

"Tell."

"OK. Here: When I blow out my birthday candles I really do make a wish, and I really do hope it comes true. I hope that's not too sad for you."

"What are you going to wish for on Tuesday?"

"Now *that* would make you blush," she teased and stood up. "We should probably start waiting for the bus, huh?" she said, and we walked to the bus stop in front of The Vagabond.

On the ride home a lingering, exhausted silence prevailed. I was watching the day turn to dusk, the sky a fading blue like in poetry.

"I'm riding into the sunset with Miranda Savitch," I thought to myself and looked at her face in profile, the cute jewbroad with the lopsided smile.

After gathering my bike from the side of her house, I walked with her to her front door.

"You still haven't told me anything embarrassing," Miranda said.

"Um, uh'all right, how about I used to have a crush on Laurie Partridge."

"And I had one on Keith. Again not embarrassing."

"Well, you still haven't responded to my statement earlier," I returned to the I-love-you thing.

"I don't know, Lance, I'm really confused right now," Miranda said, "Maybe if you call me later I'll have it all figured out."

"OK," I said.

She knew I wouldn't call.

"You're like a fortune cookie," Miranda said, as she stepped inside the house and turned to face me.

Don't make a move

She didn't elaborate.

"Bye, Lance," she said and closed the door.

A couple of weeks later when our whole group went en masse to see *Tommy*, at the Wilshire Theatre, Miranda hardly spoke to me.

None of us guys had much interaction with the girls that day, actually.

First of all, once the girls got a load of Roger Daltrey in the movie, all lean bod and blond ringlets and eyes like the sky, we ceased to exist anyway.

Yeah, we got Ann Margaret humping pillows and pleasuring herself with bubbles and beans, and Tina Turner shaking her thighs as the Acid Queen, but those were like one scene each.

Also, on the 9th Grade Court that week, an argument erupted over which was the better album, *Tommy* or *Quadrophenia*, and the two sides broke down along gender lines in exactly the same way as the argument over whether or not The Three Stooges are funny always did.

The girls all thought *Tommy* was better; the boys were more partial to *Quadrophenia*. So, at the theatre we instinctively kept separate, like at an Orthodox shul.

But beyond the general overriding tension among the group, a worse feeling was the pronounced chasm between me and Miranda.

While waiting for the movie to start, everybody started hissing when The Captain & Tenille's "Love Will Keep Us Together" started playing on the PA.

I looked at Miranda to see if she was looking at me.

She wasn't, but perhaps she had been or was about to.

Oliver Gelding said, "That's dog, dude. Shouldn't you be sitting with your girlfriend?"

"She's not my girlfriend," I said.

"What is she exactly?" Gus asked.

"I can't ever seem to figure that out," I tried to explain.

"What do you guys do when you go out?" Whit questioned me.

"We talk about stuff."

"Like what?"

"I don't know, everything. Books, music. I like turning her onto things she doesn't know about," I said, "She turns me on to things I don't know about. It's like mutual tutoring or something."

"You turn her on, she turns you on . . . sounds like girlfriend/boyfriend stuff to me," said Whit.

"She doesn't know about fucking. How about turning her onto that?" Gus suggested.

"That'd be dog, dude, if you just whipped out your dick and went like, 'Looky here, girl, let me turn you onto something new,'" Oliver said.

"Lesson #1: Suck my cock," said Sandy Clay doing a Samantha Coventry imitation.

"Yeah, and she'd go, 'Wait let me get my microcsope so I can see that shit,'" Whit teased.

"Ha ha ha," I said.

"Don't you want to fuck her?" Gus asked.

"Dang, dude, keep your voice down she's right over there," I looked over at her but couldn't tell if she heard anything.

"Don't you want to fuck her?" Gus asked more quietly.

"Jeez-louise, what do you think?" I asked.

"On the ping pong table, dude," said Oliver, thrusting his pelvis from his sitting position, "Doggy style the way she likes it . . . enh enh enh enh . . ."

I closed my eyes and waited for the movie to start.

6

Sometime between the fall of Saigon and *Monty Python and the Holy Grail* coming out, Ms. Cummings announced that the Los Angeles branch of the Modern Readers Society (L.A.M.R.S.) was sponsoring a city-wide oratorical contest, the winner receiving a $100 savings bond and a chance to go to a national competition for an even heftier prize.

The speech had to be on a quote from Goethe:

"Where there is much light, the shadows are deepest."

The only 2 requirements were that your speech specifically respond to that Goethe quote and that you support your ideas with at least one quote from a work of "literary merit."

Of course, the only two people who signed up to represent JB were Miranda Savitch and I.

We would both have to do our speech for Ms. Cummings, and she would decide which of us would go to the final round and which would be an alternate.

I started working on my speech, deciding to talk about how within every darkness there is always the promise of light, though I wanted to avoid the silver lining around every cloud cliché.

I would end up talking mostly about hope, how hope is the thing that enables us to keep on going and defeat the darkness by finding the light within it.

I remembered that line from *The Little Prince* that Miranda said was her favorite: *What makes the desert beautiful is that somewhere it hides a well.*

I thought that would be the perfect line for me to use as my literary quote, but I had to check with Ms. Cummings to make sure *The Little Prince* was considered a work of "literary merit."

A couple of days before Miranda and I were supposed to stay after school to present our speeches to see who would be the JB finalist, I went to see Ms. Cummings after school to ask her about using *The Little Prince*.

As I approached Ms. Cummings's room, I could hear the noise of voices coming from inside.

One voice sounded like Ms. Cummings.

She was chanting something like, "*bananas*," and there'd be a brief pause, and then she'd say something that sounded like, "*gotham*," over and over again.

The other voice was sort of muffled.

I tried to see through the obscured glass but detected only minimal movement.

I turned the doorknob quietly, on the chance it was unlocked, which (now to my shock) it was, and I cracked the door open just enough to see Ms. Cummings leaning back on her desk holding a crystal to her chest with her left hand and with the other hand smearing her face using blood from the spooky looking container I'd seen her with in the nurse's office following my bike accident.

"*Bananas*," she said, sort of moaning, "*gotham*."

I opened the door a smidgen more which enabled me to see someone's head up Ms. Cummings's skirt between her legs. Although I couldn't see the face up the skirt, I could tell from the straight-leg Levis and earth shoes that it was Samantha Coventry.

"I'm looking at the sky," Ms. Cummings continued to moan, "A portal, a portal, a portal for the chaos. Oh God. . ."

I was afraid to close the door for fear that I'd be heard and I was afraid to stay for fear that I'd be seen.

I kind of wanted to throw up.

Ms. Cummings then started instructing, "Now say *neither a cartooning hat is off*, go on, *neither a cartooning hat is off*, say it."

Samantha lifted her head from Ms. Cummings's crotch long enough to say "Suck my cock," and then submerged again.

Ms. Cummings got irritated and said, "Damn you, say *neither a*—" and as she began to scold Samantha the spooky container of blood spilled onto a stack of essays, which prompted Ms. Cummings to look up, her gaze, to my horror, landing directly upon me peeking through the doorway.

She sat up and pushed Samantha away, and I closed the door and ran down the hall out of the main building to my bicycle and rode home nauseated and sweating and not knowing what I'd seen or what to do.

Later that evening, Ms. Cummings called the house and told my mother she had to give me important information about the oratorical contest.

All she ended up saying to me was, "Before you talk to anybody please come to my room after school tomorrow and give me a chance to explain."

The images ran rampant in my brain throughout dinner, homework, right up to bedtime and beyond. Samantha Coventry seemingly eating out Ms. Cummings, the moaning, the witchy chanting, the blood smearing. It was at once sickening and erotic.

During that night's masturbation session I kept going back and forth between Miranda Savitch and Ms. Cummings, unable to decide where to sow my seed for the evening. I can't even remember whom I was thinking about at the crucial kaboom, but I did dream about Ms. Cummings.

In the dream I was in her classroom to ask about *The Little Prince*.

"Ms. Cummings, is-um——?"

"——Have you ever fantasized about fucking me?" Ms. Cummings asked forthrightly.

"I-um. Huh?"

"Have you ever fantasized about fucking me?"

"I'm not——"

"——When you masturbate do you entertain images of your cock in my pussy? Or perhaps it's that little dolly girlfriend of yours, Miranda Savitch, you fantasize about fucking?"

"She's not my girlfriend."

"What is she then?"

"I've never even kissed her."

"But you've fantasized about fucking her?"

"Um . . ."

"Confess."

"Um-I—"

"—Well, OK, whatever, here's the deal: I don't want you fantasizing about fucking Miranda Savitch anymore. I only want you fantasizing about fucking me from now on. Got that, son? You hear me? If I catch you fantasizing about cheating on me I will very definitely fantasize about cutting your balls off, you worthless scumbag."

"But how will you know about my fantasies?"

"I will see your thoughts in my cauldron. Do we have a deal?"

"Yes, Ms. Cummings."

"So before you go to sleep tonight whom will you fantasizing about fucking?"

"You, Ms. Cummings."

"Complete sentence please."

"I will fantasize about fucking *you*, Ms. Cummings."

"I will fantasize about fucking you doggy style the way you like it, Ms. Cummings. Say that."

"I will fantasize about fucking you doggy style the way you like it," I promised.

"That brings us back around to my original question: Have you ever fantasized about fucking me?"

"Yes, I have," I admitted, "Many times."

"Oh, my God," she winced, "you're wicked," and then after a prurient pause, "Tell me about it."

"I was fucking you doggy style the way you like it."

"Did you finger my clit while you fucked me?"

"I might have."

"Good. Keep that in mind. Oh, and next time you fantasize about fucking me?"

"Yeah?"

"Stick a finger in my ass when I'm about to come. It just makes me explode. Can you?"

"Sure."

"Awesome. Close the circuit, baby. Try that tonight and tell me how it goes."

I woke from the encounter with morning granite down below and little cartoon devils running around my foggy consciousness as well as the phrase *neither a cartooning hat is off*, whatever the fuck that meant.

I couldn't tell my parents about Ms. Cummings and Samantha because they would immediately call the prinicpal or even the police, and I wasn't sure I wanted to get the two of them in trouble.

I couldn't bring it up with my friends; they would immediately repeat the details to everyone on the 9th Grade court.

I was alone with my conscience.

Samantha Coventry ambushed me near the bike rack in the morning and begged me not to tell.

"I will totally suck your cock whenever you want if you just don't fink. Please, Lance."

I told her I was going to hear an explanation from Ms. Cummings before doing anything else.

"Please, Lance," she said again. "I mean it. Whenever you want."

I sat next to Miranda in Ms. Barrows's class, and though we were mostly avoiding talking to each other, we had, a few times over the past few days, talked about our speeches.

"You done with yours yet?" she asked.

"I'm just about there," I said, my voice in traumatized quaver.

"Are you OK, Lance?" Miranda reached over and put her hand on my shoulder.

I nodded.

"You sure?" she asked again, tilting her head, narrowing her eyes, poking my cheek, "For real? You look weirded out."

I nodded again.

"You'd tell me?" she asked one more time.

"Mm-hmm," I promised.

"I do care, you know," she said.

It almost felt like friendship for a second.

Ms. Barrows's history class was the last class of the day.

When the bell rang I went downstairs to put unnecessary stuff in my locker and get the stuff I needed for homework out.

"Be OK, OK?" Miranda said, as she shut her locker and left for the bus.

I made my way with tickling innards all the way down the hall toward Ms. Cummings' room.

I knocked.

"Come in, Lance!" Ms. Cummings said.

I entered, though I was reluctant to get too close to her.

"Come sit down. Let's talk."

I sat in the desk I normally occupy, right next to her teacher's desk. She was reading a book, *Master and Margarita*.

"Is that a good book?" I asked.

"So far, yes, wonderful."

"Neat," I said. My armpits were drenched. I could smell myself.

Ms. Cummings looked at me for several long moments.

"Do you understand what you were seeing yesterday afternoon?" she finally broached the issue.

"I think so, I-um, it looked like, um," I fumbled, and then, "you were having oral sex with Samantha Coventry," I just blurted out in a sudden gush.

"Well, yes, it might have looked that way to you, Lance," Ms. Cummings related calmly, like a teacher, "but things aren't always what they seem. 'Fair is foul and foul is fair,' as the Weird Sisters say."

"*Macbeth*," I observed. We were studying it in class at the time.

"Yes, that play explains a lot, as I think you will come to appreciate."

"Whatever it was, can I ask why you left the door unlocked? Just out of curiosity? What if I was the principal or the janitor or something?" I asked.

"Good question, my darling boy. It was mere carelessness. I was so excited to initiate Samantha, I didn't take the normal precautions. Like making sure the door was locked."

"Initiate?"

"Yes, indeed. What you saw was a very sacred ritual. Have you ever heard of 'Sexual Magic?'"

"Is that a book?"

"Ha, no. It's a method of getting in touch with all the powerful forces in the universe through your sexual energies."

"I see," I said.

"Something you should know about me: I'm a witch, Lance."

"Ah, I-um, wow. Really?"

"Yes, I am a witch. Does that freak you out?"

"Kind of, yeah. But whatever. What were you doing with Samantha?"

"Well, Samantha Coventry has a great interest in witchcraft. I recognized the latent power in her from the first day of school, but I had to wait for her to recognize me as her mistress of initiation. That happened when we were looking at the first scene of *Macbeth* in class the other day. She saw the flame aura that surrounds all those endowed with the power of the elements. She came to me later that day and asked if what she was seeing and feeling was real, and I told her it was very real and that I'd been waiting for her to approach me. And then we arranged the ceremony you witnessed."

"So Samantha wasn't eating your, I mean, performing oral—"

"—She was beholding the fire within, Lance, which requires intense proximity," explained Ms. Cummings.

"I'm feeling kind of sick," I said, a wave of nausea cresting.

I looked at the desk in silence. A desk I'd been looking at everyday since September.

There was gang graffiti carved into the desk that said *Carnales*, the name of a Mexican gang, and *Satanas*, the name of a Filipino gang, and an elaborate Black Sabbath logo hand drawn in red marker.

I wanted to vomit or cry.

My dick felt like a pencil eraser.

"So, Lance," Ms. Cummings said.

"Yes, ma'am," I answered.

"Let's figure out a way to get you to keep this incident to yourself," she said.

"I don't know what to do," I said, near tears.

"Well, here's my proposal: you agree not to say anything to anybody, and I guarantee that you will be the JB representative to the oratorical contest. How's that?"

"I don't know," I said.

I was a little dizzy, too. I was seeing stars.

"You don't agree, and Miranda Savitch goes to the final round."

I looked steadfastly deskward.

"It's the pathway to fame, Lance. Public recognition for your efforts. I know you want that. All you have to do is promise not to tell anybody about the initiation ceremony with Samantha Coventry. The *L.A. Times* will be there at the final round. This is a big deal. Local TV stations will cover it on their news report. Ralph Story is the master of ceremonies. See how it works?"

"Winners can't be choosers, in other words," I said.

"Welcome to the wilderness of sin, Mr. Atlas. Do we have a deal?"

I put my head down.

"OK, how's this: not only will you be the JB representative to the oratorical contest, but I'll also see to it that you are master of ceremonies for the graduation banquet."

I continued to writhe.

I did want both of those gigs though.

"I have the power to give you power. Do we have a deal?"

"I have to think about it," I said.

"You know you want the glory, Lance," Ms. Cummings said imploringly as I got up to go. "Oh, and Lance?"

"Yeah?" I said from the doorway.

"If your girlfriend is part of this moral equation you're working out in your soul, just remember what I told you before: she isn't worth it," Ms. Cummings said with glacial plainness.

I left the room to woozy images from *Tommy*, one of those moments where a random work of art feels directly addressed to one's own life.

You didn't hear it, you didn't see it

You won't say nothing to no one ever in your life

You never heard it, how absurd it all seems

Without any proof

You didn't hear it, you didn't see it

You never heard it, not a word of it

You won't say nothing to no one

Never tell a soul what you know is the truth

Samantha Coventry's offer was pretty much irrelevant.

I knew I'd never really take her up on it.

Mostly 'cause I wouldn't know how to.

What would I do, go up to her and say, "Um, I'd like that blowjob now?"

Although I ended up jacking off quite a few times to that scenario, the reality was I'd never collect on that one.

Rather than face the decision rationally and do the right thing, I left it up to libidinous kismet:

That night while masturbating I allowed myself to go back and forth between Miranda and Ms. Cummings, and whomever I was thinking about when I shipped my parcel would benefit from my decision.

If I was looking at Miranda's face in the blissful instant I'd tell the principal what I saw happening, and Miranda would go to the final round and Ms. Cummings would face the professional consequences.

If Ms. Cummings was that night's phantasm, I'd keep my mouth shut, and I'd be the contestant in question and the emcee at the graduation banquet.

Once more into their breeches . . .

The next day in Ms. Cummings's class, also the day of the speech showdown between me and Miranda, we were looking at some passages from *Macbeth,* and, dang, dude, Ms. Cummings was choosing shit that was just way too pointed directly at me to be accidental.

"You know there are some people who feel that the actor and businessman named William Shakespeare didn't really write the plays, that they were actually written by someone—or even a group of people—far more educated than he was," Ms. Cummings brought up in class.

"Like who?" Arabella Mayflower asked.

"Oh, there are lots of theories," Ms. Cummings said, "and I don't really buy most of them. I like to think that miracles happen, that a brilliant boy with an 8th Grade education would grow up to write the greatest literature in the English language. On the other hand, I also understand how somebody like Shakespeare might be willing to engage a bit of dishonesty in order to attain wealth and fame."

"So, if Shakespeare didn't write Shakespeare's plays, who wrote them?" Claire asked.

"Well, like I said, I don't really subscribe to any of the theories. But if I had to pick one, I'd say the theory that Christopher Marlowe wrote the plays is the one that makes the most sense artistically."

"Who's Marlowe?" Arabella asked.

"Marlowe was a playwright the exact same age as Shakespeare but who in his 20s was already writing magnificent plays."

"Like what?" Miranda Savitch asked.

"Well, probably his best known play is *Dr. Faustus*," Ms. Cummings said.

"I thought Thomas Mann wrote *Dr. Faustus*," I said, remembering the book Dolly's dad had been reading.

"Ah, thank you, Lance. Yes, Thomas Mann did write a novel called *Dr. Faustus*. But the Faust legend has been told and re-told by many."

"*Phantom of the Paradise!*" Claude Moss yelled out.

"BEEF!" several other guys shouted.

"*I know drug real from real real!*" said Gus Lagniappe to much tittering.

"The most famous story about this character is the play, or actually more of a poem, *Faust*, by Johann Wolfgang von Goethe. Lance and Miranda know all about Goethe, right?" Ms. Cummings said, looking at both of us, but especially at me. "But anyway, Christopher Marlowe wrote *Dr. Faustus* when he was only 25 years old, when Shakespeare wasn't really writing anything brilliant, but then Marlowe ended up in a bit of trouble with the British crown and was killed at the age of 29, under mysterious circumstances, after which William Shakespeare really came into his own as the greatest writer in our language."

"So Marlowe faked his own death?" asked Miranda.

"That's the theory, yes, he faked his own death and went into hiding and paid his friend, the actor and theatre owner William Shakespeare, to put his name on the plays Marlowe was writing and to keep Marlowe's hoax a secret and never tell a soul."

"You think that's really what happened?" asked Sharon Rose.

"No, actually, I don't," said Ms. Cummings, "But it's an interesting theory nevertheless. And I certainly know that if it were so, somebody like William Shakespeare would be capable of selling out his name for money and fame or whatever. I think we're all capable of that. It's a matter of making up your mind and deciding what sorts of secrets and consequences you can live with," said Ms. Cummings, looking squarely in my direction, beads of sweat gathering at her temples.

Even her sweat was sexy.

Reading the part of Lady Macbeth that day, Ms. Cummings directed her words and glances at me. Every time she'd get to a cluster of lines that were pertinent to my agonizing decision she'd take a second to look my way:

"*Yet do I fear thy nature/It is too full o' the milk of human kindness/To catch the nearest way*," she read, pausing to make eye contact, and then, "*. . . thou wouldst be great;/Art not without ambition, but without/The illness should attend it: what thou wouldst highly,/That wouldst thou holily.*"

She paced the room.

"And what does she mean when she says that Macbeth *'wouldst not play false,/And yet wouldst wrongly win'* . . . ?" she asked the class.

"He wants what he doesn't deserve but won't cheat to get it?" asked Arabella Mayflower.

"Good, Bella, yes," answered Ms. Cummings.

By this time she was standing in front of my desk, impassioned, quoting, "*. . . Hie thee hither,/That I may pour my spirits in thine ear;/And chastise with the valour of my tongue/All that impedes thee from the final round.*"

"Excuse me, Ms. Cummings," Miranda interrupted, "it says 'golden round' in my book."

"Oh yes, dear, of course, how careless, *'impedes thee from the golden round,'* that's correct, good catch." Ms. Cummings said.

After school, Miranda and I stood outside Ms. Cummings' room waiting for our session to begin. Ms. Cummings emerged from her room and said, "I need to talk to Lance before we start. Excuse us a minute, Miranda?"

I entered the room and again took my assigned seat.

"So, Lance Atlas, screw your courage to the sticking place. Have you decided?" Ms. Cummings asked me.

"I think so," I said.

"And? You going to let I dare not wait upon I would?"

"I will keep the incident to myself," I said, a new recruit to Satan's windmill.

"Excellent decision. I had a feeling you might be that way inclined," said Ms. Cummings, relieved, "You want the ornament of life, and so you shall have it, my love. Good for you. Bring Miranda in and let's get this formality over with."

"What did she want to talk to you about?" Miranda asked when I went into the hall to fetch her.

"*Be innocent of the knowledge, dearest chuck,*" I took my place in the evil continuum and escorted her into the room.

I gave my speech first, a 5 minute piece of space-junk made even less compelling by the fact that I already knew I was going to win. I talked about how within even the deepest darkness there's always light to be found. "I am reminded of a quote from *The Little Prince*," I said, looking at Miranda, whose eyebrows suddenly rose, "*What makes the desert beautiful is that somewhere it hides a well.*" I gave a speech that was, I would learn at the city finals, in fact, a totally backwards and wrong understanding of Goethe's maxim. "What keeps us striving to find the light within the darkness is hope," I said. It sounded like something Miranda would write, but I was applying it in a perfectly wrong way.

And then, much to my puzzlement, Miranda's speech sounded like something I'd write, except her speech was on target. She talked about how the most righteous are sometimes the most sinful, the shadows that are deepest, hiding in the bright lights of virtue. She quoted Shakespeare twice—"*The devil hath power to assume a pleasing shape*" and "*Look like the innocent flower, but be the serpent under't*"—and examined public hypocrisy, bringing up Richard Nixon and the other Republican turds in the Watergate scandal who painted themselves as patriots and Warriors For The Good but who were ripping off the country and trying to cover it all up. It was a talk about false idols. Essentially, she gave a Mirandafied version of my bar mitzvah speech, albeit far more amazing.

But the fix was in. The gig was rigged.

When Ms. Cummings announced her decision, that I, Lance Atlas, would represent John Burroughs Jr. High in the final round of the L.A.M.R.S. oratorical contest, I couldn't decipher Miranda's expression.

"Congratulations," she said to me, half-heartedly.

I felt like the heel of a cloven foot.

We left the building together. I unlocked my bicycle and walked her to the bus stop.

"Your speech was so much better than mine," I said.

"You know I totally stole all my ideas from you," Miranda confessed, "I feel infinitely guilty about that."

"Well, I felt guilty for totally stealing your *Little Prince* quote. I built my whole speech on your ideas. So, you know. We're all guilty of something."

"You won fair and square," Miranda said with the most endearing and painful innocence, even though I could also tell she knew her speech was better.

"*To know my deed, 'twere best not know myself*," I said.

"Huh?" she asked.

I waved her off.

"*Macbeth*," I said.

The L.A.M.R.S. oratorical contest took place at a Masonic Lodge on some generic street in West. L.A. 30 junior high schools sent contestants, and of those 30, I came in 30th.

Afterward, one of the judges approached me and told me I had gotten the Goethe quote wrong, that I had kind of turned it around backwards.

"But I like what you were saying about hope," he said, "I wish it were true."

Miranda attended the contest. She wore a dress. For the first time since my Bar Mitzvah I think.

"I only showed up in case you got sick or something," she said.

"I got the topic all wrong," I said, "Your speech was so much better. You would've won tonight."

"Aw, hell no I wun't have won. That guy who won totally wrapped himself in the flag."

"Dang, dude, when he said the Pledge of Allegiance at the end? Putting his hand over hie heart? Dang, dude. Flagrant."

"Barfaroni, yeah," Miranda answered, "So just imagine me talking bad about Nixon and the Republicans. No way I would've won."

After Miranda left, Ms. Cummings came up to me to commiserate.

"I thought you'd score higher, but they were hard-asses," she said.

"I wish you had clued me into how wrong I was about the topic."

"Hey, you wanted to be here and I got you here. I'm keeping up my end of the deal. You stay cool with yours,'K? You didn't see or hear anything, right?"

"Don't worry, Ms. Cummings. Not that I don't feel guilty about betraying Miranda like that."

"*What's done cannot be undone.*"

"Well, I feel icky about it."

"*Hell is murky!*" she quoted again, coming closer and whispering in my ear, "Get used to it."

Then Ms. Virginia Cummings kissed me on the mouth, with fire and intention, providing me with inestimable fodder for nights to come.

I felt like I was playing around in quicksand.

As the school year wound down, Miranda and I were friendly but not close.

She did ask me to sign her yearbook, and I asked her to sign mine.

But I didn't read what she wrote right away.

I'd decided that I wasn't going to look at any of my yearbook signatures until school was out.

A final formal punctuation to my years at John Burroughs.

A ceremonial farewell.

Graduation took place in the morning, and to celebrate there was a pool party at Dolly's house afterward.

At the party, I divided my time equally between being the house DJ (trading off with Sandy Clay), playing piano in Dolly's living room, and hanging out with the crowd by the pool.

Impromptu DJ'ing at a party was always a fun challenge because you had to work with the records available at whoever's house.

Sandy and I created a nice mix as a party soundtrack, music that would add atmosphere to the various activities of swimmers and schmoozers and smoochers and eaters and even a couple of sleepers.

Sandy and I took turns weaving cuts from *The Best of Bread*, *Aladdin Sane*, *Zeppelin IV*, *Pretzel Logic*, *Gorilla*, and tons from Elton John's new *Captain Fantastic and the Brown Dirt Cowboy* album.

We did our best with what we had.

We conjured the dark spirits of 1975 and commanded their presence in the air.

June gloom hung an amorphous gray haze overhead.

"We live in a crazy place," Leonard Ferris mused as he stood, in a speedo, on the back porch, looking at his daughter and her friends hanging by the pool, "I mean, June is cooler than October? What *is* L.A.?"

Sandy started spinning the song "Ain't No Way To Treat A Lady" by Helen Reddy which made all the guys giggle.

"Soundtrack of your next blowjob," Whit joked to Gus.

"Aw, that's dog dude," said Oliver Gelding.

"Da-a-a-ng!" Claude Moss choked on his own laughter, "Flagrant."

I saw Miranda sort of reclining on a lounge chair alone, and on whatever whim I decided to join her.

"Miranda Savitch," I said as I sat down next to her, and without even thinking about it I put my left arm around her. She kept her right arm tight against her body, definitely not touching back.

Dolly came skipping over to us thus entwined.

"Oh, oh, let me get a picture of the two lovebirds kissing!" she said, holding up her camera.

Sandy had put Patti LaBelle's "Lady Maramalade" on the record player, and so all the nerdy white kids had to stop what they were doing to sing along with the chorus, "*Voulez-vous couchez avec moi ce soir?*" and feel naughty.

"Dude, that's like 'let's fuck' in French," said Whitman Rust.

"It means, 'Do you want to sleep with me tonight?'" Miranda Savitch corrected him.

"Why, Miss Miranda," I turned it to joke, "that ain't no way for a lady to talk."

"Come on! Lance and Mandy. Kissy kissy! Right now!" repeated Dolly.

"*You may kiss me if you like,*" Miranda quoted Estella, looking away.

"Now where have I heard that before?" I said as I cupped the back of Miranda's head and pulled it toward me while holding the left side of her face with my right hand.

Our closed lips touched for a long moment, like a movie kiss, like a clueless duet on the Lawrence Welk Show, like a sibling reunion, like a pair of diplomats, a pose for posterity.

Nevertheless, my pals went on their predictable razzing binge.

"Solly no beava!" whooped Claude Moss.

"Don't eat that parsley!" Gus Lagniappe warned.

"SCHLITZ!" yelped Whit, making the six-pack sign.

"Soylent Green, baby!" Oliver Gelding grabbed the air.

And amid the taunts, Sandy Clay, in the DJ chair, uttered one of those dreaded suggestions, "The music is right, and the feeling is right, and the hour is right, and the fuel is right for a game of 7 Minutes In Heaven, right here on K-FUCK radio," and the intro to "Stairway To Heaven" began to emanate.

"Lance and Mandy, you first!" said Dolly, yanking both of us from the chair and leading us into the garage where a loft had been built by Leonard for Dolly and her brother to use.

7 Minutes In Heaven was an adolescent make-out game invented in like caveman days as a way for two teens to sit in the dark and look at each other or avoid looking at each other.

The idea was that for 7 minutes you'd make out or do whatever together, but the reality was most people didn't do anything except sit there in the dark.

In our crowd, the song "Stairway To Heaven" was the accompaniment, it was maintained because of the length.

But I was always fascinated by how closely the song followed the pattern of sexual excitement and release, or at least what I knew of the process from my solo jaunts.

From the slow acoustic opening, the onset of oomph, to the more insistent middle section emulating the rhythm of the wild thing, then the psychedelic transition to the raging rock and roll finale, the one-way street to imageless oblivion, and, at the very end, a return to the quietness of creation, back to that sublime garden.

I sat on a rocking chair in the loft and Miranda without prompting sat crosswise on my lap.

Through her bikini bottom I could feel her ass and stuff right up against the sprouting boner lodged in my Levi's cut-offs.

Miranda must've felt the swelling, as she moved her bottom in squirmy attempts either to turn me on or to avoid feeling the cockhardness rubbing on her sex.

Our mouths did not meet.

We merely moved in subtle avoidance of each other through the opening of "Stairway to Heaven."

But the more she shifted her ass the closer to unavoidable fruition I edged.

I tried to stay as still as I could so I wouldn't spill.

Don't make a move

"This feels really weird," Miranda said, continuing to maneuver herself, and I sensed how uncomfortable she must've been atop the sapling in my pants trying to break ground. "But, um . . . I."

"I-uh, mmm," I started to say when Miranda put her arms around me and put her lips on mine hard enough to feel the teeth and jawbone, and as she did so she turned to straddle me just enough for my arching boner to feel the whole softness of her vulva straight on through her bikini bottom, my hardness sort of wedged up against her, dang, dude, and upon that impact I shot a wad in my jeans like the boy I'd always be.

I tried to act with all pre-ejaculatory passion, but with loss of essence and my attempt to keep my now moistened crotch from her detection, the intensity of my clutch began to wane, flop sweat broke out on my forehead, and even if she couldn't sense the wetness she definitely felt my diminished force and quickly disengaged her mouth from mine before it became anything resembling a lover's kiss.

She looked at me questioningly and shrugged, slowly rose and left me in the loft alone.

A moment later, I heard Gus and Whit outside.

"Dang, dude, Lance didn't even make it to *bustle in your hedgerow*!" said Gus.

"Minute Man Service, Minute Man Service," added Whit.

Dolly came in looking for me.

"Lance? What happened? You still had like 4 minutes left."

"I had a little accident," I said, covering my crotch, sitting there with no shirt and unpresentable Levi's, "I don't really know what to do."

Dolly got my predicament and with not a sign of giggle or ridicule, said "Carry me out and jump in the pool with me; maybe nobody will see."

I stood up and hoisted a bikini-clad Dolly Ferris fireman style over my shoulder, the side of her ass against my face, cheek to cheek as it were, making sure her feet covered my spillage, and emerged from the garage roaring all caveman and shit.

I ran into the pool holding onto Dolly as we splashed amid the laughter.

She put her arms around me, and her large breasts pressed against my bare chest through her bikini top.

I began moving my hands toward them.

She gently pushed them away.

"Be good," she played.

"Thanks for the save," I said as we rolled around in the water.

"Count on it," Dolly whispered back.

Unfortunately, as clever as Dolly's scheme was, my gun-jumping hadn't escaped the notice of my overlords.

Gus and Whit called me over to the side of the pool.

"Hey, Mr. Creamjeans, come here," said Whit, gesturing me hither. I swam over to them, my cut-offs now heavy with the drenching.

"See what happens when you plant your crops before the ground has been properly tilled, sodbuster?" asked Gus.

"Lancelot Lump, No Pump Chump," Whit sang, "Dang, dude, you are the gayest fucking golita in the hemisphere."

"Fagosaurus Rex," added Gus.

I didn't see Miranda anywhere.

"Mandy left a couple of minutes ago," Arabella Mayflower told me like I'd blown it again.

Everybody was going to see the movie *Jaws* that first Saturday after graduation, but I didn't think I could handle the inevitable "Mr. Creamjeans" and "Lancelot Lump, No Pump Chump" and "Minute Man Service" jokes, and plus I'd have to see Miranda, a prospect which paralyzed me with inadequacy and embarrassment.

Instead of going to see *Jaws* with the group, I rode my bike over to the Tar Pits and read my yearbook signatures.

Like in 8th Grade, there were the requisite number of "Good Luck with Miranda" messages, which, following the 3 Minutes in Hell of the day before, only served to accentuate my humiliation.

At last, when I got to the back page of my yearbook, I saw Miranda's entry, written a couple of days before the party:

Lance,

I should have signed this last year. I really don't know why I didn't. I was going to write 'Good Luck with Miranda,' I just never got the courage. In the past year I really grew up some, and I'm glad you were part of my experience. It may sound stupid but it's serious, and if you ever want to share any more experiences, well . . . When I think of what never happened it aggravates me and makes me sad in a weird way. I'm just glad we're friends and hope we always will be.

Call me—I hope you still have my number.

Love Always (seriously),

Miranda

p.s. I hope you could figure out who wrote this already

A few yards off, near the Japanese footbridge, a bubbling crude was oozing up from below the surface of the earth onto the grass, not black gold, not Texas tea, not made from fossils but maker of fossils, a gurgle and belch and hiss of trapped gasses, an ancient presence, the smell of Los Angeles.

I breathed deep the gathering gloom.

Under the overcast sky, on the north bank of the little stream—my friend and mentor, all-wise measure of timelessness—I read Miranda's message again, trying to decide which is right and which is an illusion, hearing her rasp the words in eternal circular return—*When I think of what never happened it aggravates me and makes me sad in a weird way*—and wishing she were sitting next to me creekside at the Tar Pits, wallowing in motionlessness, grooving on love, talking about cool shit.

Mid-wish, I felt something like the barrel of a gun pressing against the back of my head.

I stiffened.

"Don't make a move," the voice said.

It was Gus Lagniappe. He'd foregone the *Jaws* outing to come hang out with me.

I turned around to see him unarmed and laughing and pointing his finger-pistol at me, dancing in the grass and making fun of my fear.

"Aaaah-ha, loser . . . You thought it was real . . ."

My Anywhere Girl Is A Geranium

1

When I look into the daylight sky I see infinite creatures of light swimming in the midst of the firmament, visible against the blue, like caterpillars or tadpoles or something otherwise larval, frenetic, spermy, sizzling with rhythm, aglow like metal smithed.

They squirm all over, on view anywhere, in the far sky, middle sky, near sky, air-on-eyeballs sky.

On my back among the Tar Pits, breathing the creatures as I see them, I observe the frenzy as a basis of meditation.

Divine choreography of angels or random energy?

Their dance is every dance and then some.

Those shifting vermicularities, I know not what they make or mean.

Beside a bubbling brook of tar that oozes ancientness (not moving so much as quivering), I stay prone to remembering, in particular remembering, through the party drug haze of last night, a breezy-warm afternoon in Malibu, four years ago. Summer of 1975.

I lay then as I lie now, on supine display, sprawled across pincushion crabgrass, hands ragged, toes wriggling, gasping for air, eyelid-movies like blossoms floating across my inner vision, a pressure on my chest bearing down like a bully demanding submission, my heart in a panic and arrhythmic as Jerusalem, hovering between verdure and azure, dipped in the river and ready for revelation.

"Son?" a voice asked, "Are you OK, son?" I opened my eyes to a circle of faces staring down at me, a halo of bent sunlight behind them.

The one who spoke was Coach Wooden, the Godfather.

"Get the wind knocked out of you a little bit?" he continued.

"Nyeah, I just . . . ran out of breath . . . while I was running . . . I dunno," I labored to say.

Although I'd been at John Wooden Basketball Camp all week, this was the first time I'd seen Coach Wooden since the opening session. He didn't interact with us much, but that day he was working with various teams on the outdoor courts, interrupting their scrimmages with instruction.

We had been playing a full-court scrimmage, my team against a much taller and stronger team.

On this one fast-break, I felt my chest tighten suddenly, followed by an equally swift dizzy brightness, and I fell to the ground.

I was aware, though barely, of being carried onto nearby grass.

My eyes remained closed until Coach spoke.

My mind hovered on the event horizon.

A premonition of death.

"Well, you're going to sit the rest of this scrimmage out. When you're comfortable enough, walk back to the dorms and rest. I think the nurse should have a look at you," he said.

"No no, I'm fine," I insisted.

Coach Wooden paused, looking into my eyes. "Well, if you're feeling better tomorrow you can play," he said as he patted my head and then my chest.

"OK, Coach," I said, "thank you."

"Very good," Wooden said and then turned his attention back to the courts.

I lay then as I lie now, though not here among the Tar Pits, rather on a grassy knoll next to the outdoor courts on the Malibu campus of Pepperdine University, the yearly locale of Coach Wooden's camp.

I was 14.

It was the first time I'd felt anything like the breathless vertigo that had just felled me.

Throughout my childhood I'd experienced episodes when my heartbeat would waver erratically, and the fluttering felt weird, but never had I gone white and then black and collapsed like that.

Regaining normal breath, I stood warily, fearing another sudden attack, and slowly walked a roundabout route back to the dorms, stopping to rest on an expansive hillside that overlooked the Pacific Ocean.

From where I sat, the sea was spread out in perfect stillness almost like on a postcard.

Lavender geraniums grew along one edge of the Pepperdine front lawn.

"Butterflies," I thought to myself, recognizing the flowers from our backyard.

My mom was into geraniums in a major way, butterfly geraniums especially.

Purple flowed out of myriad terra cotta pots placed all around the patio at our house.

I love the phrase 'butterfly geranium,' the color of its cadence, the calmness of its beauty, like a fantasy of Miranda.

When I learned about the existence of an insect called a 'geranium butterfly,' I thought about how perfect it'd be to see a geranium butterfly sitting on a butterfly geranium.

The words made flesh.

Several butterflies did flit about the geraniums and the milkweed, some landing on flowers, some on leaves, a couple of yellow and black swallowtails, a few monarchs looking like a deck of cards, one or two cabbage whites.

Were they laying eggs or sucking up nectar?

I couldn't tell.

Maybe both.

Later in the summer their offspring would come out munching.

Caterpillars hatch on the plant they're born to eat.

They destroy that which sustains them.

A fundamental lesson in the nature of reality.

Gazing at the motionless ocean, following the irregular patterns of butterfly flight along the grassy slope, I recalled my most recent encounter with Miranda Savitch a couple of weeks before coming to camp.

Claude Moss and I had taken the Wilshire RTD to Ocean Ave. and then walked down the California Incline, and directly across PCH, via footbridge, to Sorrento Beach, Lifeguard Station 8, our favorite location for body surfing, girl watching, and long hours of idle freedom.

The waves were big enough to ride but not so big they'd drown you, the burgers and fries at the Sorrento Grill were audaciously greasy, the titties were spilling out and jiggling, the asses in dazzling variety were asway, the radios were tuned to KMET, the summer felt eternal.

I was on my back, feeling empty and light, almost levitating, under the sun, as per usual looking up at the wormy wayward angels locked in their cosmic jitterbug amid the blue-gray haze above.

Claude sat ogling the flesh offerings all about us, his flabby abdomen attracting no invitations to partake.

"Dang, dude, there's Dolly Ferris and Miranda Savitch," Claude half-cackled, "Looking flagrantly foxy, I must say. And . . . dude . . . they are upon us."

I felt the recurring twinge my heart makes at any mention of Miranda's name and raised my head enough to see Miranda and Dolly come walking up in identical Bjorn Borg t-shirts over bikinis and matching flip-flops.

Their sunglasses were different though.

Dolly wore big round glam-rock shades with pink frames, and Miranda sported black pointy-framed sunglasses, the kind Lucy Ricardo might wear if she wore sunglasses.

"Hey, how's it going?" Dolly shouted to us as they approached.

Miranda startled me kneeling down at my side and blocking the sun.

"Aren't you a specimen," she said, waiting out the initial discomfort—we hadn't spoken since the incident in Dolly's loft—until finally adding, "Hi, Lance."

"Miranda Savitch. Hi," I croaked out.

She smelled of coconut suntan lotion.

"Mandy and I are walking to the pier. Wanna come?" Dolly suggested.

"Totally," said Claude, accepting for both of us.

I slipped my sandy feet, sockless, into seam-split Adidas and joined the stroll.

"Remember making the film for Barrows's class here last Christmas vacation?" Claude brought up.

"Yeah, for sure," Dolly said wistfully, catching my eye.

She seemed to share the recollection: The rubdown, the chase to the pier, the bumper cars, the merry-go-round, Claude's heroic leap off the pier into trash-ridden waters below, the movie kiss.

The seedy, sleazy wonderland of the Santa Monica Pier was in full summer commotion, a playground for vagrant fishermen, surfers done for the day, panhandlers, rotund tourists, Jesus-freaks with pamphlets and megaphones, and Samohi kids on skateboards looking for distractions.

The girls wanted to get something to drink at the cotton candy stand.

"They make the best milkshakes," Miranda said.

"At the cotton candy stand?" I asked.

"Mmhm. Share a milkshake with me?"

"Yeah, sure, I guess," I said.

"Strawberry?"

"Of course."

"Righteous," she smiled, "my treat."

Righteous was a new word for her. Where did she learn it?

In addition to the shake she grabbed two straws, handing one to me.

"You know, cooties," she explained.

"Thank you for thinking of my health," I said.

"I was thinking of my own health, dorkus. Boys are the ones who have cooties."

"Yeah, boys got cooties and girls got coochies," yucked Claude.

"Claude, please," Dolly complained.

"That's a Bozo No-No," I joked.

"Cram it, clown!" Claude answered back on cue, then, shifting focus, "I heard Wilt Chamberlain plays volleyball down at Station 17 on the other side of the pier. We should go see if he's there."

"Wilt," I said, "yeah, we have to."

We looked longingly at both ladies.

"It's Wilt," we implored, waiting, as if this were reason enough, "Only guy ever to score 100 points in a game?"

Finally they acquiesced, shrugging and whispering to each other, "Who's Wilt Chamberlain?"

They'd never heard of Wilt Chamberlain.

Dang, dude. Girls.

We crossed to the south side of the pier, between the merry-go-round and the amusement park, and took the stairs down to where Wilt was indeed playing volleyball at Station 17.

Claude was right.

A crowd of fans and fellow players cheered the big man.

He wasn't in the NBA anymore but still commanded a devoted following on the sand.

Miranda and I found a spot in the shade of the pier, apart from Dolly and Claude, to sit and drink our strawberry milkshake, nose to nose, alternately making and avoiding eye contact.

After we finished off the milkshake, Miranda looked at the sand for a few moments then lay on her back, smiling her crooked smile.

I joined her.

The crash of surf battled for prominence with the traffic sounds (sometimes also crashing) on PCH.

Side by side we scanned the heavens.

"Do you see like squirmy wormy things when you look at the sky?" I asked.

"Um . . . no . . ." she seemed to find that weird, "I see the sky," she said matter-of-factly.

"When I look at the sky I see all these doohickies moving around each other with this very intense energy. But they never collide."

"They want to touch each other but feel like they can't," Miranda said.

"Yeahzackly," I said, "That's what doohickies do. So you see them?"

"No," Miranda said, sharing an inside joke with herself.

"Sometimes I think they're angels," I said.

"You should get your eyes checked," Miranda said. "I don't think you're supposed to be seeing doohickies in the sky."

"Well maybe they're more like molecules or atoms."

"I still think you're not supposed to be seeing things in the sky. The sky is nothing but . . . sky."

"Sometimes I feel like I could touch them, but when I reach out they're always too far away. Where does the sky start anyway?" I said.

"The sky starts right here. You're in the sky. You're breathing it. It's not this far away thing," Miranda Savitch said to me.

"It's not a thing at all, right?" I said.

"Zackly."

"It's a direction."

"There ya go," she agreed.

"But what direction is it?" I asked, making one of my patently lame attempts at flirtation.

"Infinity direction," she chided in mock annoyance and added, "Isn't infinity the coolest word?"

"Totally. I remember the first time my father told me about infinity. We were at a Dodger game, and I asked him how far the foul line extends, and he said it goes to infinity. I asked him what infinity was, and he said 'Forever, but in space rather than in time.' I didn't understand what he meant back then. I still kinda don't, actually. I remember he pointed up to the sky and said those stars up there might have burned out a million years ago, but their light keeps traveling, outward in all directions. Forever. Even though the star's not there anymore. I couldn't sleep for a few weeks after that."

"Afraid of infinity?" Miranda asked.

"No, I wasn't afraid. Fascinated more like. In some ways I just loved the word and liked saying it to myself. But also the meaning, the idea, was so much to think about, and I would get all excited like I wanted to go outside and just look at the infinity of the sky. That's when I really got into stargazing. I asked for a telescope for Chanukah that year."

Miranda started dropping bits of sand on my stomach as we spoke.

"Like sands through the hourglass so are the days of our lives," she said in a gravelly voice that sounded kind of like Richard Nixon on helium or maybe Walter Cronkite. "My mother watches that soap opera everyday. I don't get soap operas. They give me a headache after about 5 minutes."

"My dad also said," I continued, ignoring her own lame flirtatiousness, "'Other eyes on other planets even farther from that star might see that same light a million years from now. Now that's what I mean by infinity.' I get dizzy when I think of that stuff too much."

"Your dad sounds cool."

"He can be. Another thing he always says: 'God is dead but the creation lives on.'"

"Dang," she said, closing her eyes. "My dad told me recently this cool story by a Chinese philosopher—I can't remember his name—not Confucius . . . anyway the story is about a guy who goes to sleep and dreams he's a butterfly, and when he wakes up he's not sure if he's a man who just dreamed he was a butterfly, or if he's now a butterfly dreaming he's a man. I was, like, whoa," Miranda said.

"Oh, I know that story sort of. I heard it on a *Kung Fu* episode. I still remember it. Grasshopper was reading it in a scroll."

"Grasshopper?"

"Kwai Chang Caine. The main character. When he's a little kid living at the Shaolin Temple."

"I never watched *Kung Fu*."

"Oh, dang, dude, *Kung Fu* is amazing. They show reruns on Channel 5. You should watch. You would like it."

"I'll have to do that," Miranda said. She continued to drop sand on me. My bellybutton was full.

"So, getting into any trouble this summer?" I rolled over onto my side, letting the sand fall off, and sort of poked her shoulder.

Her skin was soft.

I propped my head on my fist and looked at her.

I wanted to touch her breasts through her t-shirt.

"I have the right to remain silent," said Miranda, turning her head in my direction, locking me into magnetic eye contact.

I was bristling to jump her mouth yet feared the commencement of all that follows a kiss, primarily the ever dilemma of what to do next.

"Dude!" Claude's voice called out from above, "Come on, we're heading back to 8!"

Mildly irked but accepting the inevitable, Miranda and I joined Claude and Dolly up on the pier when Claude, who had been the most anxious to head back, said, "I wanna take a whiz here before we go. The bathroom at 8 smells like infected smegma."

"Lovely," said Dolly.

Miranda offered the more succinct, "Ew."

Waiting for Claude, the three of us stood at the rail of the pier looking north up the coast.

Miranda was on my right. Dolly was on my left. While they gabbed and gossiped across me, Dolly hooked her right foot around my left ankle, all the while chattering with Miranda.

And just to stoke the awkwardness, Dolly called me a couple of days later with an offer.

"I've got tickets to go see James Taylor tonight at the Amphitheatre and was wondering if you'd also be into going?" she said.

"Yeah, sure. Cool," I said. Was this a date? I didn't know. "Can I come over early and play your piano?"

"You can come over early and do anything you want," Dolly said. "Bring your trunks; we can hang in the pool before the concert."

My mom drove me over to Dolly's house later that afternoon.

I wanted to play their Steinway, but first we floated around in the pool for a while because, well, that's what she wanted to do, and my dad told me once that the best way to get along with a girl is to do whatever she wants you to do and let her do whatever she wants. So I did.

Mid-swim Dolly piggybacked onto me and said, "Take me for a ride somewhere."

I moved slowly around the shallow end, enjoying the feel of Dolly's body against mine.

She had her arms around my neck.

I thought about reaching back to hold her, but I realized my hands would touch her ass, and I didn't know if that was cool or not. And if it was, then what? So I didn't.

"How come we're not reading a book together this summer?" Dolly asked, still riding. "*Dracula* was neat last year, I loved doing that."

I shrugged, "Dunno."

"Reading anything good right now?"

"*The Collector*. It's pretty good, really creepy though," I said.

"What's it about?"

"A guy who's obsessed with this girl and kidnaps her and keeps her locked in the basement of this house in the middle of nowhere."

"Does he rape her?"

"No, he doesn't touch her. He feels like he can't. He just keeps her in his basement and tries to get her to fall in love with him."

"That *is* creepy."

"Yeah. He's into collecting butterflies. He treats her like one of his specimens."

Dolly's arms gripped a little tighter, and she moved her mouth right up against my left ear.

"Go faster," she urged, digging her heels into my thighs.

Trying to oblige I moved just slightly too far into the deep end, where the pool bottom slopes down suddenly, and lost my footing.

Dolly let go as I slipped backwards, and we found ourselves splashing to stay afloat in the deep end. She shrieked as we tumbled apart, purposely forcing water at my face.

I grabbed her by the wrists and we both sank beneath the surface, bubbles floating from our mouths.

I could tell Dolly was shouting something, I could hear a tinny noise through the water, but I was unable to decipher.

When we went back to the surface, she wouldn't tell me what she had said. "Nuh-uh, if you can't figure it out then you're not supposed to know," was all she offered wading toward the steps in the shallow end.

"Dry me off," she said and handed me her towel as we emerged from the pool.

I began toweling her back, pausing when I got to her ass and not really knowing what to do, pass over quickly or linger.

I passed over quickly, feeling for a moment its softness through the bikini bottom.

When I got to her heels, she turned around, and I made my way up the front of her body, bypassing her crotch (because, well, dang, dude, no way), lingering at the belly, stalling while trying to figure out how to handle her breasts, all voluptuous and ranging a bit beyond the confines.

As I applied the towel to her bosom, balkingly, at war with my natural reticence, she briefly prevented me from pulling away, but I got too embarrassed and pushed the towel into her face.

"We should change and get ready to go," Dolly said, throwing the towel back into my face. "Here, dry off. My parents will want to head out soon, I'm sure." Dolly went upstairs to change.

Dolly's parents were going to drop us off at the Amphitheatre and then go to a concert at the Hollywood Bowl, picking us up afterward.

I changed back into my clothes and waited for Dolly and her parents to get ready.

Sitting at the piano, playing a melody I had been working on at home, I wondered if the tune would end up being a song about Miranda, all of it muddled up with thoughts of Dolly.

Dolly's father came downstairs first.

"Lance Atlas, hello," Leonard Ferris said, "sounds good. Very pretty."

"Thank you," I said, "it's a song I think I'm writing."

"*Think* you're writing?" he queried.

"Yeah, I'm not sure."

"Any books you *think* you're reading these days? Something good I hope?"

"*The Collector,*" I said.

"John Fowles?"

"Yeah."

"Excellent book. Isn't it a little grown up for you though? Are you understanding it?"

"I don't know. It's kind of creepy. Our English teacher last year Ms. Cummings gave it to me as a graduation present."

"Great book, but an odd choice for a 14-year-old. Your teacher gave it to

229

you?"

"I think it's 'cause she knew I was into butterflies."

"Well, that book isn't exactly about butterflies."

"The main character collects butterflies."

"Yes, that's true, but . . . oh, who cares, you're reading a fine piece of literature. That's what matters."

"What are you seeing at the Hollywood Bowl tonight?"

"People on a stage wearing tuxedos and gowns and playing instruments and moving their mouths."

I laughed and then corrected myself, "What are you *hearing* tonight?"

"Well, apropos of *The Collector*, arias from the opera *Madame Butterfly* among other things. Carl Jung calls that synchronicity. I just call it a coincidence," he smirked.

"Lotsa coincidences around," I said, unsure of how to respond exactly.

The Universal Amphitheatre was a mid-sized outdoor music venue.

I'd been once before.

When I was 12 my uncle took me to see the Grateful Dead there.

I thought it was horribly boring and fell asleep about halfway through.

I have since come to love the Grateful Dead.

One particular Dead show at the Shrine Auditorium last year—once I'd morphed into a secret freak ready for the exploration—transmogrified my brain cells.

But when I was 12 the Grateful Dead was nothing but a mushy endless blur of anonymous bilge. The music never stopped. Or so it felt.

The James Taylor concert, on the other hand, was a very tight evening of recognizable tunes.

As a budding composer trying to learn how to write songs, I listened and heard all kinds of memorable lessons that night about the various architectures of melody and the singability of words.

It was like a workshop for my novice chops.

Also, Taylor's band was crisp as shit—Leland Sklar on bass, Danny "Kootch" Kortchmar on guitar, Russ Kunkel on drums, Carly Simon came out and sang on a couple of tunes—and Taylor's own guitar playing was excellent in its precision and conciseness.

His voice was a very warm nest to cuddle up into also.

Dolly and I didn't do any cuddling though.

We didn't even hold hands.

I wasn't sure if it was a date or not, so I was reluctant in that regard, a reluctance exacerbated, of course, by my inherent fear and shame at being so drawn to her.

I wanted to touch her body.

I wanted to engage her attentions.

Dolly kept looking at me when she thought I wasn't looking then turned her attention back to the music when I didn't return the gaze.

I did the same, repeatedly, when she wasn't looking at me.

We shared this avoidance.

She was wearing a lavender halter top, jeans, and leather sandals.

I liked that halter top a lot.

I imagined my hand on her smooth back.

At her house after the concert, we sat in the den waiting for my dad to come pick me up.

"Oh, here, I got the pictures from my graduation party developed," she said, grabbing two packets of photographs in paper Thrifty Drug & Discount Store envelopes.

"Is Thrifty good?" I asked. "We get our pictures developed at the Sav-On in Town & Country and it takes forever."

"I like Thrifty 'cause I also get ice-cream when I go there. The best. The pictures usually take a week or so."

The 9th Grade graduation party at Dolly's house conjured up humiliating memories for me.

The elapsed weeks since had not dampened my discomfort despite feeling Miranda's ease at the beach a few days before.

"Oh, here's the one I took of you and Miranda kissing," Dolly said. "You can have it."

"No, that's yours."

"I don't want it," she said, giving it to me.

"I like this one better," I said, pointing to a different photo, "the one where we're just sitting by the pool. You can see Miranda's face."

"Still, huh?" Dolly asked, scrunching up her eyes and nose.

I shrugged.

"I don't get you two. Whatever. You can have this one too," she said of the second photo with a decided bittersweetness and put the rest of the pictures away.

I put both pictures in my back pocket.

And yet, surprisingly, despite my tacit admission of lingering passion for Miranda and Dolly's obvious resentment, when we moved into the portico outside her front door to await the imminent arrival of my father, we faced each other, and, without a thought or a balk, our faces met, our mouths melted together, our tongues entwined, we were frenching.

Dolly's teeth felt smooth, just recently released from orthodontia, and her mouth tasted like lemon-water.

It was a natural splendor.

Dolly caught hold of my animal.

I left for John Wooden Basketball Camp a couple of days later.

Back in my Pepperdine dorm room following my reverie on the lawn, I sat on the bed and sought music, but there was only AM radio available.

I listened, suffering through "Rhinestone Cowboy" and "Love Will Keep Us Together" to get to the awesome pathos of that summer's replacements for the previous summer's "Seasons In The Sun" and "Billy Don't Be A Hero," the spiritual grandchildren of 1972's "Alone Again, Naturally," songs like "All By Myself" by Eric Carmen, "Feelings" by Morris Albert, "Wildfire" by Michael Murphy, culminating in 1975's ultimate paean to wallowing in self-sadness, "At Seventeen" by Janis Ian.

Every teenage girl in America felt that song was about her, "the "valentines that never came," "the Friday night charades of youth," the eternal condition . . .

We all play the game and when we dare

To cheat ourselves at solitaire

Inventing lovers on the phone

Repenting other lives unknown

That call and say, come dance with me

And murmur vague obscenities

To ugly girls like me

At seventeen

I sat crosslegged that late afternoon on the hard and lumpy dorm bed, touched by the whispering sweet nothingness of summer.

Worrying about my heart.

2

Something had changed when I returned from camp. I couldn't define the change exactly. The music in the air had shifted focus. The beat was turned around. Perhaps it was fear about my strafed heart, perhaps it was alternating thoughts of Dolly and Miranda. I felt like I wasn't anywhere at all.

"I think you should fuck both of them," Gus Lagniappe said with bogus authority in response to my dilemma.

He put the *Disco Baby* album on the stereo, and there, right there, was the rhythm that had shifted.

My pulse rebelled. I wasn't into it.

"Check it out," Gus air-thrusted to the music, "Doesn't this sound like fucking?"

"I'm not sure I want to fuck either of them," I said, not really sure of anything really.

"Oh, cram it, clown, you think about it all the time," he said making the pumping-fist-jack-off sign (to the beat of course).

"But thinking about it is not the same thing as actually wanting to do it," I countered.

"Nyeah, well I say you fuck both of them, like at the same time . . . *ménage à twat*, dude."

"Dude, please. I don't even know how to touch them, much less fuck them," I said.

"Fucking is touching, but just, like, in a much more major way," he said and then paused in his rumination, "I mean, you can touch without fucking, but you can't fuck without touching."

"I disagree," I said.

"You think it's possible to fuck without touching?"

"Yeah. For sure. I do it all the time."

"You mean jacking off?"

"No, that's also a form of touching."

"A major one, yeah," Gus said.

"I'm talking about language. Conversation," I explained.

"That's just flirting, that's not fucking. I say you can't fuck without touching. Talking about music and literature isn't fucking."

"It can be. And what do you know about fucking anyway?" I challenged.

"Dang, dude, you know all about my escapades with that lady last summer. Helen. In Kansas. I don't have to tell you."

"Oh, you so totally made that shit up, dude. She was living in Troy, Kansas, and her name just happened to be Helen? Dude, don't even. You are no help."

It was a hot summer day mostly spent lollygagging, playing wiffle ball on the front lawn, watching *Rifleman* reruns (an inviolable ritual in the afternoon), just me and Gus Lagniappe.

We had been looking through his Uncle Eddie's voluminous porn collection when Gus said, "We should go mess with that beehive out front."

"The one in your sycamore tree?"

"Yeah, it's been getting bigger everyday."

"I don't think it's too smart to mess with a beehive, dude," I said.

"We can scare all the bees away and then climb up and get all the honey and shit," Gus urged.

I preferred hanging out in the air-conditioning and spending more time with the limber ladies of *Beaver Slam* than going out to get the honey and shit. But Gus was insistent.

"C'mon, dorkwad, let's do something more productive than spilling jizz on glossy paper. I'll go get my BB gun."

And, for some reason, to this day inexplicable, I joined him and in fact am the one who actually did the shooting.

Rationally I knew that my shooting BBs at that beehive would not, in fact, scare the bees away, but would, in fact, compel the bees to attack and sting me mercilessly.

However, the part of me that wanted to be Lucas McCain muscled its way to my trigger finger.

In defiance of any logical behavior I fired the gun, thus bringing upon myself the wrath of terrorized apian soldiery.

I dropped the gun and ran down the street away from the buzzy tumult though soon enough was overtaken by the swarm and stung repeatedly, I'm not sure how many times exactly.

I rolled around on a neighbor's lawn which got rid of the bees mostly except the kamikazes who stung me, for they lay strewn beside me, a-twitch, on the brink of succumbing to martyrdom while I, the Empire, would survive.

By that time, Gus had taken refuge inside his house, standing in the window, pointing and laughing.

He wasn't about to come out and help me.

The bees made a busy buzz-buzz as they re-gathered at the damaged hive to begin repairs.

Beehives are the earliest form of urban living.

My parents were too astounded at my stupidity to punish me.

"I think you punished yourself" is how my mom put it.

I was distressfully uncomfortable for several days following the incident, and at night I would have apocalyptic dreams—nothing to do with bees—dreams of lonely hillsides, acres of isolation, too much room, emptiness everywhere, the absence of Miranda.

One afternoon during my convalescence from the bee stings, I was watching a *Kung Fu* rerun and realized as soon as I saw the close-up of the monarch butterfly that it was the episode I had told Miranda about at the beach, and I ended up calling her before I could talk myself out of it.

"Miranda?" I said nervously when a girl's voice answered.

"No, this is her mother. Who's this?"

"Oh, hey," I said clearing my throat, "Hi, it's, hm-hmm, Lance Atlas."

"Hello, Lance," Tamar paused, "Miranda is making a face at me right now."

I could hear the shuffle of the phone changing hands and Miranda saying, "Gimme it."

"Hullo?" Miranda said.

"Hey, Miranda, it's Lance."

"I'm shocked," she said.

"That I called you Miranda?"

"That you called me at all. Hi, Lance!"

Unsure of the proper response to that, I brought up my reason for calling: "Hey turn on Channel 5, that *Kung Fu* episode we talked about with the guy dreaming he's a butterfly story is on."

"Oh cool. Let me bring the phone into the living room," she said. "I can't believe you called me!"

"Let's watch together," I said.

"Where do I know her from?" Miranda asked of the blond girl playing mandolin.

"She was Joey Kelly on *The Courtship of Eddie's Father*."

"Oh, yeah, the tomboy. Didn't she beat Eddie up or something?"

"Right. And I'm pretty sure she played Raquel Welch's daughter in *Kansas City Bomber*."

"Now there's a name I remember!"

A silence ensued as we each watched *Kung Fu* on our respective TVs.

"Wait, what happened?" Miranda said of a sudden shift from the cowboy western action to the hazy flashback of Caine's youth in the Shaolin Temple in China.

"Caine is remembering his childhood. They do that all the time in this show. That old guy is Master Po."

"His eyes are weird," Miranda said.

"He's blind," I explained, "Oh, and that's the scroll with the butterfly story in it. Grasshopper's gonna read from the scro—"

"—Shush, I wanna listen," she said.

"Long ago Jwong Joe dreamed he was a butterfly. He was very joyful as a butterfly, well pleased with his lot, his aims fulfilled. He knew nothing of Joe the man. But shortly he awoke and found himself again to be Jwong Joe. And he could not tell whether as Joe he had dreamed he was a butterfly or whether as a butterfly he had dreamed he was Joe."

"I still can't stop thinking about that idea," Miranda said. "Like, am I a butterfly dreaming I'm Miranda Savitch right now? How do you know what's real? I wonder if my dad got it from *Kung Fu*?"

"Could be," I said, though I doubted it.

"So his name is Jwong Joe?" Miranda asked.

"That's what it sounds like, dunno," I said.

"I'll ask my dad."

Another long silence seeped between us, broken only by Miranda saying, at a commercial break, "I've gotta pee, I'll be right back."

Girls always have to pee.

"I love how they go back and forth between his past and present," Miranda said, upon returning.

"Isn't this great?" I asked.

"Totally," Miranda said, "Are they all this good?"

"Pretty much. Greatest show of all time. Or maybe tied with *Twilight Zone* and *The Rifleman*."

In one scene, Althea, the little girl, shows up at the window of Caine's cell where he's awaiting trial on murder charges. Their faces whisper close.

"It's like Romeo and Juliet in reverse," Miranda says, "Romeo's on the balcony."

"Caine's a prisoner, though."

"So was Juliet," Miranda advised. "In her father's house, being forced to marry Paris? Tell me that isn't prison," Miranda insisted hotly.

"Except they're not in love like Romeo and Juliet," I pointed out.

"Oh, she has crush on him, for sure," Miranda said.

"How can you tell?"

"It's obvious. Duh," she explained.

During a courtroom scene, Miranda suddenly said, "I think about becoming a lawyer sometimes."

"Really?" I said, "Yeah I can see that, I guess."

"What does that mean?" Miranda challenged.

"Well, I mean, " I said, searching for strategic language, "you've got a lot of, uh-hm, spunk."

"Spunk?"

"You're spunky, yeah."

"Spunky? You mean I'm a bitch?"

"Oh, no no no," I said, struggling to recover, "I mean, you know how to make a convincing point."

"Oh, my god, they're gonna hang him?" Miranda gasped, ignoring my nonsense.

"Watch," I said as they walk Caine to the gallows and ask him his final wish.

Caine facing the gallows says, *"There is nothing I wish."*

"That sounds like you!" Miranda laughed.

"Fershures fershures," I flirted.

"God, what do you think about when you're walking to your execution?"

Miranda wondered.

"What it's like to die probably," I said.

"Probly, yeah," she agreed, "and realizing, like, fuhhhhck, you're about to find out." She paused to watch then said, "I hate this on TV shows: you know he's gonna be rescued, right? 'cause it's not the last episode of the series, but you're afraid anyway."

"Yeah, like on *Gilligan's Island* you always know their plan to get off the island is going to fail or else the show would be over."

"But you want to see exactly how Gilligan is going to fuck it up," she added.

"Zackly."

We watched the tender moment between Kwai Chang Caine and the little girl after she changes her testimony and saves him from execution. He is preparing to leave town. They face each other.

"*I love you, Mr. Caine,*" says the little girl.

She pulls his head down toward her and kisses him on the cheek.

"*And I have not loved anyone more,*" says Caine.

"See?" Miranda said, "Romeo and Juliet. I told you."

"But she doesn't try to make him stay or anything," I pointed out.

"Well, she knows she can't."

"Why can't she?"

"Um, well, she's like 12-years-old to start with," Miranda said.

"This is true."

"She'll just wonder about him for the rest of her life."

"Oh, is that how it goes?"

"Pretty much," Miranda sighed, "yup. She has probably already imagined the dream house they'd live in together."

Miranda called me back later that night, and I blushed from thoughts of a fantasy I'd conjured right after getting off the phone with her that involved her and the living room couch and a *Gilligan's Island* rerun.

"Hi, Lance! Hey, so my dad said he didn't get it from *Kung Fu*, and he gave me this book by the Chinese guy who wrote that story and his name is Chuang Tzu, not Jwong Joe. I was looking through the book, and I saw this other cool thing he wrote: *'Do the clouds make the rain, or does the rain make the clouds?'* I love that."

"The rain *is* the clouds. They are the same thing," I said.

"Yeah, just different states of water. Or something like that, right?"

"Yeahzackly."

"I remember learning that in Ms. Roebuck's class. Oh and here's another cool one: *'If the universe is hidden in the universe itself, there can be no escape from it.'*"

"I don't really get that one," I admitted.

"Me neither," Miranda said, "but it sounds cool, doesn't it? Like infinity or something."

"That means one day it shall be cool, Grasshopper," I spoke with purposeful pomposity and a vague oriental accent, trying to sound like Master Po on *Kung Fu*.

Miranda didn't react. I bore the silence of my unfunniness by trying to think of something to say. Miranda got there first.

"I want to live somewhere far away," Miranda said, "I never feel right here."

"Here in Los Angeles, you mean?"

"Yeah and maybe America too. And even planet earth. I don't know. I feel like a Martian a lot of the time."

"And you want to escape back to your home planet?"

"No, more just wanting to understand Earthlings better, I guess," she answered, "And it might be easier from a distance. Perspective, et cetera."

I don't remember the rest of the conversation, but it had something to do with the impending school year, the dark mysteries of a strange new campus and much bigger kids.

Manny Shepherd and I spent the last weekend before school hanging out together.

We'd be starting high school in a few days, and we shared our deeper uncertainties, our fantasies, our fears.

Manny's older sister Leah, who made many stellar appearances in my masturbation sessions, was going into 12th Grade and provided occasional filtered insights into high school life, but mostly the onset of high school loomed with inevitable menace over our waning summer freedom.

There is a heightened sense of time as the end of summer vacation approaches.

The preciousness of every event intensifies. Knowing that soon the days of lazy free-fall will give way to schedules and deadlines and waking up in the dark, making the right decision about what to do on last days is crucial beyond measure.

When a day near the end of summer vacation goes wrong its wrongness gets magnified unto the afterlife.

Summer eludes your grasp like water.

That last Saturday afternoon we went to see *Day of the Locust* at Grauman's Chinese Theatre, which was the perfect place to view that movie, and afterward we rode our bikes over to the area around Paramount Pictures on Melrose to see if we could find the San Berdoo apartment building, or the one they called the San Berdoo in the movie anyway.

We saw a lot of great Hollywood apartments built around courtyards like in the movie, but we never did find the actual building they used as the San Berdoo.

Maybe we were looking in the wrong neighborhood even though it seemed like Tod lived near Paramount.

Manny and I decided that when we turned 18 we were going to move into a courtyard apartment in Hollywood together and live the dream of Los Angeles.

We went back to Manny's house, and he put the new Bruce Springsteen album *Born To Run* on the living room stereo, a long wooden cabinet contraption, more like furniture than a sound system, and the music came bursting forth with exhilarating perfection from the speakers.

Springsteen was everywhere at that time, in every magazine, in every newspaper, the topic of conversation, much more captivating than the presidency of Gerald R. Ford.

"Bruce is for the people," Manny said.

"Totally," I said having no idea what he meant by that. I was digging the music, though.

3

That fall we entered a more populous, scarier world, the culturally diverse and creatively vibrant campus of Fairfax High School.

Over the summer, mouths had become braceless, bosoms had blossomed, fashions had recalibrated to match the world of the older teens we'd be among.

The seniors looked like grown-ups.

The quad at Fairfax was a kaleidoscope of cliques, self-segregated according to, variously, ethnicity and gender, and then, within those broader groupings, separated again by musical tastes.

In one corner of the quad slouched long-haired kids who listened mostly to Led Zeppelin, Black Sabbath, Hawkwind, Deep Purple, Humble Pie, Pink Floyd, and other emanations of unapologetic stoner music. They were mostly fuck-ups in school. In class they were either high or asleep. KMET and KLOS ruled their lives.

Within the stoner clique was a hippy subset who listened exclusively to the Grateful Dead. The Deadheads were an intruiguing mixture, some of them brilliant students, others lost in a perpetual fog.

There was an even geekier group who were into prog—King Crimson, Henry Cow, Gong, Camel, Gentle Giant, Genesis, Yes, Emerson, Lake & Palmer—music for stoners who didn't like to admit they were stoners, stoners who got wasted every weekend yet somehow always managed to get that essay turned in on Monday morning.

Occasionally the two groups would overlap, like in their adoration of Jethro Tull and Frank Zappa.

The glam kids were still around, but their scene was in flux. Bowie was going R & B, and they hadn't yet encountered The Ramones—the band that would alter their scene drastically—though that transition was imminent. They were on the cusp of becoming punks.

R & B and Disco were creating a bit of a schism, too, with some kids staying into Earth, Wind & Fire, Kool & The Gang, Ohio Players, War, The Parliament/Funkadelic consortium, while others were turning on to Van McCoy's *Disco Baby* and KC & The Sunshine Band's "Get Down Tonight," attaching themselves to a swiftly morphing 'disco' subculture that was multiracial and cool on the one hand but distressingly plastic and soulless on the other.

But the vast majority of the student body were fairly nondescript in their cultural identifications.

They listened to whatever Top 40 songs were being broadcast at the time on KKDJ or K-100 or other such stations and didn't explore music any more deeply than that.

The *Chick Clique* remained mostly intact. Dolly Ferris, Miranda Savitch, Arabella Mayflower,, Claire Farnaway, Sharon Rose, Lorelei Lux, Justine Balthazar, et al were still moving as a pack, roaming the quad, hoping to get noticed.

"Anybody watching *Welcome Back, Kotter?*" Claude Moss asked one day early in the semester.

"It's kind of funny," I said, "but the Sweathogs are too old to be in high school. I mean, the seniors here look like grown-ups, but those guys in the show are like old."

"Really, Horshack looks around 30," Eddie Gurges said.

"And the Puerto Rican Jew—"

"—Epstein," I said.

"Yeah-and Vinnie Barbarino and Freddy Boom Boom Washington?"

"I don't think it's that funny, really," Gus said. "It's too fake to be funny."

While we talked we saw and heard a commotion at the other end of the quad near the amphitheatre.

Three stoners started chanting:

"It's a fight! It's a fight! It's a nigger and a white! The nigger can't fight, so the white's all right!"

Rudy Garlin came running over, laughing, "Oh, that whiteboy got his ass whupped," and sat down on the beige plastic bench, catching his breath while laughing.

Rudy, or "Rudy Tuesday" as he was known, was chubby, tall, light-skinned, very into The Rolling Stones (which is why everybody called him Rudy Tuesday), and he was also into the Dodgers and our beleaguered hockey team the Kings.

He had gone to Pasteur Jr. High but was immediately absorbed into the cool nerd crew from John Burroughs. "Demetrius said, 'Whap,'" Rudy gestured a punch in the face, "and the whiteboy went 'Ow' and fell down all bloody!"

"The white wasn't all right," Gus joked.

The centerpiece of the typical school day, the nexus of our collective identity, was a block of two classes: Mr. St. Jerome's 3rd period Biology class, and—my first ashram—4th period Honors English with Mr. Beauregard.

Those two classes saw a merging of our cool nerd crew from John Burroughs Jr. High, and a corresponding gaggle of equally cool nerds from Bancroft, the next closest Jr. High.

I knew some of the Bancroft kids from before, during my Melrose Avenue Elementary School days: Manny Shepherd, of course, who'd been hanging with us intermittently despite our different schools, also Bart Scribner, the epic underachiever who always knew all the answers on any test but couldn't be bothered to actually write them down.

"I've got nothing to prove," Bart would say in response to our encouraging him to work.

But there were also new faces from the Bancroft circle: Jim Lord, a brilliant wit with a vast vocabulary both sacred and profane and black curly hair that pointed in several directions at once; the intensely serene but quietly amusing Buddy Feigenbaum, a master of muttering funny shit under his breath to the merriment of the classmates in his proximity, always with an expression of virtuous innocence whenever the teacher would inquire "What's so funny?" in response to the eruption of giggles; the classically handsome Dirth brothers, Godfrey and Willoughby, identical twins born in different years, "God" (as he was affectionately called) at 11:57 pm, on December 31, 1960, and younger brother "Will" at 12:01 am, on January 1, 1961; also, there was this dude Sasha "No Shit" Sherlock. Sasha's nickname was fun to say but wildly inaccurate, for Sasha "No Shit" Sherlock was in fact supremely full of shit.

I remember once Sasha was describing the infamous and apocryphal "Cram it, clown!" incident on the *Bozo's Big Top* TV show.

In each episode of *Bozo's Big Top*, there was a carnival-style contest that promised the winner an enormous treasure chest on wheels, a clown wagon, full of toys.

Bozo would go into his "Magic Bozo Spin," twirling with his eyes closed, and would eventually point at some elated youngster who would be pulled out of the gallery of little white children and be shown all the toys in the dream-large treasure chest.

Then, the poor tyke would be subjected to some near-impossible carnival task, typically using one spoon to flip another spoon into a drinking glass or something of that nature.

The child would almost always fail and then have to endure the deflation of the treasure chest being rolled away out of reach and receiving a consolation prize like a Bozo beach towel or some such.

It was both cruel and perverse.

That particular portion of the show gave birth to the legendary "Cram it, clown!" story, a piece of notorious hearsay jacked into by all.

We had been sharing that "Cram it, clown!" myth (it was told differently every time) repeatedly during school lunch discussions since like 3rd Grade, and we'd all pretend that we had actually been watching when it happened even though it never actually did happen.

Allegedly, a kid who failed at the spoon flip said, "Oh, shit" (a big deal because *Bozo's Big Top* was done live), and Bozo answered with the reprimand, "That's a Bozo No-No!" to which the kid sassed back, "Cram it, clown!"

We hadn't heard a version of "Cram it, clown!" in quite some time, when one day during lunch Sasha started in:

"And so the kid says, 'Oh shit' when the spoon doesn't go in the glass," Sasha related, pausing to laugh at the humor of his own phony-baloney re-hash, "and Bozo scolds the kid with his fuck-finger, saying, 'Oh, that's a Bozo No-No,' and the kid says back to Bozo, 'Cram it, clown!' and then kicks Bozo in the balls, and then Bozo's all on the ground and junk and keeps saying, 'The little bastard, I'll kill that whippersnapper sumbitch.'" He continued with the knowing authority of one who was there when it happened, "And then the kid pulls his dick out of his pants and starts jacking off and saying, 'Suck on this, you whore-born, freak-ass piece of shit', and then he cums on Bozo's face and everybody in the audience goes, 'EWWWWW' and then they cut to a Whee-Lo commercial. Aw, man, it was, like, totally flagrant.'"

"Yeah, I was watching when that happened," Claude Moss fibbed, "Totally."

That kid Sasha was an inveterate liar, even beyond "Cram it, clown!"

We'd occasionally enjoy goading him into epic falsehoods by, say, talking about a *Twilight Zone* episode that we'd be just making up, and Sasha would take the bait and run with it:

"Hey, Sasha, you see that *Twilight Zone* rerun last night?" I'd ask.

"Which one was it again?" he'd ask back, searching for a starting point.

"The one about the guy who's about to blow out his birthday candles, and he makes a wish—"

"—that he'll meet his true love?"

"Yeah, that one," I'd set him in motion.

"I love that episode. The guy is played by William Shatner before he became Captain Kirk."

"William Shatner is Jewish, did you know that?" asked Jim Lord.

"Yeah, that's right," I said, "and I love how he meets her at the—"

"—counter of Schwab's where he's doing a crossword puzzle," Sasha enthused, "and his birthday cake is a lame-ass bran muffin with like 3 candles in it, right? And this lady is sitting next to him, sort of looking over at the crossword puzzle, and then she says, '69 down is pussy.' Shatner looks up startled, like, 'Uh, excuse me?' and she goes, 'Blank willow, 5 letters, pussy.' And he goes, 'Oh, yeah, huh?,' and she goes, 'Didn't you wish for me or what?,' and he goes, 'Oh shit, you're my true love?,' and she goes, ' No, duh,' and he goes, 'How can I be sure you're really the one?,' and she goes, 'Take me someplace where I can show you,' and he goes, 'Let's take a drive up to Mulholland,' and she goes, 'Righty-o' or some shit, and so they drive up to Mulholland and find a spot with a view, and he goes, like, 'show me,' and she goes, 'no, you show *me*,' and so he whips his dick out of his pants and goes, 'suck on this wishbone, you horny-ass bitch', and before she can even get her mouth on it, he cums on her face and she goes, 'loser,' and then Sebastian Cabot appears in the back seat of the car, and Captain Kirk goes, like, 'Whoa shit, no way. Mr. French', and Sebastian Cabot goes, 'I'm here to take you to Hell,' and Kirk goes, 'Cram it, Clown!' and Sebastian Cabot goes, 'I am Satan, come with me to the fiery furnace' in a ghosty-Frankenstein voice like in 'Monster Mash,' and Kirk starts going, 'Beam me up, Scotty,' and he disappears, and Rod Serling's voice comes on over the theme music and says, 'Submitted for your approval. Be careful what you wish for, and when your wish comes true, be sure you don't come on her face without warning her first, or you'll end up vanishing in shame . . . to the Twilight Zone.'"

"That's not how I remember it," I'd offer in response.

These were the typical conversations we'd have while Mr. St. Jerome was taking roll.

"What is Biology? Biology is the study of Life," Mr. St. Jerome began an early lecture, "and so the key question then is: What is Life? I can offer you my own definition—write this down: Life is the disorderly functioning of thousands of tiny enzymes. Make sure you have that right: Life . . . is the disorderly functioning . . . of thousands . . . of tiny enzymes."

We scrawled his words in our brand new spiral notebooks.

Mr. St. Jerome continued, "The other basic principle in our understanding of Life is—this is not my own theory but write this down too—Ontogeny recapitulates Phylogeny. Does everybody have that? It is from these two principles that we will make our journey this year through our study of Life.

Our approach will be from the point-of-view of science. Science is a lot like religion in several ways. Like religion, science is filled with miracles. The big difference between the miracles of science and the miracles of religion is that the miracles of science can be explained using empirical evidence, e-m-p-i-r-i-c-a-l, empirical evidence, that which you can see, hear, touch, taste, and smell, and they can be demonstrated through experiments whose results can be repeated."

Miranda raised her hand.

"Miss, um . . ." St. Jerome glanced down at the seating chart, "Savitch?"

"What's an example of a miracle in science?"

"How about a caterpillar turning into a butterfly?" Mr. St. Jerome proffered, "the miraculous lepidoptera . . ."

"But science explains why that happens. What makes it a miracle?"

"Science explains *how* it happens," Mr. St. Jerome corrected, "not *why*. In fact," he decided, "why don't we start talking about metamorphosis right now? Take notes."

Mr. St. Jerome lectured on the various stages of metamorphosis, from the embryo in the egg to the larval caterpillar ("The miracle is in the spiracle!" he elevated his voice in mock-sermon proclamation) to the chrysalis-ensconced pupa to the glorious emergence of the imago.

"The who?" asked Claude Moss, looking for a laugh unsuccessfully.

"The imago," Mr. St. Jerome repeated, "the butterfly. This change from pupa to imago is called metamorphosis."

"If the caterpillar makes a chrysalis, then what's a coccon?" Sharon Rose asked.

"Ah, a chrysalis is one kind of cocoon," explained Mr. Jerome, "We reserve the term chrysalis for the cocoons made by butterfly larvae. The chrysalis is also sometimes called a 'nympha.' Who knows what else is known as 'nympha?'"

No hands went up.

"Nympha is also the two folds of mucous membrane within the labia, at the opening of the vulva," he answered himself.

"The what?" Claude asked.

"What's that?" Whitman Rust asked.

"What's what?" Mr. St. Jerome challenged.

"Labia and vulva . . ." Whit said.

"Pussylips!" shouted Jim Lord to embarrassed laughter.

"Yes, um, Mr.," St. Jerome quickly scanned the seating chart again, "Lord, in the future let's try to use the scientific terms, as this is, after all, a science class. But you are mostly correct. The labia are the lips and the vulva the outer area of the vagina."

"I wanna pupate in your nympha, baby," Buddy Feigenbaum said to nobody and everybody.

"I'm a nympha-maniac," added Jim Lord, to a gaggle of giggles.

"Well you better start pumping that haemolymph, young imago," answered Mr. St. Jerome, "or you'll never be able spread your wings and fly."

"Mr. St. Jerome?" asked Gus Lagniappe.

"Yes? . . ." St. Jerome said, consulting the chart " . . . Mr. Lagniappe?"

"How come you never see a dead butterfly?"

"Butterflies die like we all do," said Mr. St. Jerome.

"Yeah-yeah, I know, but, like, I always see dead moths everywhere, and dead flies, like in the window sill and in the corner near the baseboard and stuff, but I never see dead butterflies anywhere, except in like display cases and stuff."

"That's a good question, and I don't know what to tell you. Perhaps you're looking in the wrong places?"

"Maybe butterflies like to die in private," Miranda said.

At the end of 3rd period, we'd shuffle en masse downstairs to Room 222, Mr. Beauregard's class, appreciating that our favorite teacher's room was the namesake of a beloved TV show deeply embedded in our collective mythology.

In addition to being our English class, 4th period was also a de facto 'homeroom,' though it was never called that, the place where school announcements were read and bureaucratic procedures and paperwork were handled.

Class would begin with 10 minutes of "homeroom activities."

Twice a week, that meant a reading of the misnamed "Daily Bulletin," a duty Mr. Beauregard assigned to me, due to my professed experience doing the PA announcements at John Burroughs.

For the next 40 weeks, I would, on Mondays and Thursdays get 4th period rolling with the rarely-changing opening of the Daily Bulletin, a section entitled General Interest, all the school-wide items of importance, to be followed by the Grade Level section, of which I only had to read the announcements pertaining to Sophomores.

"General Interest," I'd announce at the top of each reading.

And Miranda would respond automatically, "I don't have any."

I never had a good comeback for that and would meet Miranda's exclamation with a feeble glance.

Mr. Beauregard's class would often be a continuation of what we were learning in Mr. St. Jerome's class, but "from the point-of-view of literature," as Mr. St. Jerome might put it.

Mr. Beauregard was also, for most of us, the greatest teacher we'd yet encountered.

He took us to magnificent and sanctified places every day.

"*The child is father to the man*," Mr. Beauregard read out loud from a William Wordsworth poem. "What does that mean?"

I raised my hand and brought up the lecture in Bio: "It's like what St. Jerome was talking about. The caterpillar already contains the adult butterfly. Inwardly it's already an adult. It just doesn't look like one."

"Sounds like teenagers," Mr. Beauregard wryly smiled, "in reverse."

"Pharate, right?" said Miranda Savitch, "The caterpillar is like a skeleton on the outside."

"Exuvium," added Jim Lord.

"The exuvium is the empty chrysalis itself, though, isn't it?" Miranda countered.

No one was quite sure. Miranda went looking through her Bio notes.

"Chrysalis also means pussy," Buddy Feigenbaum muttered under his breath to snickers and giggles.

"Let's get back to what Lance observed," Mr. Beauregard took over, by-passing Buddy's utterance. "What is Wordsworth saying here? You, as children—"

"—Hey—" Gus Lagniappe protested, "That's not cool. "

"—No, sorry to say you are still children," Mr. Beauregard continued, "but the adult you are going to become already exists. You will, in effect, give birth to—or metamorphose into—the grown-up that's been there all along, and when you're a grown-up, I can promise you, you will be looking to the child who gave birth to you for wisdom and inspiration. Every child is already an adult, and every adult is still a child. It's all connected you see. A continuum. One of your vocab words this week if you'll recall."

The more diligent among us took notes on every word Beauregard said; others, like me, simply sat enrapt, glad to be sitting in a classroom with Mr. Beauregard and soaking in all the juice.

He was the first person to tap into our deeper being.

"Wordsworth speaks of 'the philosophic mind,'" Beauregard would say, "and you guys are right at that age when the philosophic mind, your ability to think abstractly, is ready to break out of its casing and expand outward in all directions."

"Eclosion," Miranda said, still looking through her Bio notes.

Shel Beauregard was a native Brooklynite who'd followed the Dodgers to Los Angeles in 1958 and had, since the early '60s, in addition to being a full time teacher in the Los Angeles Unified School District, also worked as an usher at Dodger Stadium (head usher by the time we sat in his classroom in 1975).

He told us stories about the exit plan for The Beatles when they played Dodger Stadium in 1966 and the mayhem that ensued when Ringo stayed on stage longer than he was supposed to afterward; he told us about hanging out with Sandy Koufax, the Dodger legend whose name, *Koufax*, was always uttered with divine reverence, especially among Angeleno Jews.

"One of *our* boys," my father would say, as he did when any famous Jew's name got mentioned.

My mother loved to tease him by bringing up more infamous examples, "Arnold Rothstein, one of our boys. Meyer Lansky, one of our boys. Bugsy Siegel, one of our boys. Mickey Cohen, one of our boys. Henry Kissinger, one of our boys," to cries of "Enough!" from my father.

"You're giving me indigestion!"

He, of course, would do the same to my mother whenever she extolled the virtues of organic food.

"Arsenic is organic," he'd taunt, "Strychnine is organic," and so on.

But nobody's name elicited that glassy god-drenched whisper like *Koufax*.

To go along with Mr. St. Jerome's metamorphosis unit, we read stories from Ovid's *Metamorphoses* in Mr. Beauregard's English class.

Of course everybody kept looking over at me when we read the story of Atlas holding up the heavens, keeping the earth and sky apart, reading my biography into Ovid's ancient myth.

"That's why your shoulders slouch," Miranda Savitch teased.

"I'm practicing for when I get turned into a mountain."

"Beware my stony gaze," she squinted at me in full on flirtation.

At the end of each school day, I left intellectual pursuits behind to play sports because somehow my Jewish ass made the "C" basketball team.

There was Varsity at the top, then Junior Varsity, then the "B" team, and, finally, the "C" team.

It was the bottom rung, yeah, but, dang, like 50 guys tried out for the "C" team and only 12 made it. And I was one of them.

Some of the guys on the team I already knew from playing basketball at Gardner Park. In fact, five of us had played together on the same team, called, coincidentally, the Lions, the official Fairfax mascot and the name of all Fairfax athletic teams.

There was the long and lanky center T'Qwan Prince, descended from Creole royalty he claimed; Trey Simple, small forward, shy and quiet but a fierce competitor on the court, a guy with a soft touch and a hard edge, didn't give a shit about basketball actually but loved to win; point guard Samuel "Ham Samich" Lee, whose ballhandling skills were modeled after Earl "The Pearl" Monroe and "Pistol" Pete Maravich, as flashy and dazzling as his electro-shock afro; Dane Almond, a long-haired, freckle-faced kid, a power forward with limber moves to the hoop (the black guys all called him Opie); and, of course, me, Lance Atlas, the other whiteboy on the team, shooting guard, nicknamed "Lax" Atlas for my decided lack of quickness.

The rest of the C team were guys I'd never met before, dudes whose massive talents on the court ensured that I'd spend all but 6 minutes of the season sitting on the bench as the last-guy-in.

Garbage time only for Lax Atlas.

There was the Japanese fireball Tatsuya Hashimoto, who went by the name of "Steve."

On the first day of tryouts, when Hashimoto's name was called by Coach Boondog, I remember T'Qwan Prince saying, "Say, man, isn't Hashimoto that little judo-mouse motherfucker?" which got a laugh (including from Coach Boondog, which was so not cool . . . teachers have to suppress shit like that; it's their job; you can't laugh when a student bags on another student; it's bad form).

Out on the court, Steve Hashimoto started sinking shots from 20 and then 30 feet and was joined by another oriental guy, fresh off the boat from Thailand, a dead-eye shooter and a ballhandling wizard named Pinot Pusyapontoon, who, when introducing himself to the rest of the hopefuls trying out that day, said, in halting English, "Jus' call me Pussy," an invitation unanimously obliged by all in the gym and honored for the next 3 years.

"OK, Pussy," guys started chortling, "If you insist, Pussy."

"Dang," Dane Almond said softly to me, "dude does not even realize what he's just done to himself."

"Peeno Pussy," I couldn't help chuckling, "dang, dude."

However, the two of them on the basketball court, Hashimoto and Pusyapontoon, oh, they shut the laughter up fast with their amazing play.

They would end up being the two starting guards.

The Orient Express, they were called, fast and accurate, lethal.

"Dang, those Buddha-heads can shoot some hoops," Samuel Lee sighed, watching his future playing time diminish with each Hashimoto swish.

There was also the Filipino sparkplug Andrew Chupoy, whom everybody called "Jewboy."

He was only a mediocre player, but his enthusiasm carried him to some great moments on the court, diving steals, snatching rebounds from 6'4" centers with his 5'9" body, a fearless lover of the game. That's why Coach Boondog picked him for the team.

You just didn't want him handling the ball with your team down and only seconds left to play 'cause he would most definitely fuck that one up.

He's the only guy I ever saw throw two airball free throws in a row.

Dang, dude.

The first game I appeared in, about halfway through the season, a game we were winning by 25 points with 3 minutes left, my name was announced over the PA as "Land Atlas," followed by the ridicule I had to suffer because Coach Boondog had spelled my name wrong on the jersey order and so the back of my uniform read "AIAS."

I got home from that game and spent the rest of the night in my bedroom writing a song called "One Moment of Glory," the thoughts of a benchwarmer who fantasizes about finally getting to play but recognizing the possibility that instead of being a hero he might fuck it all up so maybe it's better to stay on the bench.

I remember wanting to call Miranda and sing it for her over the phone, but I ended up not doing that because I thought she'd think I was a loser or something.

4

We spent a lot of weekend time that fall hanging out at Whitman Rust's house.

His parents were gone often, and the only supervision was the maid, who didn't speak English and who spent most of the time watching TV in the breakfast room.

The Rust house always smelled like air-conditioning.

Even on the coldest rainy day the air-conditioning would be on.

I kind of dug the metallic vapors that permeated the premises.

They lived around the corner from me on Mansfield, and it was there on Mansfield that our social life took on a new dimension when Whitman Rust's older brother—Bigelow, usually just called Big, a 12th Grader—summoned us into his bedroom and asked, "You guys wanna get high?"

Bigelow Rust, I learned that day, had been dealing pot to the Fairfax community for about a year, and he was offering the group of us the opportunity to sample his wares (with the intention no doubt of creating a few future customers).

I was scared but curious.

Big laid out several different baggies on his checkerboard bedspread.

This wasn't a filmstrip in health class; it was real.

There was marijuana in those baggies.

Only the fuck-ups messed with that stuff.

And yet, Big was a straight-A student as were all of his friends, and apparently they indulged, so . . .

"'Everything in moderation,' my father always says," Bigelow encouraged us.

"Taking drugs when you're not really sick is really sick," Claude Moss quoted the omnipresent anti-drug public service announcement.

Big pointed to the baggie on the far left, saying, "We call this shit Porno 'cause when you jack off high on this one it'll make you feel like you're really fucking her."

Touching the next bag, "Here's some sinsemilla, mang," he said with a cholo inflection, "Good Sense, we call it. This shit'll make you think *Gilligan's Island* is funny, my freng."

He smiled downward at the next stash, then looked up at us, "Now, this shit's from Colombia—we call it Magic Bozo Spin—this shit'll pin you to the ground and you'll feel the earth fucking rotating on its own axis, no lie."

There was a long pause until Bigelow cradled the last baggie with tender affection.

"And this here," he dangled it before us, "this is Thai Stick. This shit'll turn you into the Buddha."

"THAI STICK!" we all shouted and laughed (though we all also requested some Porno for later).

"Who wants Thai Stick?" Big intoned, holding the baggie up.

"I do! I do!" each of us responded like in the Trident commercial.

Big fired up his purple plexiglass bong, gave us a few short instructions on inhaling and holding and releasing, and launched us on our merry trip.

We ended up in Whit's room, listening to an album provided by Big, *12 Dreams of Dr. Sardonicus* by the L.A. band Spirit.

"Spirit will accompany your mind," he told us.

I was lost in the process of thought.

It was like being on a conveyor belt.

I felt myself carried into the bowels of the idea factory.

I lay on my back conjuring faces in the cottage-cheese ceiling.

Evil clown faces. Dinosaur faces. Trilobite faces. Circus freak faces. Manic Don Knotts faces. Topogigio faces. Sepia-toned famous wild west outlaw faces. Down Syndrome faces morphing into orangutan faces. Faces like the picture of the 8-foot giant in the Guinness Book of Word Records. Old people's faces in profile, all ultimately looking like Dave near the end of

2001: A Space Odyssey.

Eddie Gurges attempted to draw in his freshly baked state of brain, but the lines were all twitched like cattails.

"Dang, dude, this looks like shit I used to draw with my Bizzy-Buzz-Buzz," Eddie said.

"Whoa, shit, Bizzy-Buzz-Buzz," said Gus, "I had one of those when I was like seven. The vibrating pen!"

"Yeah, the drawing always came out stupid, but the vibration felt good," Eddie said.

"My older sister kept hers in her room and wouldn't let us play with it," Whit said.

"Mine too!" said Manny.

"She might even still have it," Whit continued, "Sometimes I hear it turning on in her room."

"Remember the Bizzy-Buzz-Buzz commercial?" Claude asked.

"Yeah, the spazz kid with the speech impediment," Whit remembered.

"I'm a Biddy-Bud-Bud," Gus lisped in faux-retard nasal reference.

"You sound deaf, not retarded, dude," Whit criticized.

"I'm a Bizhy-Buzh-Buzh," Gus tried again.

"Now you sound all Iron Curtain and shit," Whit said.

"A Russian retard," Manny added.

"Soviet spazz," mumbled Eddie.

"More like Carol Channing, Diamondzh are a girlzh bezht friend, " I sang.

"Well you do it then, dipshits," Gus retorted.

"You're a Buzzy-Bizz-Bizz," Whit got it backwards.

"A Buzzy Lagniappe," I chuckled, invoking the eternal recurrence.

"I'm a Buzzy Lagniappe," Gus repeated, in recognition.

"Totally!" Claude Moss cackle-coughed.

Stoned laughter and shrieks of "Buzzy Lagniappe!" quaked from the epicenter of Whitman Rust's bedroom that hazy cool Saturday afternoon in autumn and thence echoed across the rest of our adolescence.

A nickname was born.

From that moment on, with the exception of his family and a few teachers, everyone under the sway of the Fairfax High School mythos referred to Gus as "Buzzy Lagniappe."

By the middle of the following week, very few could even remember there ever was a Gus.

Buzzy Lagniappe hatched, latched on, and fed himself into a frenzy of voices.

Buzzy Lagniappe surrendered himself completely to a new fractured identity.

It was as if he never stopped being high after that.

"I am fuckin' buzzed," Buzzy croaked, holding his head which moved in a slow circular pattern.

After *Sardonicus*, Whit put on Jethro Tull's *Thick As A Brick*.

The music started playing, and Whit just stood there, watching the vinyl spin on the turntable.

"Dang, dude, it looks like the butterfly on the label is flying," he observed.

"It looks all blurry to me," Buzzy Lagniappe said, looking over Whit's shoulder at the revolving label.

"A blurtiful beautyfly," mumbled Manny Shepherd from the fetal position he'd assumed at the foot of Whit's bed.

Whit still had his *Willy Wonka and the Chocolate Factory* bedspread, though what had once been a childhood enchantment was now displayed as a badge of irony.

"Did you see Hilburn's review of the Tull show at the Forum the other day?" I asked.

"Totally," said Manny, quoting, "Jethro Tull Rhymes With Dull, right?"

"Flagrant," said Claude.

"Absotively Posilutely," Manny answered, "Exzackitackily."

"I can't wait to try this Porno shit," Buzzy said, holding up his little sample of aphrodisiac weed, "I pretty much spend most of my time waiting for the next opportunity to jack off," Buzzy said, "I don't know about you guys."

"That's an admirable goal," I scoffed.

"Oh, I forgot, Lance Atlas has only the purest thoughts and noble desires," Buzzy sassed, "He'd never go down under the hood and grease his own piston."

"Atlas whacks as much as the rest of us," Whit said, leaning over my crotch. "Let me see if I can tell which hand he uses . . . and . . . dang . . ."

"What?" asked Claude.

"Well, you can usually tell by which side a dude's dick is on. It's an opposite hand thing. Lefties hang to the right, righties hang to the left," Whit explained, still gawking at my groin, "but Lance's dick position is not discernible."

"You sound like Jim Lord," Buzzy said, mockingly. "Discernible, right."

"Whatever, dude. I see no evidence of Lance's penis anywhere. What, do you tuck it under or something, dude?"

"I have the right to remain silent," I insisted, thinking of Miranda.

"Hey, you ever tried to come on your own face?" Claude asked the room.

"No, but obviously you have," Buzzy cut.

"How the fuck would you do that?" Whit asked.

"You'd have to go all Jack LaLanne and shit," Buzzy Lagniappe demonstrated by going into bicycle position, supine, legs in the air, then curving his back up and his legs over his head.

We all went coyote when Buzzy did that, howling, tear-soaked laughter. When the spasm subsided, Buzzy sat back up and said, "I was out in the backyard pulling up weeds the other day, and this spider started talking to me."

"I thought today was the first time you've been stoned," I said.

"No, dude, really, I wasn't stoned, there was this big black spider hanging in its web, and it started talking to me," he claimed.

"Okey-doke, shmoke," I said, dismissing this as revisionist stoner history.

"Was the spider named Charlotte?" Eddie Gurges joked.

"Some pig," Manny added.

"I'm not lying, the spider really talked to me. His name is Flippy Killbones," Buzzy said.

"Flippy Killbones?" I asked, with great dubious attitude.

"Yeah-and he was telling me I should try to sneak back into the Garden of Eden."

"And how did Flippy Killbones propose you do that, seeing as how God is, you know, like omniscient and all?" I asked.

"All those archangels with flaming swords and shit? No way," said Manny.

"Build a tunnel," said Buzzy, matter-of-factly.

"And then what? Eat from the tree of life?" I asked.

"Hell no. Turn it into a theme park," said Buzzy. "I'd be a millionaire."

"You could have a plaque on the apple tree like 'This is where Adam and Eve lost it,' right?" said Whit.

"Rabbi Hamlisch says the Tree of Knowledge of Good and Evil was a pomegranate tree," I said.

"My rabbi says it was a fig tree," Manny countered.

"Why figs?" Eddie asked.

"I dunno, 'cause when you cut a fig in half it looks like a pussy or something, I don't really remember," Manny answered, "but it's something like that. Or no, wait, it's 'cause after they realize they're naked they cover themselves with fig leaves."

"There'd be nothing to do there," I said.

"Doesn't matter, dude. People would pay money just to walk around in paradise," Buzzy said, "don't you think? They'd be like, 'Ooh, cool, this is in the Bible' and shit."

"You could have a motel next door called The Land of Nod," Claude said.

Surprised laughter filled the hazy bedroom.

"Dang, dude, Claude was just funny," said Buzzy, "Pinch me."

"OK," I said, inching toward him.

"Do that and I'll pinch the shit out of your stowaway dick, golita," Buzzy warned.

"Plus, you'd have to install bathrooms all around the theme park," I said, ending my attempted pinch attack.

"Dang, dude, taking a dump in the Garden of Eden . . . there's something not cool about that," said Whit.

"And you'd have bad-ass dudes with tattoos eating corndogs and shit with their fat-ass girlfriends in hot pants like at Magic Mountain," Manny added.

"In the fucking Garden of Eden," said Whit, shaking his head, "No way, dude."

"Where do you stand on this issue, good Sir Lancelot?" Manny asked.

"Don't listen to the spider," I advised.

"Miranda Savitch wants Sir Lance . . . a lot," Claude jibed a few seconds too late but looking around for laughter anyway.

Eddie Gurges drew a cartoon of Bozo the Clown with a large blank spot the middle of his face.

"Dudes," Eddie said, holding up the picture, "my latest creation: 'Bozo No Nose.'"

"Cram it, clown," Buzzy mumbled.

The Jethro Tull album ended, and we decided to go downstairs to the den and watch TV.

A *Star Trek* rerun was on.

After fixing ourselves bowls of Count Chocula and half-and-half, we lay splayed across couches and along the floor.

"This is the one where Spock goes through the *Pon farr*," Whitman Rust noticed.

"Righteous. Horny Spock," Buzzy enthused, "We have to watch this shit."

"Spock wants to fuck that blonde chick, right?" said Claude Moss.

"Nurse Chapel," Eddie said.

"Spock wants to kneel in her pew," Buzzy chuckled.

"He's gonna fill her with the Holy Spirit, Glory be to God!" Whit ranted like Ernest Angeley.

"Vulcans get horny every 7 years, and this is it for Spock," Whit said.

"Time for the Vulcan cock-in-pussy meld," Buzzy giggled.

"It's the *Pon farr*, master," said Claude Moss said doing a Peter Lorre imitation for some inexplicable reason.

Buzzy snorted.

"Poon fire, dude," said Whit.

Chuckles rumbled.

"Porn fear," Claude shot off target.

"You don't get it, nads-lapper," Buzzy said to Claude, whacking him across the back of the head, "You've already used your allotment of one funny joke per year. That Land of Nod thing was on the money but shut the fuck up now."

"After a time you may find that having is not so pleasing a thing after all as wanting. It is not logical, but it is often true," said Spock.

I knew all about that having and wanting thing. Yup.

Later that night I would fuck the fantasy Miranda, on her bedspread, with the assistance of porno weed.

Bigelow was right.

Dang, dude.

Saturdays came to be like that for a few weeks: A cannabis gathering at Whit's house.

You weren't allowed to party unless your homework was done.

I mean you actually had to bring your finished homework and show it, or you couldn't smoke.

It was a cool nerd tradition, apparently, handed down through the generations, or so Bigelow taught us, and he strictly enforced it.

"I need my customers to have high GPAs," he said, "'Cause as long as you keep your grades up, you keep getting your allowances and keep on buying my inventory. You fuck up in school and get your allowances taken away, that's no bueno for business. So, like, show me your fucking math homework, dudes."

At one such session, I was walking down the hall, and I heard Bowie blasting from the bedroom of Whit's older sister Taryn. Her door was open and so I felt all right stopping in the threshhold to listen.

Taryn Rust was lying on her bed looking at the album cover.

Tight jeans. Legs extended and crossed at the ankle. She had short hair like a boy but was otherwise girly curvaceous.

She was like four years older than Whit, living at home, taking classes at LACC, and working at Aron's Records.

"*Aladdin Sane*," said Taryn, noticing me in the doorway and holding up the cardboard cover.

"*Aladdin Sane* is my Bible," I said without believing it, a flirt-move, coming out of nowhere. "Buzzy Lagniappe is also a worshipper," I added.

"Who?"

"Buzzy Lagniappe," I said pointing into the other room.

"Huh? Buzzy Lagniappe is the fat kid from *Willy Wonka & The Chocolate Factory*," said Taryn.

"Actually, that's Augustus Gloop. We sometimes call Buzzy Lagniappe Augustus Gloop as a joke 'cause his real name is Augustus."

"Oh . . . *that* Buzzy Lagniappe," she said, reality finally regaining some traction in her pot-besotted conscience.

"The Danny Partridge-looking motherfucker," I helped.

"Dang, dude, Buzzy Lagniappe *is* Aladdin Sane."

"The piano on that song," I said, pointing at the speakers when the solo in the title track launched.

"Warped, dude," she said, looking at me a good long time while the piano derailed into madness, "Mike Garson."

"You like *Diamond Dogs*?" I asked.

"Nyeah, some of it is great but not all of it."

"I dunno, this album and *Quadrophenia*, the Who album, you know?"

"No duh," she crossed her eyes at me.

"Whenever I hear them I feel like they just came out."

"I agree, yeah, totally," Taryn said.

Her eyes softened, her interest kindled.

"Girls get all horny over having things in common with you, " Buzzy had once said to me and I remembered it in that moment.

Bowie howled.

Whoooooooooo will love Aladdin Sane? Will love Aladdin Sane?

When "Cracked Actor" came on, Taryn sat up, then bounced to her feet and started dancing on the bed.

"Come on!" she waved me over to join her.

Suck baby suck

Give me your head

Taryn fell back onto her knees and then flat onto the pillow and beckoned me to get horizontal too.

You've made a bad connection 'cause I just want your sex

We lay listening to the songs unfold, she on her back, I face down next to her, eyes closed.

I wondered if I should I get on top of her and kiss her?

The sniper in the brain, regurgitating drain

Incestuous and vain

Whit poked his head in the door at that moment. "You aren't trying to fuck my big sister, are you, Atlas?"

I looked up, embarrassed.

"Come on, dude. We're gonna make stoned phonies," he said, referring to prank phone calls we'd inflict on random people from the phone book.

Usually it was Whit and Buzzy who'd do the calling; the rest of us would just sit around and giggle.

I was always vaguely uncomfortable doing malicious shit like that to people.

Whit would claim to have seen their ass in some liquor store and just annoy the shit out of them with threats like, "I'm gonna whomp you upside the head if I see your ass in Chuck's Liquor Store again, motherfucker," though often he'd break character and start laughing halfway through, and then he'd have to hang up and we'd spazz out for 10 minutes like a bunch of total fucking losers.

I got up off the bed and waved bye to Taryn.

"You've got potential," she said.

Older sisters. I swear.

Dang, dude.

As we were walking down the hall back to his room, Whit said, "Dang, dude, don't even try to fuck my sister. That'd be just too flagrant."

"I guess," I said, as we passed his parents' room.

"You can fuck my mother, though . . ." Whit said straight-faced and then paused, laughing, " . . . Psych."

5

Whenever I'd start to feel lost or unanachored, Beauregard's class would always draw me back to the solid center.

"General Interest," I read in the Daily Bulletin as usual to get the class going.

"I don't have any," Miranda replied as per the new tradition.

We had moved from Ovid's *Metamorphoses* to Kafka's *The Metamorphosis*, and, upon our completion of Kafka, Beauregard shifted gears and started to talk about Existentialism.

"You know," he said, "In Kafka you see this completely paranoid, ordered universe, where everything is connected, and only the protagonist, the main character—not just in *Metamorphosis* but in all of Kafka's writing—is left out of the knowledge; reality makes sense to everybody except him. The order itself exists, despite the hero's incomprehension. Carl Jung—a psychologist who will be coming up a lot in here and also in Mr. Megiddo's class when you have him next year—Jung said, 'In all chaos there is a cosmos, in all disorder a secret order,'" Beauregard quoted, "But then we get to somebody like Camus, the existential writer, who said that all is absurd, random, nothing is connected."

"The disorderly functioning," Lorelei Lux said and then was joined in unison by everyone else, "of thousands of tiny enzymes."

Mr. Beauregard let us have our knowing laugh and then proceeded: "I tend to side with Camus in these matters. You don't know. There could be a blood clot heading toward your heart as we speak, and you could just keel over at any second, even right now."

You could sense the discomfort as each kid in the class sat waiting for an imminent demise.

"It could happen anywhere," said Beauregard.

I had visions of dying while jacking off and my parents finding me, pants down, cock hard, dribbles of semen on my belly, a crumpled kleenex beside me.

"You just don't know anything," Mr. B. went on, "Just like there's no way of knowing what you would do if a loaded gun were pointed at your temple until it is actually happening. You might fantasize about some kind of movie heroics. You might picture that moment over and over again, of a loaded gun being pointed at your temple. Most of you are probably doing that right now, yes? But all that is just a psychodrama of your own making. Everybody in that fantasy is you, the gunman included."

He paused and let the moment hang precipitously in our heads.

"But when it's actually happening," Beauregard continued, "the gunman is not you, the outcome is uncertain, you have a direct experience of reality, a reality in which you control everything . . . and nothing."

There was considerable silence in the room.

"And as you're at home mulling it over, remember our class motto," Beauregard said, pointing behind at a placard on the wall above his desk which read:

Don't believe everything you think

With the advent of any new cultural touchstone comes the inevitable shift in clique dynamics, a rearrangement of sympathies, demarcated by who's into the new signpost and who's not.

That October the premiere episode of the late night live comedy show *Saturday Night* (called "Saturday Night Live" by so many people that it evolved into the de facto name) came screaming across our cool nerd sky like a supersonic rocket.

Some got it, others didn't.

The day after that debut, we all gathered at the Tar Pits, to have what we called a "pot-luck" picnic, not in the traditional sense of an everybody bring something to eat pot-luck, but in the subversive sense of everybody get high on marijuana pot-luck.

We pooled our scant cash to make a buy from Bigelow Rust, rolled a cigarette pack's worth of joints, and showed up on the north lawn of the Tar Pits, behind the museum, the patch of grass that abutted the sludgy black stream of tar-water admixture, laid out blankets, stayed on the lookout for tourists, museum security guards, friends of our parents who might recognize us, and inhaled the sacred fragrance to our minds' delight.

Justine Balthazar and I had taken the bus to the Tar Pits together from our Confirmation class at temple that Sunday afternoon, so we arrived slightly after things had gotten underway.

We entered the park from the Wilshire side, the more crowded area of the Tar Pits, where tourists snapped their Instamatic and Polaroid cameras at plaster mastodons posing eternally in the vast black pool that gave the attraction its name, their real life woolly ancestors entombed in the tar beneath them.

A crowd of park visitors had gathered around a black-clad white-faced mime.

He was one of those nasty mimes who perform in the park, deriving most of his humor from making fun of people behind their backs, especially the handicapped.

No lie, he imitated a guy with cerebral palsy in the classic limp-wrist-beating-against-chest 'Spazz' style.

And I swear he made fun of this group of Down Syndrome children as they were walking to the museum, mocking them with an exaggerated waddle, to everyone's horror.

And, wait, then he shuffled behind this very old man who had spent the last half-hour passing by, and the mime then looked impatiently at his watch and pretended to keel over and die.

Here's to the fantasy of mimeless parklands.

There's always hope. Remember that, Monsieur

By the time Justine and I arrived, several joints had already made their way around the gathering.

You could smell the cannabis from 20 yards across the Tar Pits.

The cool nerds were wasted and wacky.

The lookouts had abandoned their vigilance.

Anything could happen.

Nothing did, but it could've.

And that was enough danger for the wimpy likes of us.

The common question among us all: "Did you watch last night?"

"Amazing," said Sharon Rose.

"The dude who sang along with that Mighty Mouse record!" Buzzy Lagniappe referred to Andy Kaufman's mind-altering comedy routine.

"Flagrant!" said Claude Moss.

"That was most excellent," added Lorelei Lux.

"I didn't get it," said Claire Farnaway, to red-eyed silence, "but I loved Janis Ian."

"That song is totally about me," said Sharon Rose.

"Me, too, totally," said every other girl at the picnic.

"*And those of us with ravaged faces, lacking in the social graces,*" they sang in solidarity, "*desperately remained at home, inventing lovers on the phone.*"

Rudy Tuesday was sitting on a blue blanket he'd embroidered himself.

There was a red heart in the middle, and it said "Love" in white lettering below.

"I copied it from Rosie Grier's needlepoint book," he said.

He had brought his portable stereo cassette player with him and had cranked up the music.

Baby, baby, baby, you're out of time . . .

"Is that the new Stones album?" Whitman Rust asked.

"Lord, yes," enthused Rudy, "What better to listen to stoned than the Stones, right?"

"Ah, man," Manny said, "I just got that record. The Stones look like The Bugaloos on the cover. It's not really that new. It's got a lot of old stuff on it. I like it though. It's the Stones."

"So, I went with my family to San Francisco this past summer, and we drove by an apartment complex called Park Merced, and it was identical to Park La Brea," Lorelei Lux said, sitting on a big tie-dye blanket next to Rudy's, pointing at the labyrinthine Park La Brea apartment complex behind us across 6th Street.

"Trippy," said Claire.

"Probly the same architect?" said Miranda.

"No bout adoubt it," said Manny with his eyes closed.

"But I started thinking up this prank which I'm determined to pull off when I've got my own car," Lorelei said, "Chloroform a random old person sitting on a bench in Park La Brea—"

"—You could also use ether like in the Bugs Bunny cartoons," said Claude Moss.

"Chloroform," said Lorelei pointedly, "and then take him or her unconscious up to San Francisco and the corresponding bench in Park Merced and watch what happens when the chloroform wears off."

"Flagrant! Ha!" said Buzzy Lagniappe, kicking his feet with delight.

"Maybe even film the reaction . . ." Lorelei continued.

"I'd be laughing my ass off at that shit!" continued Buzzy.

The cruelty of it unnerved me.

It reminded me of the kind of shit that fucking mime would do.

I saw Miranda had risen and walked away from the group.

I followed her to the foot of a grandfatherly sycamore tree and sat down beside her.

Why do you think of the first girl you had

Some things just stick in your mind

The Rolling Stones permeated our corner of the Tar Pits.

Miranda sat and gazed at the motionless creek.

There've been so many girls that I've known

I've made so many cry

and still I wonder why

"Heya," she said without looking at me.

"You OK?"

"I think I want to sit alone for a while," she said, then looking at me, "Come back in a bit?" she requested.

"You OK?"

"Just pot paranoia, or whatever . . . I'm fine."

"Cool," I wandered back to the hive, dismissed.

'Cause you'll never break, never break, never break, never break

This heart of stone

"It'd've been cool if Vincent Price played the Godfather," said Rudy.

"The godfather of onscreen closet queens you mean?" Buzzy Lagniappe asked.

"Oh, you know it," Rudy said.

"Vincent Price was married," said Manny Shepherd, who knew shit like that.

"Uh huh," said Rudy, "Like that proves anything. He is the godfather of a whole generation of closet homosexuals who have been strutting their stuff on TV forever and nobody ever notices. I mean characters who are so obviously queer it's not even a mystery."

"Like who?" I asked, truly curious.

"OK, how about Larry Tate on *Bewitched?*" he offered.

"Oh, totally!" several among us agreed gleefully.

"Gomer Pyle," Rudy said.

"And Sergeant Carter!" Buzzy pointed out.

"No, duh," I said, "Bring us some new information."

"OK," said Rudy, ready for the challenge, "How about Floyd the Barber on *The Andy Griffith Show?*"

"I'll give you that," I said. "What about Howard Sprague, same show?"

"Now you're in the spirit, child," Rudy was elated, "Who else?"

"Reuben Kincaid on *The Partridge Family!*" shouted Claire Farnaway.

"Yes!" said Rudy, "I love when the ladies can pick up on that stuff."

"Who's on your list?" I asked again.

"Oh, well, there are unquestionable ones like Mr. French on Family Affair,

273

and of course Paul Lynde on Hollywood Squares," Rudy continued.

"You've got to be kidding me," Claude attempted an imitation of Lynde's campy delivery.

"I mean, doesn't everybody know about Paul Lynde?" Rudy went on, "And Charles Nelson Reilly on Match Game is another. Rip Taylor? Come on! Super Duh! But there are also really wayback-in-the-dark-corners closet queens."

"Like?"

"Um . . . Donald Hollinger on *That Girl?*"

"Ann Marie's boyfriend?" I asked.

"He has no sexual interest in Ann. She just looks good on his arm when he goes to parties," Rudy said. "Herman Munster is really fucked up about his sexuality," Rudy rolled on, "Uncle Charlie on My Three Sons . . ."

"Alice on *The Brady Bunch*," said Justine.

"Duh duh duh duh," sang Rudy to the tune of Beethoven's 5th.

"Jethro Bodine!" said Claude Moss.

"Nah," said Rudy, "Jethro is definitely a sexual mess, but I think it's more 'cause he wants to fuck his cousin."

"Ellie May, hell yeah!" said Buzzy, "I'd totally fuck her."

"In the sea-meant pond," said Eddie Gurges.

"You guys are gross," said Arabella Mayflower, who hadn't spoken all afternoon.

"But since we're on the *The Beverly Hillbillies*, can we talk about Jane Hathaway?" said Rudy.

"Miss Jane. Mega-Lesbian," said Claire.

"Daaaaang, dude," Manny Shepherd said, "Jane Hathaway is gayer than Aunt Hagatha and Aunt Clara, those two old dykes on *Bewitched*."

"I can never remember which is which, though, Aunt Hagatha and Aunt Clara," Candy Stoner said, "They're both freaks. They confuse me."

"Paul Lynde was on *Bewitched* too," said Claude, "Uncle Arthur!"

"And gay as quiche lorraine," said Rudy.

"As who?" Whit asked.

"Never mind," Rudy waved it off as not worth it. But *Bewitched* may be the gayest show in TV history."

"The first Darren was pretty tightly wound, too," I said.

"Oh, man, there's this lesbian bar up on Santa Monica called *Miss Jane*. It's like right near the Pussycat Theatre, too," said Buzzy. "Whit and I saw it next door when we snuck into the Pussycat this one time."

"Flagrant. *Miss Jane*," said Claude, "that's perfect."

"And speaking of which, this is my song, baby! Yeah," said Rudy, who stood up and started dancing and jiggling to the Rolling Stones song "I'd Much Rather Be With The Boys."

I left Rudy's performance to take another stab at Miranda, still pensive beneath the sycamore tree.

"Is it possible this tree has been here since dinosaur times?"

"*Ce n'est pas possible, non,*" Miranda said.

"But maybe its roots are touching soil that's been around since dinosaur times."

"*Peut-etre.*"

"The pine tree looks even older than the sycamore," I observed, pointing to our left.

"Pine trees look old even when they're young," Miranda said, sighing lightly, "like some people." She stood up, pointing. "And that tree over there," she pointed to our right, toward the Japanese foot bridge, "that thing is like from the Pleistocene."

She grabbed my elbow, tugging me in the direction of the gnarled, multi-branched, stooped-over tree that grew some weird-ass fruit that looked like figs, but, like, poisonous figs.

Tired of walkin on my own

It looks better when you're not alone

The rest of the kids were still dancing to the Stones as we took a closer look at the prehistoric fruit tree.

There must have been a dozen branches growing from the main trunk, and all of them curved close to the ground; some branches were actually somewhat embedded in the ground.

All the branches bore numerous carvings indicating couples in love.

"How many of these people are still in love, do you think?" Miranda wondered.

"How many of them are still alive?" I added.

"Yeah, huh," she said as she ran her finger along a branch, stopping gently at the path of a caterpillar making its way to a thatch of leaves at the tip.

"I think I'm a little afraid of caterpillars," I admitted.

Miranda smiled.

"*Well, I must endure the presence of two or three caterpillars if I wish to become acquainted with the butterflies,*" she said in a lilting cadence, then pausing. "That's from *The Little Prince*," she added.

"Ah, of course," I said, tagging along with her smile.

Miranda sat down at the foot of the tree and pulled me down to join her. We rested our backs against the thick trunk. It was kind of bumpy and uncomfortable, but I didn't want to move. I felt like it'd ruin everything.

You can get me if you let me

The Rolling Stones music was growing faint, pushed back into a kind of side-consciousness, as the world contracted to include just the two of us.

"Can I ask you something?" Miranda said, tentatively.

"Sure," I said, preparing myself.

"Don't take it the wrong way."

"I might, so be ready," I said, giving her a chance to chicken out.

"Just curious . . . um . . ." she was looking at my groin.

"Yes?" I said, aware of it.

"It's about, um."

"Isn't everything?" I joked and blushed simultaneously, crossing my legs.

"We were talking the other day—"

"—We?—"

"—me and Bella and Lori and Sharon, and maybe Dolly was there too, I don't remember . . . Dolly's not around as much these days . . . and we were talking about guys and how they all try to show off their . . . stuff . . ."

"Stuff?"

"Apparatus, you know."

"Dicks."

"Right . . . and someone—not me—brought you up . . . I can't believe I'm saying this . . ."

"You're stoned."

"I am," she said.

" . . . So, someone—not you—brought up my crotch . . ." I said.

" . . . and how you don't do that . . . um, show it off . . . you keep yours kind of, I don't know, hidden?"

"You talk about that junk? Flagrant," I said, bewildered and self-conscious. I bent my knees upward.

"It's a thing, I don't know," she said.

"A thing. Like boys look up skirts? That kinda thing?" I said.

"I guess."

"The promise," I reminded her.

"Something like that."

"In other words, girls get horny too," I said.

"Ew. Curious is the word I'd use," Miranda answered.

"Horny," I teased.

"Curious," she swatted at me.

"Whore Knee," I swatted back and grabbed her wrists. I could have pushed her over and rolled on top of her, but I didn't.

"Curi—"

I interrupted her, "Whore—"

"—Stop," she put her hand over my mouth and left it there. Then she touched the rest of my face.

A sublime stretch of silence between songs struck a perfect punctuation to the moment.

"I like your face," she semi-whispered and turned red.

The words fell, barely audible, out of her mouth, as if she'd tried to swallow them back too late.

"Nah. Dorky," I protested.

"I like dorky faces," she answered and caressed a tuft of my jewfro and then lightly held the back of my head but didn't attempt to draw me toward her.

I wanted to tell her she was the most beautiful girl I'd ever seen but I resisted and, instead, let another kissing moment pass.

One only gets a finite number of those before the young lady moves on, I could hear my dad saying.

How many more such moments did I have left in my account before Miranda Savitch moved on?

How many had I squandered on the shame of wanting?

When would I be left destitute with insufficient funds?

"You're stoned," I said.

I could hear Rudy singing loudly:

You're a faggy little leather boy with a smaller piece of stick.

You're a lashing, smashing hunk of man;

Your sweat shines sweet and strong.

Your organ's working perfectly, but there's a part that's not screwed on

Dolly, who must have just shown up, started asking everyone to get up in the tree Miranda and I were sitting under.

"Let's take a group picture," Dolly said as the crowd moved toward us, "I'll make duplicates for everyone so we can all have it."

I volunteered to take the shot.

"But then you won't be in the picture," Dolly said.

"Yeah, but every time you look at the picture you'll remember I'm the one who took it, right? So I'm kind of like in it," I said.

"Sort of, I guess," she said, unsure.

Everyone occupied a separate branch.

I snapped the photograph, at the time not knowing it would commemorate an arrangement that was changing, a branching out, as it were, of our individual lives.

That day at the Tar Pits was the last time we hung out together informally as a group.

After the pot-luck, our social interactions tended to happen either in class, especially during the St. Jerome/Beauregard block, or at nighttime parties that didn't afford us much soulful esprit de corps.

Parties reeked of that old bothersome bugaboo, organized fun.

Our worlds were diverging, our passions expanding, our interests exerting more sway over our time and attention.

We began to coalesce around a variety of activities rather than around one another.

Gus and Whit were spending more and more time getting high and looking for trouble.

Claude got involved in ROTC, at first as a way to avoid P.E., but then as a path and a social scene.

Dolly, Sharon, and Lorelei became Drama kids.

Claire played tennis.

Miranda and Arabella were elected into student government as 10th Grade officers.

Candy Stoner left Fairfax and ended up going to Beverly High.

Manny was in orchestra and jazz band. I played basketball and would later join the track team, though mostly I had taken to staying in my bedroom a lot, reading, listening to music, and writing songs.

Others of our circle turned more anonymously into hard-working students and consumers of mainstream culture.

There was something kind of sad about the unraveling.

But there was also the peace one finds in allowing the natural course of things to unfurl as it will.

I had been talking to Miranda in Beauregard's class (she sat next to me in there) about *Saturday Night Live* one day in early November, and she suggested we watch together on the telephone because "we haven't done that in a while, it'll be fun, I'll call you," which she did because she knew I wouldn't.

My mother glared at me when the phone rang at 11:27pm but still let me take it into my room.

"It's just starting," Miranda said.

"I know I know," I said, turning on the wobbly black & white television at the foot of my bed. The set was perched atop this metallic pole that always looked like it was about to tip over, though it never did.

We watched for a while in silence, not much laughter.

That was the thing about *Saturday Night Live*.

Most of the time it wasn't funny, but the stuff that was funny was worth enduring the sludge.

Gilda Radner reminded me of Miranda a little bit. Same sandpaper voice. Same jewbroad humor.

Neither of us thought the land shark was funny.

The TV screen turned into the video game Pong suddenly.

"Pong!" Miranda said.

"Ugh," I grunted.

"Remember the first day they had it at the Town & Country arcade?"

"Oh, yes. That was an important day," I said, recalling our virgin flirtation of 2 years before.

"Totally. I thought it was cool even though I din't actually get to play Pong that day," she said, seeming not to recall the verbal sparring that punctuated our 8th Grade attempts at flirtatious banter, "I remember watching you play though."

"You din't play?" I faked my own lack of memory.

"Hey, I'm looking in the TV guide, and you know what's on The Late Show later? *Once Upon A Time*," Miranda said, ignoring my mockery.

"I don't know it."

"It's with Cary Grant," she said, sighing romantically after.

"Judy Judy Judy," I spoke the cliché phrase in Grant-mimicry.

Saturday Night Live ended, but neither of us made a move to end the phone conversation.

It was after 1:00 am, dangerous and arousing, timeless, quiet.

A Cal Worthington commercial appeared.

If you want a better deal go see Cal

"I will stand upon my head to beat all deals

I will stand upon my head

'Til my ears are turning red"

Go see Cal, Go see Call, Go see Cal

Cal Worthington and his dog Spot—who was never a dog but always some random zoo animal—saturated the airwaves after midnight.

Buzzy, like a lot of people, used to think the Cal Worthington theme song chant was "Pussy Cow, Pussy Cow, Pussy Cow."

"Nah, dude, it's Go See Cal," I'd say to him, "It says it right there on the bottom of the screen: Go See Cal. While they're singing the song. It's pretty obvious."

There was a trashy pathos in the Cal Worthington Dodge and Ralph Williams Ford and Zachary All and Colton Piano and Bob Spreen Cadillac commercials interrupting bad movies being shown in 10-minute increments at 2am.

The pathos felt was not just for the movies or the commercials but for yourself, caught in that predicament of nowhere else to go.

You felt like you were the only person in America awake at that hour.

But I had Miranda, who ended a long silence by saying, "Whoa, I think I dozed off for a second."

"I wondered where you went," I said.

"Ha, but I think I had a weird dream just now . . .," she paused, "like I was looking at this plant, and there were flowers on the plant . . ."

"What color?" I asked.

" . . . I don't know . . . dream color . . . you know those colors like when you rub your eyes? . . . but the thing was . . . like right before I woke up just now . . . I looked more closely at the flowers and I could see they were butterflies."

"Whoa, dang."

"Totally, but like still attached to the plant . . . butterflies on stems. But when I first saw them from far away they looked like geraniums."

"Butterfly geraniums maybe," I said.

"Ha-ha, a new kind of flower."

"No no, there really are flowers called butterfly geraniums. Do you remember if they were lavender maybe?"

"Butterfly geraniums, cool. Nah, I don't know what to call the color, but they weren't lavender."

"There are also geranium butterflies," I said, "I've never seen one of those though. We have butterfly geraniums in my backyard. My mother is a geranium freak."

"How many different kinds of geraniums are there do you think?"

"Infinity strains," I said, "so fucking many."

"What makes them all geraniums? 'Cause they look different, at least the ones I've seen. What's geranium about all of them?"

"That's . . . I don't know," I said, drawing out the pause. "I have boring dreams mostly," I changed the subject, avoiding her question for fear of displaying my stupidity and ignorance, "I once had a dream about waiting in line at the bank."

Miranda laughed.

"No, really. I was with my mother. There was this girl there who looked like Dorothy from *The Wizard of Oz*. I think it was this girl I saw at Zody's once when I was 11, but I'm not sure. You know, it was a dream."

"You remember a girl you saw at Zody's when you were 11?" Miranda asked incredulously.

"I know, kinda psycho, right? She was eating a frozen banana. In real life, not in the dream. In the dream she was just standing there."

"You are a weirdo," Miranda said.

"I also have this recurring dream that I'm hiding on the garage roof. Nobody can see me up there. I love that feeling."

"You have dreams about hiding on the garage roof," Miranda said.

"Yeah. Usually someone's inside the house threatening to kill me, some intruder or something. I always take the same escape route out through my parents' bedroom onto the brick barbecue, from there to the back wall, and then I'm able to crawl onto the garage roof."

"And what do you do up there? In the dream, I mean?"

"I smoke menthol cigarettes."

"OK . . ." she paused. "You smoke?"

"In the dream, yeah. Always menthols."

"My uncle calls menthol cigarettes 'polar bear farts.'"

"Ha, that's excellent," I said.

"Yeah, my dad had this pack of Kools on the table once, and my uncle said to him, 'Those aren't yours, I hope, They're like polar bear farts.' Oh my God it was so funny, and then he was like, 'The *schvartze* who cleans your house smokes menthol cigarettes. Please tell me those aren't yours.'"

"Dang. That's flagrant," I said.

"Yup," she heavily accentuated the p.

"I actually have smoked a menthol cigarette," I said.

"No. Really?"

"Yeah, Buzzy Lagniappe and I once smoked cigarettes I got from this guy T'Qwan—he goes to Fairfax—you know tall T'Qwan on the C team? Like maybe a couple of years ago, when T'Qwan and I were playing on the same basketball team at Gardner Park he gave me some cigarettes that he stole from his dad. I showed them to Buzzy and he said we should smoke them, dude. So we did."

"And were they like polar bear farts?"

"Absotively posilutely," I said.

"S'anyway," she said, "Cary Grant is such a fox," and then fell back into another long silence. *Once Upon A Time* had started. We watched without speaking.

After a while I heard her breathing become louder and more regular. She was asleep.

I thought maybe I should hang up, but I felt bad thinking about her waking to a dial tone in her ear. And so I stayed on the line, waiting for her to wake up.

I ended up watching all *of Once Upon A Time* while Miranda slept, cornball ending and all.

Then when that was over, about 4:00 am, I fell asleep myself, still on the phone.

I was awakened at dawn by Miranda's voice.

"Lance, are you there?" she asked.

"Mmm."

"Did you fall asleep?"

"Yeah, after you did," I teased.

"How could you tell?" she was horrified, "Was I snoring?"

"I guess we can say we slept together," I said, not answering her question, trying to be flirty.

"Depends what you mean," Miranda answered.

"Let's tell everybody we slept together," I suggested.

"Uh, no," she made clear how it was gonna be.

And so nothing more was ever said about it again.

6

"General Interest," I read from the Daily Bulletin in Mr. Beauregard's class the following week and looked over at Miranda.

"I don't have any," she raised her hand.

Some days she was more into it than others.

We were reading *Catcher In The Rye* at that time in Mr. B.'s class. The day before, we had talked about Holden's obsession with Jane Gallagher.

"There is a real Jane Gallagher in Holden's past, but the Jane Gallagher he's talking about and thinking about isn't real at all; she's a myth."

"A myth for what?" Miranda asked.

"Virginity, perhaps?" Beauregard put forth, "or at least Holden's skewed notion of purity. Do you notice how he doesn't grant Jane Gallagher any sexuality at all? Like the checkers thing. Who plays checkers?"

"Children," said Rudy Tuesday. "And old people."

"Yes," said Mr. B.

"It's non-sexual," Miranda said.

"So that's why he can't deal with Stradlater trying to 'give her the time,' like he's gonna corrupt her or something?" said Manny.

"That's partly it, yes, Holden is the protector of the innocent, the catcher in the rye," said Beauregard.

"But Holden gets it wrong, right?" asked Claire Farnaway, "His version of the Robert Burns poem?"

"Yes, and what is that poem about?"

None of us had looked it up like we were supposed to. Beauregard waited long enough to exacerbate our discomfort.

"It's a poem about a girl who uses an outward illusion of purity to disguise a naughty private life. And that girl's name is . . . Jenny," Beauregard said.

"Jane," said Miranda.

"I'd say so," answered Beauregard, who then began singing:

O Jenny is all wet, poor body,
Jenny is seldom dry

"Dang, dude," said Whit.

"Flagrant," added Claude.

She draggled all her petticoats,
Coming through the rye

"Coming, heh," mumbled Buddy Feigenbaum.

Should a body kiss a body,
Need the world know?

"Mm-hmm," said Dolly with a glance in my direction.

"But what else isn't Holden dealing with?" asked Beauregard.

Silence held the classroom fast. Beauregard waited it out.

"What else?" he repeated.

Finally, Miranda raised her hand.

"The fact that . . . maybe . . . Jane *wants* Stradlater to give her the time?" she said.

"Precisely," said Beauregard, pleased, "Or maybe *she* wants to give *Stradlater* the time."

"She's curious," I said, looking at Miranda who sat to my right.

She smirked her nyeah face at me.

"I'm sure she is," Beauregard said, looking at both of us. "Thank you, Miranda." Beauregard paused, looking at a page in his tattered copy of *Catcher*. "So, whose innocence is Holden protecting?" he finally asked.

"Little kids," said Claire Farnaway.

"Not really," Beauregard said.

I raised my hand.

"Lance?"

"His own?"

"Precisely," Mr. Beauregard paused, "excellent. And why is he compelled to act out this kind of crazy mythology? Why is he so freaked out about innocence?"

"His was damaged," said Manny from the back.

"Or stolen," said Gina Dichlich. "Was he molested?"

"What do you think?" Mr. Beauregard shrugged his shoulders.

"Jane Gallagher was," said Lorelei Lux.

"Go on," said Mr. B.

"By her stepfather."

"Mr. Cudahy," said Beauregard, "What makes you say that?"

"Jane's tear hitting the checkerboard when she talks about him," Lorelei Lux said, "the silence that surrounds you when something like that is going on. Holden picks up on it."

"Yes, he does."

Mr. Beauregard looked at Lorelei Lux who turned her gaze down toward her open notebook.

"He's afraid of growing up," Jim Lord said.

"Yes. Why?" asked Beauregard, moving on but continuing to look back at Lorelei with some concern.

Nobody had an answer.

"What does growing up mean?" he prodded? "What happens when you grow up?"

"You get older," said Buzzy, half-joking.

"No, duh," said Whit, crossing his eyes and poking his cheek.

"Good answer, actually," Beauregard said. "Growing up means getting old and 'rotting' and eventually . . ."

"—dying," said Buzzy.

"Precisely," said Beauregard, "So Holden is really afraid of . . . what?"

We all muttered 'death' to ourselves.

"Holden Caulfield is haunted by death," Mr. B. said, "It's everywhere in the book."

"His brother Allie," said Miranda.

"Yes, and let's not forget James Castle, the boy who jumped out the window . . . wearing . . . significantly . . ." he waited.

"Holden's sweater," said Lorelei Lux, who always remembered shit like that.

"So it's kind of like Holden jumped?" said Sharon Rose.

"He's certainly thought about it," said Mr. Beauregard.

"Didn't James Castle get molested by that group of boys?" Gina Dichlich asked, "And that's why he jumped? That's how I read it."

"There's a lot implied there. Holden doesn't want to talk about it, that's for sure," Mr. B. answered and then paused again, looking at the book. "And remember the scene where he's in the park at night with icicles in his hair looking for the lagoon with the ducks in it and begins fantasizing about his own death and funeral?"

Miranda wrote in my notebook:

the lagoon and the ducks remind me of macarthur park!

I smiled and looked at her for a few seconds while she looked back.

"If we put it in terms of a metamorphosis, which we've been talking about a lot this semester, it's like Holden is in his cocoon, clinging to memories of being a caterpillar, but instead of using the cocoon as a nest for growth and maturation, he uses it as a hiding place, afraid of becoming a butterfly."

"Because butterflies don't live very long," said Gina Dichlich.

"And they like to die in private," I said, making a teasing face at Miranda.

"Live fast, die young, leave a good-looking corpse," said Mr. B., "that's what butterflies do, right? Ever seen the movie *Knock On Any Door* with Humphrey Bogart? No? There's a character in that film, Nick Roman, who carries that as his personal philosophy. What about the Faron Young song "Live Fast, Die Young?" Big hit, 1955? No? Anyway, a lot of times the phrase gets attributed to James Dean. Anybody know who that was?"

"*Rebel Without A Cause*," said Manny Shepherd.

"Yes, indeed, great film," said Beauregard, "You all should see it. James Dean was a rebellious figure in the 1950s, and he did indeed live fast and die young. In a car crash."

"Death is so weird," said Sharon Rose.

"But it's the one thing we all do," Mr. B. contended, "We're all going to die one day. There's nothing else you can be so certain of."

"I don't know, it's weird to think about it," Sharon Rose answered.

"Of course it is. You can't imagine the world without you in it. But let me remind you, the world got along fine without you before you were born. It'll somehow stumble along without you after you're dead," Mr. Beauregard said.

"Remember when Billy Westin got run over by a truck in front of Pink's?" Buzzy Lagniappe asked everybody who'd gone to Melrose Avenue

Elementary School.

It was one of the horrors of our childhood. The first time we knew a kid our own age who died.

None of us witnessed the event itself, but hearing about it the next day, that our classmate Billy Westin had been killed trying to cross La Brea in front of Pink's Hot Dogs, which was around the corner from school, smashed our little Eden to Kingdom Come.

There was also this kid Edward Pesky who got hit by a foul ball at a Dodger game and died.

He was in the middle of biting into a Dodger dog when the Manny Mota foul ball hit him in the head.

I'm just now noticing the hot dog connection between those two deaths.

"Do you remember the first time you realized you were going to die one day? For some of you maybe it was one of those two events, the two boys who were killed," Mr. Beauregard said, "Or maybe it was something else." He looked around the room, waiting for us to share our stories.

I raised my hand.

"Lance."

"I was nine."

"That's young," Mr. B. said.

"It was a really wet winter I remember, and the ground in our backyard was soggy."

"How did you realize you were going to die one day?"

"I spent the morning drowning snails," I said, "snails that had been destroying my mother's geraniums."

"Rock and roll," said Buzzy.

"I don't think you can drown snails," said Miranda. "Can't they live underwater?"

"We'd have to ask Mr. St. Jerome about that," said Mr. Beauregard, "but in trying to drown the snails, were you thinking about death and then applying

291

it to yourself?"

"No, the snails had nothing to do with it, the feeling of dying one day I mean," I said, "other than I got bored after a while and went inside, where I sat in the hall, and I looked through the photo albums my mother keeps in the hallway drawers just below the linen closet."

"Get to the damn point," Buzzy Lagniappe demanded.

"Digression!" shouted Jim Lord, pointing at me.

"I saw pictures from when my parents first got married, and pretty much every single one had a dead person in it. My grandma Rose. Grandpa Bernard. Uncle Hymie. Aunt Tilly. Uncle Sam who kinda looked like W.C. Fields. And while I was looking at the dead people in the pictures, I also saw a bunch of pictures of them holding me when I was a baby. And, I don't know, I started crying."

"What were you crying about?" asked Mr. Beauregard.

"Um, I guess 'cause I realized I'd never be a baby again. That was gone forever just like the people holding me," I said.

"Time moving irreversibly forward," Mr. B. said, "and what else?"

"Nyeah-and . . . well, the obvious . . . I'd be dead too one day and maybe some little kid would be looking at a picture of me and be thinking,'Weird, he's dead now.'"

"When my grandma died," Miranda said to the class, "I realized everything was going to die, including me. I remember shaking at her funeral when I thought about that."

"We do that at funerals," Beauregard picked up, "We're really mourning for ourselves. You hear the kind words being said about the departed and wonder what people will say about you. You see the body being lowered into the grave and think to yourself, 'That will be me one day.' Holden is mourning his own innocence even as he mourns his own inevitable death," said Beauregard as the bell rang.

"See you tomorrow," he said, pausing, ". . . well, maybe, you never know for sure," he laughed. We did too.

Upon Mr. Beauregard's advice, a bunch of us went to see *Rebel Without A Cause* when it played at the Continental Theatre on Melrose near Van Ness, almost right across from Paramount Studios, the area where Manny and I had once tried to find the San Berdoo Apartments from *Day of the Locust*.

Though Manny had already seen *Rebel*, he tagged along anyway.

The rest of us hadn't seen it: me, Buzzy, Whit, and also Miranda, Dolly, and Arabella Mayflower.

We had been hanging out together less, so there was approximate awkwardness all around, but we were turned on by James Dean's performance and understood the rock and roll appeal as well as the legend that had flourished over the past 20 years since his death.

But for me, the key performance was Sal Mineo as Plato.

The sad follower, the anti-philosopher, the empty yearning, the shameless wanting.

I ended up sitting between Dolly and Miranda, some kind of deliberate accident.

I felt Miranda's sensitive presence in the dark but made no physical contact, though about halfway through the film she elbowed me off the armrest.

I think I was supposed to elbow her back but instead let her lay claim to the territory.

Dolly ran her finger down my thigh, her nail dragging loudly across the denim pant leg.

This caused an immediate erection which I hid by crossing my legs despite the logistical discomfort.

When the movie was over, Whit suggested we all go over to his house.

"We'll have to call home and ask first," said Arabella, "but yeah."

"That'd be cool," said Miranda.

Dolly's mom was coming to pick her up at the theatre, so she couldn't come with, and it sort of seemed like she didn't want to be with us anyway.

She had this really impatient absence about her, even as she was scratching down my thigh.

Arabella and Miranda called their moms on the payphone in the lobby of the Continental.

"Hi, mom?" Miranda said, "Oh, it was great. Yeah, he is, but. What do you mean but what? It's just kind of ew to hear you describe guys as studs. I know it's my problem. Anyway, hey, can I go over to Whit's house for a while? On the bus. Yeah. And Lance also. Mother, please, don't even. Just can you come pick me and Arabella up later? Like near Mansfield and Oakwood. We can also take the bus home though. Yeah she already asked her mother. Yes I'm telling the truth," Miranda insisted, "Can we stay till like ten? I swear on Bubby's wall crypt I will call before ten."

The girls took the Melrose bus west to Highland, and we rode alongside on our bikes making faces at Miranda and Arabella through the bus window, past Paramount and KHJ and Lucy's El Adobe and the John C. Fremont Library.

When they got off the bus at Melrose and Highland we walked with them over to Whit's house.

The smell of garlic and oregano emanated from the kitchen of Emilio's, the Italian place on the corner as we passed.

As per usual, Whit's folks weren't home, and Bigelow was on hand to help out with some Thai Stick and the cosmic itenerary it would help us to embark on.

Miranda was mega-sexy lips-to-bong, an elemental frenching with herself and all the possibilities.

Once elevated to the realm of the sacred, we reminisced about seeing *Rebel Without A Cause* what seemed like a decade previous.

"That's the Griffith Park Observatory, you know," Manny said, "the place where Plato got killed."

"Plato was such a sad character," Miranda said.

"I couldn't tell if he was a gay golita or if he was just like retarded," Whit observed.

"We should go to the Observatory some time," Miranda said.

"I was just there recently," said Arabella. "There was the most amazing view of the whole city. I could see from downtown to the beach. Dodger Stadium and shit. I was trying to figure out where Park La Brea was, but I couldn't find it."

"Kinda like the same as being inside Park La Brea," Miranda answered.

"Totally," said Manny, "in a major way," and then he laughed the way he always laughed, on the inhale, creaking like a medieval drawbridge.

"Did you see Thurston Howell III was James Dean's father?" Arabella said.

"Jim Backus," said Manny, "He also does the voice for Mr. Magoo."

"No shit?" said Whit.

"My grandpa drives like Mr. Magoo, all slow and crazy," Manny continued, "Sometimes he drives on the left side of the road and people honk and yell, 'Hey, where do you think you are, England?' And my grandpa just laughs and says, 'Hey, ver em I? Hangland?' and then keeps driving on the left side of the street. It's funny as hell when it isn't scary. 'Hey, ver em I? Hangland?'"

"Mr. MaJew," said Whit.

"I hate Mr. Magoo. It's always the same plot," said Arabella.

"Like the Roadrunner cartoons," Miranda said.

"Yeah, but Roadrunner's cool," said Arabella, "The Roadrunner only fucks Wile E. Coyote's shit up, and the Coyote deserves it 'cause his ass is stupid."

"Hell yeah, buying all that Acme shit all the time when the shit never works and always backfires on his ass?" Buzzy added.

"But Mr. Magoo fucks everybody else's shit up. Mr. Magoo is not cool," Arabella said.

"Mr. Magoo bugs the shit out of me," I admitted.

"Probly 'cause he's blind," Miranda said.

"No," I said.

"Yes," she said poking me.

"I did used to be scared of Billy Barty 'cause he's a midget, though," I said.

"Dang, dude," said Whit, "that's cold."

"And, hey, Pepe Le Pew is always the same plot, too," I said.

"Pepe Le Pew stinks," Whit said, waiting for our laughter, which came in the form of the proverbial Three Stooges 'nyuk nyuk nyuk,' a stock response in the geek lexicon to any type of purposely lame punnery, mouthed in unison by me, Whit, Buzzy, and Manny. Miranda and Arabella didn't join in.

"Le Pew's a rapist," said Arabella, "always trying to molest that poor black cat who accidentally gets a white skunk stripe down her back in every dang episode. I mean, come up with some other story, right?"

"He's always chasing pussy," Buzzy said, trying to be Whit.

"Aw, man . . ." Miranda grimaced, "Buzzy . . . you know?"

"What was wrong with Plato?" asked Buzzy, changing the subject.

"Gay golita," Whit wheezed, mid-drag, "or retarded."

"He was just sad," said Miranda. "He wanted to be around people but didn't know how to be really."

"Loneliness," I said without thinking.

We all lay in various spots on the floor and on the bed.

A long silence ensued.

We'd run out of things to say.

We meandered off on our own little individual trips.

I was having cock-in-pussy thoughts of Miranda, getting erect from fantasies of crass comminglings, somewhat weird with her just a few feet away.

I kept coming back to us fucking on her bedspread.

What was happening in her mind?

I looked over, and she was rummaging in her purse, pulling out her same old yellowed copy of *The Little Prince.*

She began reading out loud: *"If you tell grown-ups, 'I saw a beautiful red brick house, with geraniums at the windows & doves on the roof,' they won't be able to imagine such a house. You have to tell them 'I saw a house worth a hundred thousand francs.' Then they exclaim, 'What a pretty house!'"*

I lay on my back, eyes closed, and pictured Miranda in the window of a house with geraniums at the window and doves on the roof.

In fact, later that evening, after I got home, I pulled out my favorite old box of crayons and began drawing the vision I'd had.

A girl in the window of a red brick house, though I'm a terrible artist, so the girl didn't really look like Miranda, she looked more like the girl everybody draws when they're like 5 years old, with flipped hair and and A-shaped skirt and shit. You know her.

There were geraniums in the window box except I drew butterflies at the ends of the stems instead of flowers, like from Miranda's dream. I entitled it the first thing that came into my Porno weed head: *My Anywhere Girl Is A Geranium.*

We waited out front for Miranda's mom to come pick her and Arabella up. Manny had ridden his bike home already, and Buzzy and I just lived around the corner and so were still hanging out.

Arabella was talking to Whit and Buzzy, and Miranda dragged me off to the corner of the lawn.

"Hey, so tomorrow we're going to the Huntington, and my mom said I can bring a friend. Do you wanna go?"

"I'm your friend?" I asked.

"You are," she said, "don't be a dork. You wanna go?"

"I do," I said, not sure if I really meant it and actually kind of regretting it as soon as I'd said it, and I wondered if she regretted asking me. But it was too late for either of us to back out.

We did end up having a pretty mellow time at the Huntington.

The car ride out to San Marino with her family was oddly silent, her dad, the affably quiet Henry Savitch at the wheel, her mom, Tamar, asking me briefly, "So how are you liking Fairfax so far, Lance?" but otherwise mute for the rest of the journey, her little brother Jeremy reading *MAD* and fundamentally unaware of anyone else's existence.

During a couple of sudden wide turns Miranda clutched my knee for support. That was somewhat erotic.

We didn't go into the museum itself but rather wandered the gardens.

It was a magnificent, refined wilderness.

Miranda and I ambled off by ourselves, unsuccessfully looking for geraniums.

We sat for a while in the rock and sand garden, avoiding eye contact and marveling at the lifeless beauty.

"If there's no plant life, what makes it a garden?" Miranda asked.

"Maybe 'cause it's arranged carefully," I suggested, "like plants in a garden would be and like they wouldn't be in the wild."

"May be," nodded Miranda.

"Those rocks and the sand wouldn't look that neat in the desert," I added.

"I love the patterns in the sand," Miranda said, "they're perfect. They're like a nebula."

This hippy dude in orange pants and an embroidered shirt handed us his business card and whispered, "Karma is what you are always doing," as he walked past. The card was simple, just his name:

Baron Seades, World Teacher

And there were two phone numbers in the lower right hand corner.

Miranda and I actually called the numbers on the card when we got back to her house after the Huntington, but one turned out to be the pre-recorded joke line Zzzzzz, the last entry in the phone book, and the other was a pre-recorded invitation to some Masters & Johnson seminar, narrated by a woman with what Miranda called a "fake slut voice" saying, "Come join us at Masters & Johnson for *all* the *love* you *want*." That one was a little embarrassing, listening with our heads together against the phone and me entertaining graphic thoughts of fucking Miranda or at least kissing her maybe.

I had kind of wanted to ask guru Baron Seades about the molecules I see when I look at the daytime sky. Alas.

We strolled from the absence of flowers in the sand and rock garden to a striking florescence in the rose garden. The colors were almost day-glo in their brightness.

The whole area smelled like the candy you eat in dreams.

Among the bushes there was a bronze sign that said:

The caterpillar on the leaf

Repeats to thee thy mother's grief.

   —William Blake, "Auguries of Innocence"

Miranda read it out loud.

"Cool," I said.

"What does it mean?" Miranda asked.

"It reminds me of that poem we read in Beauregard's class about 'Margaret are you grieving,'" I said, "and your mother's grief is, like, over watching you grow up, seeing you as a larva and knowing you're gonna grow up—"

"—and get old and die," Miranda said.

"Just like her," I said.

"So, it's like Beauregard's thing about how whenever you're grieving you're really grieving for yourself," Miranda conjectured.

"Yeahzackly. *It is the blight man was born for,*'" I quoted the Hopkins poem. I had copied that line into my notebook in Mr. B.'s class and had just been looking at it earlier that day and thinking about Holden Caulfield.

We spent the last portion of our visit to the Huntington sitting among the lily ponds.

"When I have my chateau in the south of France, I will defenly have lots of lily ponds like this," Miranda said.

"France, huh?"

"Oh, yes. I'm going to move to France and change my name to Guinnevere."

"Guinnevere Savitch."

"Yup."

"I like the name Miranda better," I protested.

"Then you should say it more often," she scolded, her eyes latching onto mine, "hmm?" and never have I been so transparently invited to pounce on a mouth.

The door was so completely and obviously open it required all my trepidatious wimpitude to bar myself from entering.

Miranda looked off at the roses when I didn't respond.

There ensued a moment of agony on both our parts.

"Let us sally forth, Sir Lancelot," she said finally, rising, a sigh in her voice, leading me back to the foyer where we were to reconnect with her folks and head out. She held my arm as we walked without speaking.

I hated myself in that silence.

7

"General Interest," I began with the usual reading of the Daily Bulletin that following Monday in Beauregard's class.

"I don't have any," said Miranda.

Beauregard was talking to us that week about analyzing poetry.

"You have to masticate the language," he said, "really chew on it."

It was a fitting image for him to use because when he would concentrate on meaning he'd make a chewing motion with his jaw.

"I masticate three times a day," joked Jim Lord.

"Not just *what* it means but *how* it means, the way it sounds, too," said Beauregard, ignoring Jim's innuendo, "the music, the dance."

He used terms like assonance and onomatopoeia.

"Sounds like you have to go to the bathroom," said Jim, "Onomatopoeia, I'll be back in a minute . . ." rising from his seat as if to go pee, laughter crackling everywhere, Beauregard included.

"Remember how Ms. Cummings used to say onomatopoeia?" asked Claude Moss.

"Onomatopoeeeeeeia," drawled Dolly in an exaggerated southern accent, with other John Burroughs alums echoing along in suitably genteel Cummings tones.

"That's virgin for short, but not for long," cooed Gina Dichlich also a la Cummings.

I squirmed at the mention of her name and caught eyes with Gina who, I'm sure, knew of the encounter I'd witnessed between Ms. Cummings and Samantha Coventry near the end of 9th Grade the year before.

"Who's Ms. Cummings?" inquired Mr. B.

"Our 9th Grade English teacher at JB," Claire said.

"Our *sexy* 9th Grade English teacher," corrected Buzzy Lagniappe, slapping hands with Whitman Rust.

"Not as sexy as your current English teacher, I'm sure," sighed Beauregard ironically, passing his palm across his balding pate to a few compassionate giggles. "What are some examples of onomatopoeia?" he asked.

"Shower," someone said.

"Zipper," added Rudy.

"Scissors," Jim Lord chimed in.

"Butterfly," said Miranda.

"That's a good one," said Mr. Beauregard. "In most languages, actually, the word for butterfly is onomatopoeic."

"Mariposa!" Whit shouted out the Spanish word.

"Yes!" said Beauregard, flapping his hands like a butterfly.

"Papillon," I added, "in French."

"Anyone know the Italian?" Mr. B. asked, to no response. "Farfalla," he said eventually, reprising the hand flap.

"Par-par in Hebrew," said Manny while Beauregard continued the gesture.

"And in German?" Beauregard asked and waited. "In German . . ." he said, pausing, bringing his hands to a rest, " . . . the German word for butterfly is . . . Schmetterling."

A mixture of laughter and befuddlement followed.

"Schmetterling?" asked Claire Farnaway with crooked eyebrows taking up the flapping butterfly hand motion.

"Nyeah," said Dolly Ferris, shaking her head, "that does not jive."

A general susurrus rustled among the students with the occasional half-laughed "Schmetterling?" arising from the hubbub.

"All right, people, Mr. B. is behind on his essay grading," Beauregard said, trying to calm the tittering, "let's have you do some silent reading for the rest of the period. Remember you're writing about your books in class tomorrow," he instructed, "so take this opportunity to finish up."

And so we set about our silent reading, for me *One Flew Over The Cuckoo's Nest*, for Miranda *Brave New World*.

I had chosen *Cuckoo's Nest* because the movie was about to come out; in fact, my paperback edition already had Jack Nicholson on the cover and the proclamation, "Now A Major Motion Picture."

Manny and I went to see the film together during Thanksgiving weekend over in Westwood Village where we ran into everybody, including Miranda and Arabella, who were there together, Dolly Ferris, who was with this 12th Grade guy named Aaron Wasserman, apparently on an official date, which twinged my heart a bit, I'll admit. Sharon Rose, Justine Balthazar, and Lorelei Lux were there as a threesome, all now full-fledged theatre geeks.

"You guys wanna get high after the movie?" Buzzy asked us as he and Whit made their way down the aisle, "because we are going back to Whit's house later and are going to get fucked *up*, dudes."

"Nah," I said, in agreement with Manny, "we're gonna check out this new album Manny got."

"Patti Smith," said Manny, "*Horses.*"

"Well, your guys's loss," Buzzy dismissed us as he and Whit chuckling with pity as they went to find seats in the front row.

"Hi, Lance!" I heard Miranda say, from the aisle near our seats. "I knew you'd be here! Think it'll be as good as the book?"

"Does that ever happen?" I semi-shouted back.

"You never know!" she answered as the house lights dimmed, "Oh, shoot, whoops! See you later!" she said scooting into her row, but then she turned back around and whisper-shouted, "We're gonna hang out at Ship's after if you wanna also."

I whispered back I couldn't, with slight regret but mostly glad I had an excuse not to join them.

Instead, Manny and I went back to his house and listened to *Horses* and heard transcendence.

Manny's older sister, Leah, whose wholesomeness I would often defile in sordid sexual fantasies, wasn't home, but I stopped briefly at her bedroom doorway en route to the bathroom.

Whenever at the Shepherd house I would try to get a glimpse into Leah's bedroom in order to gather details for the next round of self-pleasuring revelries.

I loved her stuffed animals.

Older sisters. Dang, dude.

Our plan for Thanksgiving weekend was to get stoned on some Thai Stick that Manny had acquired for free from Big via Whit.

"Finder's fee," Manny explained, "I sent him a new customer."

Once aloft we were planning to watch the *Twilight Zone* marathon on Channel 5, but before that we dove into Patti Smith. The journey was immediately seminal.

"Rock and roll," Manny said, and again, "rock and roll."

"Birdland" swallowed us both.

he was very different tonight

he was not human

Our eyes were closed, our heads were levitating, our hearts hit the rhythm of Patti's passion.

And he saw the lights of traffic beckoning like the hands of Blake

I thought of Miranda in the rose garden.

"Jim Morrison was really into Blake also," Manny said, "in a major way."

"We should check him out," I answered. "I saw a cool quote from him the other day at the Huntington."

"Blake? Absotively posilutely," Manny said, "You know he's a freak."

So he cried out as he stretched the sky,

Pushing it all out like latex cartoon

I felt like my namesake, holding earth and sky apart.

Am I all alone in this generation?

We were floating on the floor immune to any semblance of chronological time.

They're all dreaming they're gonna bear the prophet

I wanted to be fucking Miranda. My cock in her pussy. Pressing her into the bedspread. Spreading her. Coming buckets of hot Geronimo. The Porno weed let me smell her wetness. Dang, dude. I felt it. Her. Pussy. Exploding and foreboding deep in the imaginary vortex. Not even touching myself. Cognizant enough to keep it hands-free.

It's all gonna split his skull

It's gonna come out like a black bouquet shining

We felt capable of making art that matters.

Manny and I inhaled it together.

Patti Smith was inspiration.

We were gonna make literature.

We were gonna make music.

We were gonna be part of the creative continuum that had been going on since caveman days.

After our Patti Smith revelations, we checked to make sure Manny's parents were asleep and then went into the kitchen and pigged out on Count Chocula and half-and-half.

We crunched and slurped our snack in heavily concentrated stoned silence until Manny suddenly asked me if I was ever going to fuck Miranda Savitch.

"I'm having enough trouble working up the courage to kiss her," I answered.

"How long have you been doing this shit with her?"

"Um, just a couple of years."

"Dude, she is in love with you, in a major way, and you are like duh in love with her, so nu? I don't think you're going to get a formal invitation in the mail, dude."

For a couple of weeks Manny and I listened to *Horses* nightly together, doing our homework at either my house or his, swept up in the power of the music, discussing the call to Art invoked by the lyrics.

It was an album that solidified our commitment to constant creativity.

School remained important, especially Beauregard's class, but it became secondary to the bigger mission.

And then my heart betrayed me.

That day, in the dank hot wetness of the Fairfax gymnasium, I was felled by another collapse brought on by shortness of breath.

We were playing at home against Hollywood High, and we were trouncing them soundly enough that the coach sent me into the game early in the 4th quarter to play guard along with Samuel Lee who'd also spent much of the season riding the bench.

It was also one of the rare occasions when Miranda was among the spectators.

She waved to me several times from the stands, but I didn't wave back.

Had to be too cool to notice.

But I was well aware of her presence as I took the floor to start play.

Her breath was the sweat on the back of my neck. Her eyes were a panel of judges ready to condemn my lack of skill.

I was aware of her hair as I ran up and down the court all awkward and self-conscious.

The curse of wanting to fuck somebody.

Ball-in-hoop thoughts merged with cock-in-pussy thoughts.

Reality and metaphor at play in the pathetic dork-mind of Land "Lax" AIAS, benchwarmer and infinite loser.

I was scrambling for a loose ball when I fell to the floor, at first feeling like I had merely stumbled but then realizing that I couldn't catch my breath and was gasping, after which the world went white and I lost consciousness briefly then came to surrounded by a crowd of concerned faces, though I didn't see Miranda's among them.

The emergency room doctor used the terms 'heart murmur' and 'arrhythmia' when he was explaining the condition to my parents later, though I didn't really understand what he was saying.

He clarified, "It's called fibrillation. Crossed signals. Your heart beats the way a butterfly flies. It feels like a flutter, right?"

"It feels like the disorderly malfunctioning of thousands of tiny enzymes," I said.

The doctor chuckled, "I guess . . ."

"Yeah, but I've been feeling those flutters my whole life really."

"And you say this has happened before?"

"Yes, last summer when I was at John Wooden Basketball Camp."

"Hmm," the doctor said (I never learned his name). "It's possible you've had this since birth and it's just now manifesting."

By the time my parents arrived I was stabilized and itchy to go home.

My pediatrician Dr. Gemara showed up at the same time my parents did, and, after consulting with the emergency room doctor, advised me to give up basketball.

Also, from that day, for a while anyway, my parents used the condition to prohibit my participation in just about everything until I convinced them to let me join the track team.

"No running. Field events only," my father insisted.

I'd even freaked myself out.

For a while I was afraid to masturbate.

I already had a recurring fear of being found dead that way and now there was reasonable cause.

Upon my return to school the day after the episode, I discovered a folded up piece of notebook paper in my locker.

It was an e.e. cummings poem, handwritten by Miranda.

i carry your heart with me(i carry it in

my heart)i am never without it(anywhere

i go you go,my dear; and whatever is done

by only me is your doing

I looked around to see if Miranda was watching me read it.

you are my fate

I leaned my head against my locker.

Dang, dude.

I was her fate.

here is the deepest secret nobody knows

(here is the root of the root and the bud of the bud

and the sky of the sky of a tree called life;which grows

higher than the soul can hope or mind can hide)

and this is the wonder that's keeping the stars apart

i carry your heart(i carry it in my heart)

Below the poem she added:

Glad you're ok.

Keep on keeping the earth and sky apart, Mr. Atlas.

Love Is Real.

Miranda

p.s. Call me?

I didn't call her.

I thought about it quite a bit.

I even had a dream that I called her, but it was a dream phone call, so of course I couldn't really understand what she was saying, it was all muffled and nonsensical.

But I didn't actually pick up a real-life telephone and call Miranda Savitch.

Over the sanctified 2 weeks of Christmas vacation, Buzzy went with Whit's family up to this place near Yosemite called Mariposa where Whit's grandparents lived.

It was during break that I ran into Taryn Rust at Aron's Records.

I was combing the used bins and she saw me from her spot at the cash register.

"Lance!" she yelped my name and waved.

"I thought you guys were up in Mariposa," I said, walking over.

"Yeah, they all went, but I've got this job and stuff, so, you know, plus I'm 19 so I can do whatever I want really," she explained.

"And you have the house to yourself."

"Hell yeah," she smiled.

"Sweet deal. Have you heard this?" I asked, holding up a used copy of Joni Mitchell's *The Hissing of Summer Lawns*.

"No, not yet. You gonna get it?"

"I think so, yeah. I love Joni."

"You want to bring it over and listen at my house later?"

"I don't know."

"I have the house to myself, after all . . ." she lilted enticingly.

"Nyeah, I . . ."

"I'll make it worth your while . . ."

"As in?"

"I'll turn you on," she said, miming joint-to-mouth implying the promise of loco-weed from Bigelow's voluminous stash.

"What time?" I accepted.

Taryn smiled.

"Seven," she said.

I was there at seven.

Actually I got there about 3 minutes early but didn't ring the doorbell until 7:00.

I didn't want to accentuate my uncoolness.

Taryn Rust greeted me at the door in pink sweat pants and a button down denim shirt untucked.

"Hi, neighbor," she said like Mr. Rogers.

"Greetings, earthling," I said in dorky jewboy Martian voice like a dweeb at a Star Trek convention, even, yes, I will admit this, making the Vulcan 'Live Long And Prosper' rabbi sign as I said it, "I come bearing Joni."

"Right on," she said, taking the album from me and removing the disc from its sleeve and laying it on the stereo's turntable at the far end of the living room. "You ready to fire it up?"

"The music?" I asked.

"Everything," Taryn smiled, pointing with her eyes to the coffee table, upon which rested an elaborate bong, a pink plexiglass cylinder with dual nozzles to allow simultaneous inhalation.

She fired up Joni, then fired up the bong, and then, quite unexpectedly, she fired up me.

Anima rising

Queen of Queens

Wash my guilt of Eden

Wash and balance me

Joni sang as Taryn Rust and her satin tongue suddenly sprung a rambunctious number on my flabbergasted mouth, all tongue and teeth and heavy breath.

I didn't know what to do with my hands.

She knew what to do with hers though.

God goes up the chimney

Like childhood Santa Claus

The good slaves love the good book

A rebel loves a cause

Taryn started rubbing me through my jeans, then she very deftly unbuttoned my jeans and reached in to grab hold of my cock and remove it from its confines.

Her right hand stroked me gently as her tongue explored my mouth.

I leaned back so I could relax into the horny moment and give myself over to the release about to bring consciousness to naught.

I knew the fulcrum well and the unbalanced abandon of orgasm.

I was rather practiced at it in fact, but only in a solo setting.

In Taryn's hands I collapsed into an utter emptying; it felt like the softest bathtub.

I was even able to pretend that I was fucking her for a few seconds right before I came.

When I opened my eyes Taryn's head was on my shoulder and her right hand was dripping with my jizz.

I thought I'd be more embarrassed than I actually was to see my sperm all gooped up on someone else's skin.

She kissed me on the cheek and reached across the coffee table for a kleenex.

"You like?" Taryn asked, wiping her hand off.

"Umyeah," I croaked, my cock still throbbing.

"Your turn," she said, pulling my hand toward her crotch, which I touched through her sweatpants.

She pushed my hand against her in a circular motion as she closed her eyes.

Her clutch tightened with each revolution.

Taryn then escorted my hand up over the top of her sweatpants and into point-blank territory, my middle finger finding its own way inside her.

Taryn then guided me north toward her clit and hinted at the way to play with it.

First gentle and intermittent like a brushstroke, then pressing and relentless like a whirlpool.

She echoed obscenities to herself while moving in unison with my tidal undulations.

At her encouragement I kept at it despite my tiring finger.

"Enhyeah," Taryn moaned pretty loudly and dug her nails into my wrist as she pushed my hand away from her clit and arched her back and straightened her legs and went rigid for a second as her breathing stopped, for a second, and then resumed.

She pulled my head toward her for a long soft kiss.

Dang, dude.

That shit was bitchin'.

I've got a head full of quandary

And a mighty mighty thirst

Having missed most of *Hissing of Summer Lawns* Side A due to our escapade and its aftermath, we sort of drifted into the kitchen, frenched a few times up against the refrigerator and then the stove and then the Sparkletts dispenser, ate some Count Chocula and half-and-half, laughed about how stoned we were.

"Whenever I get stoned with people we always end up talking about how stoned we are," Taryn complained.

"Totally," I said, "Like right now."

"Dang," she laughed, "Zackly. Flagrant."

"Pot wants all of your attention. Like a nightmare girlfriend."

"Yeah-and God pulls that shit, too, huh?" Taryn added, "God pulls that shit all the fuckin' time, dude."

As I walked home I felt guilty about how not-guilty I felt.

313

Frenching Dolly Ferris over the summer had felt like cheating on Miranda, even though Miranda wasn't my girlfriend, yet getting a hand-job from Taryn Rust and then finger-fucking her did not.

Taryn and I had smoked some of Bigelow's Porno weed, and when I got home I immediately lay across my bed, held my fingers—still fragrant with Taryn's crotch sauce—up to my nose, inhaled the horny girl-fumes, and jacked off to fantasies of fucking her and not Miranda Savitch.

There were so many great possible places to fuck in the Rust home, and I imagined that action in all of them.

The living room couch. The den couch. The staircase. Her bed. Whit's bed with the Willy Wonka sheets. Best of all, her parents' bed. That one got the most play in my autoerotic cosmos.

She appeared every night for a while as the final face in a ritual litany.

Taryn Rust would be my favorite for a good long time.

8

Before 1975, New Year's Eve was an evening spent watching TV, usually *Dick Clark's New Year's Rockin' Eve*, culminating with the ball dropping in Times Square, even though when you were watching it you knew it had already dropped 3 hours before, then the anti-climactic letdown when the countdown reached zero and the dreadful sadness of the post-midnight musical portion of the show, featuring, like, Leo Sayer or the Amazing Rhythm Aces or some such.

If my parents weren't home Mimi and I would dip into the liquor cabinet to swill some horrid Kahlua or whatever bottle seemed the most full and thus least likely to be noticed if we happened to pour ourselves a glass or two.

But usually my parents were home, and so we'd repair to our respective bedrooms, underwhelmed and wondering.

On New Year's Eve 1975, however, things changed.

There was a party at Dolly's house, and I attended, though with great reluctance.

When I arrived, Dolly was arm in arm with her newish beau Aaron.

Miranda was already there and appeared to be fairly captivated by Freddy Snow, though she did look over at me several times early in the evening as if to connect, but she remained very much in Freddy's orbit.

Every time I looked at Miranda that night I had thoughts of my pumped cum dripping across Taryn Rust's fingers like oven-hot bear claw frosting.

The television was tuned to, of course, *Dick Clark's New Year's Rockin' Eve*.

During an early segment of the show, Olivia Newton-John sang "I Honestly Love You."

And while several kids scoffed about what a horrible fucking song it was, I admit I had a certain horny fascination with Olivia Newton-John, so I stood and watched her sing which also felt like cheating on Miranda even though she wasn't my girlfriend, even though she was exchanging intense body language with Freddy Snow.

In the den some people were dancing to KC & The Sunshine Band's "That's The Way (Uh-huh Uh-huh) I Like it (Uh-huh Uh-huh)," a disco song about fucking.

But aren't all disco songs about fucking really?

I was standing watching the always entertaining spectacle of white people dancing, when Diana Hitchcock came up and stood next to me, sort of moving to the beat.

"Hey, whiteboy," she said without looking at me but rather at the crowd of Caucasoid dorks in their jerky attempts at rhythm.

"That's Jewboy to you," I shot back.

"No, *that's* Jewboy over there," she pointed to Drew Chupoy, my Filipino teammate.

Diana Hitchcock had a massive afro like Angela Davis and was built like a 12-year-old boy.

I'd never met her before, but I was very aware of her existence.

I'd seen her hanging out with Dolly and Lorelei and Justine among the thespian clique and keyed into her thing immediately.

She also came to most of the basketball games, and I was aware that we were catching each other's eyes on those afternoons in the gym.

"Lance, right?" she said. I nodded yes, and then she continued, "Hey, are you part black?"

"Not that I know of," I said, "Why?"

"Lips, ass, nappy hair," she said, her eyes adazzle.

"It's a Jew thing too."

"Can you dance?"

"I'm a lame-ass loser on the dance floor."

"You wanna dance with me anyways?" Diana asked.

"Nyeah, no," I said, too uncomfortable to go for it, "Not really."

"OK," she chided with a you-blew-it sigh.

"Next time," I said.

"Yeah yeah," she said, as she walked away, "No worries. I'm patient."

I watched her ass move as she crossed the room.

She totally knew I was watching her ass, too.

Diana Hitchcock.

Dang, dude.

She'd be back.

Most assuredly she'd be back.

"I have a long attention span," she turned around and said with a final flourish.

During a party-wide group sing of "Bohemian Rhapsody," Dolly's dad shouted from the kitchen that it was just a couple of minutes away from midnight.

"At midnight you have to kiss the person standing closest to you," Dolly instructed.

I felt the dread of confrontation mingled with the shame of wanting as Miranda moved into my immediate proximity, standing under the mistletoe that hung in the threshold between the den and the entry hall. Freddy was somewhere in the crowd.

While everyone started gathering around the TV to watch the ball drop in Times Square, I hovered on the periphery, feeling removed from the nexus, off on my own trip, wanting to be home and alone.

And then, when the ball dropped and the tradition of kissing at midnight erupted, it was a moment of alien exclusion for me.

I'd never had such heightened awareness of my social discomfort and ineptitude as in that den of pleasures amidst the kissing and frivolity.

Dolly was kissing Aaron. Claude was kissing Claire Farnaway. Whit was kissing Misty Winters. Buzzy Lagniappe was kissing Justine Balthazar. Manny was kissing Sharon Rose.

Everybody was kissing everybody all over the world.

And I was standing torpid like in a tar pit.

Like a sloth in the bubble-goo.

Like a fossil in the fundament.

Miranda raised her eyebrows, pressing the question.

Marveling at how easy it seemed for others to engage with others and how impossible it was for me to engage with anybody at all (including myself), I hesitated in my approach and was beaten to the pounce by Freddy Snow who emerged from the cluster suddenly, grabbed Miranda by the jaw and sated her craving shamelessly.

Thus superseded, I averted my eyes and wandered out to the back patio, where Lorelei Lux had stationed herself as the perpetual outcast.

"You're not inside kissing," I said.

"Why would I be doing that? Kissing is gross," she said matter-of-factly.

"What're you looking at?" I asked her.

"Caterpillar spinning a cocoon," she said, "Come look."

"Cool," I said and stood by her side.

"I always wonder if it's going to be a moth or a butterfly," Lorelei said with atypical tenderness.

"This time of year, a moth. Why are butterflies magical and moths just annoying?"

"I hold the entire moth race responsible for ruining my three favorite sweaters," she complained.

"What do they think about while they're in the cocoon?" I wondered aloud, wanting to impress her with my depth.

"Maybe they dream of eating leaves," she said.

"Or of being butterflies," I added.

"Like the Chuang Tzu story."

"You know that story?" I asked.

"I watch *Kung Fu*," she said.

"Really?"

"And plus Miranda tells that Chuang Tzu story to everyone. And how you two watched that episode together while you were talking on the phone and blah blah barfidy blah. So, how did you like *The Collector*?" she asked.

"Dang, dude, you are psychic," I said, "I read that a long time ago. How did you know?"

"I keep an eye on you, Lance Atlas," she said.

"Have you read it?" I asked.

"Yep," she said, "I thought it was interesting . . ." she drawled as she took my hand and gazed at my palm, touching its lines, seeming to read them, tickling me, but I let her do it because it was sexy cool. "Interesting . . ." she paused again and locked into my eyes.

"What's interesting?" I interrupted the discomfiting energy.

"You are a witness," she said.

"Huh?"

"That's your role on earth. You are a witness," she paused, "and eventually you'll testify."

She held my hand intensely. Our fingers began to interlock. She pulled me toward her.

"Eventually you will testify, Lance Atlas," Lorelei Lux muttered, as my pelvis pushed against hers, "and confess everything to me."

The glass door slid open from the inside, and Miranda stepped out onto the patio, followed by Freddy, catching me in handplay with Lorelei.

"Hi, Lance," Miranda said, pretending not to have noticed . . . "Lori," she glared.

"Miranda," I nodded, letting go of Lorelei, "Freddy."

"Hey, dude, how's it going," Freddy said with restrained animosity.

We were in love with the same girl, so Freddy and I usually kept our distance.

"Lance was just making love to my mind," Lorelei said directly to Miranda.

"Nyeah, he's good at that," Miranda answered tartly, seemingly unfazed by Lorelei's graphic audacity at first.

"Whoa, flagrant," said Freddy Snow shifting swiftly into guy-solidarity mode, "dude, right on," and he walked toward me to exchange a hand slap which I obliged despite the underlying hostility.

He probably figured I was now going after Lorelei and so Miranda was his game alone to bag.

Miranda gave me some pointed eyebrow action then looked away with a long exhale.

"Well, we din't mean to interrupt," she said, "Bye, Lance," returning indoors, followed by Freddy.

Dang, dude.

"Happy New Year, Lance Atlas," said Lorelei, reaching her hands out to me, "Come make a resolution."

"Nyeah, I gotta go," I declined, "I promised my parents I'd call before 1."

"Maybe some other year," she said, turning to look back at the caterpillar, "See ya."

I had been dismissed.

The next afternoon, a sunny New Year's Day in L.A., broadcast across America via the Rose Parade, enticing the winter-beaten hordes to this constant mirage, I sought consolation and solitude at the Tar Pits.

I had been reading *Alice's Adventures in Wonderland* for the 3rd or 4th time, planning to use it as my next book report for Beauregard's class, and brought that along to make some progress.

School would be starting back up in a couple of days.

But mostly I just wanted to lie on my back and watch the atomic sky-show playing out against the brazen gray cloud cover.

I lay then as I lie now, saddened by the lack of Miranda, my anywhere girl, spinning inward, weaving a fortress against encroaching agony, letting Professor Dodgson provide the necessary insulation, the inviolable barrier of language, helping to keep all the heat and sound inside, away from shame.

The Caterpillar and Alice looked at each other for some time in silence: at last the Caterpillar took the hookah out of its mouth, and addressed her in a languid, sleepy voice.

`Who are YOU?' said the Caterpillar.

This was not an encouraging opening for a conversation. Alice replied, rather shyly, `I—I hardly know, sir, just at present— at least I know who I WAS when I got up this morning, but I think I must have been changed several times since then.'

`What do you mean by that?' said the Caterpillar sternly. `Explain yourself!'

`I can't explain MYSELF, I'm afraid, sir' said Alice, `because I'm not myself, you see.'

`I don't see,' said the Caterpillar.

`I'm afraid I can't put it more clearly,' Alice replied very politely, `for I can't understand it myself to begin with; and being so many different sizes in a day is very confusing.'

`It isn't,' said the Caterpillar.

`Well, perhaps you haven't found it so yet,' said Alice; `but when you have to turn into a chrysalis—you will some day, you know—and then after that into a butterfly, I should think you'll feel it a little queer, won't you?'

`Not a bit,' said the Caterpillar.

`Well, perhaps your feelings may be different,' said Alice; `all I know is, it would feel very queer to ME.'

`You!' said the Caterpillar contemptuously. `Who are YOU?'

I spent the rest of the afternoon and into the evening wrestling with that question.

"Who are YOU?"

Lance Atlas, social caterpillar.

Dang, dude.

I made a resolution to cover myself up and change into something else.

A Dodecahedron Living In A Trapezoid World

1

I wasn't sure where to wipe the blood from my hand.

I thought maybe my shirt at first.

But I ended up using the grass instead.

A pink stain remained on my fingers.

Rabbi Meshuggeneh approached me slowly.

Rabbi Meshuggeneh was this old uber-Jew who always *davened* at Gardner Park, a scruffy Orthodox guy who'd either be muttering to himself or else chanting prayers out loud with cantorial authority on the little shady patch of grass between the basketball court and the makeshift hamster graveyard.

My dad is the one who called him Rabbi Meshuggeneh.

I'd heard the name long before I knew what *meshuggeneh* meant.

I'd seen Rabbi Meshuggeneh all my life around Gardner Park, but there was this one time in particular, the time I learned his name, I saw him as my dad and I drove down Beverly Boulevard near the Pan Pacific Auditorium, and I asked who is that guy we always see and my dad said oh that's Rabbi Meshuggeneh, he's been around forever.

I have no idea what his real name was, and I don't really care either. He was just always Rabbi Meshuggeneh. It fit him.

He was definitely borderline homeless.

Usually Rabbi Meshuggeneh didn't move around in the park.

He'd just sit in his chosen spot for as long as it took him to complete his day's liturgy. Then he would pack up his reading utensils and wander out into the day or evening elsewhere in the Beverly-Fairfax area.

But at that moment he was shuffling in my direction, labored and stooped over with the weight of centuries and his ragged old-world briefcase full of scripture.

He stopped in front of me, letting his bag drop, wiping his forehead with a phlegmy handkerchief as I continued to wipe my rosy fingers on the grass.

He gestured at the world around us and looked just past me.

"Is this what God intended?" he asked in reference to something deep within his own head.

I sat in disbelief at first that Rabbi Meshuggeneh was interacting with me, asking me a direct question.

It felt like the sort of thing that happens right before someone gets murdered.

"You mean like did God intend for me to finger-fuck a girl on her period?" I wanted to say but instead just shrugged, "an Orthodox girl yet?"

He stared at some imaginary star-child in the sky for a lagging minute.

"Every night God prays, did you know this?" he said.

"I did not," I answered.

I just wanted him to say what he meant and go away.

That's how I feel about most conversations, actually.

"And do you know what God prays when he prays every night? Do you know? Can you guess?" he gestured to the heavens again.

It was a lightly smoggy April evening around sunset.

My birthday as a matter of fact.

"I give up," I said.

"I will tell you what God prays when he prays every night," Rabbi Meshuggeneh said.

He looked at me the way an executioner looks at his children when he kisses them goodnight after a hard day's work.

I let him talk.

"He prays, 'May my love of mercy outweigh my need for judgment.'"

His stare was unbreakable. A living Sphinx.

"Do you hear it?" he testified, "'May my love of mercy outweigh my need for judgment.' Isn't that perfect? That's the Lord our God praying to himself," Rabbi Meshuggeneh smiled like Uncle Fester, "You should be thankful for God's own nightly prayer. In any given moment he is in the process of saving your life."

He was a loony fruitbat, but I was now listening because that last thing about judgment and mercy was assaultingly beautiful, like something I'd heard before, something Talmudic, the sort of sentence that makes you forget where you are because you are so caught up in the rightness of it, the sort of sentence you keep quoting to other people until they're fucking sick of it.

I felt a little spooked, though, at the same time, by Rabbi Meshuggeneh.

I rose to signal my departure.

"Perhaps you will live to daven in the 3rd Temple," he said as I strolled away. "Vayikra twenty eighteen!" I thought I heard him shout afterward, though perhaps not to me.

May my love of mercy outweigh my need for judgment

Dang, dude, what a fucked up birthday.

School all day.

The unfortunate finger-fucking incident with Naomi Richter at Gardner Park.

The freaky encounter with Rabbi Meshuggeneh.

May my love of mercy outweigh my need for judgment

I had tons of homework to do so I couldn't go out to dinner or anything.

It all ruined the birthday sensation, that magic atmosphere, that fragile sanctity, the unabashed aura, the subtle penumbra, undeniably different from all other days.

That night I was so sad lying in bed I almost couldn't masturbate.

I'd gotten my homework done, though, 'cause, you know, that's what people like me do.

No matter what shit goes down, no matter what emotional hassle or social malfunction tears a hole in the cosmos, no matter what obsessive crush intoxicates the conscience, we always somehow get our homework done.

Dang, dude.

It was a Tuesday night.

Taryn Rust was up on the fantasy schedule.

I did indeed have a schedule, a prescribed schedule, of which girl I would fantasize about in my nightly sessions. Each girl was assigned a day of the week.

I called it Fuck-O-Rama, and I actually had it written down on a piece of paper which I kept folded up in my underwear drawer (a drawer that also had socks in it. And some Canadian pennies that I got back in change at Sav-On. And a Swiss Army knife my uncle gave me for my 12th birthday. And a rabbit's foot I bought at Bargain Circus on La Brea. And a broken stopwatch that fell off my shelf during the 1971 earthquake. And a black triangular stone I found at the Tar Pits which I thought might be a spearhead from caveman days. And a perfumed insert card from a fashion magazine. And a school picture of Miranda Savitch from 9th Grade—also signed by her on the back: *i'm right here. luv, miranda*).

It wasn't because I thought I wouldn't remember which girl I'd be with each night but because I got turned on seeing it in writing.

That sensation right there, getting turned on seeing it in writing, that was my future.

One time my mom was putting laundry away and came upon the Fuck-O-Rama paper.

I was reading *Flatland* on my bed, and, though horror-struck at seeing her lift the paper and unfold it, I remained agonizingly silent, not wanting to inject the moment with unnecessary provocation and presuming she wouldn't really grasp what it was. Just a list of names corresponding to days. No context at all . . . other than it said FUCK-O-RAMA at the top of the page.

My mom simply folded the piece of paper back up and returned it to its secret place in my underwear drawer.

She never said a word about it.

Sunday night's Fuck-O-Rama was assigned to Penelope Lagniappe, next door neighbor and Buzzy Lagniappe's older sister, a beguiling presence who teased me with sarcasm whenever Buzzy was around, but when we were alone together she'd be awesomely cool and somewhat into me it seemed like.

If she caught wind of me getting high on the garage roof she'd climb up and join me, sometimes bringing her own stash though usually cadging off mine.

"I thought I smelled you up here," she'd almost always say as she hoisted herself onto the roof from her backyard wall.

Sometimes I could see down her shirt when she did that.

Freckled titties, dude.

"I think my brother's crazy," she said of Buzzy this one time.

"Nyeah, ha ha, just a stoner freak," I said.

"No I'm serious, Lance, he's, like, mentally ill, like schizo, I'm pretty sure."

"I dunno," I shrugged though I knew what she meant.

"I hear him talking to himself in his bedroom."

"What, like in other voices and stuff?"

"Yeah, for sure, even though they all kind of sound like Bugs Bunny," Penelope said as she inhaled some extremely potent Thai Stick that I'd gotten from Whitman Rust via his older bro Bigelow.

"Zackly," I acknowledged, "He—I dunno—sometimes tries to tell me about 'the house next door.'"

"Yes!" she pointed at me.

"And I always say, 'you mean my house?' and he says, 'no it's a different house next door,' and I just always think to myself, whoa, dang, dude. Nigga be trippin."

We were both extremely stoned by then.

I wouldn't otherwise have used the phrase 'nigga be trippin.'

"I'm gonna call my autobiography *Nigga Be Trippin*," I said.

Penelope aspirated cannabis laughter and said, "You're the freak," while rolling onto her stomach.

"And the spider who talks to him?" Penelope said, squinting her eyes in concentration, "What's his name?"

"Flippy Killbones," I said.

"Flippy Killbones," Penelope drawled with her eyes closed, "Right."

Lately Buzzy would tell us all to be quiet in the middle of conversations so he could hear what Flippy Killbones was telling him.

He'd suddenly say shit like, "Be quiet. Flippy Killbones is telling me all about electromagnetism."

I was trying to communicate my overpowering lust to Penelope via telepathy during a long silence interrupted by a couple of obnoxious crows clearing the area of other birds.

She made some kind of weird bunny rabbit face at me and then we just sort of sat there stoned for a while and then her mother called her and she climbed back down into her yard.

"You should totally call your autobiography *Nigga Be Trippin*. That'd be funny as hell, dude," she said as she vanished.

The silence before the bunny rabbit face fueled all kinds of enraptured fantasies.

Monday nights my sultry nerd goddess was Leah Shepherd, Manny's older sister.

Dang, dude. Older sisters. It's fucked up. I can't help it. All my friends had older sisters.

Sometimes I'd assemble all the older sisters into their own separate Fuck-O-Rama tournament.

I'd do that like once a year.

One sister each night during the week surrounding the 4th of July.

The Pleiades, I called them.

Many nights I would gaze up at The Pleiades and call upon them to conjure a fire in me.

Leah Shepherd spent a lot of time studying on her bed surrounded by stuffed animals.

She got good grades and always behaved.

I thought that was sexy. Like a wall to knock down.

I always made sure to poke my head into Leah's bedroom when I went over Manny's house 'cause any interaction at all with her was future stokage for the strokage.

"Hey, how's it going?" I'd ask at her bedroom door.

She'd say, "Hey," without looking up from her book.

I'd stand there in tacit communication, my usual flirting method. You know you want to look up from your book and into my eyes right now, I'd think in her direction, "I command you to stop pretending you aren't into me and lock on like right . . . now."

Occasionally she would in fact look up at that very moment and I'd go whoa and then blush and say see ya.

The fantasy with Leah was pretty consistently on her bed, sometimes with and sometimes without stuffed animals.

And it'd usually be me swiping her books onto the floor and taking her like they do in R-rated movies. Slow motion definitely.

Tuesday night brought Taryn Rust, older sister of Whit and Big.

Taryn was already the queen of my sex dreams. She was easy to conjure.

Next up, Wednesdays, I debauched Evelyn Childs, this girl in my Geometry class.

Evelyn had the sexiest overbite and thick rich lips.

She had ice blue eyes and a crotch that called out to me.

She had a boyfriend too but that didn't stem the lust.

One time she asked me if she could borrow my eraser.

Sometimes I'd miss entire lessons because I was so distracted with thoughts of kissing Evelyn Childs on the mouth.

My Geometry grade was partially her fault.

Occupying a brief but dazzling tenure on Thursdays was Miss Graffenberg, the student teacher from UCLA who taught that Geometry class for 10 glorious weeks at the beginning of the Spring semester.

After her departure from the fantasy pantheon, she was replaced by a series of reliable substitutes like Dolly Ferris or Lorelei Lux or Laraine Newman from *Saturday Night Live*.

I reserved Friday nights for Miranda Savitch, my agony and my destiny.

Miranda Sabbath, I would jokingly call her during those Friday night raptures, pretending she was actually there.

A brief string of Saturdays belonged to Naomi Richter right up until the day I'm talking about, when I attempted to finger-fuck her while she was on her period, and that fiasco certainly knocked her off the Fuck-O-Rama roster immediately and for good.

But, dang, dude, those few raunchy Saturday night go-rounds with my frummy bunny were splendid.

Naomi was my *havdalah*.

Freedom from rest.

"Intercourse is a *mitzvah*," she actually said once to me in the library when I'd finally gotten her to talk about sex a little bit.

I put that phrase in her mouth incessantly during my Saturday night fevers.

The rule was on any given night, if an unscheduled female had provoked my horniness that day, she could replace the scheduled rendezvous for that one night.

Miranda would show up randomly on unscheduled evenings usually due to some kind of intense eye contact in English class earlier in the day or if she touched my shoulder or something but usually it was how she looked at me.

I liked to have the fallback of the written schedule, though, my totem.

It was fitting that Taryn was my birthday fantasy.

She'd given me my first handjob.

She taught me how to touch her.

"Like that," she whispered, nudging my hand that one time I finger-fucked her, guiding my motion, "make whirlpools," she urged me, "enhnyeah."

She also had excellent taste in music.

I saw her a lot while feeding my escalating addiction in the form of thumbing through the $1 bins looking for treasure at Aron's Records on Melrose where she worked.

My greatest Aron's coup was finding a copy of *Her Satanic Majesty's Request* with the 3-D lenticular cover in one of the $1 bins.

When the cashier rang it up he just kept saying, "This has to be a mistake. Somebody fucked up," and shook his head with geek chagrin. "Oh well," he said, "I guess you win."

He was one of those guys you can't tell if they're gay or not.

Triumphantly atop Taryn's girlness that Tuesday night in the throes of Fuck-O-Rama, I ejaculated into what I thought a vagina might feel like, wiped my belly dry, and stared into the ever-swirling speckled darkness of my bedroom, unable to sleep.

Happy birthday to me.

A few nights later, Saturday, my parents took me out for a belated birthday dinner at Mirabelle up on the Sunset Strip, across the street from Tower Records.

I ordered a chef's salad, no ham, green goddess dressing on the side.

"That's too much like lunch. Have something else," my dad said, "It's your birthday."

"No it's not, my birthday was on Tuesday," I answered.

"He loves that salad," my mom said, "Let him alone, it's his birthday."

"His real bird day was Doomsday," my sister Joy said.

"That's right," my dad said to Joy, starting to laugh, giving himself over to Joy's perfectly realized state.

Mimi was glowering at the salt shaker and announced she was only going to have a glass of water because she couldn't find anything on the menu she wanted to eat.

"Maybe they'll make you a grilled cheese," my father offered his usual solution to any food choice crisis.

Mimi made some kind of snorting sound.

"How's your grade in Geometry?" my dad asked me to divert attention from Mimi a-stew.

"It's ok," I said, "I had an A for a while when the student teacher was teaching, Miss Graffenberg."

"She was easier than Mr. Katz?" he concluded.

"Pretty much, yeah, I don't know, no, it's 'cause she made it fun," I shrugged.

I didn't want to tell him that the main reason I paid attention in class and got a good grade was that Miss Graffenberg was a total fox.

"Reading and music are more my thing I guess," I said.

"Pull my finger," he said.

"Theo," my mother warned, "Thou shalt not."

"My drama teacher always says 'music *is* math' whenever we're trying to figure out dance steps," Mimi said, forgetting her mood for a moment and also eating a breadstick.

"I've also been getting help with my homework from this Orthodox girl at the library," I said.

"Oh good. Just don't marry her," my dad joked.

"I don't think she's going to be coming to the library anymore," I said.

"Why not?" my mom asked.

"I tried to finger-fuck her while she was on her period," I wanted to say.

I shrugged.

"I dunno. She just said she's got other stuff to do or something. Jew stuff. I think I can still get a C without her," I said.

"A in everything else, though," my father said.

"For the most part," I hedged.

My parents never hassled me about my grades once the report card came out. They were just like whatever. But along the way, they'd encourage me to do well, try my best, give a shit, all that stuff. I appreciated their laid-back approach. I responded to it. I was comfortable with school. I liked most of my teachers. I sucked at math.

"It's humid for April," my mom said wiping her brow with her napkin, "I'm all shvitzy."

"Earthquake weather," my dad said.

"Don't be silly," my mom waved her hand dismissively at him.

"Mark my words: something's gonna be shaking soon," my dad said.

"Mimi's titties be shakin," Joy said.

"Shut up, retardando," Mimi quipped, "purple-lipped mongoloid."

"Hey, be nice," my dad said.

"That's right," my mom added.

"I'm not mongoloid, I'm Jewish," Joy gave one of her stock answers, "And you a photon foo."

"I'm not mongoloid, I'm Jewish," my dad snickered.

He often quotes that line.

I'm not mongoloid, I'm Jewish

After dinner we went across the street to Tower where I picked out a few albums, and my parents bought them for me.

That had been my preferred birthday present since I was like 10 or 11 years old.

I got Tom Waits' *Nighthawks At The Diner*, *Another Green World* by Brian Eno, which Manny and I used to get high and listen to at his house but I wanted my own copy, the Neil Young album *After The Goldrush*, another one of those records I always heard at other people's houses but didn't have, and I even grabbed *Silk Degrees*, the Boz Scaggs album, because I secretly thought it was a cool record, though I always made sure to hide it from my friends in order to avoid ridicule.

We arrived back home that night to the quiet commotion of a girl bleeding to death in the driver's seat of a rusty brown Pinto parked in front of our house.

Our across-the-street neighbor Mr. Wilson was standing next to the car waving his arms as we approached.

"Theo!" he hailed my dad, "Call for help! This girl's hurt bad!"

My mom and Mimi and Joy got out of the car and hurried inside the house while my dad and I jumped out of the car and stood next to Mr. Wilson looking into the car-door window.

An abandoned ice cream truck was parked diagonally across the middle of the street blocking access to our driveway.

"She's moving," Mr. Wilson said indicating the bloody girl.

It looked as if she had several stab wounds.

Eyes closed, she swayed her head slightly back and forth from side to side, muttering something.

Blood soaked her blouse and was spreading exponentially.

She kept touching the wounds with her right hand.

The left hand lay upon a knife in her lap.

She opened her eyes and looked at me, not imploringly.

She raised a bloody finger to me and then pressed it against her own lips.

"You can't get in?" my dad asked.

"Locked," Mr. Wilson answered.

"Did she stab herself?" my dad wondered, "Why's she locked in?"

"Weird about the ice cream truck," Mr. Wilson said, looking at the empty vehicle. The engine was still running. Music, on a loop, emanated from the tinny speakers, the treacly warped strains of "It's A Small World" from the Disneyland ride.

"I came outside to see what the hell was going on with the cockamamie ice cream truck. Then I saw this car I didn't recognize and then I saw the girl sitting inside. I was gonna ask her if she was ok but saw the blood and realized she wasn't. That's right when you guys drove up."

"I know that ice cream truck," I said.

The familiar sign, *Dinosaur Times*, was dim but recognizable by streetlight along one side of the truck.

Everything was moving in slow motion.

If this were a movie we'd be smashing the window to get her out and we'd all be freaking about the stabbed girl inside the brown Pinto. But this wasn't a movie, and we were all wondering about the ice cream truck.

On a normal day, that ice cream truck could be found either in the parking lot at Gardner Park or on Curson, next to the Tar Pits. We often joked that Happy Sam, as the ice cream man called himself, was actually pretty Neanderthal looking, so calling his truck Dinosaur Times made a lot of sense.

"Dang, dude, Happy Sam looks like he's from caveman days," Buzzy Lagniappe used to say when we'd be waiting in line to buy a 50-50 Bar or a Sidewalk Sundae from him, "with that big-ass forehead and gnarly teeth and shit."

But seeing the truck on my street, at night, illuminated by the yellowish street lamps and shifting glints of moonlight through the sycamore leaves, shook my axis with its awful wrongness.

I wondered why Buzzy hadn't come outside to view the crazy scene but remembered he was probably around the corner at Whit's house smoking pot and getting ready to watch *Saturday Night Live*.

They had invited me to join them, but I declined, partly because I really didn't hang out with them much anymore so it'd feel weird, but also because I had plans to watch *Saturday Night Live* while talking on the phone with Miranda Savitch, something Miranda and I hadn't done in a while.

My mother stepped onto the front porch and shouted, "Ambulance and police are on their way!" Joy and Mimi were watching from the kitchen window. "Is the girl ok?"

"She's still moving!" my dad shouted back.

I stared at the girl through the grimy windshield of the rusty brown Pinto.

"Do you have a crowbar in your car?" Mr. Wilson asked my dad, "We could smash the window."

"Yeah yeah, it's with the spare tire, let me get it," my dad said, trotting over to our Kingswood Estate.

The sirens grew painfully loud as the emergency vehicles turned onto our street, the police and the paramedics, along with a fire truck, all arriving at the same time, from two different directions, turning onto Citrus from Beverly and screeching to a halt next to the nearly perpendicular ice cream truck.

As the firemen attempted to force the Pinto's door open, one police officer began to cordon off the street with yellow crime tape; the other asked us what we'd seen.

"I heard the ice cream truck and came to see what was going on. That's when I saw her," Mr. Wilson explained.

"So you didn't see an assailant," the officer wanted to confirm.

"No, when I got out here it was just her sitting in the car," Mr. Wilson said.

"My son says he knows that ice-cream truck," my dad told the policeman.

"Do you?" Officer Macfarland asked me.

"Yes sir," I said, "Dinosaur Times. It's usually at the Tar Pits. Or Gardner Park."

"Do you know the ice cream man's name?"

"Yeah, it's Sam. He calls himself Happy Sam."

"Do you know his last name?"

"No. Just Sam. Or Happy Sam."

"Can you describe him?"

I didn't want to say he was a Neanderthal-looking motherfucker, so I just said he had a big forehead and kind of long hair and his teeth stuck out.

"Unibrow maybe?"

"Nyeah, I think so," I said, unsure, "maybe, yeah."

"Kind of like the fat kid from *Willy Wonka & The Chocolate Factory*? What's his name? Buzzy Lagniappe?"

"Augustus Gloop," I said, "Augustus Gloop is the fat kid from *Willy Wonka & The Chocolate Factory*."

"Really?" the cop said, "I thought it was Buzzy Lagniappe."

"No, it's Augustus Gloop. But actually, there is a kid who lives in the house next door," I pointed, "named Buzzy Lagniappe, and his real name is Augustus, and he used to be fat."

The cop looked at me for a second.

"Hey, you're the kid with the fritter," he shook his finger at me remembering.

"The fritter?" my father asked.

The cop and my father and I all turned toward the pop of a shattering window.

Flakes of rust fell from the car door as it creaked ajar. They lifted the girl out and laid her on a stretcher.

I watched as the paramedics worked with flickering speed like in a kinetoscope.

The girl began to gurgle as if to speak.

One paramedic lifted her head slightly and blood started to trickle out of her mouth. She looked at me and didn't seem scared at all, like she was ready for whatever came next.

Then she belched some more blood, gasped, and closed her eyes, her body going limp.

"She's not breathing," one paramedic said.

They attempted CPR and defibrillation, but she did not respond.

After several long minutes, there was a backing away, a shutting down.

"Radio for homicide," Officer Macfarland called to his partner who was investigating the ice cream truck.

Neighbors had been steadily gathering curbside.

Buzzy Lagniappe's old Aunt Beatrice stood scowling on the front steps next door, trying to see past Dinosaur Times.

My neighbor Lennie came running from his house on the corner and joined us.

"What the hell?" Lennie huffed, out of breath, seeing the girl on the stretcher, her face still not covered. "She dead?"

"Yup," said Mr. Wilson, "stabbed."

"Jeezis criminy," Lennie said, "how horrible. What's this ice cream truck doing here?"

I'd seen a dead body before, just a week earlier in fact, but that was the first time I'd ever watched someone die.

She looked at me right before she went out.

I watched her spirit leave her body.

It was a shake in the shape of things, a shape in the shake of things.

It hit me right in the heart of my own arrhythmia.

2

A birthday card from Miranda Savitch lay waiting to be opened on the table next to my bed.

We hadn't been talking much except sometimes in English class because she sat next to me.

Other than Miranda scribbling little messages on my desk or notebook paper—phrases like "you have eye boogers" or "Smile!" or "Mr. Beauregard looks like President Ford"—and some idle chit chat, we didn't converse on any deep level like we used to.

Not long after she'd been elected Sophomore President Miranda got deeply involved in collecting aid for victims of the Guatemalan earthquake.

Now when I read the Daily Bulletin and would begin, as always, with, "General Interest," Miranda would not always answer "I don't have any" like she had been doing but instead would more often chime in, "Guatemala," to the knowing groans of others.

"25,000 people dead, a quarter of the population homeless . . . you could at least spare a blanket or a few cans of food," Miranda scolded those who didn't contribute, "it wun't take too much to make a difference."

Miranda's passionate devotion to service turned off an inevitable segment of the student population who'd avoid her on the quad during lunch and nutrition and heckle her at assemblies when she'd speak out on some political crisis that needed our attention.

She was steadfast in her pursuit of social action, an attribute both attractive and intimidating.

As she became increasingly absorbed in student government and community service, our conversations became more one-sided with her doing most of the talking and me feeling as if my own growing passions— music, literature, art—were too trivial for her.

"The earth gets broken the way people get broken . . . We're all on this sphere together," she said to me before class in the days following the quake in Guatemala.

I tried to come up with a Bob Dylan line or something to make myself seem relevant, but I couldn't find what I needed.

I thought about that sentence a lot for a long time after she said it, though.

The earth gets broken the way people get broken . . . We're all on this sphere together

It reminded me of lying in bed the morning of the Sylmar earthquake when I was 10 years old having just woken up for school.

I had insomnia for months after that.

Waiting for the next one to hit. Or for the Soviets to bomb us. Or for something else bad to happen. I wanted to be awake for whatever it was going to be.

I was supposed to call Miranda so we could watch *Saturday Night Live* together on the phone.

I pulled the telephone into my room but was at first too freaked out about not being too freaked out about the stabbed girl.

I lay on my bed looking up at a mosquito on the ceiling.

I thought how its species has been around since dinosaur times. Its ancestors have been sucking human blood since caveman days. Serving no evolutionary purpose save the spreading of disease. How perhaps the spreading of disease is in fact an evolutionary purpose. Population control.

The music of the ice cream truck was still looping incessantly in the street, and through my window I could see the flashing glow of the cop car and the ambulance. I thought I heard the fire truck pull away. My dad and Mr. Wilson were still outside talking.

It's a world of laughter

A world of tears

It's a world of hope

And a world of fears

There's so much that we share

That it's time we're aware

It's a small world after all

The truck's music, its very existence, screamed freedom, joy, endless summer, pure pleasures, but lots of loneliness too and sad snacks and wasted time.

In the Spring of 1976 I was overwhelmed by the noxious asperities of life.

I'd also been haunted by a chronic insomnia, intensified by seeing my first corpse just a week earlier, the previous Saturday, when I heard a loud car crash on Beverly Boulevard and looked out the window to see flames coming up over the hedges at Lennie's house, just west of the intersection of Beverly and Citrus.

People were yelling for help, for someone to call the fire department and ambulance, that there was a person inside the burning vehicle.

Once the emergency vehicles arrived I joined the crowd outside and viewed the charred remains of the car crash victim, lying supine in the middle of Beverly Boulevard, burnt-frozen in driving position, foot on the brake one last inaccurate or inescapable time, both arms outstretched, hands clenched as if still gripping the steering wheel of his lime green Pacer, empty as a feather.

A fireman was squirting the burnt corpse with a hose.

Flakes of ash fell onto the asphalt from the deceased's rigid frame.

The victim had opened his eyes that morning, probably ate a substantial breakfast followed close upon by a satisfying, reliable bowel movement and headed off to his normal day, no foreboding of the fiery, violent death that would claim him in the next hour.

What was he looking forward to in the moments before the crash?

A growing audience watched the aftermath.

I wanted to scream from the deepest mortal space, the sort of scream you attempt in a dream but which emerges as a virtual silence.

I still have dreams about the sound of the impact outside.

I still have dreams about the car on fire and the driver inside floating like a silhouette among the flames.

I still have dreams about the ashen eminence, gone on the asphalt, squirted by a hose, an ember memory.

I still have dreams.

Haunted by monsters.

Monsters like the sad alone faces of dead people.

I remember trying to watch *Saturday Night Live* over at Manny Shepherd's house that night after the crash and the ashen cadaver.

When I arrived I came upon an entertaining exchange between Manny and his mother while he attempted to locate something for her.

"Immanuel!" his mother yelled from her bedroom in the back of the house, a blue bedroom that exuded the vague sense of being underwater, a complement to her eyes which looked like Gaudi windows.

"Yeah what!" he yelled back.

"Can you bring me the what's-it-called?"

"All right! Where is it?" Manny asked.

"Right next to the what's-it-called!"

"OK! Oh, wait, there's two! Which one do you want?"

"The one without the what's-it-called!" she attempted to make plain.

"Got it! You need anything else?"

"Yeah, also bring me another what's-it-called!"

"From the fridge?"

"Yes, second shelf, right behind the what's-it-called!"

"I can't find it!"

"It's not behind the what's-it-called?"

"No! There's just a thingy there!"

"Oh, I forgot," she remembered, "that's because I moved it into the what's-it-called!"

"Found it! Is that all?"

"Wait, is there also a what's-it-called in there?"

"Yes!"

"Does it have a what's-it-called on top?"

"It does!"

"Bring that too!"

"That's too much to carry!" Manny complained.

"Just put it all on a what's-it-called!"

"We still have one of those?"

"Outside the back door, leaning up against the what's-it-called!"

"OK, I'll go get it!"

"But watch out for the what's-it-called!"

"Righty-O!" Manny said, looking at me with an ironic nerd grin.

"And, Immanuel, when your father gets home tell him to hurry in here!"

"Will do!"

"I need him to stick his thingy in my what's-it-called!"

"I'll let him know!"

"Unless you'd rather do it!"

"No, that's all right, let Dad do it! He's better at it!"

While Manny was bringing his mother the what's-it-called she'd asked for, I took the opportunity to poke my head into Leah's room.

"Hey," I said, "How's it going?"

"Hey," she said without looking up from her book (on a Saturday night. Dang, dude).

I drank in her surface-nerd underlying-tigress sexual essence to savor later. I committed that shit to memory. Monday night she would be ravished in the windmills of my mind.

"Well, see ya," I wussily whispered.

"Nyeah," she mumbled.

Manny and I went out to do bong hits in his childhood playhouse in the backyard, now a great place to get high and trip out.

"Did you get this shit from Big?" I asked.

"Who else?"

"Thai Stick I presume."

"Duh."

"As long as it's not Porno."

"Naw, man, Porno's cool. I like smoking Porno."

"That shit makes me too whore-knee."

"So? Nu?"

"I don't want to be horny around you. I want to be horny all alone in the dark."

"Dude, I would totally suck your cock if you wanted," Manny gagged.

"That is the worst kind of wrong."

"No shit, dude, you could just close your eyes and pretend Miranda Savitch is giving you head."

"I'd probably be pretending it's your sister," I said.

"Dang, dude," Manny winced, "that's like incest or something. Forget it, I'm never sucking your cock ever. I take back the offer," he laughed inwardly.

We had decided to watch *Saturday Night Live* together that night because the musical guest was Patti Smith and we were freaks for Patti. *Horses* still accompanied many of our grooviest music marathons.

We were watching on the big TV in the den.

"*Jesus died for somebody's sins but not mine,*" she sang with a mournful scowl.

"Dang, dude, tomorrow's Easter Sunday," Many observed, "And Patti's singing 'Gloria.'"

"Patti is flagrant," I said.

"Patti knows," Manny sighed, "Yup."

"Dang, she's dressed like the *Horses* cover," I noted of Patti in her baggy white shirt barely tucked into black slacks, loosely hanging black tie.

"A nice Jewish boy like us," Manny said.

"She's not Jewish," I said, "and she's not a boy."

Manny laughed, "I was talking about Jesus, dude. You are stoned."

"So are you," I said. "It's weird when you realize Jesus probably looked like us."

"But with darker skin."

"Jesus was a sephardic-looking motherfucker."

"Totally. All Sabra and shit. But, dude, Jesus had the baddest-ass jewfro, right?"

"And you know everyone in the neighborhood called him Heshie."

"Yo, Heshie!"

"Whenever the subject of Jesus comes up my dad always says, 'One of our boys,'" I told Manny. "You mention Jesus or Sandy Koufax and you'll hear, 'One of our boys.' Oh, and Neil Diamond, too. One of our boys," I snickered.

"Bob Dylan."

"One of our boys," we slapped hands.

"Leonard Cohen."

Manny's inhaled laughter sounded like a castle drawbridge lowering.

"Nyeah, there's your girlfriend, dude," Manny joked as Laraine Newman appeared on screen as a news correspondent, a voice-perfect spoof.

"She is foxy."

"I'd've thought you'd be more majorly into Gilda."

"Why?"

"'Cause she's like Miranda Savitch."

"Nyeah, not really."

"Come on, dude. Admit it."

"May be," I said, "Ok. Yeah. But Laraine is who I crave."

Laraine Newman was everything sexy to me: smart and funny and dreamy-eyed and luscious-lipped and kinky-lion-maned. Not that Gilda Radner wasn't also a delectably brilliant talent (whose resemblance to Miranda Savitch was admittedly stimulating), but it was Laraine Newman who held my rattling heart when it came to celebrity crushes.

Gilda Radner, as Emily Litella, was talking about "presidential erections."

We paused to groove on Gilda and gasped with cannabis laughter.

"I love Jewish girls," Manny said.

"Oh, dude, dig it," I said, "I've been flirting with this Orthodox girl at the library lately. Naomi Richter," I said in an exaggerated New York Jew accent.

"Dang, dude," Manny said, affecting Brooklynese, "'Nye-o-mi Rickta. Big Jewish knockers?"

"Worlds unto themselves," I said, "heavenly globes."

"You gonna get some of that soylent green?" Manny said, grabbing the air with both hands.

"Haha, I dunno. We'll see I guess. She's Orthodox, dude! Soylent green is treyf I'm pretty sure."

"That'd be major if you felt up an Orthodox girl. It'd be like, I don't know, a pervy taboo porno movie or something."

"She definitely has my stomach fluttering."

"Hey, you've got the kosher beef, dude," Manny said and gave me five.

I had met Naomi Richter at the Fairfax Branch Library which shared a parking lot with Gardner Park.

I started going to the library after track practice every day allegedly to improve my geometry grade by utilizing the quiet study atmosphere, but mostly I'd stroll the aisles looking at books with random fascination.

So one afternoon in mid-March I was trying to read *Flatland* again instead of doing my homework when I looked up and sitting across the table from me was this disarmingly cute Orthodox girl.

When I say disarmingly cute I mean the kind of cute where it feels like she's your wife already, the kind of cute that reduces you to kosher gelatin, the kind of cute that fiddles with your *kishkas*, the kind of cute that wreaks havoc on the old arrhythmia.

She was vigorously at work on some crazy difficult math problem.

I don't even know what kind of math it was. Nor will I ever.

But I wanted to know her. I sat across that same table from her every afternoon.

For several days we didn't speak, but our eyes began meeting on occasion, a few seconds at a time, which became increasingly interesting, and then one time she smiled at me as if to say hi.

In a highly uncharacteristic move, I initiated a conversation with her.

"You're good at math," I said.

She looked up at me with eyes grayer than gravy.

"Yes," she said, holding my gaze, "I am."

She paused.

"I love math. It's more of a language to me than language is," she said. "In Hebrew, letters and numbers are essentially the same thing, which makes perfect sense to me."

"I suck at math," I said, "I have geometry right now, and I'm just barely holding onto a C. I'm more of a language guy."

I was nervous about the nuclear nature of our mutual gaze but I hung with it because, dang, dude, her eyes.

Naomi Richter had these snail-hazel gray-flecked eyes that jiggled my innards immediately.

"But you're reading *Flatland*," she pointed, "that's all geometry."

"I know, I um, I thought reading it would help me, but it's not really."

"I love that book," she put down her pencil, unwavering and relentless in her stare-down.

"Lineland is my favorite part so far," I said.

"Yes, especially their method of singing," Naomi said, breaking my concentration.

"Yeah, it's um," I smiled.

She smiled back at me.

I was in her power, pausing, lost.

"Lance," I introduced myself, "I forgot my own name for a second."

She laughed though I don't think she really wanted to.

I was already reverting to my loser self, the one I'd been trying to ditch.

"I can help you with your geometry homework if you want," she said, "I'm Naomi," she said. "Nice to meet you finally."

I extended my hand but she didn't offer to shake it.

"I can't," she explained.

"Nyeah I would love help with my geometry homework," I said like the biggest whore.

And so began my crush on Naomi Richter.

She was a couple of years older I think. Like 17 maybe.

Ironically, another crush, Evelyn Childs, was the one distracting me from paying attention and getting work done in geometry.

I had been trying to get Evelyn Childs to fall in love with me, but it was just not working.

Telepathy was again failing me.

The only words Evelyn Childs had thus far spoken to me in class were, "Hey, can I borrow your eraser?"

And I also had a crush on Miss Graffenberg the student teacher. It felt like cheating or something. And now Naomi was in the mix if not in the same classroom. And of course Laraine Newman danced upon my loins as well.

4 crushes. A wobbly parallelogram.

I wasn't just a crush whore, I was a total fucking full-on crush nympho.

I didn't include Miranda Savitch in my crush harem, however.

Miranda Savitch was something else.

Miranda Savitch hovered ever-present in the background.

My infatuees were unknown variables; Miranda was the constant, the remainder, the quotient left when all the other numbers in the equation cancel each other out.

Miranda was her own circumstance always. Her own conundrum.

Unsure how to make something with Miranda Savitch come together, I turned my sexual attentions elsewhere.

I grew more and more polyamorous in my fantasies in other words.

I abandoned Fuck-O-Rama for the anarchy of whoever crossed my mind.

My father once told me the secret to happiness:

"Surround yourself with beautiful women," he said mid-cigarette on the front porch one evening when I came to him with a spew of adolescent angst, "always entertain the attention of pretty girls."

I was trying to live my dad's advice by crushing on every female who'd interact with me and also a few who wouldn't.

After that first conversation, Naomi Richter and I met daily at the rectangular table near the center of the library (the rest of the tables were circular) and went over my geometry homework while finding sweet pockets of digression into each other's minds.

"I think this passage about 'Pointland' is a description of God," Naomi said, then read from the spot I had dog-eared in Flatland, "*He is himself his own World, his own Universe; of any other than himself he can form no conception; he knows not Length, nor Breadth, nor Height, for he has had no experience of them; he has no cognizance even of the number Two; nor has he a thought of Plurality; for he is himself his One and All, being really Nothing.*"

I had already read that passage and indeed thought it was cool (though it didn't make me think of God at all but rather of Buzzy Lagniappe).

"I love geometry, all mathematics really, because the beautiful rightness of it reminds me of God," Naomi said, making me horny for her brain, "God is infinitely complex. And yet utterly simple. Echad."

My plan was to shift the discourse slowly southbound from her cerebral cortex to her pudendal vortex.

It ended up being a 4 week arc of taboo sexual tension that rose from spark to flame to bloody conflagration.

Naomi Richter shook my world.

It was a time of great tremors in general for me, a series of mental temblors that knocked me up but good.

Female essence boxed me in like a rhombus rocking every thought and dream with its swaying confines.

Even though I was always in some underlying way in love with Miranda Savitch, that did not prevent my many electric moments with a multiplying coterie of bedeviling females.

I loved being around girls.

Madly pursuing my father's wisdom.

Surround yourself with beautiful women. Always entertain the attentions of pretty girls.

That was my mission, even as I was steadily withdrawing from the social scene.

3

The initial fissure from the cool nerd crew came that past New Year's Eve at Dolly's house where I just felt like something was ending.

But really it was more a slow distancing, a gradual diverging of interests and enjoyments.

There was a kind of frictional resistance, a widening rift between me and many longtime companions.

The kind of thing that's nobody's fault.

A series of oblique slips is all, each adding to the chasm with exponential magnitude.

Manny and I still got together, especially if some new album came out that we both wanted to listen to.

We were both writing songs and shared a growing seriousness about art and music and film and the whole creative continuum.

We read *On The Road* and we wanted to take off on some mad adventure. We listened to *Highway 61 Revisited* and we wanted to let our minds forge that kind of sonic poetry.

We'd take the bus to the NuArt in West L.A. to see *Breathless* and *400 Blows* and would always go across the street to Papa Bach afterward to look at books and talk about them and smell them and get off on them.

We had a kind of religious attachment to the stacks at Papa Bach. It was a hippie church of sorts, impossible to go into without engaging the muses.

Reading *The Stranger* and then *Siddhartha* in Mr. Beauregard's class back-to-back permanently turned our heads inward.

My final fracture with the cool nerd crew came at Candy Stoner's house on a coldish night in February.

I hadn't been inside Candy Stoner's house since the afternoons we spent frenching on her living room couch before her mom got home from work back in 8th Grade.

She had transferred to Beverly High, but we couldn't figure out how because she didn't live in Beverly Hills, she lived in Carthay Circle, on the same street as Dolly, Commodore Sloat, the coolest-ass street name ever.

Commodore Sloat is one of those street names you say out loud every time you pass it.

"Dang, dude, Commodore Sloat," we'd say to one another on our bikes or in our parents' cars growing up.

Whenever I was on Commodore Sloat I never knew which direction I was going.

Commodore Sloat sits inside this disorienting triangle that Olympic and San Vicente make, rendering concepts like north, south, east, west, up, down, meaningless.

But dang, dude, the name.

Commodore Sloat. The founder of white California.

When I walked into the party at Candy's house, Peter Frampton's voice singing, "*Ooh baby I love your way, everyday,*" was being its ubiquitous self on the stereo.

Whitman Rust was getting high with Buzzy Lagniappe, Manny Shepherd, and Claude Moss right in the entry hall which meant when I came in through the front door my only option was to join them.

"Remember when Buzzy first moved here from Kansas and called brazil nuts 'nigger toes?'" Whit asked them.

"Dang, dude, that's flagrant," choked Claude Moss who'd inhaled right when Whit said nigger toes.

"Awkward," Manny croaked, "Yeah."

"When was that?" Claude asked. He hadn't gone to Melrose Avenue Elementary with us.

"I came to Los Angeles in 3rd Grade," Buzzy said, "and that's what my family called them," he paused, "nigger toes," at which all four of them laughed maniacally.

"Oh, shit," Manny Shepherd wheezed.

Members of the *Chick Clique*, including Miranda Savitch were gathered in a corner and made note of my appearance.

"You know what's fucked up about girls?" Whit asked his comrades which now included me.

"The fact that they have no idea what they fucking want?" Buzzy said.

"Well that, yeah, and also they always think you should tell them the truth. What kind of fucked up bullshit is that?" Whit said.

"The only chick who doesn't want a guy to tell her the truth is Pinocchio's girlfriend when she's sitting on his face," Buzzy said.

"Ooh tell me another lie, Pinocchio!" Claude Moss falsettoed, "Tell me a great big fucking *lie.*"

"Chicks suck," said Whit.

"I can't stop thinking about them," I said, "even though they suck."

"I can't stop thinking about them *because* they suck," Whit said.

"Gina Dichlich," Claude Moss intoned as we all salaamed (which we did anytime Gina Dichlich's holy name was uttered).

"I heard you say my name!" Gina called from across the room.

"Hey, Gina, is it Ditch-Litch? Deetch-Leetch? Dyke-like?" Whit called back.

"It's Dick-Lick, as in suck my cock, you nerdball," she said pointing her middle finger at Whit.

"I love you, Gina!" Whit opened his arms to her then mimed a blowjob.

Eddie Gurges was sitting on the living room couch drawing, either the scene itself or something else entirely from his head. Eddie's drawings could come from either spigot. Like Manny and me, he was dead-on serious about art and was ever at it.

As I went over to say hey to Eddie, the girls came over as a group to intercept me.

"Hi, Lance," Miranda said.

Miranda stood next to Dolly Ferris and Lorelei Lux, and they were surrounded by Arabella Mayflower, Justine Balthazar, Claire Farnaway, and Sharon Rose.

"Hey," I said.

"We have something we want to say to you," Dolly said.

By this time the room's attention had turned our way, conversations fell silent like when the bad guy enters a saloon in a cowboy movie, though the stereo kept blasting.

"Do you feel like we do?" Frampton asked into his voice box.

Every girl in the room already knew what was about to happen.

Chicks always know that stuff ahead of time.

The *Chick Clique* all looked at each other, and on a silent head-bobbing count of three, chanted in unison:

"You. Are. A. Mimic," they pointed at me, paused, then counted again, "And We. Hate. Mimics," with scolding fingers wagging at me in rhythm to the words.

I flushed red and teary but didn't cross the line into crying.

My ears were so hot I was hearing dog frequencies.

"Dang, dude," Buzzy sighed behind the fog somewhere.

"That's cold-blooded," Claude added.

"Gnarly times nine," said Manny, "majorly gnarly."

I didn't know what to do then. Everybody was staring at me.

That long-ass Frampton song was still playing.

"We're sick of it," Claire said of my proclivity.

"Please stop," Miranda added.

"It's annoying," Dolly chimed in, "It makes us not want to be around you."

The complaint was legitimate.

I had indeed fallen into the habit of imitating the last thing people said, in a mocking tone.

I was all awkward with introverted passion and only understood how to communicate through showmanship.

A donning of the mask.

And one of my social tics was imitating people as a way to get laughs and cover my discomfort.

I was embarrassed at my own behavior, aghast that my fake personality got them bothered enough to do something about it, agonized by the fact that the shtick intended to impress them was the very shit that turned them off.

I had played a fictional character during that time and cultivated a phony persona that became increasingly difficult to sustain.

The radically true Lance Atlas lay buried under the magma flow of unexpressed love, unexpressed despite the most willing receptiveness of the exalted beloved, Miranda Savitch, ready and waiting to be taken.

The tendency toward self-sabotage akin to a psychic grand mal seizure sort of tensed up any social gathering for me.

Introverted passion is bad for the heart.

I left the party not long after.

I kind of slipped out the front door unnoticed.

Nobody knew what to say to me.

I walked all the way home instead of calling my dad to come pick me up.

That long walk was the commencement of my passage back to myself.

I would discard the persona.

I would stand alone in the universe as destiny intended.

Away from my friends.

There were so many rumblings among us that, rather than try to cling to a fake stability in the flux, instead I withdrew into a self-imposed exile.

Though I still joked around with everybody in class and stuff, and we got along fine, I exiled myself from parties and other group gatherings at the Farmers Market and the Tar Pits and the movies, hung out alone at school during nutrition and lunch, carved out a mostly solitary existence.

I had gotten a guitar at Wallich's Music City for Chanukah.

Wallich's Music City was a fantasyland of records, tapes, sheet music, musical instruments, and console TVs and stereos.

You could also buy concert tickets there at the Ticketron counter.

When I was younger my dad and I would go to Wallich's together just to browse the albums, and sometimes I would flip through the sheet music for chords to songs I couldn't figure out by ear. There were a lot of those.

Wallich's had everything I wanted.

When I was 9 & 10 & 11 I used to pick up the weekly "Boss 30, " a list of the top 30 songs for that week on Boss Radio 93 KHJ, my aural heaven. The Boss 30 each week had a picture of one of the DJs.

I wanted to be a radio disc jockey one day like The Real Don Steele.

Eventually, once my parents would let me, I started riding my gold Schwinn Sting-Ray up to Wallich's on my own and stay for hours listening to albums in the listening booths that looked out onto Sunset Boulevard.

The first two albums I bought with my own money, Janis Joplin's *Pearl*, and Simon & Garfunkel's *Bridge Over Troubled Water* were purchased at Wallich's Music City when I was around 10 or 11.

I saved my allowance for a couple of months to get those. I had saved just enough money to buy the two albums, the Joplin and the Simon & Garfunkel, at $3.50 each, and I had exactly $7.00.

But I didn't know about sales tax, and when I came up short at the register, I nearly began crying.

I had those familiar thick phlegmy inside tears at the back of my throat accompanied by the usual pencil eraser dick.

That's what always happens when I'm somewhere I don't want to be, in some situation I wish I weren't in.

I can smell that feeling still.

The cashier saw my verging meltdown and rang me up anyway and smiled and gave me the albums.

"I'll take care of the sales tax this time," she said.

A true act of kindness and compassion.

And then there was the tingly bike ride home, the anticipation, holding the Wallich's bag in one hand and a handlebar with the other, until finally I got home and gave myself over to utter absorption in the music.

The LPs were especially meaningful because I had bought them with my own money.

I listened to those albums over and over and over and over, lying on my bed, staring at the covers.

Janis was a hurricane blowing over me.

Listening to her voice was like looking up a girl's skirt.

And Simon & Garfunkel fed my nascent classical love of form. Not organization, mind you, but form. It felt exquisite.

Years had passed since that afternoon, but I could still feel the sublime loneliness of deep listening, when it's just you and the music and all that is beautiful.

Reading too was another sublime loneliness.

Leafing through my parents' art books also gave me that melancholy thrill, the Leonardo book, the Michaelangelo book, the Marc Chagall book, and, my favorite, the Gustave Moreau book.

More and more I craved the constant onslaught of sound and color and language.

I began to write songs on the guitar I got from Wallich's.

Previously, composing had been a piano-only activity. The guitar enabled me to work on songs anywhere.

I went through a period of time where the first thing I did when I got home each day was listen to "One More Cup Of Coffee" from Bob Dylan's *Desire*.

Your loyalty is not to me but to the stars above

The Emmylou Harris harmonies hooked into me.

And the image of going to "the valley below" hung in my head like a mantra.

I'd sing that line in my head upon waking, during showers, on the walks to and from school each day, while I was sitting in class.

One more cup of coffee 'fore I go . . . to the valley below

When we were reading *Siddhartha* in Mr. Beauregard's class, I walked around in a constant state of ecstatic wonder.

That book totally knotted itself into my conscience.

As a devotee of the TV show *Kung Fu*, my spirituality already leaned east, so Siddhartha was immediately familiar to me, the lone wanderer, a man on the pathless path.

When I got to the part where Siddhartha starts getting sex lessons from Kamala, pretty confused about the whole issue myself, I talked to my dad about what was happening in the book and what Siddhartha seemed to be learning from Kamala via intercourse.

"It's just friction, son," my father said without romance, "If you rub it long enough something will happen," he went on.

He had a pretty direct relationship with reality, did my dad.

"It's just the movement of tectonic plates until blammo, earthquake," he used another analogy.

My dad got off on taking the magic out of things.

"We're masses of protoplasm, that's all," he pronounced about the human condition when I asked him about the meaning of life once.

"The disorderly functioning of thousands of tiny enzymes," I added.

"That too," he said and took a drag from his Kent.

I reveled in my loneliness and made it my friend.

I lay for hours, sometimes days at a time, on my bed, listening to *Nilsson Schmilsson*, a touchstone of the era I was living, uncluttered, no hassles, breathing free, feeling the world deeply.

John Lennon's *Plastic Ono Band* was another womb for me too.

A tutorial in being uncompromisingly true to oneself.

I was gleaning daily songwriting lessons from Don McLean's *Don McLean* album, the one with "Dreidel" on it, an album unfairly overshadowed by its predecessor *American Pie*.

Randy Newman's *Sail Away*, Jackson Browne's *Saturate Before Using*, and *Tea For The Tillerman* by Cat Stevens were also my refuge and my schoolhouse, especially, for some reason, on Saturday afternoons.

Saturday afternoons have always echoed sadness for me, a heavy feather falling, a bastion of bad television, immobility, bar mitzvah receptions, little league games, shopping for clothes with mom, desperate longings for fun, always wanting to be elsewhere, desertion, doldrums, some dreary unwanted lesson to take, visiting the ancient aunt and uncle who never remember your name, naps that happen because there's nothing else to do, dad watching professional bowling on Channel 7, looking out the front window in hopes that some cute girl might walk by, awaiting the segue to Saturday night.

It was on those desolate Saturday afternoons that I plunged myself most deeply into music that emboldened my loneliness, music that harnessed my sadness for the world, a long-felt condition.

My earliest tearful sadness for the world came when I was 11 years old.

The existential pity struck me at a Lakers game in the unforgettable 1971-72 NBA Championship season, the year of the 33 game win streak, Wilt Chamberlain, Jerry West, Gail Goodrich, Happy Hairston, Jim McMillan, et al.

What a team. A season of rapture.

We had amazing seats behind the basket that night.

The Lakers were playing the newly christened Golden State Warriors, formerly the San Francisco Warriors, at the Fabulous Forum in Inglewood, and I sat enraptured with the ineffable glitzy thrill of being at a Lakers game, a thrill that never diminishes no matter how many games you go.

At the other end of the row I noticed a man who had come to the game alone.

Clad in a speckled sport coat and double knit slacks, God's lonely man sat among himself, listening to Chick Hearn's play by play on a transistor radio via a little white earphone.

In a box by his feet rested his dinner: four hot dogs and the palest piss-yellow beer.

"God, I *love* this team!" he kept saying to himself throughout.

I understood his love. And shared it.

He became an immediate and overwhelming embodiment of utter isolation.

I saw myself in 30 years.

In love with people but friendless.

Having the Lakers to jive with at least.

Maybe a couple of other sad consolations.

And as he devoured his hot dogs even while he was yelling, full-mouthed and spewing chewed bun bits and suds, "What? No FUCKING WAY, you pussy-livered son-of-a-bitch!" at the referees after what Chick Hearn would call a ticky-tack foul, I felt such an extreme sadness that I cried, right there, sitting at the game, a real deep belly cry, at his overwhelming aloneness, spilling beer on himself, the world's shadow, courageously persisting, in a place that is unaware of him, grooving on the extremely short togas worn by the usherettes, memorizing them for later, the bottom of the love chain, the common loser in all of us. I struggled with trying to hide my crying by looking away because, well, how could I explain this if asked?

"Why are you crying?" would be my father's annoyed response, thinking my outburst due, naturally, to his not having bought me the overpriced Lakers jacket I coveted.

The sobs hit spasm-point several minutes later, with breath-ending intensity. I attempted to drink my sweet Forum coke, but I was crying too hard to swallow.

My glasses were all steamed up with hotness and I couldn't see the game. The sage thing to do would have been to join him at the other end of the row, end his aloneness by sharing our love for the Lakers, cheering with him, yelling at the refs, giving each other five whenever the Lakers scored.

But I was 11 years old. An uncarved block.

I stayed in my seat. Next to my parents. Crying for this life in the void, this solitary man, lost behind his own barriers.

It is the blight man was born for

It is Margaret you mourn for

My mom noticed my tears and consoled, "What's wrong, little fella?"

I pointed to him at the end of the row.

"I know," she said.

Mom had seen and felt the sadness too.

And somehow, that little interchange, the recognition that my mom was also hip to the overwhelming tragedy of human existence, soothed my perturbed spirit and calmed my aching heart. Turning my attention back to the game, thinking, "God, I LOVE this team," as Wilt Chamberlain stuffed one right up in Nate Thurmond's face—Wilt the Stilt stuck it to Nate the Great—I squelched the outward cry.

Every school morning of my 10th Grade year I'd wake up at 6am, take a shower (always soaping the left armpit first then right armpit then chest and belly and cock and balls and so on, then around the back, sometimes trepidatious about getting soap in my ass crack because sometimes it was chafed and the soap would burn like hell), brush my teeth, and go into my parents' bedroom to blow-dry my hair. I can't remember why I had to do it in there I just remember I had to. Anyway, they'd still be sleeping, and I'd blow-dry my hair while reading the "Desiderata" plaque on their wall by dawn-light.

That Spring I walked to and from school every day because I'd already had 3 bikes stolen at Fairfax since September and just thought fuck it I'm not getting another bike.

I held dear those morning walks, acknowledging every familiar crack in the sidewalks along my route, the barren cracks, the cracks with chamomile flowers growing out of them, the cracks lifted by ficus tree roots, the cracks that sometimes form incredibly steep acute angles, the kind of shit that skateboarders love.

The morning air in Los Angeles stirred my senses which in turn inspired my brainwaves.

I'd sit in the hall, by my locker, usually reading something for Beauregard's class, before school.

Sometimes I'd work on song lyrics in the morning 'cause of the quiet and the clarity.

I was writing a song called "The Crowd" about my current situation with my friends.

The only line I remember from that song is "Once I was a part of the circle, now I am apart from the circle."

I'm actually pretty glad I can't recall the rest.

Sometimes I'd venture into Madame Couchée's French classroom during lunch—an oasis for lonely oddballs—and browse her stacks of Paris Match magazines and listen to the Jaques Brel album *Enregistrement Public à l'Olympia 1961* on her record player.

I didn't fully understand the lyrics—I was only in French 2—but I could hear the rhyme scheme and what he was doing with language in an abstract way—internal rhyming and assonance—and, of course, the melodies were hook-laden jewels.

"Hey, that's the year I was born," I said to Claire Farnaway, pointing to the Brel album cover.

"Me too, Lance," Claire snipped back, "duh."

I didn't know what was up with Claire and the rest of the *Chick Clique*, but she'd been hanging out in Couchée's room at lunch a lot, so there was obviously some kind of drama in progress, either personal or social or maybe it was the same as mine, just a falling away into one's self.

Madame Couchée pointed out that Jacques Brel's "Le Moribund" was the original source of the maudlin pop hit "Seasons in the Sun."

"You see, it's not a sad song," Madame Couchée gestured to the rhythm of the song. "Rod McKuen made it sad when he translated it."

"Bonjour, My Damn Coochie," said David Harkins as he entered Room 218.

"*Ah, bonjour monsieur, ça va?*" she said.

"Getting along quite famously thank you," said David trying to sit in Claire Farnaway's lap.

"Up, perv," Claire said, pushing him off.

One time we were listening to "Quand On A Que L'Amour," and Claire Farnaway was looking at me with a someday smile.

Dang, dude, I caught myself realizing how alluring were Claire Farnaway's big blue eyes.

I filed them away for later use.

Eventually I stopped getting invited to parties because everyone knew I wouldn't go.

On one rare occasion out in public, I went with Manny to see a screening of *The Point* at the NuArt where Harry Nilsson was going to be in attendance.

Manny and I were also hoping for an appearance by Ringo 'cause we knew they were pals and Ringo was the narrator of *The Point.*

Lorelei Lux was also there. It looked like she'd come alone.

When she saw me she squinted her usual inscrutable stare.

What was really surprising at first though was that I saw my neighbor Lennie there.

Turns out he did the voice of Count in the movie.

I might have known that and forgotten because I always just thought of him as H.R. Pufnstuf.

The Point was a great transcendental creation by Harry Nilsson, attuned ecstatic music, a hippie-sweet and righteous message, simple, sublime wisdom.

We'd seen it as kids on television when it first aired with Dustin Hoffman as the narrator. But most of us liked the Ringo Starr version better, the one we'd see once in a while when they'd rerun it on ABC.

Nilsson was in fact in the audience that night, as promised.

Alas, no Ringo.

I kept staring awestruck at Nilsson before the movie started.

That was the guy who created *Nilsson Schmilsson*, I kept marveling to myself.

He'd also made the greatest segue music in the history of television on *The Courtship of Eddie's Father*.

Dang, dude, I was sitting in the same room with Harry fucking Nilsson.

I'd only ever seen *The Point* on television, so watching those images on the big screen work in conjunction with the music—and being more than somewhat stoned—was another one of those transformational experiences, the sensation I wanted to live for always, both making and partaking of art that groks the fullness.

In particular the songs "Think About Your Troubles" and "Life Line" were exactly the sorts of journeys I needed to have that night, lonesome roads both, they soothed my soul.

"Think About Your Troubles" formed a perfect circle, from water to water, teacup to teacup.

And "Life Line" echoed the sadness of every existence, human or otherwise.

Hello, is there anybody else here?

The natural cry of all sentient beings.

After the film, Manny and I took a stroll down a side street to smoke a joint, and then we walked across Santa Monica to Papa Bach.

"Rock Man rocks," Manny said, as we imbued our heads with grassy magic and night air.

"*Let me hip you to reality*," I said, imitating Rock Man's gravelly voice, and then Manny and I said together, "*You don't have to have a point to have a point.*"

We laughed the laugh of sublime truth.

"That is so right on," I said.

When we got to Papa Bach, we saw Lorelei Lux browsing in the Philosophy section.

Lorelei was carrying a hardbound notebook which had the phrase "Upward, not Northward" written on the cover, a phrase I recognized.

"Flatland," I said, pointing to the words on her notebook.

"Correct, sir," Lorelei said.

"You into Flatland?" I asked.

"Indeed," she said.

"How'd you get turned onto it?"

"I saw you were reading it," Lorelei said, "and I need to be thorough."

"And?"

"Well, I put a quote from it on the cover of my notebook, so . . ."

"Right. Duh. I suck."

"You do and you don't," Lorelei said.

"Meaning?"

"You have to figure that part out yourself. I've already told you too much."

"Okey-doke, shmoke," I used my default I-don't-know-what-the-fuck-you're-talking-about phrase.

"To me it's a book about not fitting in, about being irregular," Lorelei said.

"Like this quote, just a second"—she flipped through her notebook—"this one: *the irregularity of a Male is a matter of measurement; but as all Women are straight and therefore visibly Regular, so to speak, one has to devise some other means of ascertaining what I may call their invisible Irregularity.*"

"Invisible irregularity, I love it," I said, "I think most people are invisibly irregular. I mean, there are a few outwardly visible freaks I guess, like Gypsy Boots and shit, but mostly there are those people you think are totally normal who are actually really weird on the inside and do crazy shit you don't know about."

I couldn't tell if she'd listened to what I'd just been saying. She continued to search her notebook.

"Wait that's not what I meant to read you, hold on"—she leafed further—"this is the one: *The life of an irregular is hard, but the interests of the Greater Number require that it be hard.*"

Manny was standing behind Lorelei circling his ear with his finger.

"You're well familiar with not fitting in, Lance Atlas, aren't you?"

"I am," I said.

Lorelei was still flipping.

"Oh and here's one I know you will especially like: *No Circle is really a Circle, but only a Polygon with a very large number of very small sides.*"

"That sounds like something Miss Graffenberg would say," I smiled.

"The cute student teacher you have a crush on," Lorelei said, "Correct?"

"How do you know Miss Graffenberg? You're not in that class. But anyway I don't have a crush on her," I said.

Lorelei stared at me to make me squirm in my lie.

"I picked that quote out special just for you. I hope you liked it," she said.

"I did, I did. Very much. Thank you."

Lorelei often creeped me out, but for some reason I had trouble breaking away from conversations with her. She had a way of hooking into me. Even as I kept waiting for her to pull out a gun.

"Well, here we are again, Lance Atlas," said Lorelei Lux.

"Uhmm, I've never been to Papa Bach with you I don't think."

"We always seem to end up in this position, don't we, facing each other, the world spinning around us."

"Or maybe *we're* spinning around *it*," I said.

"You and I, Lance Atlas, one day we will have a planet to repopulate," Lorelei said with semi-menace, slitting her eyes at me again.

"So, is that notebook like a journal?"

"No, if I wanted to keep a journal I would carry around a journal for that purpose. This is a notebook and so I take notes in it," she said, "because that's what a notebook, by its very definition, is for."

"What do you take notes on?"

"Oh many things, Lance Atlas, many interesting things, what I read, what I see, what I hear, what I think, what I fantasize about, what I long for, what I avoid, what I remember, what I'm forced to endure at the hands of my oppressors. But mostly, Lance Atlas, I take notes on you."

Manny was across the store looking at art books and pantomiming masturbation.

I wanted to laugh and go join him, but Lorelei Lux smelled so damn good, like rose petals.

She would definitely be my Fuck-O-Rama contestant that night.

"I also use this notebook to chronicle my experiments in dimensionality," Lorelei said.

"I don't know what that is," I said.

"Why would you?"

"I um—"

"Even though there is a very cogent discussion of dimensionality in *Flatland*. But, typically, you missed it."

"Yeah, I just flip through *Flatland* looking for the sex scenes."

"I can see my spell isn't working," Lorelei said, ". . . interesting," and she noted this lapse in her book, "I'll have to make the necessary adjustments."

"Can you hip me to what's happening with dimensionality?" I asked in my most sincere tone.

"You really should learn these things on your own if they are to have any real value," Lorelei scolded, but then she consented, "However, just to stoke your soul a little, dimensionality is, like, learning to experience all possible dimensions available to you beyond the simple 3 dimensions most of us inhabit."

"Oh kay," I said, presuming she'd continue, which she did.

"There is more to our physical existence than height, width, and depth. Let's just start with the 4th Dimension. The 4th Dimension is Time."

"And the 5th Dimension is a singing group," I said like Groucho.

"I knew you were going to make that lame joke," Lorelei said, "See?"

She held up a page of her notebook so I could read it.

Lance Atlas: 5th Dimension joke. 100% chance.

"Busted and disgusted," I said, raising my hands like a criminal, "I can't be trusted."

"Although 'Up Up And Away' is indeed an experiment in dimensionality," she observed, "Yes . . . interesting." She muttered to herself while scribbling that insight in her notebook.

"So you do, like, time travel and shit?" I asked.

She stared at me like I was a stupid asshole.

"Experiencing the dimension of time isn't some sci-fi H.G. Wells story, Lance Atlas. I experience all time as one moment. Like, as far as I'm concerned we're already together as a couple even though it hasn't happened yet in your limited linear-time concept," Lorelei said.

"Oh, dang, you're talking about like when Siddhartha is looking at the river and he realizes the past, the present, and the future are all, like, one ongoing event. The continuous present, *chairos* Mr. Beauregard called it. Like that?"

Lorelei almost smiled and beckoned me closer.

I leaned forward, and she whispered in my ear, "Yes."

Then she closed her notebook, slipped it into her purse and started heading toward the door.

"You leaving?" I asked.

She looked at the door, then at me, then back at the door, then back at me like I was a stupid asshole again, slit her eyes, and left hurriedly.

I walked over to Manny who was looking at an R. Crumb book.

"You know that chick is a crazy-ass bitch, right?" he said.

"I dunno, dude," I shrugged.

I liked Lorelei.

That encounter with her at Papa Bach became an evolving conversation in my head. After a while, though, I couldn't distinguish between things we actually said to each other and things I thought up later which I should have said in the moment but didn't.

4

When my Geometry teacher, the genteel milquetoast Mr. Sylvester Katz— whom we all called Mr. Pussychin due to his prominently dimpled jaw— handed the class over to Miss Graffenberg the student teacher, he apologized, as if by learning from a student teacher instead of him we'd be missing out on something (which was most definitely not the case).

A sister in the Sigma Tau Delta sorority at UCLA, with red hair, aquiline nose, oval mouth, eyes that defied you to identify what shade of green they were, Cecilia Graffenberg had a body that moved across several fault lines.

She thought math was the greatest thing ever.

She wanted everybody else to love it as much as she did.

"Math is just a game, you guys," she'd say when we'd grumble about the difficulty of proofs, "Turn it into something fun."

We had competitions, did art projects, wrote stories using geometry vocabulary.

All of us did better because of her creative love for numbers.

It was fun to be in her class, and I also really wanted to have sex with her.

I kept thinking of that line from the Simon & Garfunkel song, *"Making love in the afternoon with Cecilia up in my bedroom (making love)."*

And I would picture making love to her not in my own bedroom but rather in this weird imaginary bedroom, a very spare romantic boudoir with a fluffy white bed and the wind blowing in through the curtains and Miss Graffenberg beneath me like a river.

It was Miss Graffenberg who first talked to us about how parallel lines do eventually intersect.

"Take Lance and Miranda," she didn't say.

"Due to the curvature of space," she did say. "Geometry isn't really about straight lines, it's all about curves. A circle can turn into any shape, depending on where it chooses to straighten. Everything fits comfortably inside a circle. Whereas a dodecahedron trying to fit into a trapezoid is mighty uncomfortable. Right?"

She then attempted to draw what that would look like.

"Are we gonna have to do a proof for this?" Heaven Sender groaned.

"No, this is just for fun," Miss G. promised, "absolute geometry."

In Period 3 Bio, Mr. St. Jerome had told us that the shape of the universe might be a dodecahedron.

"Or maybe the universe is a trapezoid," Miss Graffenberg said in retort upon hearing this, "and we life forms here on planet earth all together form a kind of dodecahedron, 'cause, you know, maybe you haven't noticed," she lowered her voice, "we don't exactly fit in with the rest of that airless vacuum out there in space."

Everyone was paying attention, even Evelyn Childs, the crotch goddess, her outlined pudendum in my line of sight whenever I could muster an excuse for looking behind me.

When Evelyn faced forward with her legs straight her crotch was a perfect equilateral.

But, dang, dude, when she'd lean to one side or the other it'd go all isosceles and shit, I am not joking.

"Don't you want to reconfigure that hypotenuse?" Jim Lord whispered— having caught me staring at Evelyn's delta—and flicked a cunnilingus tongue in her direction.

"All 180 degrees, dude," I said.

"Fahrenheit?" Jim quipped back.

"That'd be my guess, yeah," I snickered.

"Burn your mouth worse than pizza," Jim said, holding out both hands for slapping.

Heaven Sender sat in front of me. I did not register on her sexual radar. She liked dudes who could grow beards.

Buzzy Lagniappe was really into Heaven Sender, obsessively at times, but he too caused not a quiver in her sphincter.

Geometry class was voluptuously endowed with girls I didn't normally see in my other classes, girls like Heaven and Evelyn, Amanda Guff, Laurel Bay, Loki Vartmann, wonderfully slutty badass bitches all. Evelyn was slightly different though. Less badass. More injured.

As a 10th Grader in Geometry, I was a year behind in math, but most of the other kids in that class were a year or more behind in everything.

It was the only class I had that wasn't honors and I didn't really know anybody else in there except for Jim Lord who also sucked at math.

Two fellow language guys consigned to sit amid this preponderance of pussy, this panorama, this parade.

The *Chick Clique* girls were all in Algebra 2 already.

These less academically inclined girls were foxy as fuck though.

Made it hard to concentrate.

I had Naomi Richter to help me, and our tutoring sessions were heating up.

One silky sweet afternoon that Spring I was sitting in the library waiting for Naomi to arrive, working on lyrics to a love song I was writing for Laraine Newman.

"*My emotional sterility abbreviates the pain,*" I sang in my head to hear if it fit the melody.

Naomi slipped into the chair next to me.

She had her hair tied back in a tight bun.

Her olive skin was unusually clean for 5pm.

White blouse buttoned to the top.

Long pleated skirt whose hem was closer to her ankle than her knee.

White Keds.

She smelled like fried fish and cooking oil.

"I'm presuming you're Jewish," Naomi said once she'd gotten herself all situated, "Reform obviously."

"I'm of the tribe, yes," I said, "But come on, you already knew that. You couldn't tell?"

"Just making sure," Naomi smiled and looked around the library at the other kids, some of whom were classmates of hers.

Her smile slipped into grimace.

"I don't really fit in with the Orthodox girl paradigm," Naomi confided, putting her head down for a second.

I wanted to kiss the back of her neck and make her shiver.

Turning to face me, head still down on the table, she said, "Every Shabbat, when I look at the crowd of boys milling around on the sidewalk outside my shul, all I can think is, 'Someday I'm going to have to have intercourse with one of them for the rest of my life.'"

"Ah," I said, flustered at the unexpected frankness.

"That's my destiny," she said, sitting up and facing me.

Naomi sighed, placed her left elbow on the table, rested her head against her left fist, and looked at me, beautiful and tragic in the midst of her existential woe.

She wore a gold Mogen David around her neck, also a charm necklace with separate Hebrew letters.

"You know, I'm really not even supposed to talk to you," she informed me.

"But here you are," I said, "doing it."

"I am," she answered.

"What does your necklace say?" I asked.

"Come on, you can read Hebrew, can't you, Reform boy? You at least had a bar mitzvah. Right?"

I sounded out the letters, "I moan . . . "

"Right to left," she scolded.

"Ah, Naomi, right," I corrected myself.

"Oh, you knew that, you're just being rude."

I pretended she was right by smirking, hiding my idiot bad-Jew ignorance.

If I knew how to say 'fuck me' in Hebrew I'd have put those words in her mouth during my Saturday night Fuck-O-Rama sessions with her.

Maybe Manny would know how to say 'fuck me' in Hebrew.

His mom was born in Israel back when it was still Palestine or "back when it was still what's-it-called," as she used to say.

"Judea," Manny would always have to finish the joke for her.

"Or Canaan," Manny's dad would sometimes add laughing like Jerry Lewis.

It was a recurring shtick in their house.

"What do you do when you're not at school or here?" Naomi asked me.

"I read a lot," I said, "and listen to music and also write songs."

"What instrument do you play?"

"Mostly piano," I said, "but I've been writing songs on guitar lately."

"I'd love to hear your music one day," she said.

"Nyeah, I'm not any good. I just keep on doing it because it's impossible to stop. It's like always going on in my head," I said, "So it's really a matter of sanity."

"You are always a little bit elsewhere I've noticed."

"I guess," I said, "yeah."

"Math is my music," Naomi said, "so I know that place you go. I go there too in a way. It's a fine line between *ab*straction and *di*straction. It makes it hard to have conversations with people when you're not really in the same place they are. You know what I mean?"

"And yet here we are, doing it," I noted again.

"We are."

The faintness of her library whisper forced me to lean in closer to her.

Our faces were breath-close.

I believe we almost kissed in that moment. And I enjoyed imagining that maybe she believed the same thing.

"Where's your favorite place to sit and think?" Naomi asked, breaking the gaze and creating some distance.

She wanted to know about me.

She was getting off on breaking rules, I could tell at least that.

She was flirting with a boy. A secular boy. Naughty.

"I sometimes go to the Tar Pits, but my friends hang out there, and I don't really want to run into them," I told her.

"But they're your friends," Naomi said.

"Nyeah, they are but I dunno, I talk to them in class and stuff, but I'm not into hanging out with them these days. I don't fit in either. That's not what I want to be doing. You know?"

"Something else we have in common," she said.

We were majorly staring at each other.

We did a lot of that.

"Do you wanna hang outside for a while since we're not really doing geometry?" I invited her.

"Yes maybe," she said rising with me, "That'd be . . . yes."

She looked around the library for spies.

We walked out into the last of dusk, and sat on the grass near the makeshift hamster graveyard.

The grass was a little bit wet in the twilight.

Rabbi Meshuggennah lumbered past us muttering something about *loshon hora*.

"Rabbi Meshuggennah," I said, pointing.

Naomi laughed, "That's not his real name."

"Does he have a real name?"

"My dad told me once but I can't remember. My dad says he davens here because his son drowned in the pool," she pointed in the general direction.

"Oh, man. Now I feel bad."

"Guilty is what you feel," she mockingly shook her finger at me.

We Jew-shrugged at each other.

The universal, "Nyeah, nu?"

"Unh?" I grunted in question, pointing my finger at my own head which made her smile, "Unh?"

Dang, dude, her eyes.

"Hey, Lance," Naomi paused.

"Yerz," I dorked.

She looked away and paused.

"Did I tell you about the time this guy streaked past my shul on Shabbos?" she asked, though it was obvious that's not what she'd wanted to say.

I shuddered, as I had a feeling I knew the very incident she was referring to. In fact, I was pretty sure I had been a participant.

"What shul do you go to?" I asked in order to confirm my suspicion.

"Beth Emet," she said.

Yup. I was involved.

It was like 2 years before, 8th Grade, during the streaking fad that was sweeping college campuses at the time, back when Ray Stevens had his hit record "The Streak," and we threw our very own streaking party, which amounted to a bunch of us contributing money toward paying our friend Danny Samuels to streak down Beverly Boulevard, on Saturday, at noon, when the congregants of Beth Emet and other shuls would be breaking from morning services and milling about outside.

We all met at Grady Mason's house on Poinsettia that morning.

Danny was going to make a naked statement (for pay), and we were going to film it with somebody's dad's super eight movie camera.

Danny came through like a visionary, shedding his clothes on Grady's front porch, dashing toward Beverly Boulevard, with different bunches of us stationed around the synagogue—I was the one holding the camera—as witness to Danny's grand declaration, turning the corner onto Beverly Boulevard and past a crowd of congregants assembled on the sidewalk.

He stopped briefly in front of a gaggle of shrieking girls (one of whom must have been Naomi)—suddenly interrupted in the midst of gossiping about which boys they might have to have intercourse with for the rest of their lives—by this secular Yid helicoptering his shlong like a propeller at Kitty Hawk.

Leaving the shocked maidens, Danny turned left on Alta Vista as three men tailed him, threatening to call the police, then he cut back across to Poinsettia through the alley behind the Beth Emet, running barefoot across gravel and broken glass like Kwai Chang Caine, losing his pursuers, and on up the street back to Grady's porch, where he put his clothes on, with all of us, now *en horde*, running after, nauseated with cackling laughter.

"My friends and I thought it was funny, but we had to pretend to be outraged and traumatized," Naomi said.

I half-laughed but didn't tell her of my involvement in the prank.

She semi-undid her bun so there were these stray loose strands all around it, and, dang, dude, it was flat out sexy. I wanted to kiss her really hard on the mouth.

Then, without looking at me, Naomi cleared her throat and said, "So, anyway, I like you."

"Yeah?" I said, getting that embarrassing heartbeat you can hear on the outside.

"Yes," she said. "I do. I always look forward to seeing you."

"Nice," I said, "Same here."

"I feel kind of weird about it, though," she admitted.

I swallowed a few times unnecessarily.

"Me too," I said.

"I find myself thinking about you quite a bit lately," she said, gazing straight ahead.

I didn't respond to that because, dang, dude, I didn't want to say the wrong thing and fuck it up.

Naomi hard-changed the subject, rescuing both of us, "My grandfather always used to say, 'The Jewish People have survived because we understand the value of two things better than anybody else: education and real estate.'"

"My dad says we've survived because we migrated to Europe and intermarried with Caucasians so now we're able to pass for white."

Naomi shook her head.

"That's a good one. But I'll go with the education and real estate theory. I remember when my grandfather called my father the day of the earthquake and said 'Buy a house now.' And my dad did. Got a great price. Remember the earthquake?"

She didn't need to provide anything more specific. Everyone knew that 'the earthquake' meant the Sylmar quake on February 9, 1971.

Earthquakes defy geometry.

Euclid is useless in an earthquake.

The Pythagorean theorem ain't nothin' but a megathrust among the bedding and cleavage.

The insomnia that followed the Sylmar quake—the months of being afraid to fall asleep, as if my staying awake would prevent another earthquake from happening, my mom playing cards and listening to music with me until I'd finally drift off—was longer lasting than would be the latest insomnia, though the current condition had a heavier gravity dragging at it, the drag of mortality.

Being totally high on Manny's grass had allowed me to drift off into all these myriad thought-clouds, but the closing theme music of *Saturday Night Live* yanked me back into the always present moment.

I noticed that Manny had conked out on the den couch.

Rather than wake him, I left him a little note that said, "Thanks for the great blowjob last night, loverboy," grabbed my sweatjacket, made a last attempt to look into Leah's room but by then her door was closed, and left the Shepherd house.

After I left I realized that his parents or his sister might wake up before he did and see the note. But I had no way to get back in to remove it.

I rode my bike home, taking a slight detour to get an apple fritter from Winchell's on Melrose.

Two cops sitting inside Winchell's kept their eyes on me as I waited to pay.

A 15-year-old riding his bike and buying a doughnut at one o'clock in the morning had piqued their attention.

"Are you on your way home, kid?" one of the cops asked.

"Just getting an apple fritter first," I said, "Yeah."

As I exited with my fritter, the cops followed me out.

"We're going to make sure you get home ok," said Officer Macfarland, the one whose name tag I could see.

I pulled out onto Melrose, and, indeed, the cop car cruised slowly behind me.

A red light pulled them up even with me at the corner of La Brea & Melrose.

The other cop made eye contact with me and waved me forward when the light turned green.

As a student at Melrose Avenue Elementary School I had crossed that intersection twice daily for years, and afterward it continued its prominence in my Angeleno meanderings.

The smell of Pink's hot dogs, the cornucopia of candy and baseball cards at Rudolph's drug store, the Gordon Theatre, Len Jac's Auto Sound, Aaron Bros. Art Mart, landmarks of that golden crossroads.

Across the street from Pink's was where Billy Westin got run over by a truck when we were in 6th Grade.

I remember how weird it felt hearing about it.

Dude, Billy Westin got killed last night. Run over by a truck near Pink's.

Turning onto Citrus that night all was quiet (unlike the spectacle that would greet my homecoming a week later).

I parked my bike on the porch, waved to the police who drove slowly away, went inside, put my apple fritter in a sandwich bag to save for breakfast the next morning, and lay down on my bed to fantasize about Naomi Richter.

I think I only got like one hour's sleep that night. The insomnia had severely kicked in.

5

A week later, there I was in my bedroom again, insomniac and exhausted, this time with the phone, putting off calling Miranda.

I finally opened the birthday card she'd given me belatedly and which I'd also postponed reading for a couple of days for some reason.

I'm not sure what I was hoping it would say.

It was not actually a card but rather a note on her still extant *Little Prince* stationery.

Dearest Lance,

Of course I wish you a happy birthday and all that, because you deserve everything special, but really I want to apologize for participating in the mimic thing (I know duh 2 months later). I'm soooo soooooorrry. I want to cry I feel so rotten about it. Lancelot Link, Secret Chimp, I miss you and we need to change that situation immediately because it's making me sad and I don't like to feel sad. So make me happy and say you forgive me.

I Love You (I know you don't believe me but it's true),

Miranda

It was 11:25. *Saturday Night Live* was starting in 5 minutes.

Miranda had gotten a phone in her room with her own number so I didn't have to be nervous about her mother answering. But making a telephone call took courage always nevertheless.

The last time Miranda and I had talked on the phone was back in February, right before the mimic incident. She'd called me when Sal Mineo was murdered. We both loved his performance as Plato and just had a really great time that day and evening, though as usual with us, it didn't turn into anything.

Right after the party confrontation we didn't speak at all for a while which made things especially awkward sitting next to each other in English class.

That Miranda was part of the ambush—and had obviously been in on the planning of it—made me skittish about talking to her at all for a while after.

But after a couple of weeks I said something funny in class and she laughed at it and our eyes met and we were friends again sort of.

Even with the warmth slightly back, though, we didn't talk much outside the context of English class.

So, we were joking around on Monday about the *Saturday Night Live* episode that had just aired, Patti Smith, Emily Litella talking about presidential erections, etc., and Miranda suddenly said, "Let's watch together this Saturday!"

I was surprised by her suggestion but also definitely into it and immediately agreed to the phone date.

"The weirdest thing happened tonight," I said to her right off when I called.

"Tell me, what?" she answered.

"Oh by the way I loved your birthday note," I said.

"Well, you know. I mean it."

"And I forgive you."

"Yay!"

"But anyway this weird thing happened."

"Oh, yeah yeah yeah, tell me."

"This girl got stabbed outside my house."

"WHAT?"

"Yeah I got home from my belated birthday dinner tonight, and there was this stabbed girl in a Pinto parked in front of my house."

"Whoa, shit," she said, "That's cray-zee."

"Nyeah, crazy amounts of death lately, right?" I said, "Sal Mineo getting killed. Claudine Longet accidentally murdering Spider Sabitch—"

"—Please don't say it," she inserted, fearing I would be yet another person who'd jokingly call her Miranda Sabitch 'cause of the news story that had fueled gossip mongering for the past month since Claudine Longet shot her ski champ boyfriend. Miranda had endured it for weeks, the sniggers, haha, Miranda Sabitch, haha.

"I was thinking the other day, I don't know why, about being Spider Sabitch at that moment he realized Claudine Longet was really going to do it, that she was going to pull the trigger and that he was going to die."

"Well, that's kind of creepy to think about," Miranda said, "But in a way, yeah, I guess I get it, wanting to put yourself in that moment."

"Oh you know it," I said.

"But the girl who got stabbed. Did she die?" Miranda asked.

"Yeah, I watched her die actually."

"Whoa shit."

"Yeah."

"What was that like? You ok?"

"She died really quietly, like it was no big deal. I was most surprised at how calm she was, how easy it was, almost like she welcomed it. The thing is, last Saturday I saw another dead body."

"Aw, baby, that's awful. Tell me."

We both held silent a moment when she said that.

Dang, dude.

I continued past it, "Yeah, this guy in a car accident on my corner burned to death and when I ran out there they were hosing down his burnt corpse," I said.

"Dang, did I just call you baby?" Miranda asked aghast.

"Yes, I believe you did, honey," I salved her slip with an ironic endearment so we could keep talking.

"Well, I meant it like 'aw, poor baby,' but anyways."

A longish pause followed.

"Dang," she said.

The show was underway. Raquel Welch was finishing up her monologue. John Belushi came out as Joe Cocker.

"Your ex," Miranda joked.

"Va-va-voom."

"My middle name's Raquel."

"I know."

"You do? How? Did I tell you?"

"Haha, it says 'Miranda Raquel Savitch' on your stationery."

"Oh yeah huh," she said, "I'm such a spaz."

Dan Aykroyd did a funny bit where he was presenting "The Decabet," a metric alphabet, a simplified version of our lettering system.

It made me think about Naomi Richter and how she liked numbers better than language, but then I felt guilty thinking about Naomi while talking to Miranda.

"Celebrity crushes are kind of a weird thing," Miranda said, "being infatuated with someone you don't know."

"My first one was Marlo Thomas in *That Girl*," I said, "After that Raquel Welch. And as I've previously confessed to you, I briefly dabbled with Laurie Partridge. What about you?"

I didn't bring up my current Laraine Newman fascination.

"Ummm . . . well like I said I'm not into celebrity crushes, for sure not these days, but when I was younger, let's see, probly Davy Jones from the Monkees was my first one. David Cassidy. After that, uh, Jack Wild from H.R. Pufnstuf."

"You know H.R. Pufnstuf lives across the street from me?"

"Yeah, you've told me that before."

Miranda squealed her glee when the next sketch turned out to be, as Don Pardo announced it, "The Claudine Longet Invitational," a ski tournament that saw each participant getting "accidentally" shot by Claudine Longet.

"Whoa, shit," I said.

"No way!" Miranda giggled, "They must've been eavesdropping on us."

"*Uh oh*," Chevy Chase shouted as shots rang out and a skier fell to the snow, "*it looks like he's been accidentally shot by Claudine Longet!*"

"That's hilarious in a way," I said, "Kinda wrong too in a way."

"Nyeah, the thing is," Miranda said, "you know, we're joking about it, but he's dead. He stopped. He doesn't know the stories we're telling about him. He's just dead. He doesn't know the difference. He doesn't know he died. He doesn't know anything. There is no He anymore."

"His family knows, though," I said, "I don't think his parents find this very funny."

"This is true," Miranda agreed.

"But maybe they don't watch *Saturday Night Live*."

"May be. Let's hope."

Gilda Radner did her Baba Wawa spoof on Barbara Walters during the Weekend Update portion of the episode, making fun of Tom Snyder's hair.

"How old do you think Gilda Radner is?" Miranda asked.

"Around 30 maybe?" I said, "I dunno."

"30 is almost dead."

"We're 15," I said, "We're halfway there."

"We're halfway to almost dead," said Miranda. "Dang. That sucks."

After Lorne Michaels announced on the air that he would offer The Beatles $3,000 to reunite on *Saturday Night Live*, there was a solo Gilda segment.

"Gilda reminds me of you," I said before I could stop myself.

"All us nice Jewish girls look the same."

"It's mainly her voice."

"Ah."

"I love your voice."

"You do?" Miranda said.

An expectant silence lingered.

"Yeah," I said.

"Well I love *you*," she said.

I think I was supposed to respond to that but I didn't.

"You make me cray-zee," she said, "But I love you. I can't help it."

"Sorry."

"Jeez, don't apologize, just ask me out already," she said, "and we can take it from there."

"I have to make that happen," I said, "Yes."

"Up to you, dude."

"I will," I said, knowing I wouldn't.

Then, during a commercial, out of nowhere, Miranda said, "So Lori said she saw you hanging out with an Orthodox girl at the library."

"Huh?" I stalled, trying to figure out when Lorelei Lux might have been there and what she might have seen.

"Yeah, she said it looked like you guys were having an, um, 'interesting' time."

"I don't remember seeing Lorelei at the library."

"Of course not. She's Lori. Duh. She was probly lurking in a corner spying on you."

"Dang, dude."

"So? What's the story?"

"Nyeah-um," I groped for the proper response, "I'm embarrassed to say I'm getting geometry tutoring from this girl named Naomi, and yes, she's Orthodox. But, um, yeah. That's it."

"Is the tutoring helping?"

"It has been a little, yeah, but it's ending."

"Why?"

"She can't come to the library anymore."

"Why not?"

Two roads diverged in a yellow wood at that moment, and the emerging artist-rebel in me wanted to say, "Because I tried to finger-fuck her while she was on her period," but the nice Jewish boy in me who also loved Miranda said, "I don't know, she has responsibilities in the weeks between Passover and Shavuos, like extra Jew shit she has to do, you know, Orthodox stuff."

"Best not mess with Shavuos," Miranda said deadpan.

"Hell no," I said, "gotta commemorate our journey from slavery in Egypt to slavery under the covenant."

"Damn straight," Miranda laughed.

While John Sebastian was singing "Welcome Back," I said, "Hey, I read in the TV listings in the paper that there's a movie called *Miranda* coming on at 1am on Channel 9."

"Cool. Don't know if I can stay up that late. I'm kinda zonked."

"Oh, come on, there's a movie called *Miranda* and you're not going to stay awake and watch it?"

"Probly not, no."

Both of our energies were flagging. The silences elongated.

"It's a full moon tonight," Miranda said, "I'm going to go outside and look at it before I go to bed."

"Likewise," I said because I couldn't think of anything else to say at that moment.

"Hey I think I'm going to run for Junior Class President next year," she said, at this point grasping for conversation.

"You will win and be amazing I have no doubt," I said, "You are a mover and a shaker."

"God, I miss talking to you, Lance," Miranda said, "really really really really."

"We talk in Mr. B's room," I said.

"No, I mean like this, when it's not built-in automatic. I feel like we've drifted so far apart, like you hardly know me anymore."

"Well, I've been, you know, doing my own thing, and you're really busy with student council and earthquake relief and all that."

"Nyeah, I know, but it still makes me sad. I don't want us to lose each other just out of inertia," she said, using a Mr. St. Jerome word.

I changed the subject in order to avoid saying something that would make both of us miserable.

"So, the Guatemalan earthquake relief effort is still going on?" I asked.

"Oh, for sure, so many homeless people, especially kids. I might join a group that's going down there this summer to help with some of the rebuilding that needs to be done. That is if my parents let me. There's a youth contingent being assembled right now. I've got my name on the list."

With that, Miranda began telling me about the situation in Guatemala, in great detail. I didn't need to do anything but listen.

Some of what she said was interesting, but the sound of her voice and her seductive intelligence were also making me horny as hell, and since I had to drop Naomi Richter officially from the Fuck-O-Rama pantheon due to the utter loss of hope and insurmountable level of fucked-upedness following the atttempted finger-fucking, I gave Miranda a Saturday night guest appearance. Right then. During her Guatemala spiel.

I masturbated to fantasies of fucking her while she was telling me about the lack of sanitation in the homeless camps and the shortage of potable water.

I kept my mouth away from the phone so she couldn't hear my heated breathing, and I came as silently as possible, without a grunt or groan. I squinted my eyes really hard to compensate and felt it in my loins tremendously.

About that time I had learned to keep rubbing my dick while I was coming to make the orgasm last longer.

I tried to mop up my groin without letting Miranda detect my movements.

"Just imagine how scared those kids are," Miranda said, "Especially with the mudslides and everything. I mean, I was scared enough by the Sylmar quake. Didn't sleep for a long time after that one."

"Me too," I said, wiping myself off.

"That's how I got really good at solitaire. I'd just sit on my bed and play solitaire until I'd finally fall asleep. Remember when we played solitaire together?"

I wanted to say, "I just finished a game right now, baby," but withheld the cryptic deliciousness of that and just said "Yeah of course."

After I came I didn't really feel like talking to Miranda anymore.

"So you're gonna call me again, right?" she asked, as *Saturday Night Live* came to end.

"Uh huh," I grunted.

I had nothing else to say. I wanted to roll over and go to sleep for the first time in a week.

"And we're gonna do something together soon."

"Unh-huh," I managed to croak.

"Someone's falling asleeeeep," she teased.

"Pretty much," I said.

"This was great," Miranda said, "I'm glad we did this."

"'Twas," I said, "Me too."

"Bye, Lance. Call me when you wake up."

I didn't want to do that and wouldn't.

She hung up before I could say bye back.

I tried to watch the *Miranda* movie but lost consciousness during the opening credits.

Glynnis Johns was in it. That's all I remember. When I woke up at 4:30am the Indian test pattern was on.

The next day, after wasting another precious Sunday morning at Confirmation class, I rode my bike to Gardner Park, partly to work on a new song, partly to revisit the scene of Tuesday's sexual humiliation.

I wanted to sit on that lawn and take it all back.

I wanted to say, "I'm sorry, Naomi."

But I knew I'd never see her again.

"*I'm a shape with no corners,*" I sang the lyrics to the song I was working on, "*I'm a space with no borders,*" I continued, "*I'm a dodecahedron living in a trapezoid world.*"

I would dedicate that song to Naomi Richter when it was done.

My concentration was wobbly because I couldn't stop thinking about last Tuesday, just behind the public pool, just a few yards from that very spot where I was sitting on the grass amid the gloriousness of a lovely Spring Sunday in Los Angeles.

I put down my lyric draft, tucked up my legs and grabbed myself around the knees, still haunted by trauma, and gave myself over to the memory of my unfortunate faux pas.

Dang, dude, it had been going so well.

Naomi and I had started taking longer study breaks and hanging outside the library, sometimes just in the parking lot, other times sitting on the grass near the public pool.

On that fateful Tuesday, we stood together behind the public pool at the back of the park, away from foot traffic, along the fence that looked out over a large vacant lot of gravel, broken glass, and urban tumbleweeds, across to the Gilmore Drive-In on the other side near Farmers Market.

The sunset looked like a bowl of Froot Loops.

"You've talked about who you might *have* to have intercourse with for the rest of your life. But how about who you would *want* to have intercourse with?"

"I would never admit to having such thoughts," Naomi said.

"Oh, come on. It's my birthday. Make it my present. Tell me."

"You want my dirty secrets for a birthday present?"

"Yes. I do. *Tell me something good*," I sang like Chaka Khan, "*tell me tell me tell me*."

"You're a good singer," she said and placed her right hand on my hip and lay her left palm on my chest.

Naomi was right up against me. It had taken me weeks to reel her in.

We were transfixed in the circumference of each other's eyes. There was no periphery.

"What would your parents say if you told them you were in love with a non-Orthodox guy?" I asked her, "theoretically speaking, of course."

"Oh, my," she looked away, "Well, my father would go crazy and yell and forbid me to leave the house except for school or shul I'm sure, and my mother would side with my father at first but eventually say something like, 'At least he's Jewish,' and then eventually persuade my father that it's OK. Theoretically speaking. I guess. I don't know."

"Like *Fiddler On The Roof*," I observed.

"I haven't seen *Fiddler On The Roof*," Naomi said.

"Dang, I thought every Jew saw *Fiddler On The Roof*. Like it's a requirement or something."

She silently shook her head no and then with big wet eyes came at me full steam.

"I do have a present for you, actually, even though I didn't know it was your birthday until just now," Naomi said as she leaned toward me and our mouths melted together.

Our tongues met in a velvet exchange and she reached up and held the back of my head with her right hand.

I backed her up against the fence and lodged my hard bulge against the vicinity of her crotch, but the folds of her skirt prevented any meaningful frottage.

My hands, before they could sickly o'er with the pale cast of thought, reached for her breasts.

Through the shirt counts if you're groping an Orthodox girl, I'm pretty sure.

With one hand continuing at a breast, I journeyed my other hand down her torso and pressed gently against a vulva buried deep beneath the layers of fabric.

I gathered her long skirt slowly upward inches at a time until I had access to the holy land.

I reached in over the top of her tights and slipped my hand under the elastic waistband and on down Pisgah to a land flowing with, well, not milk and honey . . .

"You don't want to do that," she said, yanking in panic at my arm to preempt disaster.

Regardless, I forced my way to her fertile crescent long enough to discover she was in the time of her uncleanness.

"Stop," she said, pushing me away and straightening herself out, glancing at my bloody fingers.

"I shouldn't have done this," she huffed, backing away.

"—Naomi, I—"

"I didn't know you were going to—" she scurried off, not looking back.

"I'm sorry!" I tried say loud enough.

I knew I'd fucked up, but I was also disturbingly turned on in a way by what had happened.

My cock was peeking over the peninsula like Gibraltar.

I stayed behind the pool to masturbate the agitation away.

It was my first time jacking off outside. I could so totally have been caught. But that was part of the thrill.

I could hear Rabbi Meshuggeneh chanting in the background as my mind wandered Naomi Richter's wilderness of sin.

In my fantasy's crescendo I was finger-fucking Naomi, working relentless circles, fiddling with the gist of it until the milk and honey I'd been promised flowed forth abundantly.

It was one of those intense orgasms where you pretend it's her coming. Like you become the girl for those milliseconds.

Afterwards, I sopped the stuff up with the bottom of my shirt and looked around to make sure nobody had seen.

I wandered out from my covert den of lechery, hand (and now dick) bloody, and sat near the makeshift hamster graveyard.

I will admit I felt a little bit proud of myself.

But then, almost immediately, I grew overwhelmed with sorrow, as I wiped my scarlet fingers on the grass, at losing Naomi forever in an instant, before I even had her really.

I felt the ground open up, a perfect circle, beneath me.

Rabbi Meshuggeneh was on approach.

Near Misses

1

"In 1770 the Comet Lexell flew within one million miles of earth, pretty darn close in cosmic terms," said Mr. St. Jerome in his most serious lecture of the school year, "hurled at us by big bad Jupiter. There's a reason that massive planet is named after the Roman god of gods, the holder of ultimate power. Jupiter rescues us everyday from extinction by deflecting deadly comets and asteroids, yet at the same time," he paused and looked above our heads at the windows overlooking Genesee Avenue, "the gargantuan guy also tosses some pretty calamitous boulders in our direction."

He stared us down for a drawn-out moment.

"It's a good thing Jupiter doesn't have very good aim," he smiled, helping to disrupt the doomsday scenarios playing in everyone's heads at that moment.

"We do live in a fairly dangerous neighborhood, though," he went on, "rolling through space just like all the other rocks."

Mr. St. Jerome took off his glasses and wiped the lenses using his lab coat.

"I'm always puzzled by people who talk about 'going into space.' I want to say to them, 'Where do you think you are?'"

Mr. St. Jerome gestured upward with both hands.

"It's important to remember you're already there," he said to us as the bell rang to end Period 3, "Don't let the atmosphere fool you, you already *are* in space! Here *is* There!"

I shuffled reluctantly to Period 4.

I had been dreading Period 4 all morning.

In Period 4 I was going to inform Miranda Savitch that I had to flake on our Kiddyland date because my parents were making me go to this temple youth group Shabbat "experience" with my Confirmation class on Saturday and I couldn't get out of it.

Punished by the covenant again.

I figured she'd be pissed and give me the "Dang, dude" look, but amazingly when I told her she just said "Why don't we do it on Sunday then?" like it was no big deal.

"Cool," I said, praising Jupiter for the rescue from a close one, "Let's do it."

"Defenly," she said, "Sunday."

We touched fingers.

"And you're allowed to call me between now and then too, you know," she added.

"Totally," I said and looked down at the same scuff in the linoleum I'd been looking at all year, the one that cut across the space between our two desks.

Mr. Beauregard was handing out a poem.

"This is something by Lord Byron," Mr. B. said, "I thought it would go well with Mr. St. Jerome's lecture today. He did talk about comets and asteroids and near-earth events, yes? I have my days right?"

Most heads in the class nodded.

"Good. This is perfect then. It's called 'Darkness.'"

He read out loud.

I had a dream, which was not all a dream.

The bright sun was extinguish'd, and the stars

Did wander darkling in the eternal space,

Rayless, and pathless, and the icy earth

Swung blind and blackening in the moonless air

"What do we have here?" Mr. Beauregard paused and asked us.

"Doomsday," Gina Dichlich said.

"That's some end-of-the-world type shit right there," Buddy Feigenbaum muttered softly so Mr. B. couldn't hear.

"Something apocalyptic," Miranda said, "I remember you were talking about that the other day."

"Yes," said Mr. B., "when I was telling you guys about *A Canticle For Leibowitz.*"

"Armageddon," said Crystal Nabors.

"Post-nuclear," Claude Moss offered.

"Byron wouldn't have known nuclear weapons, however," Mr. B. said.

"That's right, dorkwad," Buzzy hissed at Claude and smacked him on the back of the head.

And men forgot their passions in the dread

Of this their desolation; and all hearts

Were chill'd into a selfish prayer for light

"*A selfish prayer for light,*" Mr. Beauregard repeated, "Is that what it all comes down to in the end? Just that? *A selfish prayer for light?* Is that what we all do in the final moment?"

"That'd be a bummer to think that," Manny Shepherd said from behind me.

"I can't accept it," Miranda said.

"What can't you accept?" Beauregard asked.

"That we end up losing our love and concern for other humans," she said, "I don't think that would happen."

"I think different groups of people would sink into savagery at different intervals in that kind of situation," Lorelei Lux said.

Gina Dichlich and several other girls who didn't like Lorelei rolled their eyes.

"Depending on what?" Mr. B. asked.

"Food and water," Lorelei Lux answered.

"What about food and water?"

"Uh, how much they have," she said.

"So available resources then," Beauregard said.

I wanted to say yes to Beauregard's original question—Is that all it comes down to in the end?—but was afraid my voice might break or tremble because the poem was reading my dreams.

I wanted to hear more.

A fearful hope was all the world contain'd

I reached over and poked Miranda's arm and she poked back while keeping her eyes on the poem but I saw her smile.

All earth was but one thought—and that was death

Just at that moment I looked across the room and Lorelei Lux was looking right back at me, I had no idea why, and then we quickly went our separate ways.

The world was void,

The populous and the powerful was a lump,

Seasonless, herbless, treeless, manless, lifeless—

A lump of death—a chaos of hard clay.

How many times had this very image haunted my thoughts.

In any given end-of-the-world fantasy I became inevitably always the trampled remnant of humankind.

A bystander to Armageddon.

A mannequin contraption.

I had many dreams of being a scarecrow.

Situated in witness.

Mr. Beauregard spoke the last few lines of the poem slowly.

The waves were dead; the tides were in their grave,

The moon, their mistress, had expir'd before;

The winds were wither'd in the stagnant air,

And the clouds perish'd; Darkness had no need

Of aid from them—She was the Universe.

We all dwelled in silence a moment.

Just a bombardment of desolate dead world images all day that day.

"Trippy," Manny Shepherd mustered, "but, dang, dude."

"Indeed," said Mr. B., "I wish we could spend more time with it."

The bell rang for lunch.

Manny and I would definitely be talking about that poem later.

I was going to ask Mr. Beauregard if I could keep my copy.

"You didn't chime in," Mr. Beauregard said to me as he noticed I wasn't getting up to leave.

"I felt too close to it," I said.

"What struck you about the poem?" he asked, sitting at his little writing table.

"I've been thinking about that stuff a lot lately," I said.

"What stuff?"

"The end of everything," I said.

"What do you mean?"

"I mean like some doomsday thing happening, like an asteroid striking the earth, and how nothing that ever happened on earth would matter after that, how no one would ever know about any of it; it'd be like we never existed."

"Ah, that kind of stuff," Mr. Beauregard said, seeming concerned. "How often do you picture those sorts of events in your head?"

"Oh, off and on, whenever things get quiet," I said, "and I have doomsday dreams sometimes."

"Do you picture yourself surviving in those scenarios?"

"Yeah, usually, or, well, always, yeah."

"That's good, good, that's a good thing," he said.

"I guess," I said.

"We are insignificant," Mr. Beauregard said.

"Sure feels like it."

"Is that what bothers you?"

"Nyeah, I guess."

"And what do you want to do about the fact of our utter insignificance?"

I shrugged.

"Well, let's put it this way: If you knew the world's end was imminent, what would you most want to do with the time left? Other than the obvious I mean."

I smiled as if to say fuck.

"I'd want to turn it into music," I said, "I'd want to be playing the piano while it's happening."

"Chronicle and accompaniment. You're a hopeful romantic."

"Haha, not me," I said.

"An artist then."

"Nyeah, I dunno."

"Is that what you are, an artist?"

"Creativity is the only thing that makes me happy, so," I said.

"How about girls?"

"Girls confuse me."

"Ah, well, there you have the subject of most art, so you're going into the right line of work."

I smiled again which made him smile also.

"Is Miranda Savitch your girlfriend?"

"I don't really, uh, I dunno. Miranda's a complex story."

"Oh, I suspect it's more than one story."

"For sure, yeah," I sort of laughed, "it's been going on for a while now."

"Well, I can feel it from way over here, so if she's not your girlfriend now then she either once was or probably should be. It's pretty obvious."

"I dunno, I'm always kind of into her but then I turn off when we're on the verge of making out. I am an endless source of disappointment."

Mr. B. just nodded and looked at me.

"It's much easier to be alone and listen to music and write songs and watch *Rifleman* or *Kung Fu* reruns. That's what I'd always rather be doing, no matter who I'm with."

"You like to do your own thing," he said.

"Mostly, yeah, but it's, like, more than that, though, I'm—"

I paused because I didn't know how to describe it.

"—It's like I'm always thinking about whatever new thing I'm working on, the melody will spin in my head while I silently try out lyric ideas, and it'll be happening even while I'm having a conversation with someone."

"Like right now?"

"No, right now I'm all here."

"Ah, well, I feel honored."

"And when I'm with Miranda there's this side of me that's always apart but there's this other side of me that's right there with her and into her and what she's talking about and also there's the side of me that wants to touch her body and stuff, you know, and still another side of me that says no don't give in."

"Give in to what?"

"I dunno, like, it's embarrassing to be human or something, to want things."

Mr. B. nodded.

"A sign of weakness maybe?"

"I started writing a song called 'The Shame Of Wanting' and it's kind of about that, but I don't think I'm gonna finish it."

"Maybe it's just lack of experience, your trepidation," he said.

"No but, like, I have actually gone pretty far with a couple of girls or well really this one girl. She's kind of older."

I would've said Taryn's name but I remembered she'd had Beauregard when she was at Fairfax.

"And were you ashamed?"

"No, it was just like blam it's happening."

"You weren't thinking about it."

"Nyeah it was just . . . happening."

"Thinking gets in the way of some things."

"Or more wanting to stand back and observe, I dunno. I feel very distant from most people even though I like them. Or even love them."

"There's a Eugene Ionesco line, 'Solitude seems to oppress me. And so does the company of other people.'"

"Pretty much, yeah," I laughed, "It's true. That's good."

"That kind of tendency can make it difficult to have friends," Mr. B. said.

"I'm finding that out," I said.

"You need to find other people who share your passion. They'll be equally preoccupied. That can make for a perfect friendship. They won't require anything of you other than hanging out once in a while between projects."

He rose and walked over to his filing cabinet.

The manilla folders in there looked like ancient scrolls.

He pulled something out and handed it to me.

"This is for you to read more carefully later," he said, "I'm sure you will study it with Mr. Megiddo in 12th Grade. You are going to take him, yes?"

"My counselor told me I'm going to have him in 11th and 12th Grade," I said, "American Lit next year and AP in 12th."

"Perfect," he said, "You will love Mr. Megiddo. A couple of years from now you'll be ready to digest the full scope and depth of this poem, but in the meantime I thought you'd like the images. They go well with 'Darkness.' You can just read it for the visuals. Fodder for a new song maybe. This poem gets to the heart of things."

I looked down at the mimeographed copy of "The Hollow Men."

"Can I keep this copy of 'Darkness' so I can xerox it and bring it back?"

"Just go ahead and hang onto that one," he said.

I wanted to say thank you to Mr. Beauregard but ended up not.

I was a little embarrassed I had talked about that stuff with a teacher and also hoped I didn't scare him too bad.

For the rest of lunch I found a sweet solitary spot in the courtyard near the library where nobody ever hung out.

I went back to thinking about Mr. St. Jerome's lecture on Jupiter which earlier had stirred my head, not only because of the doomsday scenarios he was provoking, but also because I was presently obsessed with the Gustave Moreau painting *Jupiter and Semele* which I discovered in the Moreau book my parents had.

When I looked at that painting I wondered what kind of mother Semele would have been had she not gotten robbed of the chance by the power of divine majesty, had she not given in to the temptations of Juno, had she not demanded proof of Jupiter's divinity, had Bacchus not been from his mother's womb untimely ripped.

That painting is a phantasmagoria of outrageous detail.

I could tell Jupiter was totally tuned in and grooving on his own godhood too, looking like a Sephardic Jesus.

Olympus a wacked-out frenzied landscape of gods and fruits and flowers and maniacal angels all dressed up as pagan gods but with Christian halos emanating also.

I loved the mayhem surrounding the deity, the bedlam of the god-brain.

I would watch the painting vibrate. At times I felt it was breathing with me.

If I let my eyes blur a little it became 3-D looking.

The sky behind Jupiter was the sky I saw every night at the top of my mind right after ejaculating.

Every speck of canvas was a detail.

"Imagine looking at this shit on acid," Manny Shepherd said once pointing to the print of "Jupiter and Semele" in the book which pretty much lived in my room now.

"We've never dropped acid," I said, "so how would you know?"

"Yeah but still," Manny said, "You know it'd be major."

"I guess maybe, I don't know," I said because I couldn't just pretend.

I don't remember why I was feeling ornery that day.

"Thanks for turning me onto this painting, dude," Manny said.

"*Jupiter and Semele*," I nodded and did a thumbs-up thing.

"It's, like, depicting pagan idolatry but the look and the vibe is all Christian and shit."

"Nyeah but being filtered through the mind and eyes of a 19th Century freak," I said.

"Totally," Manny concurred and handed me this cool little hand-held bong he'd just bought.

"Dang, that's the smallest one I've ever seen," I said, took a hit, and gave him the bong back, exhaling, "just like your dick."

"It gets the point across dude," he said as he took his own hit, "and that's all I care about," he wheezed, "it gets the fucking point across."

"The bong or your dick?" I asked.

"Well you suck on both of them so you tell me."

"Haha you're talking like Buzzy Lagniappe type shit now."

I got up to open the windows and turn on the fan and also light some incense.

"What is up with Buzzy, man? He is out there lately," Manny said.

"Yeah, something is definitely up," I said, "but I don't really know what."

"I don't know how that dude can take so many drugs and still get straight-A's."

"He's Buzzy," I said.

"This is true," Manny said with Hindu inflection.

It made me sad to think too much about Buzzy.

Such a puzzlement.

I realize now of course I was watching someone go insane.

I hadn't had a conversation with him in a couple of months other than joking around in class.

I hardly ever saw him next door.

I supposed he was spending a lot of time at Whit's house—I knew they got high and did their homework together—and at school the few times I'd venture outside at lunch I'd notice he was hanging out with the prog-rock dudes on the quad, long-haired nerds who were serious students but who also dabbled in major hallucinogens quite regularly on the weekends.

One time I ran into him at Aron's Records when he was selling back a bunch of his albums.

We said hey and when he got his store credit he joined me in browsing the $1 bins.

He was looking for Henry Cow stuff and Gong but doubted he'd find anything.

"You like Gentle Giant?" I asked him. Manny had recently turned me on to them, "Free Hand? Great fucking album, dude."

"Oh hell yeah. I already have all their shit."

"All?"

"All there is to get, yeah. I mean there's always the bootleg shit, but I'm not that geeky. Or at least I try not to be."

"Sorry, dude, you are to the geekhood born and you know it."

Buzzy nodded.

"So have you fucked Taryn Rust yet?" he asked me.

"Huh?" I feinted.

"Dude, she wants your cock in her pussy. It's yours. Take that shit. Trust me. I heard her say it."

I blushed and looked around to make sure she wasn't working that day.

"Dang, dude," I said, "that's bogus. She's like 19."

"For real, dude. All the better. You could make it your own. I'm telling you. Me no lie. Imagine your cock in that. I assure you that pussy knows what it's doing. Right?"

I gave a wide-eyed nod, the kind that is effective in seeming to agree with people so they'll get off your back.

"So what's been going on, man? I never see you around the next door. Where are you hanging these days?" I asked him.

"I dunno, walking around a lot by myself when I have time. Disappearing into the wilderness."

"Disappearing into the wilderness," I said.

"Yeah, that's where I go, man . . . I'm just like disappearing into the wilderness. I don't know how else to put it. I go places."

"Like where?"

"To the house next door."

"You mean, like, my house?"

"No, man, it's a different house next door."

We'd had this exact same conversation about the house next door several times over the past few months.

It gave me a creepy kind of sadness like in Thomas Inge plays.

After we parted ways outside Aron's, both empty-handed, I missed him even more, disappearing as he was into the wilderness.

"See you next door," he said as he walked off.

"I'm not sure what Buzzy's thing is," I said to Manny who was still staring at *Jupiter and Semele.*

"Well, anyways he's mental, dude," Manny said, "majorly mental."

"*Jupiter and Semele,*" I pointed to the painting, "that's some majorly mental shit right there though."

"Hoo-laws," Manny went supine on the carpet, "I'm gonna be dreaming that shit tonight," he slurred with dry mouth, "In fact, Jupiter's eyes, dude, in that painting, I fuckin' already have dreamt that shit before, dude, I swear, I have fuckin' seen that dude, dude."

"Right on," I said and lay upon my back as well.

I knew what he was talking about.

2

On the Saturday that I had to go to the youth group Shabbat thing with the Confirmation class at my temple, my father dropped me off in the parking lot and drove away and said something like "have fun" or "bye, son"—I couldn't tell which—as I got out of the car.

My mother had packed me a lunch.

Salami sandwich on rye. Pickle. Carrot sticks.

I walked into the courtyard where we were supposed to mingle with our fellow temple youth until the planned rigmarole began.

I scanned the scattered groups around the courtyard and felt the encroaching agony of having no one to talk to.

I hadn't made a single friend in all my years of Hebrew school other than Justine Balthazar, but I went to regular school with her also and we hung out and stuff so she didn't really count.

A girl waved at me but it was just that gnarly bitch Yocheved who always sat next to me in Hebrew class every year, so I didn't wave back and perched on one of the stone benches and had a look at the flowers.

I also began to plot my escape.

I would just slip out through the parking lot and walk around all day until the Shabbat experience was supposed to be over and then get back in time to meet my dad in the parking lot.

I stared at the clusters of impatiens in the flower bed next to the bench.

At first I was just pretending to be interested in the impatiens but then I became quite sincerely interested in the impatiens and their ability to make such vibrant colors in the shade and then I said fuck it I'm leaving.

Sitting on that stone bench alone, dreading the impending awkward bonding activities the heinous day ahead was sure to hold in store, I was moved to stand up and slip unnoticed out of the courtyard, across the parking lot, and out onto the street, there to begin my long day's ditch.

I ducked into St. Mary Magdalen's to get some quiet and map out the day.

There were a few people praying but otherwise the cathedral was desolate.

I considered staying for the next mass and trying to take communion.

How would they know I wasn't Catholic?

Ultimately I decided not to attempt communion because I realized there was probably some prayer or catch-phrase or code-word you're supposed to say when the priest gives you the wafer thingy and I wouldn't know what it was and then I'd be busted.

I chose instead to mosey on, leaving the cathedral to merge with the profane, exhausted city of Los Angeles.

I had brought with me a joint of this new pot Bigelow Rust was selling called School Night.

"It's mild, but, like," Big insisted, "it definitely gets you thinking, you know, a very mellow buzz, and you can still get your homework done. Ergo, School Night, dude."

It was indeed mellow but it had a lot of seeds in it which was a pain.

I ducked into the alley behind St. Mary Magdalen's and smoked about half the School Night joint and thought about my next day Kiddyland date with Miranda Savitch.

The Kiddyland date thing was all because she'd come to see me high jump one afternoon.

She had told me earlier in the day that she was going to watch the track meet after school, and even though I tried not to be nervous I kept looking up into the bleachers to see if she was there yet.

I was warming up with Harold Monarch, the other high jumper on the C team with me.

Harold Monarch was this wiry guy with legs like springs and you knew he'd be Varsity next year and All City and all this and all that.

He was serious as shit about jumping.

"Why you looking so nervous, man?" Harold asked as we stretched, "You need to get loose."

"Oh, this girl I know might be coming," I said.

"A girl you know might be coming," Harold Monarch said, "meaning a girl you wanna fuck."

"It's not like that," I said.

"Man, it's *always* like that."

"Ha ha," I responded.

"You've jacked off to her, right?"

"Well, yeah."

"Then that's a girl you wanna fuck, man."

"I guess."

"What you mean you guess? You ever jacked off to a girl you *didn't* wanna fuck?"

I was tempted to say yeah.

"No," I said.

"'Cause that'd be some crazy fucked up bullshit right there. But all right then. Just don't be thinking about fucking her while you need to be thinking about your jumps, man. Bitches can and will fuck up your timing," he said as he stood up to take some practice jumps, "it's always like that, dude."

"I concur," I said.

"Say what?"

"I dig what you're saying about how bitches can and will fuck up one's timing."

"You talk funny, Atlas," he said as he trotted away.

During the meet, Jack Hunter was walking around the field taking pictures for the *Colonial Gazette*, the Fairfax High newspaper.

"Hey, Atlas," he said, "can I get a shot of your next jump?"

"I guess," I shrugged. I didn't care.

I missed the jump of course, just barely, caught the pole with my heel on the way down.

I made it on the second jump at that height, though.

"Thanks, man, got a good one," Jack said as he moved on to other events.

I did not have a good day jumping, but Harold Monarch took first in high jump and in long jump, and our runners did well, so overall we won the meet even though nobody cared what the C team did. Our scores didn't count for anything.

I knew I was finishing up my last stint in organized sports.

I would not be going out for basketball or track in 11th Grade.

I had reached the age where athletic mediocrity pronounced itself loudly enough for the nondelusional to accept their fate.

Only the truly talented advanced from that point on.

After the meet Miranda was waiting for me on the outdoor basketball courts where we all cut across from the field to the locker room.

"Hi, Lance!" she said, waving, "I made it. I saw you jump!"

"Ugh," I said, "I sucked."

"Shut up," she said, "You feel like hanging out?"

"Sure, yeah, let me change," I said.

When I came back out of the locker room she was standing next to her backpack.

She smiled and waved again.

"Yay," she said.

"You can't be cheering my performance in the meet today," I said.

"No I mean yay we get to hang out."

She took my arm and we walked out onto the now deserted football field and looked at the photochemical iridescence of the Los Angeles sunset.

We lay back, perched on elbows both of us, alone together, and breathed the breezy air.

The days in May were getting warmer, but the evenings remained cool.

"*I am very fond of sunsets. Come, let us go look at a sunset now,*" Miranda intoned.

"Um, we are looking at a sunset," I informed her.

"*Little Prince,*" she informed me back.

"Ah," I said.

The moon was orange as it rose.

"The sun and moon are in the same sky right now," I pointed.

"Mmm, shivers," Miranda said and stretched her legs. "Look behind us, it's already dark back there," she said, hanging her head back eastward.

We lay side by side gazing upward at the approaching dusk.

"I remember when I was little I'd look at the moon with my father sitting in the backyard," Miranda said, "When I asked him what the moon was, he said—I still remember this—he said the moon is all the dirt from when they dug out the Grand Canyon."

"That's sweet," I said.

I really needed to french her brains out right then.

"I pictured shovelfuls of dirt being scooped up and made into a big balloon that they then let go in the sky," Miranda said, "And you're the one who's sweet," she said, sitting up as if to leave.

"Where are you going?" I asked.

"I should probly call my mom and tell her not to worry," Miranda said.

"Yeah yeah," I said, rising with her.

"Maybe we can go have dinner at Canter's or something," she said, "You into it?"

"I guess yeah," I said.

We walked over to the pay phone on campus which was in a dark corridor between the cafeteria and the theatre room, G-90.

"Uhmm, do you have a quarter?"

"Um-yeah," I fished for a coin.

"Do you think D-Lux and Mr. Hill are doing it?" Miranda asked.

"Huh?" I said, handing her the quarter.

"You know, do you think Deirdre's getting it on with Mr. Hill?"

I shrugged.

"You mean, like, now?" I asked.

I was a little freaked out about the darkness surrounding us.

Mr. Hill was the drama teacher who taught in G-90.

Deirdre "D-" Lux was the older sister of Lorelei Lux and she was always hanging around Mr. Hill.

"When we ask Lori she just says she's got no idea," Miranda said.

"Yeah, um, I dunno, I haven't really thought about it," I said.

"Boys," scoffed Miranda as she dialed, "Dang, I can hardly see."

I remained on the lookout for hoodlums and other would-be attackers.

"Hey, mom, I'm . . . mom I . . . mom . . . mom . . . I'm sorry I didn't call earlier. I . . . yes I know I promised . . . sorry . . . sorry . . . yeah ok . . . hanging out with Lance . . . yeah . . . of course . . . mom, stop . . . ok ok . . . all right . . . soon," Miranda said and hung up looking dejected.

"She pissed?"

"Nyeah, a little. I forgot I promised to stay with my little brother tonight so my folks can go out. S'anyway I have to go home. Walk with me to the bus?"

I was kind of relieved 'cause I didn't really want to go to Canter's and plus I didn't have enough money even if I did want to go, so that worked out ok.

I pretended to be disappointed though.

We walked down Fairfax toward Beverly where she wanted to catch the Fairfax bus because the closer stop at Melrose was too creepy for her. Scuzzy Russian pervs in leisure suits and resident hobos as she described it.

"I can stand guard and protect you," I offered.

She grinned as if to say, "Ha! You?"

"You gonna stay up and watch the meteor shower tonight?" she asked.

"Not sure, maybe."

"I wonder when the next collision's gonna happen."

"Yeah, I think about that shit all the time," I said, "I kind of do believe that's how it's all going to end."

"You mean it's all gonna end with a big bang."

"Our Ironic Cosmos" I spoke like a documentary narrator.

"Methinks you are wrong, Sir Lancelot."

"I haveth not refutation, m'lady. But the meteor shower will be way cool."

"Are you really that hopeless about the future?"

"Nyeah, no, not really, or I guess I just like the imagery maybe," I said, "I dunno."

I shrugged.

"That's how Beauregard would read it," Miranda said.

"Totally."

"I'm scared to go into Mr. Megiddo's class next year."

"Why? I heard he's great. Mr. B. told me I'd love him."

"Yeah, you maybe."

"I dunno, I'm excited about it."

"I'm gonna miss Mr. Beauregard."

"Of course," I said, "But a new experience is good too."

"I'm always afraid of letting go of things," Miranda said, "'Cause what if I end up wanting them back?"

"Nyeah, I always feel like I'm trying to get back what I never had," I said, feeling like a total dick because I'd turned her statement into another way to talk more about myself.

I was doing my gender proud.

"That's weird," Miranda said, "But then you're a weirdo so it actually makes sense."

"It does?"

"Well, not the statement itself, but the fact that you said it, yes," she leaned in, trying to get me to put my arm around her which I didn't, "So explain the statement to me. Where does that come from, trying to get back something you never had?" she asked me.

I said, "I dunno when I was like 5 years old I had this birthday party at Kiddyland—"

"—I loved Kiddyland!" she said, "and the pony rides next door!"

"That's the place, but, see, actually I hated Kiddyland. It was one of those places I had to pretend to like because we spent so much time there and I didn't want my parents to feel bad when they took me. And, dang, the flavorless vanilla ice cream in those little cups and the wooden spoons that gave me shivers when my teeth would touch them. Kiddyland sucked."

"So what happened at your birthday party?" Miranda focused me.

"Yeah yeah, I was off by myself playing with the gravel. The gravel was the only thing at Kiddyland I liked. The entire grounds were gravel. I could play with it near the rides my party guests were going on. I loved the way it felt as it fell from my hand."

"And then . . ." she prompted against my digression.

"Oh, so I heard a kid screaming and looked up just as the screaming kid's white balloon sailed up, and I followed it all the way up there until until there was nothing but blue, and the whole time the kid is screaming 'cause he lost his balloon. I felt bad for him because of his balloon but I also wanted him to stop screaming because it was annoying me. Right then my mother called me over to the table with all the stuff for my party, including Batman and Robin from the *Batman* TV show on my cake, and she started to hand me a red balloon on a string, saying, 'Here, little fella, this is for your birthday!'"

"Little fella?"

"Yeah," I skidded past her question, "and she starts to hand me this red balloon on a string."

"I know what's coming," Miranda winced.

"Of course. I wrap my fingers around the string and it slips from my grip and the red balloon goes up up and away. Into the 5th Dimension. Totally."

"It had to happen," she said.

"I remember watching the red balloon go up and feeling weird, maybe some kind of sadness or something, but all I know is I still have dreams about the red balloon getting away."

"Getting back a thing you never had," Miranda said, "I get it. Yeah."

I couldn't tell if she was bullshitting me or not.

"I dunno, it's stupid," I shrugged.

413

"It's not stupid," Miranda said and touched my shoulder as we passed Damiano's Pizza.

I did not reciprocate.

"It's weird 'cause I was just thinking about Kiddyland the other day. I liked Kiddyland. I loved it. I had several birthday parties there," she said.

"Me too, duh, and went to bunches of others."

"There's no way we weren't there at the same time sometimes," Miranda said.

"Oh yeah no way," I agreed.

"All those near misses," she added.

"Totally," I said, wanting to kiss her very hard on the mouth, "Maybe I even threw gravel at you as you passed by. That's how I flirted when I was five."

"You still kind of do a version of that," Miranda teased.

We passed the last block to the corner of Fairfax and Beverly in silence.

"Let's go there together," she said as we stood at the bus stop outside Crocker Citizens bank.

"Where?"

"Kiddyland."

"What, the abandoned ruins? There's nothing really there now but old rusty junk from the rides. Plus it's like trespassing or some shit."

"Yeah," she said, "I think it'd be creepy and cool. Don't you? It'll be like our playground date at Hancock Park Elementary only crazier."

"May be."

"Oh, come on, Lance, let's do it, a Kiddyland date."

"Are you asking me out on a date?"

"Nyeah-I'm not asking you out on a date per se, I'm just making a suggestion that we visit the holy ruins of ancient Kiddyland together. It

414

doesn't have to be a date."

"I-uh—"

"—It doesn't have to *not* be a date either," she said.

"I'm-uh—"

"—I mean why can't it be a date? Let's go out on a date and do what boys and girls do when they go out on dates."

"I don't know what boys and girls do when they go out on dates—"

"—other than frenching which you know plenty about," she interjected, "i.e. Candy Stoner."

"And Dolly Ferris and Taryn Rust and Naomi Richter," I never had any intention of saying out loud, but, dang, dude, it danced distractingly in my head.

"I mean like all the other stuff," I said.

"Me neither. We'll figure it out," she was tapping my knuckles with her fingers, "Come on, Lance," she tried in her adorably dorky way to be enticing.

I waited with Miranda until the Fairfax bus came.

"Kiddyland next Saturday," she said, stepping into the stairwell.

"Not tomorrow Saturday."

"Right. A week from tomorrow Saturday," she grabbed my face, "a date!"

I smiled.

"Bye, Lance!" she said as the bus door closed on her.

A part of me wanted to walk home and think about Miranda in the sweet night air, but I succumbed to laziness and hopped the Beverly bus.

I should have walked though.

Thinking about Miranda on the bus wasn't nearly as satisfying as doing it while walking would have been.

The fluorescent lights were giving me a headache.

Plus this old man wearing a bathrobe threw up in the back of the bus like right when we passed El Coyote.

There was stringy stuff hanging from his mouth like pizza cheese probably.

He used his finger to break the web.

I got off a couple of stops later, but, dang, dude, it was flagrant.

I had to walk a few blocks down Beverly to regain that slow Friday ease of having nothing to do tomorrow and the weekend feels like it'll last forever.

I sort of regretted saying yes to the date mostly because now I didn't know how to act around Miranda for all the next week.

I should have told her not to come to the track meet. Dang.

My next jaunt on the long day's ditch was over to the Wiltern Theatre to see if there was anything good playing, something that would save my day, like a Bruce Lee triple bill maybe, or a Three Stooges marathon, or maybe a daylong showing of all the *Planet Of The Apes* movies. That saga always held my attention.

Alas, the Wiltern was not going to rescue me that day, as the theatre was playing host to a live talk by Maha Roger, this hippy guru dude who was on Johnny Carson sometimes.

I had been seeing his picture everywhere like on billboards and shit of late.

He was a Jewish guy who'd bribed his way to enlightenment on an ashram in India and had packaged the schtick for American consumption.

Manny Shepherd used to call him The Rama-Lama-Ding-Dong.

"How can people believe in gurus and shit?" Manny said once when we were talking about the Rama-Lama-Ding-Dong and maybe Scientology came up too.

There was this weird poster up around town that showed Maha Roger flying across the sky and in his wake the words "The End Is Here . . ."

Mr. Beauregard had a similar poster on one of the walls of his classroom which said "*A screaming comes across the sky* . . ." but instead of Maha Roger it was a rocket.

I stared at that sentence often.

I was staring at that sentence just before I started reading the daily bulletin this one day in Period 4.

"General Interest," I read to my inattentive classmates.

"I don't have any," said Miranda, who was listening sort of.

"Uhhh, neither does the bulletin," I said, "The General Interest section is blank. The whole thing is prom announcements for the Seniors."

"Fuck '76," said this Samoan kid who had somehow kept his name a secret from everybody the entire school year.

We would beg teachers to tell us his name but none of them would.

"I bet he's a narc," Claire Farnaway said.

We didn't know for sure if the Samoan kid was actually Samoan. We couldn't tell what he was.

One time Buzzy Lagniappe flat out asked the Samoan kid, "What are you and shit?"

And the Samoan kid answered, "The one who's fucking your mama's loose coochie every night . . . ooh and I be tearing that shit up, I mean, like, dang, dude."

"Defenly a narc," Miranda joked quietly.

"I heard that," said Mr. Beauregard who was chatting at the classroom door with Mr. Whiteswallow, the Fairfax counselor responsible for the middle of the alphabet.

"K and L drive me crazy," I overheard Mr. Whiteswallow saying once in the hall, "I've got 42 Kims and 57 Lees."

Manny thought 42 Kims would be a great name for a band.

Beauregard was going to be handing back our poems on that day, and we were all anxious to hear his reaction to our creative work because usually we just wrote expository essays for him.

He had given us this assignment to write a poem that included the phrase "always playing the game."

Form was up to us.

I chose to do a song lyric.

I knew I wanted to do something with the idea of an aloof kid, an outsider and born that way but still sort of connected, "always playing the game."

I felt like I should write it at the Tar Pits, but I was still avoiding the cool nerd conclaves that would often take place there.

I mapped out some possible corridors that'd be safe for a Tar Pits visit.

Saturday morning seemed a likely shot at solitude.

The crowd would most definitely not be partying at that time.

I took the bus over to the Tar Pits that day, guitar in hand, and some folded up pieces of notebook paper in my back pocket for lyric writing, my Bic 4-color pen ever at the ready.

"The guitar pits," I kept amusing myself silently on the bus.

My holy patch of grass by the little stream that doesn't move was relievedly free of all people.

I sat alone at the center of Los Angeles.

Where music emanates from the ancients.

I needed to plug into that essence.

An E minor essence.

Birth was his take-off

He was destined to lead a life up in the air

I knew I wanted that to be the opening line. I'd written that walking home from school the day before.

I also already knew I wanted to call the song "Flying Solo."

Like a loose balloon he rose

And though far out was still aware

That was the first line that came to mind once I'd settled onto the grass.

Then a shift from E minor to E major and a different rhythm and meter.

He didn't want to blend because he hated to pretend
To be one of the same
He wasn't gonna win 'cause he had trouble fitting in
But he was always playing the game

That formed the basic structure of the verse.

I sketched out a second.

Back to E minor.

His life was an orbit
He went spinning around lost in space
Something told him to hold back
And stay apart and hide his face

And then to E major.

He tried to keep his distance from the others in existence
A gnome without a name
He refused to choose because he knew that he would lose

But he was always playing the game

Then the chorus would pop as only E-major can pop.

On a flight plan to infinity

There is nowhere to go

No matter how high he traveled

He was always flying solo

Flying solo

Flying solo baby

Flying so low . . . .

I wrote the whole thing that morning.

I added a droning A major bridge after writing the chorus but changed my mind and made the A major drone a solo section with no lyrics.

I revised a few lines before I turned the song in but mostly it was made right there that Saturday morning at the Tar Pits.

We sat in anticipation of Mr. B. handing back the poems and perhaps reading a few examples out loud.

"Listen to this line," he said, holding what I could already see was my paper, from a poem called 'Flying Solo:' *Birth was his take-off. He was destined to lead a life up in the air.*"

Nobody commented.

"It's all up in the air, you see, and yet destined. This is the existential moment right here. And the internal rhyming, in the second half of each stanza. Where did you learn that?" he asked me.

Everybody looked my way as my authorship was revealed.

"Dr. Seuss mostly," I said, "Oh, and Stephen Sondheim a little bit. Jacques Brel too."

"Jacques Brel?"

"Yeah, great internal rhyming," I said.

"In French?"

"Oui. You can hear the rhymes even if you don't get what the words mean. I listen to him at lunch in Madame Couchée's room."

"My damn coochie," Buddy Feigenbaum to his neighbors who giggled.

"Well, a great piece of work," Mr. Beauregard said.

After class he told me, "You are what you think you are."

I headed off to Madame Couchée's room to listen to Jacques Brel and browse a copy of Paris Match while reveling in Mr. Beauregard's acknowledgement and wondering if Miranda was impressed or maybe resentful because he didn't read her poem out loud.

When I asked her later that day if she'd let me read it she said no.

The long day's ditch continued.

After rejecting any notion of going to see Maha Roger preach, I continued my foray turning north onto Western Avenue, where I felt for the first time like an alien in my own city.

I remember the moment I touched that chilling bone of discomfort.

The wandering Jew, the invading Gringo, passing shops whose Spanish and Korean signs I couldn't understand, the past and future of Los Angeles.

And yet in many ways it was no more foreign to me than the culture of the private school kids in my Confirmation class at temple.

I spoke to almost no one on the long day's ditch.

This is what the rest of my life will be like, I remember thinking, ambling aimlessly and alone. I couldn't imagine any other outcome for me.

I sat at a bus stop on 6th Street for two hours, feeling bad every time a bus would arrive, stop, open its doors for me, and I'd wave it on, continuing to sit, like a schizoid homeless person who has forgotten his mother ever existed.

I ate my packed lunch at the bus stop.

Time lies still in such circumstances.

I wasn't thinking about anything, just receiving the audio-visual stimuli as they passed through my field of perception.

In a bizarre act of thrill seeking, I dared myself to walk all the way home, look at my house from the corner, and then trek all the way back to temple.

I walked along 6th Street which, heading west, switches from a gritty commercial conglomeration of mom and pop operations—laundromat, grocery, burger joint, shoe store, toys, flowers, discount apparel—to the palatial homes in Hancock Park.

We lived one street west of Highland, so we weren't officially in Hancock Park; we were considered in the Fairfax area.

At Highland I headed north to Beverly Blvd, 1 block from my house.

The odyssey finally brought me to Citrus and Beverly, the closest intersection to my house, having an absurdly perverse moment in my already deviant history.

Flirting with discovery.

That epic rush of an open secret.

I stood on the corner, in front of Lennie's place, and looked across the street at my house.

The driveway was empty.

Somebody wasn't home.

At any moment either one of my parents could emerge from the house and see me or else arrive home driving right past where I was standing.

Neither happened.

I was both relieved and disappointed.

I'd never felt more perverse.

Thus utterly rudderless I began a zigzag path back to temple.

I was visited again by a heightened sense of aloneness, a lack of true connection to any human being, a sensation which can either nauseate or inspire depending on one's astrological sign.

On the corner of 6th & Western there was an evangelical dude with a megaphone quoting scripture and admonishing the sinners.

He stood in front of a poster board sign that said "I am Alpha and Omega, the beginning and the end."

As I walked past him he said into his megaphone, "Nevertheless I have somewhat against thee, because thou hast left thy first love," and he was pointing at me when he said it.

I tried not to engage, but he kept pointing at me.

"I know the blasphemy of them which say they are Jews, and are not, but are the synagogue of Satan," he said still gesturing in my direction.

He was like Rabbi Meshuggenneh only Christian.

"And round about the throne were four and twenty seats," he then said.

"Hey 4/20 is my birthday," I said, trying to break the spell.

"Who cares if it's your birthday? I mean big whoop. La-dee-dah it's your birthday. Come hither; I will show unto thee the judgment of the great whore that sitteth upon many waters."

"Cool," I said, "take me to her."

"Are you ready for Jesus?" he asked and meant it.

"I think I'd be more into him if I had a better idea of what Jesus actually looked like," I said.

"I think Jesus probably looked like the fat kid from *Willy Wonka & The Chocolate Factory*—What's his name?—Buzzy—?"

"Augustus—"

"—Lagniappe?"

"—Gloop. Augustus Gloop is the fat kid from *Willy Wonka & The Chocolate*

Factory," I said.

"Oh, I could've sworn it was Buzzy Lagniappe."

"No, it's Augustus Gloop. But actually I know a guy named Buzzy Lagniappe, and his real name is Augustus. And he used to be fat. Kids would sometimes tease him and call him Augustus Gloop back when he was fat. But whatever, I actually think Jesus looked like me with darker skin. Sephardic Jewboy sporting a way-out fro."

"Once you have accepted him as your personal savior it doesn't really matter what he looked like in his bodily human form on earth for thereafter he is transfigured in your eyes."

"Well, for the time being I'll pretend he looked like me," I said.

Sensing my flippant mockery, the ragged evangelist shook his head and said, "Well, you do that, and may the grace of Jesus Christ open your heart enough to let him in someday. May you know his love and glory in the salvation that is his alone to give."

He blew me a kiss and went back to his megaphone.

I wandered on and became enraptured with the myriad passings at the corner of 6th and Kingsley, cars and people and stray animals.

It occurred to me that an invisible divinity was hovering among the bustle.

I saw this geeky girl wearing Spock ears and a Star Fleet Academy shirt. She was carrying some kind of makeshift electronic contraption that required her to stop every few yards and rest.

Dang, dude.

It looked like she'd been eating licorice.

If only she'd come sit on the bench with me and talk about Star Trek. Or about what her contraption was for.

But I did not exist in her galaxy. Nor would I ever.

The Lord was more present at this atavistic intersection than in the gothic awfulness of the domed sanctuary back at temple.

I think the next God prophecy, the next significant wisdom tradition to emerge, will be delivered unto (and thus emerge from) someone sitting at a bus stop in Los Angeles.

God will speak in a Spanish-Korean dialect and he will have gills.

Religion will move in a new direction thereafter.

The new liturgy will be openly metaphorical, composed of mythic hymns all sung to the tune of "Rama-Lama-Ding-Dong."

The long day's ditch came to an end at sunset.

I re-entered the temple grounds and found the hallway of classrooms where the various discussions and experiences I'd avoided had been taking place.

Kids were emerging from the rooms at the event's conclusion and making their way to the temple parking lot where parents were lined up waiting to collect them.

As I walked down the hall, blending in with the crowd, as if I too had spent all day in their midst, like the guy who jumps into the last 100 yards of a marathon as if he'd run the whole thing, I was asked by a bewildered parent where his daughter was.

"I think she was in the last room at the end of the hall," I said with presumptuous authority, having no idea whom he was talking about, "on the left."

Several temple teens stared at me, trying to process why they were suddenly seeing me after my utter absence from the day's activities.

Justine Balthazar, who was enthusiastically into the whole Jewish youth group thing and Jew camp and all that shit, came up behind me and whispered, "Yocheved said she saw you here earlier, dude. Where did you go?"

And behind Justine, with stern countenance, stood Miranda Savitch, who wasn't a member of our temple.

"I only came here as Justine's guest so I could see you," Miranda said.

"This seems weird I know," I said.

"Where the fuck were you?" Miranda asked.

I'd messed up yet again.

"Uh, so is our date still on tomorrow?" I asked because she seemed angry enough to cancel and I didn't want to talk about the long day's ditch.

"Oh hell yeah, you have to double make this up to me, so you better be amazing tomorrow," Miranda warned, thereby guaranteeing diappointment.

"Yes, m'lady," I said trying to get her to not be mad at me.

"And bring me a present."

"By all means, m'lady."

"Bye, Lance," she said as she and Justine stepped into Justine's mom's car.

My dad picked me up and we went over to Cassel's because my mom wanted us to bring home burgers for dinner.

My dad had the radio tuned to KMPC. I sang along to "My Eyes Adored You," a song that always reminded me of Miranda. KMPC played hits from like 2 years before and always the corniest shit, but my dad dug it. He was really into Dick Whittinghill's morning show but also usually had it on in the car unless there was a Dodgers or Lakers game on and we'd listen to that.

"Is there anyone in particular you like these days?" my dad asked me.

"Musically you mean? There's this band called the Ramones I'm getting into a lot."

"I was thinking of young ladies."

"I dunno I like a whole bunch of girls right now."

My dad smiled.

"I bet," he said. "But nobody who stands out?"

"No," I said, all crazy about Miranda, "not really. I like thinking about lots of girls."

"I remember those days," my dad smiled to himself mostly.

Later that night I lay on my back in the dark, wishing on Miranda.

I believed that if I jacked off romantically enough—like to a whole involved scenario and shit—and came really intensely Miranda would feel it

426

somehow, especially if she was sleeping.

Like voodoo or something.

Manny had lent me The Ramones album and that was blaring from my stereo while I had my way with thoughts of Miranda pulling me into her and holding me tight as we both came really hard together.

I fell asleep and had dreams of lonely hillsides.

3

Because of the youth group Shabbat the day before, there was no Confirmation class on Sunday morning.

I asked my dad to drive me over to The Frigate to find something offbeat to give Miranda, something that would surprise her.

I was always sure to find the perfect thing at The Frigate, that hodgepodge wonderland.

Proprieters Sid and Marty were both in the store when I entered.

"Sid, it's our handsome friend," Marty hailed his partner.

"What's the object of your hunt today?"

"Cool and unusual. Music. Funny even."

"For yourself?" Sid asked.

"Nyeah, for a girl."

"A girl friend? Or a girlfriend?" he asked.

"I'm not exactly sure," I said.

Sid smiled.

"What's her name? Have you told me before?"

I had told him before.

"Miranda," I said.

"Miranda," he paused and then moved over to a bin of singles, "Well, here's a camp classic," he said, holding up a 45 entitled "Miranda," sung by Adam West who played Batman on the TV series.

I grabbed it immediately.

"I used to idolize Adam West. Batman was my favorite show when I was five."

"A fine man indeed," Sid said.

"I was more partial to Burt Ward myself," Marty said, "The Boy Wonder."

"Well, you were always sluttier than I was, darling," Sid answered, "I go for the more dignified gentlemen."

"You don't realize how perfect this is," I interjected, "You guys always come through for me. Thank you."

"Keeping the magic alive since 1965," they said together.

I waved bye from the doorway.

"Good luck with your friend," Sid said as I left.

My dad dropped me off at Beverly and Fairfax where Miranda and I had planned to meet at eleven.

Miranda had taken the bus down and was already waiting in front of Bargain Fair.

She approached the car as my dad pulled over.

"Hi," Miranda waved in at my dad who waved back.

"Thanks, dad," I said and closed the door.

"Hi, Lance," Miranda said and pulled me over to the bus stop.

"No buses have stopped since I got here so the next one is probly soon. Sunday schedule is a drag."

"Here I got you something," I said and handed her the record.

She looked at the cheesy cover and smiled.

"Oh, far out, thank you, you are the coolest," she said and kissed me on the cheek, putting the record into her suede shoulder bag, "You got me a present," she smiled. "You didn't really have to. I was semi-joking about the present part yesterday."

"You know it's gotta be hilarious," I said, "Adam West singing?"

"Totally. Can't wait. Cool name for a song, too," Miranda said and then we were silent for a while and exchanged some awkward eye contact.

She was wearing powder blue Dittos and a tucked in Roger Daltrey t-shirt, righteously tight. She was wearing some kind of leather shoes girls wear but I don't know what they're called.

Oh and she had on these earrings that looked like arrowheads made from lava-rock.

Those would most definitely get in the way of nibbling on her earlobes later should the afternoon end up coming to such circumstances.

I'm not into earrings.

They just, like I said, get in the way of things.

I need those lobes to be bare and waiting and ooh.

We got off the bus at the corner of Beverly and La Cienega.

The Smokey Joe's sign loomed over the intersection, a robotically operated cigar sticking out of a round-faced black dude's mouth and making what looked like real smoke.

"Do you think that sign is racist?" Miranda asked.

I shrugged.

I'm bad at political stuff. I get all flustered and don't know what I'm talking about. I stick to film, art, music, and literature; otherwise I'm lost.

I liked the sign.

When Smokey Joe's closed not long after our date it turned into a place called Crosby's Pizza and it was as if Smokey Joe's had never been there.

All the magic of that corner was swept away with its demise. First Kiddyland and the pony rides and then Smokey Joe's.

Dang, dude. That's what always happens eventually. Magic goes away.

"Buzzy and Whit snuck in here once," I said as we looked for a way onto the Kiddyland grounds where we wouldn't be seen, "and they said around the back, like behind the furniture store, there's a hole in the fence you can crawl through."

The only way to get back there was to go all the way around the front of the furniture store to the back parking lot through the gravel driveway it shared with Standard Shoes.

The parking lots, in front and in back, for both stores, were all gravel too.

Just like at Kiddyland.

The entire block was covered in gravel in fact.

It was really weird behind the stores because their property butted up against a field of oil derricks pumping away, looking like dinosaurs drilling for their very own residue.

We found the promised hole in the fence and crouched through.

The gravel was still there but was overgrown with weeds, some of them our height.

We crunched our way across the long-shuttered grounds, among the rusted cockpits from the copter ride, rotted wooden boats that used to go in a circle, the forever frozen ferris wheel, the faded carcasses of cars, the ones that went on this lame little road and I could never figure out what the fuck was fun about that, a choo-choo train on its side (the black and yellow one where they let you clang a bell), two grounded rocket ships, dinky little motorcycles, the abandoned Dad's Root Beer stand, and most of all a thundering silence.

"Sonny and Cher used to bring Chastity here," Miranda said, "and now it's a junkyard. I've never seen so much rust in one place before."

This is where I lost the balloon," I said, standing near the dilapidated Haunted House in the vicinity of where the party tables used to be, now just scraps of metal and stacks of soggy wood.

"That story makes me sad," she said, "Knowing that you're always feeling like you've lost something you never had."

What I didn't tell Miranda was that I wasn't the boy in the story, I was the balloon.

Up and away in heartache, past the grabbing, soaring, ascending in spirals, forever lost, vanishing into the upper distance, consigned to a lonesome eternity.

"It's amazing how small it is," Miranda said as we strolled the derelict perimeter of the park.

"Yeah it's like a total mind time blitz," I said.

"A mind time blitz? What the hell does that mean?"

"Nyeah, nothing, just making shit up trying to impress you."

"You don't have to try to impress me."

Miranda grabbed my hand pulled me toward her, but I put up my habitual resistance.

My skin felt prickly and seemed to be tugging at me.

I looked at the merry-go-round behind her.

"You ever go on that thing?" I pointed at the decrepit relic.

"Yeah of course. Who didn't?"

"Me," I said.

"Let me guess."

"It made me too sad."

"You and your organized fun complex."

"Hate it."

"So you've told me."

"It's nothing compared to the Miranda complex," I'm glad I didn't say to her.

"Ever been to the one in Griffith Park?" she asked.

"I've seen it but never ridden it."

"It's very Catcher-In-The-Rye. Brass ring and everything. We should go!"

"Nyeah maybe."

"We can do that and go see Laserium!" she said.

"I dunno."

Miranda grunted.

"Come on, you know you totally want to make out with me at the Observatory," she said.

"I'm not entirely opposed to the idea."

"You are such a doofus," she said.

"You hungry?" I asked, maneuvering my way out of another close one.

"Totally," she said, "All I ate for breakfast was the leftover Jiffy Pop from last night, so yeah, starving."

"Nutritious," I said, "Let's grab a bite."

"What's good around here?"

"We could either go to Jan's or to Smokey Joe's."

"Oh Smokey Joe's for sure," she said, "Jan's is boring. Jan's is where you go for lunch with your grandma after she takes you shopping for tights."

"Ah," I said, having never had such an experience.

"Eating at Jan's is like shopping at Britts."

"I get it. But the great thing about shopping at Britts was then we always get to go to Andre's afterward."

"Andre's salad dressing," Miranda sighed.

"Dang, dude," I concurred.

"Another place my grandma always takes me is Stats, over where Wilshire and San Vicente cross," Miranda said.

"Ugh, I hate that place. It's, like, not a coffee shop and not a restaurant. What is it?"

"Right? And they serve potato chips with your sandwich instead of french fries. Lame-o."

"And you have to be accompanied by someone 65 or older to get in," I added, laughing.

"Ha ha, yeah, like Nibbler's."

"Oh, man, Nibbler's. That's where your *great*-grandmother takes you," I said.

We chuckled and used that time to think of other things to say to each other.

"So what did you like to do when you were a kid?" Miranda asked over her cheeseburger, "since organized fun wasn't your bag?"

"Uhmm, I guess I was usually happiest playing alone in my bedroom."

"Dang, what did you do in there?"

"When I was really little I was majorly into dinosaurs and I created this whole primeval world in a corner of my bedroom with a whole bunch of plastic animals. My favorite was the triceratops."

"That's everybody's favorite," she said, "Just like Saturn is everybody's favorite planet."

"Not mine," I said.

"Oh yeah, you're a Jupiter guy. Right? Even after Mr. St. Jerome's lecture last week? Big bad Jupiter and all that? Hurling death rocks at us?"

"Pretty much, yeah. Jupiter's still my dude, dude."

We looked at each other for a sweaty moment.

I wanted to say my favorite planet is Uranus but couldn't.

Miranda said, "I'm glad we're here," and she sort of reached out for my hands a little.

"Me too, I love Smokey Joe's," I said..

"Ugh," Miranda grunted.

"What?"

"Nothing," she covered her eyes.

"I loved moving the dinosaurs around the carpeted marshland and imagining the things the dinosaurs were thinking about one another."

Miranda lowered her head, heavily.

"Another thing I did alone was my war on the ants."

"Your what?" she said, looking up.

"I declared war on the ant population in my backyard."

"How?"

"I would kill the ants in my backyard one at a time with a hammer."

"Really?"

"Yeah."

"For how long?"

"I dunno. Several months?"

"No joke?"

"Yeah. Every day after school."

I probably shouldn't have, but I went on at great length about my war with the ants as Miranda sat and maybe listened and maybe didn't.

The Battle of Sonoma Beach I decided to name the war 'cause when you're 10 or 11 you think shit like that is funny.

We always used to say son-of-a-bitch with a foreign accent so it sounded like Sonoma Beach.

"I keel you you sonoma beach," we'd bark at each other.

We thought that was the funniest shit ever.

That and talking like Aunt Bee from the Andy Griffith Show.

I fought the war like a Japanese monster movie. I was the forbidding menace visiting death upon the pismire population relentlessly and with no mercy like Godzilla or Mothra or Rodan.

Yes, every day, after school, I would go into the kitchen and search through the gallimaufry drawer, which contained a dozen rubber bands, a box of wood screws, a can of 3-in-1 oil, a book of matches from *The Wich Stand*, a spool of kite string, a buffalo nickel and that 1909-S VBD penny that I planned to sell one day, Chanukah candles from 6 years ago, a couple of moist towelettes, loose thumbtacks, the good scissors, a free soap sample that came with the newspaper, a never-used wedge of sandpaper, a pin cushion, 2 screwdrivers (one phillips, one flathead), a pair of rusty pliers, and my weapon of choice, the hammer.

My afternoons were spent smashing ants with a hammer.

While the other kids were doing their homework or riding their bikes or skating or watching Popeye reruns or hanging out at the park or practicing the piano, I was in the backyard at war with the formicants.

I can't imagine what my parents must have thought of my oddball solitude.

What did my mother wonder when she'd look out the bathroom window at her son down on his hands and knees on the concrete smashing ants with a hammer?

Even at that age, I was asking philosophical questions.

I'd hover the hammer over my chosen ant, and I'd wonder if that ant knew it was about to die.

What would its last little ant-thought be?

I was fascinated by their utter vanishment under the hammer.

There weren't even remains left.

Just emptiness.

Or the times the hammer would strike just off the mark, the ant never knowing how close it came to obliteration.

I rarely missed the second time.

I enjoyed killing all those bugs.

I feel terrible about it now.

I'm sure the room reserved for me in Hell is full of thousands of ants with hammers waiting to greet me and say, "Remember us?"

I recall my sadness when the last ant was eliminated.

Now I would have nothing to do after school.

Several months later, a new ant colony invaded our yard, and so I buckled down to fight World War II.

As I had moved on, though, to other after-school pursuits (primarily watching reruns of *The Rifleman* on Channel 5), I wasn't much interested in a prolonged engagement.

And so, WWII would turn out to be nuclear.

A different kind of Japanese monster movie.

The Battle of North Fork I called it because that was the name of Lucas McCain's town in *The Rifleman*.

The whole thing lasted about 5 minutes, from the time I opened the garage, pulled out the can of lighter fluid, doused the anthill and the entire marching column as far down my driveway as I dare, set a match to it, watched and heard the formal whoosh that spread across the concrete and then onto the lawn, to when I managed to quench the last ember with water from the hose.

Afterward, I was still alive and walking amid the desolation but none of the ants were.

"Who *are* you?" Miranda asked.

"Then the fake radio show in my bedroom sort of took over everything and listening to music also," I said, not wanting to answer her question even though it was probably rhetorical.

"Yeah, I remember you told me about that. I remember thinking that you were perhaps the cutest human being in the world right then," Miranda smiled at me, "when you were telling me about the radio show. Macarthur Park."

We stared across the table at each other.

"I can't tell if you look bothered or bored," I said.

"Neither. Just trying to figure you out, Lancelot Link."

After lunch we walked across the street to Owl Rexall, a drug store like no other.

There were always these same two guys out front.

A black dude who wore a pork pie hat and only had a few teeth and sold the *Herald-Examiner.*

And an intense wiry white guy with an anchor tattoo on his arm who sold the *L.A. Times.*

My dad always said there was nothing you couldn't find at Owl Rexall.

"This is my favorite place to shop," Miranda said.

"I like to come here even when I'm not shopping and just look at stuff."

We cruised the corner candy section, almost like its own little store.

I bought Miranda a pack of wild cherry Now & Laters because she was constantly sucking on them at school so I knew she loved them.

"You can really get anything here," she said, pointing, "I love that counter over there, pipes and tobacco, watches, film, cameras, wallets & purses."

"Who needs wishes when you have Owl Rexall," I said.

"For sure," she said popping a Now & Later into her mouth.

Now & Laters made her lips extra red, and I think that aspect of the candy was as important to her as the flavor.

I imagined what her kiss would taste and feel like.

We both fell into a blushed silence as we walked down the condom and tampon aisle.

"I always get my back-to-school supplies here," Miranda said.

"It's the only place that has Pee-Chee folders these days, and I use those exclusively, so yeah, me too. My only school supplies are Pee-Chee folders, notebook paper, and a few Bic 4-color pens. That's all I need."

"Oh no, I like to have extensive supplies. It makes me feel like I'm gonna do better," she said, "like if I have the right erasers and colored pencils and a binder with properly marked dividers and lots of college rule notebook paper I'll be able to get all my work done and keep up with things."

"I don't like taking notes; I try to remember everything," I said.

"If it works," Miranda said.

"It doesn't always," I said.

We weren't really talking about anything.

I was thinking about this new song I was writing in E minor.

I was obsessed with E minor.

All my thoughts were in E minor lately.

We exited Owl Rexall and contemplated our next escapade.

"We should go check out the Pan Pacific Auditorium," Miranda said, "since we're into sifting through ruins today."

"Let's make it our theme," I said.

"Yes, do let's," Miranda said like a girl in a British movie, "our motif."

"Pan Pacific, cool, yeah," I said, "I haven't poked around there in a while."

Once glamorous and then tawdry, it had ended up an abandoned shell.

"My dad took me to the auto show there once I remember when it was still open," Miranda said.

"Yeah I went to that," I said, "Now it's just hobos and junkies prowling around."

"A cool movie would be about a whole secret culture that develops in the abandoned Pan Pacific Auditorium," she said.

"Totally," I said, "Like a community of schizophrenics who have learned how to coexist."

"That would be far out," she said.

"Like they have found a way to make it look like they are interacting," I said.

I know I feel that way sometimes about the whole world.

"Yeah, I get it," Miranda said, "that'd be bitchin'."

"Did you just say 'bitchin'?'"

"Yeah. I've decided to bring it back."

"Dang, dude, bitchin'. That's ancient," I said, "but I use it sometimes too. It just works."

"Zackly."

"Like sometimes things are still groovy."

"Oh, yeah. I still defenly use it unironically. Groovy is groovy. There's no other way to say it."

We sat down together on the bus stop bench and our hands kind of touched each other.

"So where did you go yesterday when you ditched the Shabbat thingy, you rat bastard?" Miranda asked me.

"I may be a bastard, but I'm a bitchin' bastard."

"Of course. But where'd you go though?"

"I dunno, I just walked around. I sat at a bus stop for a couple of hours, on 6th Street. That's where I ate my lunch. I talked to a street corner evangelist. I also walked all the way home. I mean, I actually stood at the corner of Beverly and Citrus, looking at my house from across the street. It was quite awesome."

"Dang, dude, that is flagrant," Miranda said.

"It was godlike."

She was looking at me all goofy-eyed.

"I mean the experience not myself," I said, "of course."

And she kept on looking at me.

Luckily the bus came.

We rode the RTD down Beverly to Gardner Street.

When we got off the bus, I saw Naomi Richter walking toward us with a couple of friends.

I knew that was bound to happen one day, but the timing was especially bad.

I had but nanoseconds to determine whether or not to allow eye contact.

I was pretty sure she'd probably already seen me.

As she neared I did look over at her, and she was in fact looking my way too.

She waved shyly as she passed with a half-held-up hand but I could derive nothing from her face.

"You know her?" Miranda asked immediately.

Girls, dude. They notice everything.

"No, I, well, yeah, ok, she was my tutor for while."

"Oh my god, you were going to lie to me just now," she said, "and you changed your mind."

"I told you about her before," I said, annoyed like every guy when girls bust you on your bullshit.

"The girl from the library."

"Yeah, that one, math tutor," I said, omitting the frenching and finger-fucking incident and wanting to change the subject.

I knew Lorelei Lux had told Miranda she'd seen me with an Orthodox girl at the library because Miranda had interrogated me about it once before already.

When we got to the Pan Pacific we discovered it had been effectively fenced off.

"You wanna try to find a way in?" I asked.

"Nah, I don't think it'd be worth it really," she said, "I'd rather just walk back over to my house from here and hang out in my room. That's what I want to do."

She took my hand and dragged me onward.

"Sounds good," I said in this painfully dorky way I don't even know how to describe other than I was embarrassed as soon as I said it.

Our walk took us past the box office of the Pan Pacific Theatre, where Claire Farnaway worked.

Logan's Run was playing.

"Isn't that the one where you have to die when you're 30?" Miranda asked.

"Yeah, very cool movie," I said, "Manny and I saw it in Westwood back in like January or February."

"And 30 is almost dead," she said referencing our joke.

"We're halfway to almost dead, yes," I filled in the rest.

Miranda and I visited Claire briefly in her little ticket kiosk.

"So, are you guys on a date?" Claire asked, catching eyes with both me and Miranda separately.

I shrugged, but Miranda volunteered, "Yes!"

"Ooh I'm telling everyone," Claire said.

Miranda poked her cheek and crossed her eyes and I figured it was some kind of secret girl code thing.

"Go away for a second," Miranda said, pushing me away and putting her face against the box office glass and speaking quietly to Claire.

We all pretended to laugh as we waved goodbye even though all three of us were sad for different reasons.

"Wanna take the bus back to Fairfax and transfer?" I asked, leaning toward laziness.

"No, let's just walk to my house from here . . . it'll make our date last longer," Miranda said.

We walked down Gardner, though I steered her away from walking through the park 'cause of the Naomi incident there.

We crossed 3rd Street and braved a foray through Park La Brea.

"Hancock Park playground," Miranda said.

"I remember," I said, "That was a really great day."

"Best day ever, next to this one," Miranda said and knocked into me with her shoulder.

Our pinkies latched briefly but then fell apart. Miranda touched the side of my arm but didn't hold on.

We got through Park La Brea without getting lost and ended up at the Jack-In-The-Box on Fairfax near her house.

As we walked into Miranda's bedroom, Miranda's mom heard us and came down the hall.

"Lance, your mom called here looking for you," she said from the doorway.

"Yeah, I said I'd be back about an hour ago. Oops."

"I'll call your mom and let her know you're here," she said as Miranda closed the bedroom door on her.

"Thank you," I said, raising my voice a little.

Miranda and I weren't ready to part ways yet.

It was dusk, beautiful blueness in her room.

We left the lights off.

"Let's listen to the Adam West record," I said.

Miranda pulled Silk Degrees out of its jacket and put it on the new stereo she'd gotten for her birthday.

She'd told me about it but it was my first time seeing it.

It was kind of too dark to tell what it looked like.

"I want to listen to this first," she said, lowering the needle.

442

The opening piano strains of "We're All Alone" made it feel like a movie scene.

"This is my favorite song right now," Miranda swooned, "Oh man, it's so bloody romantic . . ."

She tried to pull me up from the bed, I presumed to dance with her while she sang.

Close the window, calm the light

And it will be alright

No need to bother now

Let it out, let it all begin

Learn how to pretend

"Come on," she said, "Stand up."

I resisted, I don't know why.

She sang.

Once a story's told

It can't help but grow old

Roses do, lovers too

So cast your seasons to the wind

And hold me dear, oh hold me dear

"Dance with me," she said, still tugging, "Come on," she tugged again.

I declined and stayed seated.

She sat down on the bed next to me and sang along.

Close the window, calm the light
And it will be alright
No need to bother now
Let it out, let it all begin
All's forgotten now
We're all alone, all alone

She lay on her back and I reclined on my side facing her.

Our eyes found each other in the deepening blue darkness.

"Hi, Lance," she said and smiled.

Our fingers were just intertwining and kissing was imminent when Miranda's mom knocked on her door.

"Mandy?"

"What?" Miranda ugh'd.

"Lance's dad is on his way right now to pick him up."

"Now?" Miranda complained.

"Yes, now," her mom said, "They want him home."

"Okay, we'll be out in a sec," Miranda said fairly despondent.

I stood up.

I had the biggest hard-on.

"Dang, dude," Miranda sighed.

She wasn't looking at my crotch although it would've been cool if she was.

Saying "dang, dude" is always somewhat existential, but occasionally it can be utterly existential, like the way Miranda meant it right then.

We walked downstairs and waited for my dad out on the front porch.

I don't think we said anything other than "nice night" for the few minutes it took my dad to get there.

She was borderline upset.

I remember she said "See ya" instead of "Bye, Lance" when I got into my dad's car.

That was always a bad sign.

At home later I masturbated to a festival of thoughts about Miranda, in particular fucking her on her bed in the beautiful indigo light of dusk and wondering if she could feel it.

4

The day after the Kiddyland date, just like every aftermath between us, was awkward and uncomfortable.

When I read the Daily Bulletin in Period 4 and got to General Interest, the usual "I don't have any" from Miranda didn't arrive.

I looked over and saw she was talking to Claire Farnaway.

I didn't know if I was her boyfriend or not and if yes what I was supposed to do.

When I went back to my seat Miranda looked at me.

"Why didn't you call me last night?"

"I didn't know I was supposed to," I said.

"It's not a *supposed to* thing," she looked away, "but whatever."

"Here's a poem by Percy Shelley," Mr. B. rescued me, entering the room with a stack of fresh dittos.

We would all cop that fresh mimeograph buzz momentarily.

He distributed the dittos and we each subtly inhaled the ditto fluid fumes.

"Ozymandias," he said and read the rest out loud.

I met a traveller from an antique land

Who said: "Two vast and trunkless legs of stone

Stand in the desert. Near them on the sand,

Half sunk, a shattered visage lies, whose frown

And wrinkled lip and sneer of cold command

Tell that its sculptor well those passions read

Which yet survive, stamped on these lifeless things,

The hand that mocked them and the heart that fed.

And on the pedestal these words appear:

`My name is Ozymandias, King of Kings:

Look on my works, ye mighty, and despair!'

Nothing beside remains. Round the decay

Of that colossal wreck, boundless and bare,

The lone and level sands stretch far away"

"Now I get the poster," Gina Dichlich said, pointing to the wall behind me where hung a picture of a stone head and two stone legs scattered and shattered in the desert and the words as if etched "Look on my works, ye mighty, and despair!"

"Correct," Mr. B. said, "What's the poem about?"

"A broken statue," Gina Dichlich offered.

"There is one in the poem for sure. But what's the poem *about?*"

"How nothing lasts," I said, "and our accomplishments are meaningless."

"Eventually," said Mr. B., "yes."

"Then why bother to do anything?" Lorelei Lux asked, "I mean if it all just comes to nothing?"

"Well, there is this moment we're living in, for one thing," he said, "and just like we're sitting here reading a 150 year old poem and liking it—I hope"— he looked around the room—"so too can we create and do things that future humans will be able to love and relate to and be comforted by in the midst of all this insignificance."

"Like a time capsule," Miranda said.

"Good," Mr. B. pointed, "And, look, the plaque survives in the poem, the warning, the unintentional wisdom. Ironic isn't it that what lasts is only the warning that nothing lasts," Beauregard said.

"So wisdom is eternal?" asked Lorelei.

"Precisely," Mr. Beauregard said.

"What if no one is left to receive it?" I asked and looked across the room at Lorelei who slit her eyes at me.

Mr. Beauregard raised his finger, paused, lowered his finger and said, "Good question."

In the ensuing silence most of us looked back down at our copies of the poem.

"Here's another poem that addresses what I was just talking about," Mr. Beauregard reached for a manilla folder on his desk.

He got up and distributed the new poem while we all passed "Ozymandias" up to the front.

"This is one by A.E. Housman," he said, "from one of my favorite books of poetry, *A Shropshire Lad.*"

He read:

I hoed and trenched and weeded,
And took the flowers to fair:
I brought them home unheeded;
The hue was not the wear.

So up and down I sow them
For lads like me to find,
When I shall lie below them,
A dead man out of mind.

Some seed the birds devour,
And some the season mars,
But here and there will flower
The solitary stars.

And fields will yearly bear them
As light-leaved spring comes on,
And luckless lads will wear them
When I am dead and gone.

"Aren't you glad we have this poem?" he asked, "that Housman transcended his own insignificance and wrote about that very thing and made it seem hopeful."

"I think it's sad," said Gina.

There were grunts and nods.

"Is it?" Mr. B. asked, "Nobody wanted what he was selling but here we are reaping his crop today, just as he predicted. You see? Impermanence shouldn't make you sad; it should inspire you."

There's always hope, remember that, monsieur

"Yeah," I said and Mr. B. understood that I understood.

Suddenly he changed the subject.

"Don't know if you saw in the news, but just a couple of days ago 2 planes almost collided near LAX, a small plane crossing into the flight path of a jet on approach," Mr. Beauregard said, "Disaster averted, but everyone on those planes and lots of people on the ground would have had their lives ended in an instant. It didn't happen but it could have. No one in the path of that near miss was planning on dying that day. Death doesn't wait for our permission."

"Jeez-o-man, you are just a bundle of happy thoughts today, Mr. B.," Claire Farnaway said.

"I make the daily mistake of reading the newspaper," he answered.

The discussion was interrupted by Jack Hunter delivering the new issue of the *Colonial Gazette*.

Then as he was leaving, Jack said to me, "Turned out great, man, take a look. Back page."

I turned, slowly, to the back page, where the sports stories were, trying not to look too anxious, and, indeed, there was a picture of me doing the high jump.

The shot was of my ascent.

The caption said, first, "Fax Sophomore Lance Atlas in a high jump attempt," and then, for no discernible reason, the caption continued, "Atlas did not successfully complete this jump."

I could hear the giggles around me.

"Dang, dude, that sucks," said Claude Moss.

"They didn't have to write that," Miranda said.

I looked over at her.

She tilted her head but I don't know why she did it or what she meant by it so I just kept looking at her.

"Dipshits," said Buzzy Lagniappe.

Manny Shepherd and Claire Farnaway also criticized the Gazette editorial staff.

Claire added, "Jack Hunter is such a dweeb."

Most of my classmates were laughing, though.

Miranda was looking at the picture.

"I like it," she said to me and put the Gazette in her backpack.

A couple of weeks later, although I didn't really want to, I attended opening night of the Spring musical, *Anyone Can Whistle*, a really old Sondheim show whose score I didn't know. Actually I didn't even know of its existence until Dolly and Lorelei and Justine started talking about it.

I loved Stephen Sondheim. The lyrics to *West Side Story* and *Gypsy*, and also everything about *Company* and *Follies* and my favorite at the time *A Little Night Music*, were deeply inspirational to me.

Dolly wasn't in the show, but she was one of the assistant directors, along with Deirdre Lux, and she wanted me to be there.

"I cannot keep track of what is going on with you and Mandy," Dolly said when she called one night.

"Well-um, it's always kind of the same thing, great conversations that go nowhere."

"You guys are silly," she said. "You should just kiss and get it over with."

"Nah, it's me. I'm inept. Miranda just keeps putting up with it."

"I miss you," Dolly said.

"Well you've been busy with play production and Aaron and stuff. How's that going by the way, the Aaron thing?"

"It's going great," she said, "That doesn't mean I don't miss you though. I saw you in the *Colonial Gazette*," she said.

"I'm totally embarrassed about that picture."

"The picture's great. The caption sucks," Dolly said. "You know Miranda has that picture up on her wall."

"I didn't know that, no. I hope she cut the caption off," I said.

So, Miranda Savitch went to bed each night with a vision of my failure.

As I feared, Miranda was in attendance at *Anyone Can Whistle* on opening night.

I hadn't called her or anything since our Kiddyland date and over the past couple of weeks we had gone back to just talking at random moments in Bio or English or French, mostly about stupid stuff, nothing about us.

I'm not sure but I think Dolly begging me to come to opening night was supposed to be my cue to ask Miranda to go with me. Or something. Or I don't know.

Anyway, I did go, but not with Miranda.

When we all stood around talking in the Rotunda before the show Miranda was noticeably distant. She didn't even say hi to me when I first walked up to the group.

When the house doors were opened, I didn't know if I was supposed to sit next to her or not.

As soon as I'd made up my mind to go sit next to Miranda, though, Freddy Snow slipped into the seat I was aiming for.

Once again I'd missed my shot.

Miranda seemed happy enough sitting with Freddy.

Lorelei Lux, Sharon Rose, and Justine Balthazar were all in Play Production but didn't get cast in the musical and so they were ushers that night.

I wasn't paying much attention to the show because I kept thinking about how I'd fucked up again with Miranda and I couldn't stop myself from looking over at her and Freddy.

But then some Sondheim lyrics caught my ear.

Anyone can whistle,

That's what they say-

Easy.

Anyone can whistle

Any old day-

Easy.

It's all so simple:

Relax, let go, let fly.

So someone tell me why

Can't I?

I have never been able to whistle and consider it a great failing. But deeper down it was like the epitome of all my other failures.

It was a metaphor made for me.

What's hard is simple.

What's natural comes hard

A very short and simple song, it poked me in the solar plexus and I could feel my heart twinge, almost as if I were heading into one of my fibrillation episodes, but instead I just started tearing up.

I was glad nobody was sitting next to me to see my little catharsis.

Mr. Beauregard once said, "Catharsis can sometimes be the result of seeing your own weaknesses, or sins if you want to call them that, depicted in art, and recognizing them as such to the point of purging."

"Is an orgasm catharsis?" the Samoan kid asked in class that day.

Undaunted, Mr. Beauregard said, "I suppose it could be under the right circumstances."

"Just playin'," the Samoan kid said.

What's hard is simple, what's natural comes hard

Yup. That's my saga right there.

After the show we all waited around the stage door to say hi to the actors.

"Hey, whiteboy," Diana Hitchcock said as she walked past me, running her hand across my back and shoulder blades and passing on.

Diana was a dynamo in the play. Amazing singing voice that filled the room.

Dolly came over to where I was standing with Whit and Buzzy and Miranda. For some reason Freddy had split right after the show.

"Hey, a bunch of us are going to the Observatory for Laserium next Friday night," Dolly said. "I know you don't do that sort of thing anymore, but maybe you'll join us?"

"Dude, totally. Come with. We want Atlas back," Whitman Rust said, "Come on, school's almost out. You don't have any homework to do."

"Make your boyfriend come, Mandy," said Dolly.

"That's the basic idea, yeah," joked Whit.

"Good advice," added Buzzy Lagniappe.

"That's not what Dolly meant, guys, jeez," Miranda blushed, "and he's not my boyfriend."

"Make him come anyway," Whit said, and he and Buzzy gave each other five.

I had my answer.

"I'll come," I said.

"Really?" Miranda said, dropping her mad mask.

Claude Moss had just gotten his driver's license and would be driving one group up to the Observatory in his mom's station wagon.

After I agreed to go along on the Observatory/Laserium outing, Miranda got back to answering "I don't have any" to my "General Interest" proclamation in English.

"Word number one is conundrum," Mr. Beauregard said as he started to go over the last vocabulary list of the year with us.

"A difficult problem or question," he said.

"Like a puzzle?" Gina Dichlich asked.

"Yes, though I tend to use it when describing puzzles for which there are no solutions, or at best obscure or strained solutions," Beauregard explained.

"Like?" Gina asked.

"Which came first, the chicken or the egg, that sort of thing. Or the question that underlies all philosophy: Why is there something instead of nothing? Or the meaning of the sentence 'All generealizations are false.'"

"My dad loves the conundrum 'Can God create an object so heavy even he can't lift it?'" I said, "He always asks it at parties when there was somebody new to try it on."

"That's an old one, yes, but good," Mr. B. said. "What do you think? Anyone have a solution to that one? Can God create an object so heavy even he can't lift it?"

"The answer has to be yes because God can do anything," Crystal Nabors said, "He's omnipotent."

"Then he should be able to lift the object," Buzzy Lagniappe said.

"Of course," Crystal said.

"So then he can't do everything. He can't make an object so heavy even he can't lift it," Buzzy said.

Crystal was quietly thinking.

"This conundrum is God's kryptonite," Jim Lord said from the back wall.

Crystal was miffed at all the blasphemy flying around.

Miranda raised her hand.

"Do you have a solution?" he pointed to her.

"No, I was just wondering why you use He to mean God?"

"A convenience of grammar," said Mr. B.

Manny raised his hand.

"God's name in Hebrew is both masculine and feminine," he said, "and past, present, and future too."

"Interesting," Mr. Beauregard said as Lorelei Lux took notes. I needed to talk to Lorelei about what she saw me doing with Naomi Richter and what she had told Miranda about it because I was seriously fearing the worst.

"Miranda's question is good though. Do you have a guess as to why we default to the masculine pronoun when talking about God?"

"Because men wrote the Bible?" Miranda said.

"Precisely. Men controlled every lever, not just language."

"They still do," Miranda said.

"You are correct for the most part I suppose," he said.

"But we can use She if we want, right?" she asked.

"Feel free," he said, "Though remember it's just as inaccurate."

Crystal Nabors was uncomfortable with the idea that human beings had anything to do with the writing of the Bible other than taking dictation, in English, from the Almighty, but she saw herself outnumbered by secular Jews, lapsed Catholics, and a hodgepodge of other heathens, so she stayed quiet.

But when Beauregard continued to pursue things, she spoke up.

"In philosophy, there is a conundrum that is sometimes referred to as 'the problem of evil,'" he said.

"Evil is a big problem," Crystal said, "What is puzzling about that?"

"No the problem of evil is this: If God is all good, how could he even conceive of evil?"

"God can do anything," Crystal Nabors said.

"Except make an object so heavy even he can't lift it," Buzzy said.

"Which God are we talking about?" asked Mr. Beauregard.

"Jesus," she said.

"Jesus can do anything?" Mr. Beauregard asked.

"Yes," she affirmed, "with Jesus the world was made fresh. That's what my pastor always says."

Beauregard smiled. "The world was made fresh . . . I like that," he said.

You could tell he was looking for an exit.

"Why don't we all ponder these questions," he said, "Who or what controls the universe? Is there any control?"

"It's the disorderly functioning of thousands of tiny enzymes!" Claire Farnaway joked..

"When I went to Catholic school, I used to think people were saying inaccurate conception," Arabella Mayflower said.

"You mean like Jesus was born in the wrong womb," Mr. B. said.

"Yeah I guess so," Arabella said, "or something like that."

"That happened to me," Buzzy said, "I was supposed to be a dolphin. Something got screwed up."

The class laughed but I knew Buzzy actually believed that to be true.

"The thing about Judaism, Christianity, and Islam is they all claim a common forefather, Abraham. I think of their neverending jostling as a kind of sibling rivalry, each one trying to claim 'Dad likes me better,'" said

Mr. B.

"A kid in my Sunday School class asked Pastor Steve if Adam had a bellybutton," Crystal Nabors said, "That's like a conundrum, right?"

"Sort of," Mr. Beauregard said, "although that's a fairly simple one to solve," he tried to be gentle. "But my favorite conundrum is this sentence," and he walked over to the chalkboard, writing, "I always lie," and then turned to face us. "I invite you to stay up very late tonight working *that* one out," he smiled.

I always lie.

"*You're a conundrum,*" Miranda wrote on my vocab list.

5

That Friday in the early evening I joined the old crew on an outing to the Griffith Park Observatory to see Laserium.

We all piled into Claude's mom's green, wood-paneled Ford station wagon.

Dolly and Claire were in the front with Claude, sharing the bench seat.

Dolly's boyfriend Aaron was curiously absent.

Miranda and Lorelei and I sat across the back seat.

Whit and Buzzy had the way-back.

"Let's stop at the merry-go-round first," Miranda said.

"It closes early," Whit said, "Buzzy and I tried that last time."

"Bummer," said Miranda.

She leaned toward me.

"I wanted to ride that with you," she said.

"We'll have to make that happen someday," I said.

"Right," Miranda halfway snorted.

"I don't know why I'm here," said Lorelei Lux with her eyes closed.

"Don't even start with the existential metaphysical bullshit now, Lori," Dolly admonished from the front seat, "We came here to have a good time."

Claude was driving way too fast for the curves, nearly missing, first, a car coming downhill and, then, a steep cliff over which he almost sent the car.

I thought about my parents being informed of my death.

I continued to think about it as we pulled into a parking lot filled with cars being driven by stoned teenagers.

The atrium of the Observatory had a huge pendulum that swung back and forth.

It reminded me of when we read "The Pit & The Pendulum" in English class.

"The Pit and the Pendulum. Cock-in-pussy, dude," Buddy Feigenbaum mumbled behind me that day to the giggles of all except Miranda who said, "Gross."

Mr. B. read the entire story out loud, stopping every few sentences for analysis.

"At the end of that first paragraph," Beauregard said, "that last sentence, is that reminiscent of something we've read before?"

Then silence, and stillness, and night were the universe

"Lord Byron," I said, "'Darkness.'"

"Yes, *Darkness had no need of aid from them——She was the Universe.* Good," Mr. B. said.

"Ultima Thule would be a great name for a heavy metal band," Manny

Shepherd said, pointing out that image from the story.

I remember Beauregard's summation after reading the final sentence was, "The godfather of all near misses, right? That's called a 'deus ex machina' ending, god from the machine, referring to ancient dramas when Jupiter would come down from the rafters of the stage and rescue the hero or make everything right. Usually such endings are trite or lazy, but, I don't know, in this story it works. What do you think?"

"I don't know whether technically it's a good or bad ending, but it was good for suspense, I was anxious to see if he'd get rescued," Miranda said.

"Well, it *is* a 1st person narration told in the past tense, so you sort of know he survived," Beauregard said.

"True," Miranda said and blushed a little.

In the echoing atrium of the Observatory Miranda and I stood next to each other at the giant pendulum and waited for the doors for Laserium to open.

I think Miranda might've said something to me, but I wasn't listening 'cause I was thinking of Beauregard's class, so when she asked, "What do you think?" I answered "I'm cool with it" and hoped I hadn't just agreed to something I'd regret.

Laserium had become the event to experience stoned.

"It is so fucking trippy, dude," Buzzy said. He and Whit had gone a couple of weeks before and were way wasted.

We had passed around a joint before we got out of the car so we arrived inside appropriately blitzed.

Shadoe Stevens, one of the Boss Jocks from the 93 KHJ Boss Radio days, did the introduction to Laserium.

The only classical music I recognized was "The Blue Danube" which I knew from the *2001: A Space Odyssey* soundtrack. I had that soundtrack and listened to it obsessively when I was younger.

My grandfather had given me a Panasonic cassette player/recorder for my 9th birthday, and my parents took me to Wallich's Music City to pick out a couple of tapes to listen to on my new machine.

I got the *2001: A Space Odyssey* soundtrack, and my dad suggested a Martin Denny tape which I agreed to.

All that year I fell asleep nightly listening to either *2001* or Martin Denny or 93 KHJ or Vin Scully calling the Dodger game..

Or sometimes I would lie awake listening, unable to sleep, freaking myself out thinking about infinity.

2001 provoked my insignificance. Especially the 2 Ligeti pieces. "Requiem" and "Lux Aeterna."

When "Set the Controls for the Heart of the Sun" started blasting from the Laserium speakers, the surfer dudes in front of us started hooting "Floyd!" which they repeated when "Echoes" started a bit later in the program.

There was also a really weird version of "Gimme Shelter" which I dug a lot but other people were saying what the fuck is this shit. It was a jazz rendition.

The laser lights were trippy as anything, and whoever designed that shit fucking knew the cannabinoid condition well.

It was masterfully synched to that particular alteration in consciousness.

The program ended with a third Emerson, Lake & Palmer song.

Buzzy told me what it was but now I can't remember.

"ELP, dude, fuck yeah!" some proggy stoner yelped from the back row during the last song of the show.

A whole bunch of other kids who looked like they were from the Valley started hooting "Yaow!" and making chimpanzee sounds.

Soon everyone joined the caterwaul which devolved into hysterical stoned laughter.

The Observatory had a smash-hit evening on its hands.

There was money to be made providing the soundtrack and visuals calibrated to entertain a room full of kids on drugs.

Afterward everyone sort of wandered apart, stoned and separate, around the Observatory grounds.

Somehow we'd all find our way back to Claude's mom's car eventually.

Miranda and I ended up walking together behind the Observatory where you get the single best view of Los Angeles possible.

This was a sort of overcast June night, however, so the panorama was hazy but goddamn romantic as hell.

The yellow glow of the city's streetlights was cinematic.

Miranda trotted ahead of me, backwards, taunting, "Nyeah nyeah nyeah-nyeah nyeah," like a sassy six-year-old.

I picked up my pace, and she turned forward and shrieked running away.

I caught her easily from behind and put my arms around her but didn't know what to do next.

I almost reached up to cup her breasts but decided not to in case she didn't want me to do that.

"Lance has a girlfriend," she chanted the same universal melody as "Nyeah nyeah nyeah-nyeah nyeah."

"I do?" I said.

"I'm just playing," she answered and turned to face me.

"There are allegedly stars up there," I said, pointing to the misty gray sky, and we both looked out upon the sprawling city and the cloudy horizon.

"Like a diamond in the sky," Miranda sang way off key.

"I loved your movie from last year," I said, "It was amazing. I think of it whenever I hear that song. Like right now."

"Thank you," she said and smiled, as usual, with downcast eyes.

"You ever notice that's the same melody as 'Baa Baa Black Sheep' and the 'ABC Song?'"

"What is?" she said looking at me with a certain degree of fervor.

"Twinkle Twinkle Little Star," I clarified.

Miranda closed her eyes and sang to herself.

"Oh yeah, huh?" she said and looked at me some more and also touched my forehead for some reason, "But who the fuck cares really?"

461

That hurt my feelings a little bit but it was cool whatever.

Maybe she didn't, but I *did* care about stuff like that, like songs having the same melody.

"You know, this is where the last scene of *Rebel Without A Cause* was filmed, the scene where Sal Mineo gets shot."

"Yes, Lance, I know, we talked about that when we saw the movie. You do remember we saw the movie together, right?"

"Oh yeah yeah, I was just saying," I stalled, and then continued, "It's weird he also got shot in real life."

"Yeah, we've talked about that before too, not even that long ago," Miranda was tugging subtly at my sweatjacket.

"When I was younger my relatives used to say I looked like Sal Mineo," I said.

"You're much cuter than Sal Mineo," she said, "and not as gay."

"Haha," I said, not pouncing on her.

"Although the way you're acting now, I don't know," she let go of my jacket and turned to face the view.

An oppressive silence hung between us for a hellishly long time until she turned to face me again and closed her hands around my neck in a fake strangle.

"What is wrong with you?" she released her grip and leaned against the wall, "Grrrr. You make me cray-zee."

A part of her was a little bit angry, I could tell.

"I don't know what else to do," she said.

"I guess I don't really know what to do either," I said because there was nowhere to hide. "I guess it's partly fear."

"Fear of what?" Miranda asked, "Please don't say rejection."

"No, I—"

"—because, dang, dude, come on. You know?"

"No, I—yum, I guess I'm, uh-afraid of what happens once this starts."

"Why don't you just kiss me and let's see what happens?" she said, caressing my face, "Maybe it'll be way cool, right?"

All desire left me.

I went all mannequin contraption on her.

Miranda waited a few moments for me to do *something*, and when I stayed frozen she walked away.

"Bye, Lance," she said, waving backwards at me Italian style.

"Ciao bella," I said too softly for her to hear.

I followed her quietly through the dark to Claude's mom's car.

On the way back home Miranda sat up front with Claude and Dolly, and I sat between Lorelei and Claire in the back seat. Buzzy and Whit had the way-back again.

The girls were laughing about something.

"What?" I asked.

"You are surrounded," Claire said and put her head on my shoulder while Lorelei patted the top of my head.

I never did understand the joke.

The last few days of school were, as Manny Shepherd put it, "majorly lazy."

Textbooks were turned in, grades were being tabulated and submitted.

Most teachers just gave us free time to sign yearbooks.

Miranda and I hadn't exchanged many words since the Observatory.

Even in English class the silence hung with tepid emptiness, neither friendly nor unfriendly.

But on the very last day of school Miranda handed me her yearbook to sign in Bio and so I gave her mine in return and we both retreated to our seats in order to commemorate another year of our intensely near misses.

Honestly, I don't remember what I wrote in hers other than I know it avoided reference to our romantic misfires and how much I liked hanging out with her and I made a bunch of inside references to Kiddyland and the Pan Pacific and that I hoped we'd get to listen to the Adam West "Miranda" record together eventually.

Hers was much more direct.

Lance,

This whole school year when you've been reading the Daily Bulletin and saying 'General Interest' and I've been saying 'I don't have any,' I've been lying. I have a general interest, and it's you. Not only is your picture on the wall of my bedroom, but your picture is on the wall of my heart. I'm still hoping and dreaming of you . . . (and me?).

Love forever and whenever,

Miranda

6

I spent the early part of the summer mostly writing melodies and occasionally lyrics during the day and reading at night.

I finally got around to Beauregard's suggestion of *A Canticle For Leibowitz.*

Once summer school started, the early part of the day was taken up with that.

I had Driver's Ed and this stupid required class called Guidance, which was mostly just taking aptitude tests and reading college catalogues.

All I cared about was that I was done at noon and could get home to my reading and music.

When I saw on the news about the earthquake in China I thought of Miranda right away and without really battling my cowardice all that much I called her to talk about it.

"Hey, it's Lance," I said when she answered.

"Oh, heya hey," she said and paused, "Lance Atlas, he who hates the telephone, is calling me on the telephone? Am I dreaming this?"

"May be," I said.

Even though Miranda was also going to summer school, getting her fine arts credits out of the way by taking ceramics, we didn't hang out on campus at all.

"What might I do for you, m'lord?" she asked, "Wherefore callst thou me, secret chimp?"

"I saw on the news about the Chinese earthquake," I said.

"Ah."

"And it made me think of you."

"How flattering."

"Nyeah-I mean I remember you were involved in the Guatemalan relief effort and dang dude I dunno what the fuck."

"It's bad there. More than half a million dead."

"Shit yeah I saw that. Cray-zee."

"I wish you didn't need an excuse to call me," Miranda said.

"Are you going to be involved in the relief effort for this one?" I diverted.

"Probly," she said, letting me divert, "I dunno."

Her breath was getting fussy.

"Whatever," she said.

I was grasping for a roadblock.

"And all the stories of the people who narrowly escaped," I tried.

"Always, like after every plane crash there's interviews with all those people who missed their flight who are all freaked out about their lucky brush with death."

Another slow-motion silence transpired.

"I'd love to see you," Miranda said, "We should hang out."

Regrettably, I uttered, "Wanna come over tomorrow?"

"Really?" she said.

"Uh, yeah. After summer school maybe," I said 'cause it was too late to do otherwise.

"I'd love to yes," she accepted.

Dang, dude. Now what?

"Walk home with me?" I said.

"Mmm-yeah," she said.

For a second I pretended she was trying to be lascivious.

That night I dreamed the Samoan kid's name was Rumpelstiltskin.

I was looking in the yearbook and there was his picture among all the other sophomores and his name was listed as Rumpelstiltskin.

In the dream I thought, "Dang, dude, Rumpelstiltskin isn't a Samoan name, must be a narc."

I woke up laughing.

I went and looked in the yearbook just in case the dream was real but no the Samoan kid was not in the yearbook.

Miranda and I met in front out on Melrose after summer school ended.

She was wearing a calico blouse and Levi's cut-offs and flip-flops.

I usually walked home down side streets and took Oakwood most of the way, but Miranda wanted to walk along Melrose.

A few blocks in I learned we took Melrose because she wanted to shop for pants at Aardvark on the way.

Chicks.

Dang, dude.

They always always have to build side-errands into whatever the main activity is. Like doing just one thing is not enough or something.

She did find a very cool pair of jeans with the moon and stars embroidered up and down both legs.

"Shopping is fun but then you have to carry the bag around the rest of the day," she said.

"Want an apple fritter?" I asked her as we passed Winchell's.

"Nah I'm fine," she said, switching the bag to her left hand and hooking arms with me.

"M'lady," I said, patting her hand.

When we got to my house no one was home.

I took her into my bedroom thinking damn we are going to make out for sure but when we got in there I realized it was a bad idea.

The room was suffused with the aroma of "fartosis," the admixture not just of fart remnants but also dirty gym socks and unwashed jeans.

I suggested an immediate alternative.

"Hey we should walk over to 3rd Street and climb up the air raid siren near Mansfield. There's an observation basket up there. Really cool view of rooftops. Like in Mary Poppins."

Miranda agreed to it but I couldn't tell how into it she was.

When we got to the siren pole I cupped my hands for her to step into.

"Here, I'll hoist you up. Grab hold of that first rung and then just keep climbing until you get to the platform near the top."

"Then how will you get up?"

"I can shinny up to the first rung," I grunted as I lifted her.

"Shinny?"

"Yeah."

"That's a funny word. Shinny. Sounds dirty."

We stood close together in the basket just below the yellow shell of the siren looking out at the rooftops.

I put my hand on her back which is quite different from putting one's arm around somebody.

"I can see Park La Brea!" she enthused.

"Remember the air raid drills?"

"Last Friday of the month at 10am. Or something like that? All the way through elementary school at least."

Miranda and I had attended different elementary schools, but when the air raid sirens went off on those Fridays at 10am, like all students in the L.A. Unified School District, we got under our tables and crouched, wondering how that was going to protect us from Soviet radiation.

The sound of the sirens was spooky like a herd of dying robots.

The whole city could hear it, the surreal sadness of it.

"I wonder how many times the president's finger has been on the red button," Miranda said, "how close we've really come to all out nuclear war."

We were children in the age of instant annihilation at any time.

"It's weird but ever since Ford became president I don't feel as afraid of a nuclear war. It's, like, who'd attack good ol' Jer," Miranda said.

"Yeah, President Ford is like a holding pattern."

"I feel like the whole country's in suspended animation right now."

"Pupal diapause," I said.

"I always thought of the horizon when the sirens went off for some reason," she said.

She was at her most beautiful right at that moment, right when she said that.

"That's weird and cool at the same time," I said because I couldn't tell her she was beautiful.

"You're weird and cool at the same time," she poked me and then put her hand on my shoulder as we looked west, sharing another afternoon sky all bronze and hazy and starting to sparkle with the colors of sunset.

It would have been a memorable moment to kiss.

We didn't.

Back at my house, still wanting to avoid the fartosis in my bedroom, I led her up the driveway into the backyard where she loved my mom's geraniums and the Japanese garden decor.

We wandered among the array of pots and I told her the names of the various geraniums, at least the ones I knew.

"Show me the garage roof," Miranda said once we'd made a circuit of the yard.

"For sure," I said, "let me grab some puffage," and I ran into my room to retrieve a little baggy of grass and my wooden totem pole pipe. For some reason I'd been carrying the lighter around in my pocket all day.

We climbed up via the brick barbecue onto the back wall of the yard, from there hoisting ourselves onto the roof of the garage.

Sitting near the edge of the roof we looked west again, as we often did together, inhaled some kind bud and faced each other cross-legged.

After a few minutes of eye lock, Miranda lay back and reached out her hand to me.

I lay down next to her, turned toward her, wanting to kiss her unashamedly, I mean like french her brains out.

There was rustling in the bushes next door.

"I thought I smelled your foxy ass up here," said Penelope Lagniappe, my frequent companion on the roof, ". . . Oh, shit, sorry," Penelope surveyed the scene, and then disappeared quickly into her backyard.

I looked at Miranda as if to dismiss that little intrusion as nothing.

"I'm pretty sure I told you about her before—"

"—This is your usual rendezvous spot, I take it," Miranda said, cutting me off, unamused, "you and your foxy ass. Wasn't that Buzzy's older sister?"

She let go of my hand.

Followed by the worst silence of my life.

"I don't think I can do this anymore," Miranda said, sadly, sitting up.

"Do what?" I asked.

She shook her head, looking like she was suppressing the most painful laugh.

"This. This pretend thing we do. I need a real boyfriend."

She started to climb down from the roof.

"Do you need help?" I asked.

"No no, I've got it. I'm going to call my mom to pick me up. Can I use your phone?"

"Yeah of course. It's at the end of the hallway inside."

I sat on the edge of the roof, looking into the yard of the house in back of ours. They had a pool.

I was pretty sure I'd fucked things up for good, like it was really ending this time.

Dang, dude.

"Hey, Lance," Miranda called up to me, "my mom's on her way. You coming down?"

"Yeah yeah," I said, scurrying, "wait for me," something she'd been doing for several years already.

I walked her out to the front yard.

We stood beneath the sycamore trees not looking at each other.

She was crying.

"You think you're the Scarecrow but you're really the Tin Man," Miranda said suddenly, "You've got plenty of brains."

"But no heart," I finished for her.

"Oh, it's there," she knocked her fist against my chest with restrained hostility, "But you've gotta let it make a sound once in a while."

Miranda's mom pulled up in front.

"Hi, Lance!" Tamara Savitch shouted and waved.

I smiled and waved back but couldn't muster any voice.

Dang, dude, this was it. The final falling off place.

"Bye, Lance," Miranda said, looking away, disappointed yet again, as she ducked her head inside her mom's car and closed the door.

I didn't bother to say bye back. She'd've never heard it.

I stood on the front lawn and waved feebly to no one.

From then on I knew there'd be nothing but distance.

ABOUT THE AUTHOR

Barry Smolin is a native of Los Angeles, California. He is the author of "Wake Up In The Dreamhouse" (2011), a novella composed one sentence at a time on Twitter, "Always Be Madly In Love" (2011), selected poetry culled from the years 1988- 2010, and "Narcissus In The Dark" (2012), another novella. Since 1995 he has been the host and producer of the radio shows "The Music Never Stops" (1995-2012) and "Head Room" (2012-present) on KPFK 90.7 FM in Los Angeles. He has also released four albums of original music under the name Mr. Smolin: "At Apogee" (2004), "The Crumbling Empire Of White People" (2007), "Bring Back The Real Don Steele" (2009), and "Heaven's Not High" (2013), as well as setting chapter 1 of James Joyce's *Finnegans Wake* to music in collaboration with the band Double Naught Spy Car as part of the "Waywords and Meansigns Project" (2016). His music has also been featured on the Showtime television series "Weeds." He can be found online at www.mrsmolin.com

www.ingramcontent.com/pod-product-compliance
Lightning Source LLC
Chambersburg PA
CBHW071217250626
47163CB00001B/25